Spencer's List

Spencer's List

LISSA EVANS

VIKING
an imprint of
PENGUIN BOOKS

VIKING

Published by the Penguin Group
Penguin Books Ltd, 80 Strand, London WC2R 0RL, England
Penguin Putnam Inc., 375 Hudson Street, New York, New York 10014, USA
Penguin Books Australia Ltd, 250 Camberwell Road, Camberwell, Victoria 3124, Australia
Penguin Books Canada Ltd, 10 Alcorn Avenue, Toronto, Ontario, Canada M4V 3B2
Penguin Books India (P) Ltd, 11 Community Centre,
Panchsheel Park, New Delhi – 110 017, India
Penguin Books (NZ) Ltd, Cnr Rosedale and Airborne Roads,
Albany, Auckland, New Zealand
Penguin Books (South Africa) (Pty) Ltd, 24 Sturdee Avenue,
Rosebank 2196, South Africa

Penguin Books Ltd, Registered Offices: 80 Strand, London WC2R 0RL, England

www.penguin.com

First published 2002
1

Set in 12/14.75pt Monotype Dante
Typeset by Rowland Phototypesetting Ltd,
Bury St Edmunds, Suffolk
Printed in Great Britain by Clays Ltd, St Ives plc

A CIP catalogue record for this book is available from the British Library

ISBN 0-670-91202-6

For Keith

With thanks to Gerard Reissmann, who kept me right on the medical bits, to family and friends, for putting up with my regular defeatist moans during the writing, to Georgia Garrett, for her unparalleled guidance, both on and off the page, to Juliet Annan, whose enthusiasm and encouragement is unflagging, to Clare Parkinson, so meticulous and thoughtful, and to David Hastings, for coming up with 'Hung and Heavy'.

I

The estate agent's letter was one of a handful that dropped onto the mat on a mild September morning. Fran, still in her socks, passed the bathroom where her brother was clearing his nasal passages with a series of avian honks, and padded down the stairs to the hall. She sifted through the post on her way to the kitchen, binning the junk, dropping Peter's copies of *Home Plumber* and *Journal of Health and Safety* onto the table and hesitating over a fat airmail letter postmarked Denmark. She pinched the edge to confirm that it held more than the usual sheaf of folded paper and, swayed by curiosity, opened it and teased out a small photograph. It was a close-up of a cornflower growing beside a dusty footpath and the scrawl on the back read: *Fran, this speedwell is as blue – but no bluer – than your eyes.* She looked at the photo again and frowned slightly. It was quite definitely a cornflower; she could even see the characteristic pseudo-radiate capitula.

She tucked the unread pages into her bag for later and, switching on the kettle, stood for a while with the other letter unopened in her hand. It was in a nasty, flimsy Lion Brand envelope with a second-class stamp and a big smudge on the back, where someone had pressed on the flap to make the cheap glue hold. Eighteen months ago, when she and Peter had bought the house from Brown and Baddeley, all their correspondence from the firm had been typed on creamy, textured paper, almost as thick as cardboard, and the folder they kept it in had eventually split under the strain. This letter drooped limply in her grasp, and only the hand-stamped motto

– Your Home is in our Hearts – was unchanged. She stuck a finger under the flap and felt the same queasy anticipation that had preceded opening her A Level results.

She hadn't wanted a valuation; she knew it could only be dreadful, but Peter, with his usual formality, had insisted that they stuck to Paragraph 4 of their original agreement, the one stating that 'eighteen months after purchase, the current value of 33 Stapleton Road should be ascertained and if either or both of the parties so wish the house re-introduced onto the market.' The wording had been courtesy of a solicitor friend of Peter's and the agreement amicably drawn up during the nine days that elapsed between exchanging contracts and watching the property market plummet into a death spiral.

The kettle clicked off while she was still hesitating, and with a surge of cowardice she decided to grant herself three minutes' grace; she would read the letter once she had a mug of tea in her hand. She filled the pot and wiped a swathe of condensation from the kitchen window. Just a few yards away, on the other side of the garden wall, her neighbour was hanging out a row of huge shirts, doubling the sleeves over the line to prevent them dragging on the ground. As Fran watched idly it occurred to her that Iris had been living in that same downstairs flat for fifteen years. She looked at the envelope again; it was possible, she realized, it was really, horribly, possible that the contents might condemn her to a similar fate.

'Fran!'

It was a muffled call. She looked up to see Iris waving and pointing.

'What?' she mouthed.

Iris pointed again, indicating something high on the wall of the house. Heart sinking, Fran chucked the envelope on the table and opened the back door.

'Have you seen your roof?' asked Iris, as soon as she was outside.

Face braced for the shock, Fran looked up.

During the night a length of guttering had come loose from the eaves and was hanging down in a giant diagonal, like a slide for sparrows, the lower end resting snugly on the bath overflow pipe. A sludge of ancient leaf mould had dripped from the broken section, forming a stinking blot on the wall, and beneath it on the concrete lay an old nest that had landed intact and upright. It contained the tail end of a mummified mouse.

'Tremendous,' said Fran, flatly. It was only a month since a chunk of her bedroom windowsill had fallen off, and not much more than that since her brother had put one of his size twelves through a bathroom floorboard. Like a very old lady who has never seen a doctor, their house was disintegrating piece by piece. All their DIY – all their hammering and gluing and slaving and fiddling and following the instructions over fifteen illustrated weekly parts – had merely constituted so much first aid; it could surely only be a matter of time before one of the major organs failed. Or possibly the whole building would suddenly implode like the house at the end of *Poltergeist*, leaving a pulsating black void strewn with corpses. At least it would be quick, she thought, at least it would spare them the current relentless decline.

'Sorry to be the bearer of bad news,' said Iris, resuming her shirt-hanging.

Fran shrugged, resignedly. 'That's next weekend sorted, anyway.' Out of the corner of her eye, she saw a pigeon flutter down to the blackcurrants and she smacked her hands sharply to frighten it. It clattered off, and the black cat from number 39 bolted out of the broccoli and leapt over the back wall.

'Vermin,' said Fran. 'I should get one of those bird-scarer

shotguns that automatically fires every ten minutes. I suppose the neighbours might complain though.' Iris laughed through a mouthful of pegs. She was dressed for work, in a longish, darkish skirt teamed with a paleish, vaguely crumpled shirt that sported a brown smear on the collar. Fran pointed it out.

'Oh Lord. I bet it's Marmite.' She held out the collar and tried to focus on the stain, just below her chin. 'And I ought to iron this top really. Does it look terrible?' Fran hesitated. 'I'll iron it,' said Iris. She yawned and ran a hand through her hair, and then patted it down as though she'd remembered she wasn't supposed to.

'Mu-um.'

'What?' asked Iris, over her shoulder. Fran saw the pale, sleep-creased face of one of the twins look round the back door.

'We're out of cereal.'

'Look in the cupboard behind the pasta.'

'It's their eighteenth on Sunday, isn't it?' asked Fran, suddenly remembering.

'Saturday.' Iris hung up the last shirt, veiling herself from Fran's sight.

'Mu-um. There's none there.'

'I'll get a card,' said Fran. 'Cards, rather.'

'Mu-um? There's *none there*.'

'I'd better go,' said Iris, lifting a shirt-sleeve and looking at Fran through the gap. 'Your courgettes look lovely, incidentally.' She let the sleeve drop again and a couple of moments later Fran heard her say 'Look, just behind the spaghetti,' with barely a trace of impatience.

The courgettes did look lovely, thought Fran, snapping off a strand of fennel to chew and taking a moment to admire her produce. Over the course of a year she had turned a sad little stretch of balding grass into a square of textbook fecundity,

4

and it had been galling when the valuer's sole comment on the garden had been 'no lawn'. She winkled out a couple of snails that were hiding among the broccoli florets and threw them against the wall – a quick, organic death and a satisfying noise to boot – and then, unable to postpone it any longer, turned back to the house.

Probably the only advantage of 33 Stapleton Road, indeed probably the only selling point still remaining, was that a bus stop stood only twenty yards from the front gate. It was served by the 92A, which started in the City and ground uphill through Dalston and Tottenham to the green edge of London that still smudged the map between the North Circular and the M25.

For the first half of her journey, Fran sat staring out of the window, still trying to absorb the contents of the estate agent's letter. The bus was full of schoolchildren, and beside her sagged a teenage boy whose lardy buttocks restricted her to a tiny section of the seat and whose enormous voice, raised in conversation with a friend three rows in front, seemed to fill the whole upper deck.

On the High Street the shops were just starting to open. There was a breakfast queue outside the twenty-four-hour fried-chicken takeaway cum minicab office, the *Watchtower* sellers had taken up position in the doorway of Iceland and the man with the orange lady's coat and the airport trolley was already sitting outside the British Legion with a can of Strongbow.

'Your face, right,' shouted the boy next to her to his friend, 'your face, MY ARSE.'

They crawled past the blackened shell of what had first been a Pound Store, then a charity shop and finally, briefly, Deelite Electrical Goods, where Fran had once bought a suspiciously cheap cassette player made by a company she'd never heard of. By the time the rewind button had jammed in the 'on' position – three days after purchase – the shop had already burned down. 'Insurance company "has doubts" about origin of Deelite Fire' as the local paper had put it. She'd binned the player.

At the Point Break snooker hall, the bus emptied, and a river of black blazers poured along the pavement towards the gates of Abalene Grove Comprehensive. The remaining passengers seemed to expand with a sigh, and Fran, unable to face brooding any longer about her future in Dalston, took Duncan's letter from her bag and smoothed out the six closely written pages.

Dear Fran,
Low, dark hills – deep woods – shifting cloud-shapes in still pools
– a white gate, painfully bright against the tangled undergrowth –
can you see Jutland as I'm seeing it?

She had been to Denmark, once, on a field trip, and her chief memory was of how tidy the countryside had been, and how expensive the ice cream.

I've been camping at a dairy farm, rising at dawn to capture the
first threads of the sun as they weave the day's new light, and the
cloud-puffs of the cattle's breath as those gentle beasts watch me
with unblinking eyes. My third eye – my camera – blinks only
when I ask it to – a steady friend, who keeps watching even when
the beauty makes me turn aside.

There was a lot more of this sort of stuff. Fran speed-read through to find something more concrete.

I miss you, Fran, I miss your body next to mine and your small,
cold feet curled beneath you. I miss your stubborn face and your
sun-scrubbed cheeks and the level blue of your gaze. I miss the
curve of your back and the rough skin of your practical hands. I
want to hold those hands and scour them across me, I want to

'Scuse me.' She budged up slightly to allow a cadaverous,
rather trembly man to sit down. He spent some time shifting
around in the seat, arranging himself, and then lifted an aged
Boots bag onto his lap and started to look through it, emitting
the while little plosive sounds between pursed lips, like a pan
starting to boil.

She returned to the letter.

I want to hold those hands and scour them across me, I want to
lick the salty sweat from your breasts and feel your nipples like
raspberries against my tongue. I want to taste the

'Prick.' The man beside her was starting to form whole
words. 'Prick. Prick. I gotta prick.' He said them briskly and
without any particular emphasis, as if reciting a telephone
number. 'Prick, prick, that's my prick.' The bag rustled
ominously.

I want to hold those hands and scour them

'Prick, prick, balls, prick.'

I want to hold those

'Prick, prick, prick, prick,prick,prickprickprickprick . . .' The
rustling started to speed up.

'Excuse *me*,' said Fran, loudly and coldly, pushing past him and trying not to look at what the bag might hold. He barely paused in his rhythm, and she turned her back on him and went downstairs with what she hoped was dignified haste.

There were no seats on the bottom deck, and she held on to a rail, stuffing Duncan's letter back into her bag and bracing herself with one hand as the bus rounded the corner by Safeway's. She glanced automatically over to the service alley between the supermarket and Billo Shoes, through which it was possible to glimpse her raspberry canes arrayed beyond the chain-link fence. They weren't there. She strained towards the window, but could see only the side of the hen house, normally invisible from this angle. The bus lurched forward again, but just before the view disappeared she caught a glimpse of a large pig running across the gap.

She arrived at the gates of Hagwood Urban Farm at a run, her face red with a mixture of exertion and fury. Claud, the farm manager, had obviously been hovering by the car park in anticipation of her arrival, and he intercepted her, hands outstretched pacifically. 'He's in. Porky's back in and it's . . . it's –' he paused, clearly straining for a phrase that wasn't a direct lie '– it's not as bad as it looks. I think we'll find that with a real group effort we can . . .'

Fran dodged round him and jogged past the classroom, the hen house and the compost heap before halting abruptly in front of her domain. The vegetable patch was smashed flat. Everything that had previously been vertical was now horizontal. Everything that was now horizontal had bits missing. A row of pumpkins looked like the aftermath of an alien road accident and the ground was sprinkled with a few tiny, saliva-flecked pieces of carrot. The lettuces had simply disappeared, as if sucked up by a giant hoover. There was a large, ragged gap in her newly planted hawthorn hedge and the wicker hurdle that had previously bordered the pond was now bent in half at the bottom of it. A long muddy smear ran the length of the wild-flower meadow, punctuated at one end by a flattened red bobble hat.

Claud appeared at her elbow and she threw him a pinched glance. 'Which bit, precisely, isn't as bad as it looks?'

He looked trapped, but smiled sweatily. 'Well, obviously at first glance it's pretty shocking but I think with a bit of work we can pull together and . . . and straighten a lot of it . . . straighten quite a bit of it . . .' Fran picked up a snapped stem of Swiss chard and held it directly in front of him.

'Well, er . . . obviously not, er, that er . . .' his voice trailed away.

Fran chucked the stem to one side and stood with her arms folded, struggling to hold back tears of frustration. To visiting school parties, her end of the farm was known as 'the boring bit'. On a sensation scale, with the size of Porky's genitalia at the top, the baby ducks a close second, and the smell of the manure heap a hilarity-inducing third, the average ten-year-old could barely remain conscious when confronted with a bunch of plants. In her teaching sessions, she sometimes felt as if she were pitching the plot of a European art film to a group of Hollywood movie executives: they wanted sex, blood and car chases, and she was trying to sell them thought-provoking dialogue. The way to do it, she had discovered, was to wrong-foot them, to present botany and ecology with the degree of brio and the elastic range of imagery more often used by sports commentators. It was sometimes exhausting, but part of her reward was the wall of felt-tipped pictures in the staffroom that showed the sun issuing instructions to the vegetables through a megaphone almost as many times as they showed Porky weeing.

She could hear him now, above the roar of traffic on the

North Circular, grunting with contentment as he scratched himself against the fence. At her elbow, Claud shifted anxiously as he waited for her reaction.

'How did it happen?' she asked.

He stalled for time. 'You mean er . . . ?'

'I mean how – did – the – pig – get – out – of – the – pen?' she enunciated, separating the words with great clarity.

Claud took his time replying. His managerial style, if he could be said to have one, was that he wanted everyone to be friends, all the time. He removed his glasses, cleaned them on the bottom of his t-shirt, replaced them and cleared his throat. Fran stood with arms folded.

'There was a . . . a misunderstanding.'

'Oh yes?'

'I thought that the weakened stretch of fencing had been mended, whereas, in fact, almost certainly due to some kind of mix-up, there was a –'

'You mean that you'd told someone to mend it and they didn't?'

'Well, it all depends on whether you view the word "told" as an appropriate –'

'Who?'

Claud shuffled miserably. 'I don't think we need a scapegoat for this particular –'

'I'm not asking for a scapegoat, I'm asking who was told to mend it and didn't.'

'I'm really not sure we want to –' A police car howled by, making speech impossible for some moments.

Fran changed tack. 'OK. Was it Costas?' she asked in a reasonable voice, naming the most reliable person on the farm.

Claud was startled into frankness. 'Costas? No, of course it wasn't.'

'No, I didn't think so. You'd have told me if it had been someone competent or useful, because they'd certainly have had some kind of excuse.' She impaled Claud with a look. 'So it must have been someone who's a total waste of space.'

He opened and shut his lips a couple of times, but nothing came out.

'I'll kill him.' She turned and marched towards the staff-room, Claud bleating ineffectually behind her.

Barry had the foresight to look slightly worried when Fran banged the door open. He was by the sink, wiping mud from his waterproof jacket with the washing-up sponge, his curly hair haloed by the morning sun.

'Hiya,' he said, cautiously. 'I was just going to make you a mug of tea. I thought you might need one,' he added, with a humorous little lift of the eyebrows.

Fran pushed the door shut behind her, blocking Claud's worried face from view. 'I'd like a word with you.'

'Sure.' He smiled, exuding his usual sleepy charm – the sleepy charm that Fran had stupidly assumed was jet lag when he'd been interviewed for the post of Agricultural Education Assistant Grade 5. He'd just come back from a holiday in Australia, and it had seemed a reasonable explanation for his excessively relaxed approach to the panel's questions. Unfortunately it had turned out that he was always like that.

She sat down, and gestured brusquely towards another chair.

'Sure you wouldn't like a cuppa first?' He waggled a mug at her.

'No.'

'Right.' He seemed to sense the seriousness of the impending conversation and, sitting down, clasped his hands on the table in front of him and leaned forward with an earnest expression, as if auditioning for the role of a social worker.

'What's the problem?'

'I'll give you three guesses,' said Fran.

'It's about Porky, isn't it?' He looked at her sympathetically. 'Yeah, I'm afraid he made a bit of a mess of your veg. We just couldn't get a grip on him, you see. I must have fallen over about fifteen times, that coat's never going to be the same again.' He tried a smile, and then put it away again.

'And why was Porky out in the first place?'

'Oh right, right. I see.' He nodded, as if everything had come clear. 'Yeah, I just hadn't had time to get round to that fence, I'm afraid. Sorry about that, Fran. Claud asked me to do a poster for the autumn open day and then there was that kid yesterday I had to take for a tetanus jab and then I had to get off early for my girlfriend's birthday so . . .' He shrugged ruefully. 'You know how it is when things get in the way.' He looked at her, apparently waiting for an understanding laugh of assent.

Fran felt a neurone snap somewhere deep within her brain. 'Oh for fuck's sake, Barry,' she said, with a vehemence that made him jump, 'don't be so ridiculous. An enormous great pig has completely wrecked my section of the farm and it's all your fault because you're a stupid, lazy, spaced-out berk.' The last word was a shout and as she motored on she felt a certain pleasure at the shock on his face. 'You know, when I think of all the students we interviewed for your job I could bloody well weep. We could have thrown a stone in a –' she cast around bullishly and spotted a poster above the sink ' – *donkey* sanctuary and hit something with more ability and common sense than you.'

Barry recoiled slightly, as if he'd been punched.

'You've been given chance after chance but you think just because you've got a nice smile you don't have to do any bloody work. Everything you touch is botched. You can't lift a potato without needing a fifteen-minute tea break. The least you could be doing now is trying to restore some of the damage instead of sitting here cleaning your bloody coat like a member of the landed gentry. God, the work I put into that garden . . .' She gulped for breath and tried to restore her breathing to a normal rhythm. Barry sat as if stuffed. 'So why aren't you out there? Go on, get out there.'

Like a very old man, Barry got to his feet. Under the remains of the tan his face was pale, and his eyes flinched away from Fran's as he passed her. Following him to the door, she watched him tramp down the long, sloping parallelogram of the farm, past the hen house where Spike was collecting eggs, under the flyover, whizzing with cars like a vast abacus, and towards the dented patch of green where Porky had frolicked.

Fran glanced at Claud, hovering beside the boot scraper, and then looked away. Down by the pond she could see Barry starting to fish for the hurdle.

Claud eased himself towards her. 'I'm not sure . . .' he began.

'I know,' said Fran, tiredly, leaning against the doorpost. 'I'd had a bad morning, even before I got here.'

'He looked a bit upset.'

'*I'm* a bit upset.'

'Even so, I think that maybe . . .'

A passing juggernaut gave a great blast of its air horn. Claud tried again.

'I think that maybe you should have a . . . a calmer chat with him. After all, it wasn't as if he . . . he deliberately allowed Porky to . . .'

Fran nodded, slowly.

'Perhaps you could make him some tea. Bring it down to the pond and –'

'Yeah, OK.'

'Peace offering.'

'OK.'

'I think we've got some biscuits.'

'*OK*, Claud.'

'Good. Good.' He clapped his hands together. 'Right . . . well, all hands on deck for the great restoration. I think first of all I should . . . er, perhaps call some kind of informal meeting to, er, discuss . . .'

2

It was a thin afternoon for tourists in Trafalgar Square, and the birdseed man, who was wearing thermal gloves and a baseball cap with 'I Love New York' on it, sold Spencer two bags of yellow grit for the price of one. He said, 'It's your lucky day,' as he handed them over, and Spencer asked, 'Starting from when?' but received no reply. The Square looked rather fine in the low sunlight that streamed along Pall Mall, turning the windows of South Africa House crimson and jewelling the KFC boxes that blew between the fountains.

Spencer positioned himself just under Nelson's Column, filled both hands with birdseed and held them out at arm's length, feeling like a combination of the crucified Christ and the Scarecrow in *Wizard of Oz*.

For a moment nothing happened, and then there was a mild commotion in his immediate vicinity and two smartish buff-coloured pigeons landed on his right hand and started devouring the seeds with cartoon-like velocity. Next a hideously diseased, possibly leprous, one-legged grey pigeon landed on his left hand, balanced precariously on its warty remaining foot and quite deliberately pecked Spencer on the wrist. He shook his hand violently to dislodge it, dropping most of the seed as he did so, and suddenly every pigeon in Greater London was in the air, heading towards him like a bomber squadron, wheels down, flaps set, tails flattened for landing. The sky was black with bodies, and the world only fitfully visible behind a screen of wings. He cringed as pigeons banked and swooped and landed and took off again; the ground was hidden beneath a shifting carpet of feathery backs and the air vibrated with the throaty calls that he had always found pleasantly soothing, and which now sounded like the rallying cries of an army crazed with bloodlust.

Covering his head with his arms, he ducked and ran. The carpet exploded into a wall of wings and then he was through, and safe, and all at once aware that he was being videoed by a party of Japanese pensioners. He counterfeited a casual wave and walked away, trying to look like someone who was really enjoying himself.

His other assignment was within easy reach. The London Pride ('Sixty Sights in Sixty Minutes') was a double-decker bus painted in an ill-advised combination of yellow and purple. It departed at twenty-minute intervals from just outside the National Gallery, employing a very old man in a fake Beefeater costume to stand on the pavement shouting, 'London Pride, *HAWL* the Sights,' at passers-by.

Spencer hesitated for a while, overwhelmed by inertia at the prospect. There were only three passengers on the lower deck, and two of them had their eyes closed. The third, a small child, stared fixedly through the window at Spencer, her finger up her nose to the second joint.

On some invisible signal the Beefeater changed his shout to 'London Pride, departing in *FUHIVE* minutes' and the engine started. Spencer climbed on board very slowly.

'How much is it, please?'

'Three pounds downstairs five pounds upper deck,' said the driver in a monotone, his eyes fixed on a far and invisible horizon.

'Five pounds, please.' He placed a note on the change tray.

'No drinks or ice creams, no standing up while the bus is in motion, no getting off except at designated stops.'

'Right.'

'Commentary is in English.'

'Fine.'

'In the event of traffic problems the company reserves the right to alter the route.'

'OK.' A green ticket whirred from the machine by the cash tray. 'Anything else I should know?' asked Spencer. 'Any hints or tips?'

The driver swung his head round with the weighty slowness of a JCB and looked at him through half-closed eyes.

'Just checking,' said Spencer. 'Thanks.'

His favourite seats – or rather Mark's favourite seats – the ones right at the front that gave the illusion of driving the bus, were already occupied by a group of Americans – west coast queens by the look of them, tanned, fit, gorgeous and dressed in the kind of subtly expensive colours that people who regularly sit on London bus upholstery know not to wear. One of them was in the middle of an anecdote, and Spencer was given only the swiftest of inspections, five pairs of eyes registering cursory approval, before he sat down a few rows back and the storyteller picked up the thread.

Spencer hoped they appreciated their privileged position. He had once witnessed Mark paying two small boys a pound each to move, just so he could sit there and enjoy his usual thrill of going round corners six feet ahead of the front wheels, the nose of the bus apparently veering psychotically into the opposite lane before swinging round in a majestic curve.

'London Pride departing in *THUREE* minutes.'

There was a five-pence coin under the seat in front. Spencer picked it up and used the milled edge to scratch at a crusty stain on his left shoe. Earlier in the afternoon he'd been stitching up a cut on a drunk's hand when the man had flopped his head over the side of the couch and been copiously sick all over the floor, the wheels of the dressings trolley, and Spencer's Birkenstocks. He'd run them under the tap but had obviously missed a few spots. In fact now he looked at them closely, he realized that the laces would have to go through the washing machine before they were presentable. As would his trousers, which had a pink stain just below the left knee, incurred when he'd accidentally knelt in a puddle of Hibiscrub, the lurid antiseptic soap of which they used gallons in Casualty. He'd been in the process of scrabbling around on the floor helping to pick up a pile of X-rays which had fallen off the reception desk and slid in all directions.

'Better get them in order, or we'll be ripping the spleen out of someone with a sprained ankle,' as his consultant, Mrs Spelko, had remarked jovially. Since she had a voice that could vibrate lamps in the next room, there had been a volley of worried looks between the waiting patients.

It was the kind of remark that meant that Spencer, now into the second month of his contract, was learning more about damage limitation than emergency treatment. Mrs Spelko was tiring to work with; she was wide and vigorous and brought extra noise and panic to a department that was already lacking in neither. There was an easy brutality about her, as of someone who'd learned their bedside manner on the battlefield, dipping bleeding stumps into hot tar, and when she surged through the waiting room, patients leaned away as if avoiding the scythes on her chariot wheels. It was her voice, though, that caused most of the trouble; she seemed to lack an internal volume control, so that all statements, however mild in intent, emerged with booming clarity. Thus 'Dr Carroll, you smell of vomit' and 'Can someone get rid of that idiot in cubicle seven' could both be heard within a ten-metre radius. The man in cubicle seven – a fretter, rather than an idiot, who had unshiftably decided that a pulled muscle was a heart attack – had turned out to be a solicitor's clerk, and Spencer was unsure whether the apology he'd managed to wring from Mrs Spelko ('if I had to apologize to every stupid patient I'd be here all day') would be sufficient to prevent litigation.

'London Pride departing in *WUHUN* minute.'

The front row of the bus began a noisy count-down.

'British seconds,' shouted one of them, 'remember they're *much* slower than US seconds.'

Spencer dropped the coin on the floor again and looked out of the window at the weaving lights of the rush-hour traffic circling Trafalgar Square. It counted as the first sight of the promised sixty, he supposed, a tiny tick on the list.

'Fifteen . . . fourteen . . . thirteen . . .'

Spencer heard the slap of the doors closing downstairs and the bus eased forward into the stream of traffic. There was a cheer from the front row, and then ironic boos as it stopped immediately at a red light. 'England's full of goddam reds,' one of them shouted in a John Wayne voice.

The pedestrians streamed across, the amber light began flashing, and then the roar of a motorbike tore past the bus, changing almost at once to a scream of rubber followed by the horrible, distinctive crump of metal and glass colliding. The bus, which had just started forward, stopped with a jerk, and Spencer glimpsed the riderless bike scraping an arc on the tarmac just in front of them.

There was a collective, horrified 'Whoah' from the front seat, and then Spencer, mentally gritting his teeth, was hurrying down the stairs. As he flipped the emergency exit lever on the bus door, the driver shouted 'Oi' and for a moment he heard a stampede of feet above him.

A crowd had already assembled, and he pushed himself to the front with a series of 'excuse me's. There was a lot of shouting going on, but in clearly defined strands, like the layers of a soundtrack. The ground was strewn with plastic shards and the bike lay with its front wheel tucked under the stove-in boot of a black cab; beside it knelt the cabbie, swearing monotonously. In the centre of the road stood a tiny elderly nun, leaning on two sticks and repeating the word 'Maniac' over and over again in a clear but tinny voice, like a stuck record. The biker lay prone with his head almost under one of the wheels of the bus, but he was clutching one of his knees with both hands and a reassuring stream of muffled obscenities was audible from beneath the helmet. A woman squatted by him, fiddling with the visor.

'I'm a doctor,' said Spencer, kneeling beside her.

'So am I,' she said, and lifted the plastic shield.

'My *fucking* knee,' said the biker, clearly.

'Hi there.' It was four of the Americans from the bus, arriving in a pale flurry of cashmere and leather.

'Hello,' said Spencer, confused.

'We're doctors,' said the one with the floor-length camel coat, 'can we help?'

'I *know* it's fucking broken. I don't need six fucking doctors to tell me.'

'I think we've got it covered, thanks,' said Spencer.

'Oh, OK.' The spokesman straightened up amiably.

'Need a hand?' A plethoric man in a double-breasted suit was waving from the second row of spectators. 'I'm a GP.'

'Just fuck *off.*'

'We're fine thanks,' said Spencer.

'No skin off my nose,' said the man, disappearing into the crowd again.

'Is it hurting anywhere else or is it just the knee?'

'Maniac.'

'Fucking leave me *alone*,' shouted the biker, desperately, at

20

the little nun. She had shuffled over and was poking one of her sticks at his midriff. Spencer caught the rubber ferrule before it could do any damage, but with surprising energy she pulled it out of his grasp. He caught it again. She used the other stick to hit him on the knuckles. He grabbed the other stick as well. There was an impasse.

'Tenner on the nun,' shouted someone in the crowd.

'Excuse me, sister.' The fifth American had emerged from behind the bus and was extending a hand pacifically towards her. 'Do you think you ought to come and sit down? You've had a very nasty shock.' She turned a whiskery face towards him.

'What?'

'You've had a shock,' he repeated, more loudly, and in what Spencer realized was an English accent. 'You should come and sit down.' She looked at him, doubtfully, her jaw trembling, and he placed a reassuring hand on her arm. 'I'm a doctor,' he said.

The crowd stayed on, but there was no blood and, apart from the appearance of a troop of Danish Venture Scouts with first-aid experience, little drama, until the ambulance emerged unexpectedly along the wide pavement beside St Martin-in-the-Fields, the siren eerily amplified by the high wall, and the blue light beating off the pillars. Spencer stood to one side as the crew scooped the biker onto a stretcher with breezy skill.

'Busted patella?' said one, after the woman doctor had spoken to him. 'You'll be playing football in a couple of months.'

'Thanks,' muttered the biker, subdued. The police had just been over to take his details, and were now huddled with the Americans, one of whom was drawing a diagram.

As the ambulance drew away, Spencer could see the fifth

member of their party, the English one, sitting on the steps of St Martin's beside the nun. Taken in isolation he was clearly not as glossy as the others, and sported a bristly black crew-cut and a Nivenesque moustache. He caught Spencer's eye and waved, then was obscured for a moment as a yellow-and-purple bus drove between them, venting a huge cloud of exhaust from its rear end. It took Spencer a second or two to realize it was the London Pride.

'Hey!' he said, feebly, but the bus had already swung round the corner and headed off towards Pall Mall, the lit upper deck completely empty.

'I believe the tour-bus driver can be dragged through the courts on a number of counts,' said Greg conversationally, his personalized ballpoint poised above a notebook. The party was wedged in the corner of a smoky pub on the Strand, all swirly carpets and chipped glass ashtrays, a couple of hundred yards from the site of the accident. With much the same speed and efficiency as the ambulance men had displayed, Spencer had been scooped up by the American party, introduced to each of them, congratulated on his role as Good Samaritan and bought a double vodka.

'Count one, failure to give a statement to the police after an accident. Count two, theft of property – that is, the burnt-orange scarf which my aged maternal grandmother knitted for me with her own, arthritic hands and which I left draped over the back of the seat. And count three, failure under the trades descriptions act – is that the correct name for it, Miles? –' the Niven-moustache man nodded ' – failure under the trades descriptions act to deliver the stated promise of sixty sights in sixty minutes.'

'We saw one sight in one minute,' said Miles, 'so I suppose the ratio was correct.' He had an occasional twitch, Spencer noticed, a tendency to screw up his eyes and then blink rapidly.

'I always hated that scarf,' said Greg's partner Reuben, a spectacularly handsome blond. 'I'd say it was worth paying five pounds never to see that scarf again. I might even have paid twenty.'

'You never told me.'

'I didn't want to hurt you, Greg, because I know how sensitive you are about your grandmother's presents. Besides, if you got rid of it she might have knitted you another one in an even uglier colour.'

'Oh it all comes tumbling out now . . .'

Under the laughter, Miles leaned across to Spencer. 'Are you all right?' he asked, quietly.

'Yes, fine.' He'd started to think about how long it was since he'd been in a pub, just sitting and chatting. Months, probably. Maybe as long ago as Easter. 'Just drifting off a bit.'

'Doing long hours at the moment?' Seen in close-up, the moustache was more George Orwell than David Niven.

'Peculiar hours, really.' Miles raised his eyebrows interrogatively. 'I'm working in Casualty, so it's a shift system – we do a whole day, then a morning, then a whole night, then an afternoon. It's a clever way of ensuring that we're all tired, all the time.'

'So you're a surgeon?'

'No, no, thank God,' said Spencer, horrified at the suggestion. 'A GP trainee – I start in General Practice in February. This'll be my last hospital job ever, I hope.'

'I heard that "thank God",' said Reuben accusingly. 'You realize that if it wasn't for surgery we wouldn't be here? We actually met Miles at a surgical conference in Carmel. Admittedly he thought it was just a casual acquaintanceship and didn't realize that three months later we'd arrive on his doorstep demanding entertainment.'

'But he's *such* a gentleman,' said the one with the beard, whose name Spencer had forgotten. 'Never a word of complaint. Not even when he realized we were staying the extra month. And bringing the maid.'

They all laughed and Miles twitched modestly.

'What sort of surgeon are you?' asked Spencer.

'Eyes,' said Miles. 'I don't know anything about legs, so I stayed clear of the accident.'

Spencer stared. Blinky Blaine. It had to be.

'We're walking in London at *night*,' said Reuben excitedly, as they left the pub. 'Everyone told us not to do it because it's supposed to be too dangerous. But look, here we are!' He waved his hands in mock terror.

'You're a bunch of fucking poofs,' said a passing man.

'Thanks for the info, Mr Ugly,' replied Reuben.

'If you're going to Piccadilly then the theatre's on your way, isn't it?' asked Miles. He and Spencer were slightly ahead of the others.

'Mmm,' said Spencer, distracted. He knew he had to do it. 'Can I ask you something? You're not . . . your surname's not Blaine, is it?'

'That's right,' said Miles, surprised. 'How did you know?'

'Because you used to treat a friend of mine.' And he used to do impressions of you for days afterwards, he didn't add. 'I don't know if you remember him – Mark Avery?'

'Mark? Oh, of course I remember him.' Miles blinked, and gave his moustache a stroke. 'He wasn't the forgettable sort.'

'I know,' said Spencer.

'I heard he'd died. I was very sorry.'

Spencer felt his eyes begin to fill, as usual. 'Yeah,' he said lamely, 'me too.'

'How long ago was it?'

'Four months.'

'Not long.'

'No.'

There was a pause, during which his nose began to run in sympathy. He searched ineffectually for a tissue, and was rescued by Miles, who wordlessly passed across a handkerchief. It was the ironed, monogrammed kind, on which it seems sacrilegious to wipe one's snot, and Spencer dabbed tentatively rather than blew.

'Thanks.' He wondered what to do with it; he could hardly give it back.

'You're welcome. My mother gives me twelve every Christmas.'

'Oh, OK. Thanks.' He tucked it into his pocket and smiled awkwardly. 'It was the double vodka, I think.'

'Nothing wrong with a good weep.'

'Yeah, that's what I tell myself. About eight times a day.'

'So how long had you known Mark?'

'Oh – about ten years now.' He found himself sighing involuntarily – a deep, almost theatrical exhalation – something he did so often lately that last week he'd spent a fruitless couple of hours rooting through the hospital library trying to find a physiological explanation for the habit.

'And where did you meet?'

'An ABBA concert. Such a cliché, I know. I was standing behind him in the choc-ice queue and he needed some change. He was wearing an Agnetha wig and a badge that played the first line of "Fernando".'

Miles nodded in recognition. 'I had one of those.'

'And we were lovers for a while but that didn't really work out. And then we were friends, and that . . . lasted.' He nodded, too many times.

They walked in silence for a while, retracing their steps past Trafalgar Square. Behind them Greg and Reuben were struggling with the harmonization of 'Feed the Birds'.

'Mark wasn't a doctor, was he?' asked Miles, suddenly.

'No, a civil servant. Why?'

'I was just remembering – he always came to see me with a typed list of questions, with the medical terminology absolutely correct, all very well researched. Was that you?'

'Well, I helped. But he was a great list man. Never happy without a ruled page in front of him. You know the type.'

Miles nodded.

'In fact . . .' Spencer hesitated. Mark was his specialist subject, his favourite topic; given the slightest encouragement, he could talk about him all day, every day, any aspect, any amount of detail. Yet sometimes, mid-monologue, he would detach himself, draw back and wonder whether the listener was actually listening, or whether they were simply indulging a grieving friend, letting him yammer on therapeutically.

'What?'

He realized that Miles was still waiting for him to continue.

'Oh, well . . . he's the reason I was on that bus at all. He organized this year for me. He said he didn't want me moping round, so he made out a list of all the things I'd never done in London. I promised to tick them off within twelve months.'

'What sort of things?'

'Oh, touristy things . . . Madame Tussaud's . . . Harrods Food Hall . . . the Tower of London . . . Pie and Mash shop –'

'You're kidding!' Laughter increased the twitch.

'Oh, I'm barely scraping the surface here. It's two pages long: Changing of the Guard . . . Billingsgate fish market . . . Lord Mayor's Show . . . Cockney Pub –'

'What's that?'

'Fake pearly kings playing the old Joanna.'

'Oh my God.'

'He said he wanted to break me of my middle-class gay cultural snobbery. And get me out of my flat.'

'And how many have you done so far?'

'About half a page.'

'Any recommendations?'

'Yes, don't go and see *The Mousetrap*. It's shit.'

Miles laughed and then stopped suddenly, as if bitten. 'Oh. I just got it.'

'What?'

'Mark and Spencer.' He caught Spencer's eye. 'Sorry.'

'Good to meet you, and many thanks for the display of traditional nun-wrestling,' said Greg, shaking his hand as they stood amidst the crowd outside *Phantom of the Opera*.

'And are you two going to stay in touch?' asked the bearded one, archly. Spencer glanced at Miles, a bit embarrassed, and then looked away.

'Spencer knows where I work,' said Miles, with dignity. 'And if he wants company when he watches the Changing of the Guard, he can ring me there.'

'Guards? Changing?' said Reuben, looking round wildly. 'Where? And why wasn't *I* invited?'

Spencer could hear the phone ringing as he approached the outer door of the thirties mansion block in which he lived. His flat was on the ground floor but by the time he'd fiddled with two sets of keys, the answerphone had clicked on and he entered the living room to the sound of his god-daughter's piercing voice: 'Helloo! Spence-a!' then, aside, 'There's no one there,' and Niall's voice hissing in the background, 'Leave a message then.'

Spencer picked up the phone. 'Hello, Nina, I'm here.' There

was breathing at the other end. 'It's really me,' he said, 'not the answerphone.' There was a further pause, and then Niall took the phone.

'Well you've really puzzled her now. Not there/there; she's completely thrown. (Do you want to say hello to Spencer? No?) She's off, I'm afraid, no stopping her, straight to the kitchen to see what Nick's doing. Anyway –' he took a pause for breath '– how are you?'

'All right.'

'Only all right?'

'Well,' said Spencer cautiously, 'all right's quite good on the scale of things, I think.'

'How's that list going?'

'I've fed the pigeons in Trafalgar Square and . . . well, just the pigeons really, since I last saw you.'

'Are you up for a bash on Saturday? We thought we'd go to a salsa club. The sitter's booked. You could stay over, see Nina at breakfast.'

Spencer paused. 'Can I think about it?'

'Ah no, that means you won't come, I know you. Go on, it'll do you good. It's only the Cally Road – two stops on the tube and you're there. Bit of a dance, tip a few beers down you, see those Brazilian boys in their little shorts.'

'Well I'm not –'

'And Nina was only saying yesterday that she wanted to show you her new backpack with the teddies on that she currently only takes off to get into the bath, and to be honest the bloody thing's going to disintegrate before too long so you should take your chance while you can.'

Niall was like a tidal wave, and Spencer gave up. 'All right then.'

'Yes! Result, Nick!' He heard a distant cheer. 'Right, well I'll give you a ring on Saturday, make the arrangements.'

'OK.' He wondered if he'd be able to fake a last-minute cold. Or a bout of gastroenteritis.

'See you then.'

'Bye.'

Spencer put the phone down, and stood for a moment, listening to the chirrup of the crickets. He'd grown so used to the sound that these days he only noticed it after the cessation of something loud, like Niall, or when it ceased altogether, signalling a visit to Pet World. He roused himself to inspect his inheritance, which took up most of the wall space in the living room: a series of glass tanks containing, respectively, a spider, a small green lizard (together with three as yet uneaten crickets), five African landsnails, and a very expensive chameleon that remained resolutely the same colour despite the wide variety of attractive backgrounds that Spencer had provided. On the wall above them was a colour-coded chart, detailing in Mark's four-square handwriting their hygiene requirements and dietary whims.

None of them seemed to have died or deteriorated since the morning, but it was rather hard to tell. As pets went, he had to admit they were pretty dull; he looked after them conscientiously and, in return, they stayed in exactly the same place, twenty-four hours a day. The chameleon sometimes swivelled its eyes, and Spencer had once seen the spider apparently biting its fingernails, but that was it. The only one to whom he'd become attached was the tortoise, who lived not in a tank, but behind the magazine rack. He was also the only one to have a name: Bill, after Mark's grandfather, reputedly the slowest driver in the world. On first moving into Spencer's flat, Bill had roamed widely, often taking up a hopeful position just beside the fridge, and occasionally venturing as far as the bedroom where he had lurked among the shoes. After Spencer had stepped on him, one bleary contact lens-less morning, Bill's chosen territory had narrowed, and now he was seen only rarely, a wrinkled head peering round the edge of *Reptile Monthly*, checking that Spencer's feet were nowhere in sight. This evening he was invisible, though the pages of one of the magazines were moving slightly.

Spencer kicked off his shoes and went into the kitchen. He kept the London list pinned to the tea and coffee cupboard and he put a tick by 'Feeding Pigeons'. His pencil hovered beside 'Sight Seeing Bus'. Did this evening's micro-journey count? He had a horrible feeling that it didn't. After all, if he'd paid for his ticket for *The Mousetrap* and then the performance had been cancelled due to a bomb scare, he wouldn't, in all conscience, have been able to claim he'd seen it. Though he'd still have been able to guess every single jackbooted nuance of its apology for a plot. 'I could've sicked up a better play,' as Fran had put it. No, it was the act of actually sitting through the experience that really counted. He compromised by appending a very small tick, and then put the pencil back in the drawer.

Next to the list was a photo of Mark, and he looked at it for a while. It had been taken only a couple of months before he died but it showed someone who appeared not ill, but introspective. A shadow pattern of leaves lay over his face, softening the sharp cheekbones, camouflaging the Kaposi's that splotched the left side of his nose, and he looked at the camera with gravity. A beautiful look, full of self-knowledge and dignity. And yet . . . the leaves were those of St James's Park, and Mark's reason for going there was in the hope of seeing one of the resident pelicans swallow a pigeon whole, as they were rumoured occasionally to do. Spencer smiled faintly, and then it suddenly occurred to him that Miles was probably the last person, ever, who would make the Mark and Spencer joke.

He took half a lettuce from the fridge and, returning to the living room, dropped it into the snails' tank. Horns weaving, they glided towards it and began a slow-motion feast, gummy mouths pasting the leaves with mucus. He peered closer. What had appeared at a casual glance to be tomato seeds scattered across the glass floor seemed, on closer inspection, to be clusters of glutinous eggs. The phone rang, and he reached for it without taking his eyes away from the tank.

'Hi, Spence.'

'Oh Fran, I'm glad it's you. I think my snails are having snails.'

'What, right now? Are you sending out for towels and hot water?'

'No. They're still at the egg stage. Hundreds of them.'

'Kill them now.'

'Do you think I should?'

'Well they're not going to be easy to find homes for. Maybe nearer Christmas . . .'

Spencer sighed. 'How do you think I should kill them?'

'A doctor asks me that.'

'Ha ha.'

'Pour boiling water over them. That's what I do with slugs – they sort of dissolve.'

'Oh God, how disgusting. Let's change the subject.' He sank onto the sofa.

'You all right, Spence?'

'Yeah. Just tired. What about you?'

'Gotta have a talk. I've just found out I'm in Dalston for life.'

'What?'

'Can we meet up? I haven't seen you since we went all the way to Poets' Corner and it was closed.'

Spencer ignored this dig. 'Daytime? I could do tomorrow afternoon.'

'Yeah, all right, I can wangle that. They owe me at the moment. And Spence . . .'

'Yes.'

'Can *I* choose the venue?'

He sat limply on the sofa for a while after putting the phone down, listening to the soft crunch of snails eating lettuce. After a while, another sound penetrated his consciousness, a slow rustling. He concentrated hard, and tracked it down to the magazine rack; Bill was eating the back cover of *Hung and Heavy*, working his way up a chain of small ads. There seemed no enthusiasm in the task, no light in the boot-button eyes – it was as if he were at work, in a dull and relentless job with no holiday on the horizon. The cucumber and carrot which had been placed on a saucer beside him only that morning, lay limp and ignored. Was he missing Mark too? Did tortoises eat paper?

3

'Do tortoises eat paper?'

'Is this Bill we're talking about, or some theoretical tortoise?'

'Bill.'

'I don't think so. *Pigs* eat paper. Pigs eat bloody anything.' The perforated walkway of the Palm House clanged beneath their feet, and through the holes a verdant blur was visible. The air was warm, damp and earthy, and Fran savoured it, snuffing the bouquet like a sommelier.

'This is lovely,' she said. 'It's ages since I've been to Kew. I'm sure they didn't used to have parrots.' There was one just a few feet in front of them, swinging upside down from a custard apple, sweeping its tail to keep balance as it stripped the flesh from the seeds.

'I give him all sorts of treats,' said Spencer, as if she'd never spoken, 'Kiwi fruit. Sorrel. Those funny little orange berries in paper lanterns –'

'Physalis.'

' – and he just ignores them. He's eaten the whole of the back cover now.'

'Wasn't there a study about rats eating –'

'Cornflake packets, yes. Probably apocryphal, and anyway they're made of cardboard. This has got that thick shiny paper, very toxic-looking.' He pulled at his lower lip. 'Maybe he's missing some vital nutrient. Maybe he's a Greek tortoise, and I'm subjecting him to an African diet. The only manual I could find was written for seven-year-olds; it's got cartoons of people holding out carrots, and tortoises saying "thank you".'

There was a fretful note in Spencer's voice that was quite new to Fran; she glanced at him, covertly. He was looking tired and pasty, his hair was sticking up at the back, and he seemed to exude an air of watchful anxiety, like a guard with no one to report to. These days she saw only occasional glimpses of the amused detachment which she'd always regarded as part of his nature and which had sometimes made her feel like a performing flea by comparison, hopping wrathfully around his knees.

'So what did Mark feed him on?' she asked.

'Oh, I don't know, any old rubbish I think.'

There was a pause.

'I know, I *know*, I'm not being logical,' said Spencer, 'but he's had a change of environment. Maybe he's disturbed.'

Fran gave him a look. 'You are kidding.'

'Well, how would we know? He could be going psychotic.' He mooched a couple of paces. 'Very, very slowly.'

Fran cackled, slightly relieved, and then leaned over the rail, her attention caught by a school party thirty feet below. Although she could only see the tops of their heads, the body language of the group was horribly familiar – the still, small central core of attentive students, notebooks poised, eyes fixed on the teacher; the restive nature of the next couple of rows, whispering amongst themselves, sharing crisps, leashed to the nucleus only by a lack of bravado; then the fraying edge of the party, the drifting outer layer of serious inattention and potential vandalism; finally the free radicals, already out of voice range, and hidden from horizontal view by the vast leaves of a banana tree. As Fran watched, the free radicals darted to the door of the Palm House and ran outside with an audible crunch of gravel.

'How do you cope?' asked Spencer, nodding in the direction of the escapees. 'You must get this kind of stuff all the time.'

'I don't do what gingernut there's doing, for a start.'

Spencer peered at the red-haired teacher, who was pointing limply at the soaring trunk beside him. 'What do you mean?'

'Oh, he's ignoring the troublemakers and only speaking to the swots. The back row's never going to be spontaneously interested in –' she groped for an example '– osmosis versus capillary action, or whatever he's talking about, so he ought to be dragging them in to the subject – asking them direct questions, using analogies, making them swap places with the front row.' She paused for breath.

'Getting a bit passionate?' suggested Spencer.

'Yeah. And purposeful. He's just hoping that if he doesn't look at the problem, it'll go away. He's not addressing the issue.' Her voice was firm with conviction.

Spencer straightened up and stretched. 'The first time we met –' he began.

Fran swung round with the start of a grin. 'I know what you're going to say.'

'– I was watering my window box, happy in my own little way –'

'I know. That was the funniest thing about it.'

'– nurturing my own little patch of green, when this severe voice from the next window along –'

'Hey.'

'– informs me that everything in my window box is a weed –'

'Not just *a* weed.'

'– and that I should bin the whole lot and start again.'

'A particularly malicious and rampant and non-native, *wind*-dispersed weed that was liable to spring up in every window box within a forty-mile radius if you didn't destroy it.'

'As you conveyed to me in a passionate and yet deeply purposeful way.'

'Bastard.'

'No, it was impressive. And slightly intimidating'.

'Oh rubbish.'

'You'd be surprised. After all, I've never forgotten it.'

'Well I'm glad,' she said, rather primly, 'otherwise North London would now be a sea of waist-deep Himalayan balsam and it would all be your fault. Shall we go and get a cup of tea?'

They passed the school party on the way out and had to push their way between blazers as if through dense undergrowth.

'If you compare the porous surface of this leaf with the thick waxy covering that we saw on the succulents in the previous –' the door clanged on the teacher's earnest, ineffectual voice.

'He was quite cute,' said Spencer.

'Oh, I've never really gone for ginger.'

'He was one of mine anyway.'

'How do you *know*?'

Spencer shook his head mysteriously, declining to pass on the secret. It was a long-standing grievance of Fran's, this purported ability of Spencer's to instantly gauge the sexuality of any male within fifty yards.

'The trouble is,' said Fran, 'we've got no way of proving it.'

'I don't need proof. I *know*.'

From the Palm House, avenues of trees radiated like the ribs of a fan, a carefully planned vista at the end of each. They set off toward the Orangery, walking beside a row of vast horse chestnuts that flickered with squirrels.

'So what's this about Dalston?' There was a lighter note in Spencer's voice, as if he knew he was about to be diverted.

'Oh bloody hell. Well we've just had the house valued.'

'And it's bad, is it?'

'It's worth thirty thousand less than we paid for it. *Thirty thousand*. So that's that, we'll never sell it. We'll be there for ever – I'll be dragging my Zimmer frame to collect my pension in bloody E8.' She turned a gimlet eye on Spencer. 'Please, please don't say "I told you so" – though you did, obviously.'

'I just said I thought it wasn't a good idea buying with someone you didn't know all that well. In your case, your brother.'

'I know,' she said glumly.

'I wasn't sure what you'd find to talk about.'

'I know.'

'And I didn't know why you wanted to live in Dalston.'

'*All right.*'

'Sorry. What I was trying to say was, I didn't predict the market was going to crash. Anyway, go on.'

She shrugged her shoulders, as if settling a burden. 'Well, you were right of course. As usual. Infuriatingly. We don't have anything to talk about – it's not that we fight or anything, it's just that we can't . . .' She paused, mentally reviewing their stiff little conversations about work or films or newspapers, none of which ever seemed to flow into anything easier or more profound.

'You can't banter?'

'Yes, that's part of it. We can't be trivial, we can't have a laugh. It all has to be topics.' She booted an early conker several yards, and it rebounded off a tree trunk and split apart.

'Good shot.'

'It's as if we're working through a list of subjects. And he's so slow. I don't mean dim, he's obviously not dim, just . . . steady. One-paced. He has to think through everything. When I'm talking to him I sometimes feel like one of those dogs that runs three hundred yards for every ten feet the owner walks. They both get to the same place but they never cover the same ground. And he broods over things. Brings them up weeks later when I've forgotten all about them.' She paused before her final accusation. 'And you can't take the piss out of him.'

'No,' said Spencer, 'I can see that.' He always felt a bit sorry for Peter, whose social life seemed to consist solely of visits to B&Q and whose large, round, rather troubled face always reminded him of a radar dish, swivelling ponderously to follow the conversation.

'I mean, he's a *nice* man,' amended Fran, struggling to be fair. 'He is, isn't he?'

'Very nice,' agreed Spencer gravely.

'And I know he works terribly hard on the house and he never complains. And apart from the gargling . . .'

'And nose-blowing,' added Spencer, who had stayed over a couple of times.

'And nose-blowing, thank you Spence, he's quite easy to live with. It's just that now I know that we *can't* move . . .'

'He's not the cell mate you would have chosen.'

'No.'

They walked a while in silence together. Spencer remembered that when he had voiced his initial fears, Fran had confidently – even loftily – assured him that it was a *business* proposition and that she would treat it as such. 'Like going to work in Saudi Arabia, Spence, but with looser alcohol laws.' She had never, as far as he was aware, ever taken the slightest notice of anyone else's advice, but had thrown herself headlong into problems, mastering them through sheer force of personality. He aimed a kick at a conker, missed and took an awkward extra step forward, shooting out his elbows to keep balance. Fran's mouth twitched.

'The trouble is,' said Spencer, 'that your usual response to difficulties is to pick up your pitchfork and go wading in, whereas this is a situation that requires retrenchment and calm. As far as I can see, it's not immediately soluble. It may even require a change of government –' Fran snorted '– but in the meantime you need . . .' he hesitated over the apposite phrase, 'a modus operandum. It's quite a big house, there's only two of you. If you regard Peter as a reasonably quiet lodger with one or two irritating habits then it might seem quite bearable. After all, what would you be doing if the price *hadn't* dropped? You'd have held out for a bit longer, wouldn't you?'

'Suppose so.'

'Unless, say . . .' he paused, as if searching for a random example, 'you'd decided to move in with Duncan.'

'Oh very funny. Anyway, he's living in a tent at the moment. In Denmark.'

'Poor Duncan, used for sex and then flung aside like an old shoe.' He shook his head and gazed wistfully into the distance. 'Lying in a Danish bog, his heart broken.'

'Pity his biro isn't broken as well,' she said, sourly.

He looked at her with affection. 'It's amazing. The woman who complains about being sent love letters. Bet you read them all, though.' It was impossible to make Fran blush, but she looked discomfited.

'Most of them,' she muttered, and Spencer laughed.

They sat outside with their teas, at a plastic table, one of a cluster. Most were unoccupied, the flyblown tops dotted with sparrows, but at the one furthest from the Orangery door sat the two escapees from the Palm House, hands clasped, foreheads almost touching, eyes intertwined. Fran nudged Spencer to make sure he'd seen. He looked at them, ruminatively, and then turned back to her.

'Have you ever fancied someone with a twitch?'

She laughed and then stopped. 'Oh, you're serious?'

'Yes.'

'What sort of twitch?'

'Quite minor – bursts of blinking.'

'Well . . . that sounds OK. If he looked like a Greek God and was tremendous in the sack I could probably cope. Who is he, then?'

Spencer fiddled with the plastic spoon. He had thought about Blinky – Miles – a couple of times since yesterday, rather in the way that one lifts a plaster and checks a wound to see whether it's started to heal. 'Oh no one really,' he said. 'It's all hypothetical at the moment.'

'Is it?'

'Yeah.'

'Why's that?'

He shrugged. 'I'm just . . .' What could he say? That his emotional life currently felt as rich and vivid as an empty cardboard box? That his libido was taking an open-ended sabbatical? That his tortoise was the only *Hung and Heavy* fan still living in the flat? 'I'm just not interested.' He downed his tea like medicine and set the cup back on the saucer with a clunk.

Fran looked at him narrowly. 'You can't just drop this bloke into the conversation and then run away.'

'Which bloke?'

'The Hypothetical Blinking Man.'

'Oh him.' He waved a hand dismissively, wishing he hadn't brought up the subject; Fran's terrier instincts had been roused.

'Who is he, then?'

'Oh he's a . . . fictional character.'

'Really? Do tell me.' She folded her arms and leaned forward.

'He's the hero of a little-known fifties sci-fi film. Cult viewing. A gay scientist walks through a radioactive cloud while out shopping.'

'Shopping for what?'

'Table mats.'

'Where?'

'Selfridges.'

'*Right*.' She nodded with well-faked understanding. 'Well, that all hangs together nicely. Thanks for explaining.'

'No problem.' He stood and straightened his jacket. 'Shall we go?'

By the lake, a Burberry-clad elderly lady was feeding tiny cubes of sponge cake to a yelling, stamping mob of Canada Geese. Spencer, reminded of the pigeons, stopped to watch.

'Look how leathery their feet are,' said Fran.

'Yeah, they look like they're wearing biker boots.' Behind the squabbling ranks, two dark leggy birds were mincing around, radiating disapproval. 'And those ones –' he said.

'Moorhens,' supplied Fran.

'– *they* look like they're wearing high-heeled mules. And they're hanging around, waiting for the Philippino maid –'

'That's a mandarin duck.'

'– to get the cake for them.'

'What about the pigeons? What do they wear?'

'Trainers,' said Spencer, firmly. 'Supermarket own brand.'

'Sparrows?'

'Barefoot.' His eyes met Fran's in unspoken acknowledgement; this was exactly the sort of conversation Mark had always enjoyed, though his suggestions would have been far ruder.

They resumed walking towards the Victoria Gate, where the turnstile was a bottleneck of buggies.

'So what's next on the list, then?' asked Fran, weaving between toddlers. 'Mark's list, I mean.'

'I'm going to bite the bullet and do Madame Tussaud's.'

'On your own?'

'Are you volunteering?'

She looked at him nobly. 'Spence, if you want me I'll be there.'

'Thanks, friend.' He gave her arm a squeeze. 'I'll try not to ask. Madame Tussaud's and then the Lord Mayor's Show. And then the Norwegian tree that goes up in Trafalgar Square at Christmas. Oh God, and the sloth, I must visit the sloth.' He had a sudden vision of Mark propped up by pillows in his hospital bed, on the phone to London Zoo. He had wanted to sponsor an elephant for Spencer to visit, but was defeated by the price. 'Have you got anything smaller and cheaper?' he'd asked, as if to a greengrocer, and had finally settled on half a sloth – the other half had already been adopted – as an ironic comment on Spencer's sleeping patterns. 'I want you to treat that sloth like a brother,' he'd said, quite sternly. 'I'll be watching.' 'So Madame Tussaud's, the zoo, the Lord Mayor's Show and then the tree. I ought to make a list. I'll buy a notebook at the station.' He felt suddenly jittery, obligations rising out of the ground before him like mist.

Uncharacteristically, Fran took his arm as they walked up the road to the tube, passing alongside the plane trees that cast shadows across the road like the stripes of a zebra crossing.

'What happens at the end of that sci-fi film?' she asked. 'Does he get the boy?'

'Oh, I couldn't be bothered to sit through it,' said Spencer.

4

The resolutions – a litany of failure – were recorded on successive pages at the back of her address book.

1986
1. Get up 15 minutes earlier
2. Evening class
3. Make boys eat more fruit
4. Wash kitchen floor <u>twice</u> a week

1987
1. ?drop Friday visit to Dad
2. Encourage boys to watch less TV
3. ?Evening class

1988
1. ?Evening class
2. talk to Dr Petty re raise
3. <u>Talk to boys re college options</u>
4. ?suggest 1 night a week no TV
5. Make boys eat more fruit
6. ?drop Friday visit to Dad
7. Get up 10 minutes earlier
8. ?new kitchen floor

1989
See 1988

Iris turned over a page, wrote:

1990

at the top and then stared for a while at the blank space beneath it. She added:

1

and then decided, after a further pause, that she really ought to clean the flat. For an hour or so she gathered up items and dumped them in their correct places and surged round with a hoover and banged cupboard doors, secure in the knowledge that nothing that didn't involve actual explosives was capable of waking the boys on a Saturday morning. She even removed a pillow from under Robin's head, changed the pillowcase and then replaced it without any alteration in the rhythm of his breathing.

Feeling self-indulgent, she paused for a moment and watched him sleeping, his expression placid, a couple of scabbed shaving cuts just under his chin. She sometimes tried to see the twins as others saw them – friends had told her that they were quite handsome – but it seemed to involve a trick of the eyes, a de-focusing equivalent to that of visualizing the 3D shape in a 'Magic Eye' picture, difficult to sustain for more than a second or two and resulting in an image much less recognizable than that of a leaping dolphin. Occasionally she caught a glimpse of two square-jawed almost-men, but most of the time she could see only Robin and Tom, enormous versions of the scarlet roarers who'd arrived seven minutes apart, seventeen years, three hundred and sixty-four days and fourteen hours ago – still hungry, still dependent; quantitatively but not qualitatively changed. As she watched, Robin

44

sneezed in his sleep and turned over, dislodging an avalanche of dirty washing from the end of the bed. Iris scooped up the crumpled clothes and returned with them to the kitchen, stuffing them into an already overfull machine. Then, as the steady whirl and thump reverberated through the room she returned to the open address book.

She was still pondering the blank page when there was a tapping on the kitchen window and she looked up to see the wavering tip of a long bamboo pole. At the other end, on the other side of the garden wall, was Fran.

'I tried waving but you were concentrating so hard you didn't see me,' she said, when Iris had opened the back door. 'What were you doing?'

'Oh just, um . . . a shopping list.' The concept of writing New Year's Resolutions in September was too complicated to explain.

'I wanted to give you these.' Fran handed two envelopes over the wall, and a bottle of Australian champagne. 'It is today, isn't it, that they're legal?'

'That's right. Thanks, Fran, they'll love that.'

'Are they up yet? Or is that a stupid question?'

'They were at a party last night.' They'd returned at about 3 a.m. and let themselves in with the exaggerated quietness of the truly drunk. Iris had woken when one of them dropped his keys in the hall, and had stayed awake long enough to hear them giggling hysterically in the kitchen as they tried to make toast with crispbread (now fused all over the inside of the toaster).

'So it's a stupid question then,' said Fran. 'Say happy birthday from me and tell them mine's a vodka next time we're in a pub together.'

'Would you like a cup of tea?'

'Can't. We're supposed to be fixing this bloody guttering.'

'Fran?' Peter's sonorous voice called from the shed next door.

'Coming.' She rolled her eyes. '*God*, it would be nice to spend just one weekend not propping the house up. See you.'

Back in the kitchen, Iris picked up her pen again and added a full stop after the number 1. Four years ago, the first time she had written the resolutions, it had been on an impulse and she had rattled out the first ideas that came into her head. Her mother had died just the month before and the boys' birthday had been the first remotely pleasant event for a very, very long time. It had seemed a hopeful new starting point, a potential hinge on which she could begin to turn her life and, even in retrospect, the items had not seemed overly ambitious. The next year, when it had become clear how much support her father would need, she had toned them down a little; the year after that, gripped with frustration, she had come up with twenty-eight suggestions (including 'tell boys to stop growing' – a response to a terrifying bill for school uniforms) and then ripped out the page and started again. The year after that had been too demoralizing to even think about. This year, she had decided, there were to be no repeats. This year every resolution was to be new and all of them achievable.

1. Do all the housework myself

This was not (she told herself) the supine gesture it appeared, but a positive step. She had tried cleaning rotas, and they had always failed. Neither of the boys appeared to see any point in keeping the flat tidy. Their vast shoes lay like reeking tank traps across the hall, tripping anyone who came in. They experienced no revulsion at the sight of toenail clippings scattered across the living-room rugs and the smell of damp towels screwed up into a bundle and left under the bed for two weeks seemed scarcely to register. They were happy to drink tea out of cups encrusted with coffee grounds and when Tom dropped half a packet of sugar onto the kitchen floor, he'd considered that kicking the spilled grains under the washing machine was an adequate response; three weeks later Iris was still peeling her shoes off the lino every time she used the kettle. There was no malice involved; they just didn't *think*.

Of course, they liked wearing clean crease-free clothes, but never evinced curiosity as to how these things appeared in the cupboard. Iris had stopped ironing once, but had resumed after five days when the enormous pile of washing actually prevented her from getting to the sink. Neither twin had apparently noticed this, but then the sink was merely the place where you fished around in cold scummy water to find the can-opener. She knew that to an outside eye – Fran's for instance – her inability to enforce any kind of regular tasks seemed feeble. But what Fran – in her determined way – had never really grasped was how tiring it was to try and be the boss all the time. Begging, nagging, baffled tears – none of these things were worth it. The boys would very slightly alter their behavioural patterns for a couple of days (say, trying to aim for the bin when cutting their toenails in the living room) before reverting to exactly the same irritating habits that had prompted her outburst in the first place. Iris would be exhausted, and nothing would have changed.

How much easier, then, to do it all herself. Instead of determining that Robin and Tom would or should have household responsibilities, she was going to work from the baseline that nothing got done unless she did it. She would no longer be living a lie and, as far as she could see, her workload would be exactly the same. It would be freedom of mind rather than body, but would mean that any action by the twins – anything at all, from the merest lifting of a pair of pants into the linen basket, to the rinsing of a jam knife before it was used for marmite – would be a bonus. It would be a victory born of defeat, and she wished she had thought of it years before.

2. Dress appropriately

This resolution had been prompted by an incident at work, some weeks ago. It had been raining heavily, and she'd been shaking off her old blue anorak prior to hanging it on a peg. The part-time receptionist, Ayesha, had glanced at it in passing as she carried an armful of notes into the filing room. 'Nice coat,' she'd said, as the door closed. Iris had actually looked round, assuming that Ayesha must have been speaking to someone else. 'Nice coat'? From someone who had a pierced nose? She'd looked at the anorak anew. It was dark blue and had a zip and a quilted lining. In an identity parade, its only distinguishing features would have been a 'Save the Children' sticker, now bent in half and covered in fluff, and the crumbled remains of a shortbread in one of the pockets. 'Nice coat'?

That evening, she had checked with Fran. Could Ayesha's remark have been sarcastic?

'No, people wear these now.'

'Do they? You mean, not just people like me?'

'What do you mean, "people like you"?'

'People who've been wearing the same coat for seven years. Longer than that, actually, because it was my mother's. She thought it was sensible, though – she wouldn't have worn it for a social occasion.'

'Well, its time has come. You are officially finger on pulse.'

Iris had pondered her trendiness. 'Does that mean it's been *un*fashionable for the whole time I've been wearing it?'

Fran had hesitated. 'Not so much unfashionable as –' She'd struggled for a description.

'Frumpy?'

'No. More . . . *a*fashionable.'

It was a scientific distinction that Iris could appreciate, describing not so much the opposite of fashion, as the total absence of it. She'd taken a moment to absorb this. 'Could you tell me when its time has gone again? Maybe I should know. I don't want to become an embarrassment.' Like Mrs Simms, she had thought suddenly, a neighbour from her childhood. Mrs Simms had taught the piano, had been to Oxford and was reputed to know Anglo-Saxon; she was famous locally, however, for dressing like Wurzel Gummidge. No item of her clothing ever seemed to have been selected with reference to any other item. An average outfit might consist of a beret, a nip-waisted 'New Look' jacket, a dirndl, ribbed tights and patent-leather sandals; it was as if she dressed in the dark. 'Her mind's on higher things,' Iris's mother had once explained, kindly. Sitting in the kitchen with Fran, Iris had felt a presentiment that she might turn into Mrs Simms – so unaware of fashion that she ended up creating her own.

After the conversation she had looked critically through her wardrobe – at the items of clothing chosen solely for their practicality, or the ability of their pockets to hold a paperback and a tube pass. Style simply hadn't entered it. At eighteen she had at least had an awareness of what someone of her own age was supposed to wear, even if she never seemed quite the right shape to carry it off. Her nickname at school had been 'Lanky' and it was still a reasonable description. 'You could be a real clothes horse,' a friend had said once; it was supposed to be a compliment, but Iris had instantly imagined one of those wooden concertinas, draped with damp washing.

After the twins were born, for many years her clothes seemed to have been covered in mashed potato, and by the time they had moved on to packed lunches she had somehow lost the thread; she no longer knew what she was supposed to look like. What did thirty-seven-year-olds wear?

The boys were hopeless; they seemed to view her as a separate species, one to whom the normal rules did not apply. When prodded, they'd occasionally offer the phrase 'you look nice', but in much the same way as one might praise a Martian's tentacle-protector, if a comment were demanded. What she needed was a guide, someone who could point the way through the maze, so that at least she'd be going in the same direction as everyone else. She thought, in the meantime, that she might start buying some magazines and looking at the pictures, to get her eye in, so to speak.

3. Limit

'Oh Godddd.' Eyes half closed, hair randomly flattened, Tom shuffled into the kitchen. 'Have we got any aspirin?'

'Happy birthday,' said Iris.

'Oh,' he nodded very slowly. 'Ta.' He was dressed in Tom and Jerry boxer shorts and a huge baggy jumper, his arms wrapped around himself.

'Paracetamol's better for a hangover – there's some in the bathroom.' He shuffled out again, hunched over as if battling against a strong wind.

3. Limit Dad's phonecalls

'I can't get the top off.' Tom reappeared, pathetically holding out the paracetamol container. He sank into a chair as Iris lined up the arrows and flipped off the top, and watched pallidly as she filled a glass of water for him.

'Thanks, Mum.' He made a great play of swallowing the tablets, jerking his head back and retching as they went down. He had always been terrible at taking medicine, and she had dreadful memories of the time he'd had impetigo, when she had had to invent a different ploy for every single dose of antibiotic: mashing in jam, liquidizing in syrup, crushing in ice cream.

'I think I'll go back to bed,' said Tom, barely moving his mouth.

'Do you want your presents now?'

'No. Later.' He stood up carefully and made his way out of the kitchen, one hand on the wall to support himself.

Iris still liked to maintain a semblance of surprise when it came to giving birthday presents, so the boys would specify a narrow range of goods, among which she was allowed to freely pick her gift. Robin had requested a subscription to either *Viz* magazine or *The Face* (she had chosen the latter) while Tom had asked for a Nike t-shirt, v-necked, short-sleeved either in dark blue with a white neckline or white with a dark blue neckline. Even though it made shopping easier, she yearned for the days when there were so many things they wanted that she could scarcely decide which to get. Flying in the face of experience she still bought them one or two extras – books they would never read, key-rings for losing, videos for taping over – but the resulting pile of gifts, supplemented only by Boots' tokens from her father and a five-pound postal order (between two) from Auntie Kath, seemed woefully little compared to the mountains of electrical goods and clothing reportedly received by their friends.

'IgottaincarstereoanerwalkmansixpairsofCalvinKleinpants anerRolextypewatchthanksforaskinMissisUnwin,' as Tom's friend, the fast-talking but always impeccably polite Leon, had informed her recently.

'How on earth does his mum afford it?' she'd asked after he left. ('ByeMissisUnwinthanksforhavinme.')

'His uncle nicks it,' Tom had replied, laconically.

3. Limit Dad's phonecalls to half an hour

She'd given up trying to cut down the frequency of her visits; her father was lonely, her work was only five minutes' walk from his house and there was therefore really no excuse not to pop round for supper on Tuesdays and Thursdays and for at least a cup of tea on Fridays, though the latter was not an absolutely rigid appointment. Sunday lunch, on the other hand, was immutable; the roast went in the oven before her father went to church and she would arrive just in time to make the gravy, a task which she rather enjoyed. After lunch, she'd do the washing-up and her father would take 'ten minutes' and then he'd garden and she'd read, and then soon enough it would be Monday again. And if there were moments when she panicked at the encroachment upon her own life, when she wondered what would happen when the twins left home – whether he'd expect her to visit *every* night – on the whole it seemed simpler just to go along with his routine rather than live with the guilt of breaking it. The problem (the problem that she wanted to tackle this year, anyway) was the phonecalls. They were getting longer.

On Mondays she rang her father; on Saturdays – and often on Wednesdays – and sometimes even on Sunday evenings, he rang her. As they had always only just seen each other, there wasn't an awful lot to say, and he took such a very long time to say it.

He had never been much of a conversationalist, in the dictionary sense of giving and receiving information in a relaxed and entertaining way, and on her visits they would often maintain a comfortable silence for long stretches; but of course that wasn't possible on the phone, and his calls were more in the nature of slow monologues, which she would prod along with supplementary questions. She had recently splurged a frightening amount of money on a cordless phone and had thus found that during one of her father's *average* calls she was able to empty the washing machine, hang the clothes on the line, take them in again when it started raining, cut an irritating snag off her left thumbnail and peel a panful of potatoes, all the while saying little more than 'uh huh' and 'really?'

He was holding back the silence, postponing the moment when the phone would go down and he'd return to an empty house, and as a result she knew about every aspect of his life, knew which shoe polish he used and where the best pork chops could be bought. She knew his favourite weather forecaster (Michael Fish) and where he got his lawnmower repaired. Most of all she knew about Mr Hickey, the hated neighbour whose garden backed on to his own and whose fence was, according to her father, creeping inch by inch across his herbaceous border.

Robin and Tom had long since ducked out of the Sunday visit, but still dutifully talked on the phone to him once a week, calls in which her father tried to resuscitate his moribund conversational skills.

'Hi, Grandad.

'It's Robin . . . yes I know, everyone says we sound alike.

'Ha ha.

'Fine.

'Art, Media Studies and General Studies.

'Ha ha.

'Six foot five.

'OK, bye then. Here's Tom.'

'Hi, Grandad.

'Yup.

'Six foot five, yup.

'Same as last week, Geography, Spanish and Theatre Studies.

'Don't know yet, depends if I pass them.

'Yup, she's called Samantha Fox, we've been going out for two years.

'You told me that one last time.

'OK, bye then. Here's Mum.'

Frowning at Tom, she would take the phone. 'Hi, Dad. How's things?'

Apart from 'Oh yes, and what did he say?' that would be almost her last contribution to the conversation. Towards the end of the call he would usually remember to ask her a couple of questions about work or finances, but was completely thrown if she replied with anything other than the blandest of assurances. Detail rattled him.

'What do you mean? Processing what?'

'Word-processing skills. It's just a three-day course, so I can keep up with new –'

'Dr Steiner saying you're not skilled at the moment, or what?'

'No, it's just that we're computerizing the –'

'It's a vocabulary thing, is it?'

'No it's a –'

'He knows you got a place at university, doesn't he?'

'It's not that, it's –'

'I used to learn a word a day. You should get the boys to try that. Start at A in the dictionary and work through . . .'

It was not – she told herself – that her father didn't care, just that he found it hard to focus on other people's problems. It was as if her crisis of eighteen years ago was still quite enough to be going on with thank you very much, the shockwaves still reverberating.

She looked at the resolution again, and then – feeling brutal – crossed out 'half an hour' and substituted '20 minutes'; there was no point in being half-hearted about this. She had to be ruthless in pursuit of this year's aims – ruthless, bold, bloody and resolute as she reclaimed her life.

Though as to her method of prising him off the phone, she had no clear strategy. There was a limit to the number of overflowing milk pans or unexpected visitors she could claim, and she really didn't feel ready (just yet) to tell him the truth.

54

4. Widen my outside interests
She paused for a moment, crossed the item out, and substituted:

4. Acquire an outside interest
And then, because it looked such a pathetic statement, such a
spineless admission of defeat, she scrubbed it out again.

The trouble was there was no time, there was never any
time; meeting a friend for lunch, finishing a book, watching a
TV programme without being interrupted every thirty
seconds were the peaks of her ambition. The window of
opportunity which had opened when the boys were at last old
enough to be left in the flat by themselves had been slammed
shut by her mother's protracted illness, and then by the
amount of time she spent with Dad. She was no longer sure
what she was interested *in* – it was such a long time since she
had actively pursued anything other than the dullest necessi-
ties. Other women her age went to clubs and wore leather
trousers and took drugs. Or had weekend cottages in the
country and dogs and au pairs. And husbands.

In just under a year the boys would be off to university and
everything would change. Suddenly she'd have spare evenings
and Saturdays – vast empty echoing spaces of time to fill with
activities not involving laundry or vegetable preparation. The
flat would triple in size, and those moments of solitude which
– at present – she so relished, would become the norm. She
needed to prepare.

The washing machine began the groaning drum-roll which
denoted its spin cycle. It was almost as old as the twins and
had begun to emit ominous twanging noises on unloading.
Clothes were starting to emerge without their buttons, and
the machine would subsequently disgorge them in small
pieces, like teeth after a fight. Under the thunderous climax of

the spin, she could hear the fragments rattling round some-where deep in the interior. Recently, and for the first time, she had managed to push her savings account over the £300 mark; it was rather depressing to think it would all go again on a new washing machine.

She looked again at the ruined page and decided to use the remaining space to make a list of the things she enjoyed doing most. She had got as far as 'Going to the library' and 'Having a bath' when Robin emerged.

'Hi, Mum.' He gave her a stubbly peck on the cheek. He was both more affectionate and more gloomy than Tom.

'Happy birthday.'

'Ta.' He lowered himself into a chair. 'I'm getting old. Eighteen's *old*.'

'Robin, what do I enjoy doing?'

'What?'

'If someone asked you what I was interested in, what would you say?'

'What you're interested in?'

'Yes.'

He wiped his nose and sat in a stupor indicative of deep thought. Almost thirty seconds went by.

'It doesn't matter,' she said, closing the address book with a snap. 'Bacon sandwich?'

5

The trampled vegetable patch had made an incomplete recovery. When all was safely gathered in, the harvest comprised four pounds of plums (too high for Porky to reach), a wizened pumpkin imprinted with a trotter-mark and a small bucket of root vegetables. Of the five carrots which had survived, four were deformed.

Fran allowed a junior school party to feed the latter to Porky, in the interests of recycling, and cut the remaining one into twenty-eight pieces so that everyone in the class could have a bite.

'I don't like things what aren't cooked.'

'I can't eat this, I'm allergic.'

'Lee's spat his bit out, Miss.'

'Miss, my mum said I shouldn't eat things off the ground.'

Pieces were dropped, thrown, trampled in the mud and offered to the ducks. The teacher, a weary-looking woman in her forties with a wool suit and a laissez-faire attitude, rolled her eyes at Fran. '*I* think it's delicious,' she announced, crunching her own portion, 'and it's very kind of this lady to give her carrot to us, isn't it?'

There was a low drone of 'yesses' from most of the class and a soft but distinct 'This garden smells of shit,' from a very small boy in a red woolly hat. When the wave of thrilled giggles had died away, Fran made the most of the opportunity.

'There's a very good reason why it smells like that. Anyone know why?'

'Cos it's your toilet,' said the same boy.

'It's not *my* toilet,' said Fran, when the class had finished shrieking, 'but when Porky the Pig goes to the toilet, we scoop up the poo and we dig it into the earth here.'

'Uuuuuuuuur'

'Because animal poo helps plants to grow.'

'Uuuuuuuuur'

'That's disgusting, Miss.'

'So Porky eats vegetables, and Porky's poo helps new vegetables to grow.'

'Uuuuuuuuur'

'I ain't never going to eat a carrot in my life no more,' said a horrified girl.

'And something which helps plants to grow is called a *fer-til-ize-er*.'

'Who can remember that word?' asked the teacher, with little hope in her voice.

As the class was shepherded away towards the hen house where Spike, the farm's animal expert, would take them through the basics of embryology, Fran started to prise the bits of carrot from the mud.

'That was really superb.'

She spun round, startled, and trod on Barry's foot. 'What?' she asked, irritated. He had taken to standing directly behind her during teaching sessions and she always forgot he was there.

'How you took the reaction of those children and turned it into something they'd never forget. It was superb.'

'Yeah, well, thanks.'

'I mean it.' He looked at her earnestly.

'OK. Well, thanks.'

'I learn *so much* just by watching you.'

He seemed to be standing closer to her than was strictly necessary.

'Like using the word "poo" a lot with the under tens?' she asked facetiously, trying to break the atmosphere.

'Your whole rapport with them. It's wonderful to watch.'

'Good. Well, that's . . . good.' Hoping the conversation was at an end, she bent to retrieve another piece of carrot; Barry dived simultaneously and they avoided cracking heads by a millimetre. He shot up again, knocking her with his shoulder and causing her to stagger a couple of feet and drop all the bits she'd already picked up.

'Bloody hell, Barry!'

'Sorry sorry. Let me do it.' He fell to his knees and scrabbled in the mire at her feet and she shifted awkwardly, feeling like Marie Antoinette with a serf.

'Here.' Still kneeling, he proffered a muddy handful and then scrambled up, looking anxious, poised for the next task. Fran wondered how to get rid of him. 'Tell you what, I'm going to give these to Porky. Can you carry on with seed-head collection in the meadow?'

He practically jumped in his eagerness to obey.

Up at the pigpen, now reinforced with stakes sunk deep into the ground and steel-mesh fencing, she took a little rest and scratched Porky's scaly back as he snuffled at the trough. She bore him no ill-will for the destruction he'd caused: he was a pig and had done what pigs do; their motivation was always so blissfully transparent. Porky rechecked the corners of the trough for unnoticed shreds of carrot, sniffed hopefully in Fran's direction and then with a curiously slow-motion action, toppled sideways into a puddle and lay there flapping his ears.

This was the first clear morning after days of constant rain, and the normal jobs of the farm had been sidelined by the necessity of holding back the mud. The area was naturally boggy and only the constant application of chopped bark, builders' rubble (broken down with sledgehammers), shredded hay and home-made duckboards kept the paths from reverting to their primeval state. The staff, of course, wore wellies; their visitors, on the other hand, wore their most treasured possessions, and it had been known for a child to refuse to get out of the school coach because of the danger of dirtying his trainers.

From her vantage point by the sty, Fran could see her colleagues labouring in the swamp: Barry, in a bright red jumper, crouched in the sodden grass with a supply of plastic bags and a pair of scissors; Claud, bald head shining in the sun, wheeling a barrow full of rubble past the classroom; Spike, by the chicken coop, inverting an indignant hen for the edification of the junior school class; Mick scooping dead leaves out of the pond with a fishing net, watched by a group of restless fourteen-year-olds; and Costas, a volunteer in his sixties, laying duckboards with rigorous perfection, as if tiling a patio.

Costas's council flat overlooked the farm, with the result that he viewed it as his own back garden and spent a great deal of time making sure it looked nice for the neighbours. He also owned an allotment, on which he grew vast vegetables with the aid of as many chemicals as were legally available. Sometimes Fran would turn round from forking-in her carefully sieved compost to find Costas watching her with a mystified expression. 'How you expect your potatoes get big like this?' he'd asked contemptuously last week, gesturing at her with a King Edward the size of a rugby ball.

Claud completed the last few yards up to the sty at a run, dropped the barrow with a thud and leaned over, hands on knees, to catch his breath.

'Where d'you want this unloaded?' asked Fran. He waved his arm at the patch of ground beside the tool shed. It was rampant with ragwort during the summer and much enjoyed by the hens, although Fran had caught Costas lurking there a couple of times, obviously dreaming of Weedol. She started to throw the lumps of rubble into a heap.

'I'm glad I caught you,' said Claud, when he'd got his breath back and had helped her sling the last few pieces onto the pile.

'Oh yes,' she said, cautiously. The last time Claud had used that phrase, she'd ended up agreeing to be press liaison officer, resulting in an article in the local paper entitled 'Farmer Fran' and illustrated by a photo of her bending over to pick up a shovel, making her arse look the size of Porky's.

'Just wanted to say that you've done a fantastic job with Barry, I mean he's . . . he's –' they both turned automatically to look at the distant figure, bent humbly to his task '– he's now a fully contributing member of the team. It's really a very impressive achievement.' He nodded affably at her and wiped the sweat off his forehead with a grubby hand, leaving a long smear where he'd once had a hairline. Fran felt a bit awkward.

'I didn't actually do anything, Claud.'

'No, no, I think it's terribly important in these sort of cases to give credit where it's due. After all, I mean, directly following the . . . the . . .' he fumbled for a non-inflammatory phrase, 'incident, I have to admit that I thought we might have to have a . . . a . . .' his lips hesitated over the letter p (punch up? wondered Fran, prayer meeting?), 'plenary session.'

'Oh right.' Well, thank God they'd avoided that option. She'd attended one last year, purportedly to discuss local residents' complaints about noise pollution – specifically a very loud cockerel – but with Claud's boneless arm at the tiller they'd drifted right off the subject and spent nearly an hour deciding what to call the twin lambs they'd just acquired.

'But we've all seen how much time you've been . . . er . . . putting in with Barry.'

'Seriously – all I did was shout at him. And then I took him a cup of tea. You saw, you were there.'

'But since then it's pretty obvious that you've more than made up for –'

'Since then I haven't done anything. He follows me round. I can't shake him off.'

Claud smiled knowingly and gave her a stagy little thumbs-up. 'Good work anyway. In this sort of situation, I think it's always important to –'

She gave up the struggle. 'Thanks.'

Claud smiled rather sweetly and trundled his barrow away for the next load, skirting the pen where Delboy and Rodney stood bleating incessantly, impatient for their lunch.

On the day of the pig escape, Barry had apologized to her so many times that she'd eventually told him to shut up and forget about it. She thought she could date his transformation into a human dynamo from that second. He arrived at the farm before Fran, ate his lunchtime sandwich on the move, and was still at work when she left at 5.30, usually somewhere in her own domain where he seemed to regard every gap in the vegetation as a knife to the heart. She had once come across him pathetically staking individual stalks of barley with tiny bamboo canes. 'It *might* work,' he'd said, looking at her with the kind of expression that Bullseye reserved for Bill Sykes.

At the morning meetings, he not only listened but actually wrote down the day's tasks in a specially bought spiral-bound notebook. He washed up mugs, he volunteered to buy biscuits and he'd spent the whole of a weekend drawing a poster for the autumn open day (it showed Hagwood as a sort of Noah's Ark in a sea of concrete, the assembled animals welcoming the visitors with outstretched trotters and wings). It was neatly done and much, much better than Claud's prototype design:

a piece of paper with the words 'Please come to day of community fun and action at Hagwood Farm' written on it in black felt tip.

There remained a significant gap between Barry's enthusiasm and his competence; what he most resembled was one of the brooms in *The Sorcerer's Apprentice*, lacking in any marked skill or initiative, but able to apply himself endlessly to a single task until redirected. 'You can stop doing that now, Barry' was a phrase never far from her lips these days.

Porky heaved himself up and nudged her in the back with his snout, grunting enquiringly. She showed him her empty hands before dusting the dried mud from them and starting back down the hill. As she neared the meadow, she could see that Barry had inadvertently dropped three of the plastic bags; one of them had already blown into the pond and the other two had been caught by a breeze and were cartwheeling across the grass like giant dandelion puffs. She called to him and gestured, and watched with a mixture of irritation and amusement as he lolloped after them.

'Maybe I *can* take some credit,' she said to Peter that evening. 'Shouting at him was obviously the nudge he needed.'

Peter, a screw between his teeth, held out a hand and she snapped a red plastic rawlplug off a chain of twenty and placed it in his palm. He was replacing a bathroom shelf – one of the original fittings, much lauded in the estate agent's description – which had collapsed under the weight of a new bottle of shampoo, hosing the linoleum with toiletries and taking a picture down with it.

'What do you think?'

He tapped in the rawlplug carefully, and removed the screw from his mouth.

'I'm not sure shouting is ever worth it.'

'Aren't you? We're not supposed to, obviously; it's not a recognized teaching practice these days, but I can't help feeling it did him good. Gave him a metaphorical kick up the arse.' Her brother was silent. 'The only trouble is, I think he's imprinted me – you know, when orphaned baby ducks think the farmer's their mother and follow him round the entire time.' She sat on the edge of the bath as Peter screwed the brackets onto the shelf, carrying out the procedure with his usual slow thoroughness. If the profession of Health and Safety Officer hadn't existed he would have had to invent it, the job fitted him like an insulated glove with special grips on the palm. He looked up at her only when he'd put away the spare screws, and counted those remaining to check that he hadn't left any rolling dangerously around the bathroom floor.

'Have you tried asking him?'

'Asking him what? Whether he thinks I'm his mother?'

'Whether he thinks it did him good for you to shout at him.'

'Oh.' Fran paused. 'No,' she said, reluctantly.

'Perhaps it would be a good idea if you did.' There was an edge of reproof in his voice.

'All right, all right. God, you're such a head boy sometimes.' He looked slightly hurt, and she added, 'Only joking,' although she wasn't. The serious figure who – without raising his voice – had single-handedly eliminated smoking in the bogs during his reign at Rose Everett Comprehensive, had changed only minimally. The gravitas, the deeply felt but plonkingly expressed morality which had set him apart from his contemporaries, were still present. His advice on a given subject was never given lightly, but considered, weighed and carefully prescribed. If followed correctly, the outcome was usually good. There was just something about the way it was proffered that made it terribly hard to take.

'Yeah, well I might give it a try,' said Fran, after a while. She wasn't sure that she really wanted to know what Barry thought.

'I've got something to tell you,' said Peter as he replaced the tools in the box he'd received from their stepfather last Christmas.

'What?'

He hesitated a moment, apparently trying to work out whether the twelve-inch Philips screwdriver went in to the left or the right upper storage tray and eventually fitting it in with the precision of a watchmaker. His face was so heavy in thought that Fran wondered if something serious had happened. It was a fear of hers that she'd scoff once too often at his hypochondria, and end up apologizing to him in intensive care.

'What?' she asked again.

'I've met someone.'

For a moment, she didn't catch his meaning and then he smiled a little shyly, looking suddenly five years younger.

'What, a *girlfriend*?'

'Well, we've just started seeing each other,' he said with his usual caution.

Fran laughed in exasperation. 'I thought you had bad news. I was just about to make you some hot sweet tea.'

'That's no longer the recommended treatment for shock.'

'I *know*.' They grinned at each other for what felt like the first time in ages.

'So, tell me about her,' she prodded. 'What's her name?'

'Sylvie.'

'And what's she do?'

'She's a music therapist.'

'And where did you meet her?'

'At choir. She's our new accompanist.' Peter had a thin but tuneful baritone and claimed that regular singing helped free up his sinuses.

'How long have you been seeing her?'

'Just a few weeks.'

'And what's she like?' Fran was accustomed to this crumb-by-crumb method of extracting personal information from her brother, but now he paused for so long that she started to wonder if he'd misheard the question. She was about to repeat it when he opened his mouth.

'She's . . .' he began, and then stopped. A beatific expression settled across his features, like a tarpaulin over a swimming pool.

'You're smitten!' said Fran, with delight.

Looking absurdly pleased with himself, he finished packing the tools and snapped the box shut. 'Would you like to meet her?'

'Of course I would.'

'Are you around on Tuesday evening? We could come back here after practice.'

'Great. I'll cook if you want.'

'Thanks.' He looked suddenly worried. 'She can't eat cheese. Or wheat products.'

'No problem.'

'Or chocolate. She gets migraines.'

'Right. What about fish?'

He hesitated. 'I *think* she likes fish.'

'Well why don't you phone her and check?'

'OK. Thanks, Fran.' He hefted the toolbox cautiously, with straight back and bent knees as specified by the Practices at Work poster he had recently put up in the hall. Fran started replacing the bottles on the shelf.

'Do you want all these?' she called as he clumped down-stairs. 'You've got three different sorts of dandruff shampoo.'

'Maybe I've got three different sorts of dandruff.'

She grinned; on Peter's scale of emotions, that remark was the equivalent of turning cartwheels.

6

Apart from the regular rasp of his breath, the young man on the examination couch had made no noise since the ambulance men had plucked him off the street. A scarlet stain matted the hair above his left ear and extended in a tacky film across his cheek and temple, and he lay in the recovery position, eyes closed, head on one side, his right arm curled and his left arm dangling over the side of the couch. Spencer gave it little push and it swung back and forth.

'I know you're awake,' said Spencer.

There was no change in the rhythm of the breathing. Marsha, the night sister who had started to clean up the head wound, folded her arms and tutted loudly. She had dropped the soiled dressing into a pot of antiseptic, turning the pale pink liquid a violent crimson. 'Waste of everyone's time,' she said to no one in particular.

'It's surprisingly easy to tell when someone's pretending to be unconscious,' continued Spencer, conversationally. 'For instance, the muscle tone in your eyelids is completely normal. Also, once you get under a good artificial light it becomes obvious that red gloss paint looks absolutely nothing like blood. It's a lot more difficult to remove, for a start.'

'A *lot* more difficult,' repeated Marsha. 'The doctor's coat is completely ruined, I hope you realize that. Also the sheet. Also, I was on my break till they brought you in and now my toasted sandwich will have got all cold.' She turned to Spencer. 'Do you want a psych consult? Dr Jayaram's already here with the aspirin OD.'

'Might as well.'

Marsha wheeled the dressings trolley away with as much noise as possible, managing a final high-decibel collision with the door jamb which made even Spencer jump. He started to fill in the casualty card. 'Unless you tell me your age,' he said to the figure on the couch, 'I'm going to put forty.' This tactic had worked occasionally in the past, but only on women and gay men. There was no response and he put '30-ish' in the space on the card. 'I'm writing in your notes now that I can't find anything physically wrong with you. That you appear to be fit and healthy.'

It was odd how cases turned up in clusters: no perforated ulcers for months, and then two in adjacent cubicles; a flurry of broken ankles, and then nothing but elbows for a week. This was the third feigned ailment he'd seen in as many days. The first had been a case of driving-test avoidance, subsumed into an unconvincing wrist injury, the second an embarrassingly poor stab at appendicitis, enacted by a writhing student who couldn't face telling his parents he'd failed his re-sits. Spencer had tempered scepticism with paracetamol, and both had gone home. The current patient was more of a challenge.

There was a quiet knock, and the door opened just enough for Vincent's narrow frame to slide in. He gave Spencer a tiny wave. 'Hello, friend.'

'Hello, Vincent.'

'Hello, young man. Sister Leonard has been telling me about you.' Vincent went up to the figure on the couch, and – as Spencer had done ten minutes before – gently raised one of his eyelids with a long finger. Then he bent towards the red splotch and sniffed delicately. 'All right, I think I get the picture.'

'I'm going to leave you with Dr Jayaram,' said Spencer. He pointed in the direction of the office and mimed lifting a teacup. Vincent nodded and mimed two spoonfuls of sugar. Spencer mimed a biscuit. Vincent smiled beneath his moustache, shook his head and waved him away.

At the reception desk, Marsha shuffled through the cards of the waiting patients like a croupier. The department was in its 5 a.m. lull; the after-club fight victims had been X-rayed, stitched and booted out, and the sea of chairs was three-quarters empty.

With a sinking of the heart, Spencer noticed a familiar figure stretched across three of them. The night sister followed his gaze.

'Yeah, he's back.'

'What's he presenting with?'

'Haemoptysis.'

The stench of glue projected a good ten feet around Callum Strang, and the other occupants of the waiting room had given him a wide berth. He lay on his side, hands in the pockets of his greatcoat, chest heaving in and out with a bubbling wheeze that was audible above the whine of the coffee machine. Amidst the wreck of his twenty-two-year-old face – the dirt, the premature lines, the shiny halo around the mouth and nostrils – there was still only one thing that drew the attention: the poorly executed tattoo above the eyebrows that read 'EVOSTIK'.

'Hello, Callum.'

His eyes opened at once, but seemed to take a while to focus. Then he smiled widely, looking genuinely pleased and revealing a wilderness of chipped and missing teeth. 'Heyyy, Tsocter Carroll. I hoed you were on.' The blurred words floated out on a miasma of glue, and Spencer swayed away involuntarily.

'How have you been, Callum?'

'Alrigh. I was alrigh. I was tsoing alrigh. I was offit an I was savin a bit. Then lars coupla tsays I been coughin blood again.'

'Where have you been sleeping?'

'Allover.' He took a hand out of his pocket and flapped it around. 'Anyfuckinwhere. Issnot cole. Sorry for swearin.'

Marsha joined them. 'Do you want to take a look at him?'

'Yes,' said Spencer, depressed at the prospect.

'I was offit and savin,' repeated Callum.

'Anybody else I should see right now?'

'I carn tsake it when people stare . . .'

'Nah. You take ten minutes while we clean this fella up a bit. Have a coffee. Change your coat. Eat my cold sandwich.' She gave him a little shove towards the office, and started to haul Callum upright.

Smoking in the office had been banned for over a year, but the ceiling had not yet been repainted and was still a deep-yellow reminder of the tensions of the past. Spencer made two cups of tea and then drank one while sitting on the desk, his back to the window that overlooked the empty ambulance bay. He'd cleared a space on the desktop by dumping everything onto a chair, the 'everything' consisting of the nurses' night report, Marsha's sandwich and the pharmacology textbook and notes he'd brought with him, purportedly for studying during his 2 a.m. lunch break.

In the event he hadn't had a lunch break, but in any case bringing the notes into work had been a desperate measure prompted by the total lassitude which overcame him every time he set foot in the flat. His exams were in May and he hadn't done any serious revision for weeks. In fact, the only things he'd managed to read with any thoroughness were the letters pages of *Reptile Monthly* and a surprisingly homoerotic Dick Francis novel he'd found in the hospital waiting room. Yesterday, after he'd awoken from a muddy swirl of dreams into the disorientating half day left to him before night shift, it had taken him two hours – *two hours* – to get washed and dressed. He'd kept stopping halfway through tasks to remember other tasks that he ought to have done yesterday and which needed to be written down if he wasn't to forget them again today. The milk bill. Hoover bags. A box of crickets. A lettuce. A third-birthday present for Nina. Contact lens solution. Another lettuce. A mountain of trivia that had to be conquered before he could even start to think about anything remotely important, like whether he should try and get Bill to a vet or what to do about the snails.

God in heaven, the snails . . . He had meant to find an alternative to Fran's suggested method of killing the eggs, but had not got around to it, with the result that the tank now held not five but one hundred and thirty-seven snails. The babies were only the size of peas, and looked rather chic with their pearly, almost iridescent shells, but he was now buying two lettuces a day and the tank was a sea of slime.

He was, to use a phrase of his grandmother's, Letting Things Slip. The flat was starting to look neglected, if not shabby. Unanswered messages were piling up on the answerphone. And over the last four weeks he had ticked only one item off Mark's list. He'd chosen a rainy Saturday (and what a perfect illustration of his thought processes *that* decision had been) to visit Madame Tussaud's, and out of a kind of willed misery had decided to go alone. The queue had been gargantuan and fizzing with youthful hilarity and he had stood under a dripping umbrella feeling like a man out of a Magritte painting. It was nearly ninety minutes before he'd actually entered the building and joined the shuffling procession. At first he had been staggered by the sheer awfulness of the waxworks, their orange skin pitted with what looked like ants' footprints. But with no one to nudge or exclaim to, without Mark to fake a collapse in front of Mrs Thatcher or grope Mel Gibson's bum, the glacial slowness of the queue had soon become unbearable. The crowd was too thick to allow overtaking and, driven to desperation by the prospect of a room full of Australian soap stars, Spencer had spotted a fire door, ducked between Desmond Tutu and Nelson Mandela, and exited into a rain-swept alley behind Baker Street tube. The door had clanged shut on a row of startled faces. He felt obscurely that he had let Mark down.

'You're very deep in thought,' said Vincent, standing in the open door of the office.

'The opposite really,' said Spencer. 'Just paddling around in the shallows.'

'Is this my tea?' He indicated the pallid cupful beside the kettle.

'Yes. It's not great, I'm afraid. Cheap teabags and no pot.'

'No pot?'

'Someone dropped it last week. Me, actually.'

'It doesn't matter, I've tasted worse.' Vincent took a second sip. 'Well, maybe not. Incidentally, I've waved goodbye to the man with the paint on his head.'

'Really? Already? How did you do that?'

'I adopted a kind of Agatha Christie approach to the problem.'

'Right. Well pretend I'm one of the less educated servants standing at the back of the library, and explain it slowly.'

Vincent folded himself onto a chair and allowed a well-judged dramatic pause before speaking. 'Instead of asking "Why is this well-dressed and perfectly healthy adult male pretending to have a head injury?", I altered the question and asked myself "Why would someone *want* this well-dressed and perfectly healthy adult male to pretend he has a head injury?"'

'Ingenious. Obviously, I have no idea what you're talking about.'

'You have to allow the explanation to unravel, Spencer. Agatha gives these things several pages.'

'Sorry.'

'You see, it struck me that it wasn't a *normal* case of feigned unconsciousness. It's usually a teenage strategy, it suits the melodrama of the adolescent psyche. Is your family ignoring your needs? Why not fake a brain haemorrhage and make them really pay attention?' He took another mouthful of tea, and winced. 'So, back to our man. He comes in unaccompanied by distraught family and friends. He has no form of identification. And the red paint could only possibly have passed for blood in the darkness of the street. So, what's going on?'

Spencer shrugged extravagantly.

Vincent leaned forward. 'I concluded that the whole stunt was a decoy. Our man applies the paint, phones an ambulance to report a mystery accident and then staggers into the street and collapses. An excited crowd gathers, the noise builds, the siren approaches, the drama grows – and meanwhile, somewhere in the vicinity, an accomplice is quietly carrying out a crime, unnoticed by everyone. All our man has to do is lie low, keep silent, and look for an opportunity to make an unobtrusive exit –' Vincent walked his fingers to freedom along the edge of the desk ' – into the night.'

'Very good,' said Spencer, nodding appreciatively. 'Very Poirot. So did you tell him all that?'

'No, I just told him that I had to leave the room for a couple of minutes, and when I got back he'd gone.' He stood, and tipped the rest of the tea down the sink. 'You know, now that I think about it, it's quite surprising there are no Asian detectives in the classic canon. There's a guru-like quality about the best sleuths, don't you think – all those near-mystical pronouncements? All those answers for those who thirst after truth? And who traditionally does that kind of thing best? Elderly ladies? *Belgians?*' His voice was scathing.

'More tea?'

'I won't, thank you.' Vincent sat down again and yawned, and after a moment Spencer yawned too. Theirs was a night-time friendship, forged over tired conversations in the echoing canteen, their first link a shared, scabrous opinion of Mrs Spelko, their second, and strongest, something different altogether.

'I've just read a detective novel,' said Spencer. 'Do you know it's the first book in six months I've actually finished.'

'Well done. So, who did it?'

There was a pause as Spencer tried to recall something – anything – about the plot. 'I can't remember,' he said eventually, defeated. 'I think he had a beard. Concealing an untrustworthy chin.'

Vincent smiled and reached across for the textbook on the chair. 'And how's the studying going? I could test you if you wanted.'

'There's no point.'

'Still can't concentrate?' His tone was gentle.

'It's more . . .' Spencer tried to analyse his failure '. . . it's more that my brain keeps short-circuiting. I can't think about anything new without ending up in the same old place.'

Vincent nodded, leafing absently through the pages. 'I think the electrical analogy's very good, actually; there's definitely a neurological element to grief – some kind of re-wiring. Though it's probably idiosyncratic.' He closed the book and laid it aside. 'After Anita died I could manage textbooks, but not fiction. And fiction was what I really wanted to read. I wanted the chance to go somewhere else, mentally – to escape for a while.'

'But you couldn't?'

He shook his head. 'No one else's story had the intensity of my own.'

'But you read now, don't you?' asked Spencer, groping for some kind of future normality.

'All the time,' said Vincent, flatly. He examined a thumbnail and pushed back the cuticle. 'All the time.'

'You should get out more. That's what everyone says to me.'

'With whom?' asked Vincent. 'That's what I say to them.'

They smiled at each other, a little grimly. 'The Widowers' Club' Vincent had dubbed it, one night as they swapped symptoms over plates of tepid lasagne. 'Exclusive membership.'

'What I wanted to ask you,' said Spencer, 'was if there's a point when –' Headlights swooped across the wall, and he turned to see an ambulance rounding the corner from the main road. He groaned.

'To be continued,' said Vincent, getting up slowly. 'Unless this is for me, I might try and get some sleep.'

'All right.'

'Spencer?'

'Yes?'

'You won't forget to eat occasionally? Greens?'

The ambulance contained a man with a suspected broken ankle and Vincent went off to bed. Frank Barron's injury was unremarkable; Spencer noted a bit of swelling, a bit of bruising and no obvious deformity. His wig, on the other hand, was spectacular, the type of wig which would have made Mark, who had regarded wig-spotting almost as a hobby, happy all day. It was beige, with a uniform shiny finish, a crisp, crinkle-cut edge, and a visible seam at the front, which rested just above Frank's eyebrows.

'How did you come to hurt your ankle, Mr Barron?'

'What happened was, I was in bed with my wife. We've got a shop, you see, and we've got a flat just above it, so the bedroom's right over the stockroom.'

'Right.' Spencer folded his arms and rested one buttock on the couch. He recognized instantly the symptoms of a born storyteller.

'And we were busy. If you know what I mean.' He gave Spencer a man-to-man wink.

'Yup.'

'And then Margaret said, "I can hear something, there's someone in the shop."'

'Right.'

'I mean I couldn't hear anything and I was all for carrying on, but you know women, once they're distracted you might as well throw in the towel.' He paused, and Spencer realized he was waiting for a comment.

'Uh huh.'

'So I put on a pair of trousers and went downstairs, and I picked up the broom on the way, just in case I had to defend myself.'

'I see.' He wondered when the wig had gone on. Or perhaps Frank kept it on for sex.

'So I banged on the door with the broom handle and shouted – "I've got a gun," and there was a real scuffling noise and I thought, aye aye, it *is* burglars, because theft of exotica's a growing problem in the trade.'

'OK.' Spencer started to drift off. The thermostat, he thought. He really needed to adjust the thermostat in the chameleon's tank, to allow for the colder weather. A vision of a red electricity bill suddenly entered his mind. When had that arrived? He could remember opening it, but what had he done with it then? It could be anywhere. Last month he'd found the phone book in the fridge.

'. . . and I'd tripped over it. The turtle was all right, but I couldn't stand up.'

'Turtle?' He was suddenly all ears.

'Yeah. You know, like a big terrapin. It must have shifted the top of the tank somehow and got out.'

'You've got turtles?'

'Just a couple. I specialize in birds, really. Cockatiels, budgies, you know.'

'So you've got a *pet* shop.'

Frank looked at him warily. 'Yeah. Like I said.'

'Have you got tortoises?'

'No. Not at the moment.'

'But do you ever have tortoises?'

'Sometimes.' He sounded cautious.

'Do you know anything about them?'

Frank looked around as if for help, his wig rotating significantly less than his head. Seeing none, he looked unhappily back towards Spencer. 'If this is about imports I never touch them.'

'No, no it's –'

'I've been RSPCA inspected.'

'No, honestly. It was about what tortoises eat.'

'What they eat?'

'Yes, mine only eats paper. It can't be normal.'

Frank rotated his jaw a couple of times as if chewing cud. 'I don't know about that,' he said. 'If it was a lovebird, I'd have said you were operating under a misapprehension. You see, they tear up paper and you might just get the impression that they're eating it. They're not, though, they use it in their mating rituals.'

'Yes, but I've got a tortoise,' said Spencer.

Frank tutted, as if that had been a bad decision. 'Can't

help you, I'm afraid. They eat them in Togo,' he added, inconsequentially. 'Boiled, apparently.'

The rows of seats were beginning to fill again, and after Frank had been X-rayed and sent home with a tubular bandage, Spencer rallied himself for the last two hours of the shift. It was easy, towards morning, to let the pace drop but he knew how demoralizing it was for the 9 a.m. staff to be greeted by a bulging waiting room, and he rattled through the list with as much efficiency as he could muster. Finally he hefted Callum's notes – a four-inch thick bundle bristling with staples and extraneous bits of paper, and held together with a rubber band – and opened the door of Examination Room 3.

Marsha's team had worked very hard and the room reeked of antiseptic soap, beneath which only the faintest hint of UHU was detectable. Callum was asleep. He was dressed in clean clothes and his face looked almost babyish despite the tattoo. Spencer laid the notes on the table. He knew the whole pathetic history well; Callum told his story to everyone who would listen. He had been on glue since the age of twelve, but had lived at home in Musselburgh until five years ago, when a mate of his had done the tattoo with a pin and a biro, creating a symbol almost as potent as a leper's bell.

Spencer lifted one of Callum's hands and looked at the swollen and bluish nails.

'You're *always* interested in my nails.'

Callum had woken, and while he still looked terrible – the whites of his eyes yellowish, his lips a web of cracks – the slurring had largely dissipated.

'It's because you've got clubbing,' said Spencer, tilting the hand so Callum could see the nail bases. 'You see how puffed up the ends of your fingers are?'

'What's that mean then?'

Spencer hesitated. 'It means your lungs are . . .' He groped for the right word.

'Totally fucked?'

'Yes, they're not in great shape.' He pulled his stethoscope out of his pocket. 'Can you sit up and let me have a listen?' Callum struggled up and lifted his shirt to reveal a skeletal though surprisingly hairy chest.

'Take a deep breath in.' The normal quiet sweep of air entering the lungs had been transformed into a mess of liquid crepitations, as if a giant with wet hands was squeezing a family-sized bag of crisps.

'And out.' The giant blew through a straw into the last dregs of a milkshake.

Spencer took out the earpieces.

'What do you cough up normally, when it isn't blood?'

'Green stuff. Wi' big yellow lumps in.'

Spencer hesitated over the notes card, his pen describing little circles in the air. After ten years of glue and five living rough, Callum's lungs resembled tea strainers clotted with pus and his X-ray was regularly shown to medical students as a horrible example. If admitted, he absconded in under a day, in search of glue. He was probably incapable of finishing a course of antibiotics, since the tablets could be passed off as painkillers and sold.

'I went to see a plastic surgeon.' Callum was back on his favourite topic.

'Oh yes?'

'He wanted twelve hundred quid to laser it off.'

'Right.'

'So I went to a charity.'

'Uh huh.'

'And they said they'd only pay if I got off the glue.'

'Right.'

'And I said I couldn't get off the glue with this on my head.' He smacked the tattoo with one hand. The skin on his forehead was criss-crossed with scars and burns where he'd attempted self-removal in the past, and Spencer doubted if anything less than an extensive skin-graft could get rid of it. No sane doctor would dare put him under general anaesthetic; the plastic surgeon and the charity were most likely figments of Callum's imagination.

'Did you try going to that hostel? The one in Clerkenwell.'

'I went,' said Callum. 'I *went*. And it was *real* kind of you to arrange it, Doctor –' he raised a hand in acknowledgement '– but it was full of filthy fucking smackheads with their fucking AIDS-y needles and I couldn't take it. Sorry for swearing.'

Spencer nodded resignedly. Callum's only source of pride was that he'd stayed off heroin.

'You do realize that unless you get off the glue there's no real point in treating you.'

'I know, I know it, but how can I with this on my face? All I need is the money for the laser and I'll be all right.' His eyes were wide and guileless.

Spencer had once looked all the way through the great wodge of notes. They were an A to Z of doctors' attitudes: the sympathetic, the unsympathetic, the boneheaded, the useless. Over the course of a single eventful month, two years ago, Callum had been thrown out of Casualty by the police; interviewed by the social services; sent away with three different types of medication; referred to the hospital chaplain, and booked into a plastic surgery clinic. He had failed to attend the appointment. Since a run-in with Mrs Spelko last year when she had referred to him, within earshot, as a waste of NHS resources and he had counter-attacked by calling her a bloody great heifer (this was not in the notes, but had become part of Casualty folklore) he had stuck to night visits, and as a result often managed to get a few hours' sleep and some breakfast.

'Tell you what,' said Spencer, 'if I phone the Salvation Army Hostel, and then I arrange for the prescription to be sent to the warden –'

There was a knock at the door, and Marsha stuck her head round. 'Thought you might like to know that Mrs Spelko's in.'

'Already?' Spencer checked his watch, and Callum almost threw himself off the couch and started fumbling for his boots, coughing violently as he bent over.

'It's her orthopaedic clinic on Tuesdays.'

'Oh bugger. Hang on, Callum.'

He was almost at the door, coat over his arm, laces trailing. Marsha blocked his way and he peered over her shoulder, nervously. 'It's all right,' she said. 'I won't tell her you're here.'

'Honest, Nurse, I've got to go.' He coughed again, a great ocean of sound which turned his face dark red. 'Honest,' he repeated, when he got his breath back. '*Please*, Nurse.' With a sigh, Marsha removed her arm and let him shuffle away.

'I should have seen him earlier,' said Spencer, annoyed with himself. In the distance he could hear Mrs Spelko talking on the phone, the volume of her voice rising with every sentence until the words 'it's absolutely confidential' ricocheted around the department.

Marsha shrugged. 'I guarantee you'll see him again.'

7

The shopping expedition turned out to be a bit of a disappointment; in fact if Iris had not become inured over the years to
life's dull and regular setbacks, she might have felt quite
depressed. The Saturday after making her New Year's list, she
took the bus to Hanley Cross with the aim of buying a
completely new outfit. It was pouring with rain; the bus was
packed and the interior foggy with condensation. Everyone
got off at Shopping City and she passed with the herd between
the automatic doors, through a wall of hot air which instantly
dried her face to a taut mask, and into the roaring void. The
centrepiece of the mall was a lavish gushing fountain beneath
a high glass roof, the pool fringed with palms and surrounded
by a low wall occupied exclusively by winos whose empty
cans of Diamond White bobbed in the foaming water. Next
to it was a map which detailed the shops available over the
three levels.

During the week she'd bought a sheaf of expensive fashion
magazines but her studies had only led her to the usual
observation that everyone in the world was younger than
herself, and that most of them wore lycra. In desperation,
she'd moved downmarket and bought a *Woman's Weekly*.
Besides a double-page spread on cut-price power dressing (the
only fashion in the world, she felt, that would suit her even
less than leggings) she'd found a minimally helpful article on
colours – 'Which season are you?' – picturing readers holding
swatches of fabric against their faces. 'It'll be obvious when
you find *your* range of tones: your skin will seem to glow,

your eyes brighten, you'll gain an almost visible aura.' When the twins were out one evening, she had experimented with as many colours as she could find in the flat. While some were obviously wrong – a fuchsia book jacket sucked the colour from her face, while Robin's orange t-shirt made her look like a carrot – her aura remained resolutely absent. Whatever the hue, she looked just like herself.

It was hard to gauge from the list of shop names precisely who they catered for. How old was the She of What She Wants? Did Oasis specialize in beachwear? Was Wallis for men or women? She went there first, mysteriously drawn by a vision of Wallis Simpson in the thirties equivalent of a power suit, and was reassured by the age of the clientele, most of them comfortably into their thirties.

'Are you looking for anything in particular?' asked an assistant, and she didn't know how to answer. A whole new image? Appropriate attire for the current season? A polyester/wool dress in midnight blue that can be teamed with a tailored jacket for a sleek evening look? 'Something green,' she said.

She left Shopping City two and a half hours later with a skirt and a top, and the uneasy sensation that they were not really her choice but that she had merely caved in under pressure. She had bought them from a relatively empty store called Heaven Sent, situated in a mercantile backwater between a shop that sold glue-together model aircraft kits, and a seating area full of slumped pensioners. When Iris had wandered in, one of the assistants had detached herself from a bored group by the till and approached her like a heat-seeking missile. There was no escape; only by continually repeating the mantra 'I can't spend more than £40' had Iris got away with less than an entire winter wardrobe.

At the bus stop, she furtively opened the bag and examined the contents. The shirt was plain enough, navy blue with small shiny buttons, but the patterned skirt which had seemed rather subtle, almost dappled, in the harsh shop lights now appeared to be a rioting yell of colour, a vigorous mixture of greens and blues overlaid with textured mustard-yellow blotches, as if someone had glued a handful of cornflakes to the material. She drew it up to the mouth of the bag to get a better look.

'Nice,' said the old lady standing next to her.

'Do you think so?'

'Oh yes. Bright. Youngsters nowadays just wear black, don't they? You'll cheer the place up.'

Back at the flat, she tried on both shirt and skirt, and walked into the living room where the boys were watching football.

'What do you think?'

They looked at her for a moment and then Tom slumped backwards on the settee, clawing at his face. 'Blind, I'm blind. For pity's sake help me, my eyeballs are burning up.'

'Seriously, what do you think of it?'

'It's a bit bright, Mum,' said Robin. 'I mean, you look *nice*, but . . .'

By the time she'd returned to Shopping City and been informed by the now tight-lipped assistant of the unalterable 'Exchange but No Refund' policy, and spent twenty minutes trudging round the racks *on her own*, trying to avoid another sartorial disaster, it was too late to go on her usual Saturday pilgrimage to the library. She watched the wide oak doors slide past the bus window, and glimpsed the notice on the wall announcing reductions in opening hours. She felt as if she'd failed to visit the sickbed of an old friend.

She wore the new outfit to work on Monday, but since it consisted of a dark blue skirt and a dark blue shirt over which she wore her most comforting jumper, nobody at the surgery noticed. In any case, she spent most of the day tucked away at a small desk in the filing room, engaged – as she had been for the past two months – in computerizing the practice records. The narrow shelves bristled with notes, creating a wall of paper that deadened and displaced every noise, so that the click of her fingers on the keys seemed to come from yards away. Every once in a while Ayesha would crash open the door from the waiting room, and search through the shelves, muttering a running commentary on the patient whose notes she was attempting to find: 'Old lady old lady old lady old lady . . . yes!' Through the open door could be heard the autumn soundtrack of coughs and phlegmy throat-clearings.

'You all right there, Iris?' Ayesha's head would be cocked to one side, her tone bright and patronizing.

'Yes I'm fine. Any problems?'

'Nah. You can stop worrying.'

She'd swing out again with the notes, bumping the door shut with her hip and leaving Iris gritty with irritation.

It was seventeen years since Iris had started working at the Sarum Road Practice, and in that time she'd graduated from part-time secretary to full-time administrator, a job description that encompassed everything from cleaning out the fridge to organizing the payroll. Until the Great Computerization, she had also worked on reception three times a week, and had been vastly relieved to hand the job over to Ayesha. 'When the surgery's full, it can be really nightmarish,' she'd warned at the interview. 'There might be someone on the phone shouting at you *and* someone in the waiting room shouting at you. Patients are far more likely to take out their frustrations on you than on the doctor.'

Ayesha had shrugged. 'I worked on the desk in a club, there was always people giving me grief and I always kept my calm. My rule was if they get mouthy at me, I never get mouthy back. That way, I stay in control. Also,' she'd added, breezily, 'my mother's from Jamaica and my dad's from Scotland so I always see both sides of everything.'

Duly appointed, Ayesha had turned out to be efficient and fearless, handling verbal aggression by standing with folded arms and averted eyes, like a mother sitting out a toddler's tantrum. She dealt with phone rants by holding the receiver away from her ear and scrutinizing her nails until the stream of abuse had slowed to a trickle before resuming the conversation at exactly the place she'd left it. 'There's totally nothing I can do about it' was her favourite phrase to patients, and the only time Iris had ever seen her lose her cool was when a child had been sick on the waiting-room floor. Ayesha had bolted into the staff kitchen, hands over her mouth, and remained there until every last trace of vomit had been removed. 'I can't take it,' she'd said afterwards, 'my stomach's too delicate.'

'Surely Jasmine must be sick sometimes?' Iris had suggested.

'I don't touch it. My husband cleans it up.'

She treated Iris like a slightly dim elderly maiden aunt, one who has been gently nurtured and knows nothing of the ways of the world. Which was, Iris admitted to herself, possibly understandable, though hard to take. 'This man was swearing away in here about his test results not being back, Iris, and I told him to shut his mouth before you came back in.'

'I've heard swearing before, you know.'

'Yeah, but this was *strong*.'

She had never met Robin and Tom, and a strange look would creep over her face if Iris ever mentioned them, as though she suspected her of making them up. 'Why aren't you married?' she'd asked once, in the filing room.

'Oh I don't know, it just never happened.'

'You don't live with no one then?'

'Well . . . I live with my sons.'

'Oh yeah, right. Do they ever see their dads then?'

Iris had felt herself start to blush, and kept her face turned to the computer screen, though she'd imagined the perspex reflecting a reddish glow. 'No. And they're twins.'

'Oh yeah.' Ayesha had giggled. 'One dad then. But if you don't want to talk about it, that's OK.'

'Thanks,' Iris had said, grimly typing.

Her only other visitor that Monday was the junior partner, Dr Steiner, who loomed round the door once he'd finished afternoon calls. 'Are you staying on, Iris?'

'Uh huh.' She saved what she was working on and turned towards him. He was wearing an astrakhan hat pulled low over his ears, the dent in the top inverted so that the material stuck up in a long crest. 'I'm going round to Dad's this evening, but he's out at indoor bowls till six.'

He zipped his green quilted coat up to the last possible tooth and started to pull on a pair of large, stiff, sheepskin gloves. 'How is your father? I haven't seen him for a month or so.'

'Oh . . . up and down. Mainly down, actually. Last week would have been their ruby wedding anniversary so he's been a bit depressed.'

He nodded sympathetically, and then rocked on his toes a couple of times, having run out of conversation. His gloved hands stuck out like garden forks. Iris half turned back to the keyboard. 'Any problems?' he asked, suddenly.

'What?'

'With the computerization?'

'Oh, right. No. It's fairly straightforward.' The silence lengthened, broken only by the hoarse honk of a passing train, clattering towards Liverpool Street on the embankment track that overlooked the surgery. Patient opinion of Dov Steiner was divided sharply into those who (like her father) assumed that his absence of small talk was a professional choice which freed up his intellect for brilliant diagnosis, and those who (like Ayesha) referred to him as The Martian. Iris had become adept at judging into which camp a new patient would fall, and would divert people who required regular communication to Dr Petty, who liked talking so much that he rarely did anything else.

As she wondered whether she could resume work without appearing too rude, a low buzzing noise gradually became audible which, after a few baffled moments, she identified as Dr Steiner humming. There was no particular tune, but the sound rose and fell in pitch as if a distant stunt plane were looping the loop. He was staring past her shoulder, apparently at the computer, although his glasses had caught the light in such a way as to be completely opaque; he looked as though he had taken root.

'Is there anything I can help you with, Dov?' she asked, tentatively. The humming stopped.

'No, no. Nothing. I was just thinking.' He scratched his nose with a rigid finger.

'Only I really do have to get on.' She riffled some pages of notes to back up her statement.

'Right.' For a moment, nothing happened, then to her relief he swivelled on the spot and disappeared back into the waiting room. He walked like a pair of scissors, hinged from the waist and almost on tiptoe, and his diminishing staccato footsteps became lost under the noise of her fingers on the keyboard. Then the exterior door slammed, and she was left on her own.

The surgery stood on the edge of an artisans' estate, built in 1889 for the 'hygienic and practical habitation of foundry workers and their families'. The phrase was quoted on a ceramic plaque screwed to the side of the house that Iris grew up in, and it was the first prose that she had ever learned by heart. The foundry had long gone and the estate had reverted to the council, but the houses were still deemed hygienic and practical enough to have spiralled in value, and the fourteen streets contained an uneasy amalgam of tenants and owners. Her father had long been retired when the opportunity to buy presented itself, and it was his running, bitter refrain that he could have been sitting on a diamond mine by now.

As she set the alarm and locked the surgery, Iris's heart sank at the thought of this evening's visit. She never normally saw her father on a Monday, but yesterday she had tried to enforce the twenty-minute cut-off resolution during his phonecall, and the result had been awful. He had been in the middle of a rumination about which items of clothing he could spare for the church jumble sale, and had become very huffy and hurt when she tried to ease the conversation to a close. 'I'm sorry if I'm keeping you from something,' he'd said.

'No, no it's just that –'

'No, if you're busy you must get on. I know how full your life is.'

'It's just that –'

'No, no – there's no need to say anything. You just ring me when you can spare a little bit of time.' He'd put the phone down, leaving her wincing. He was so quick to take umbrage, he always had been, but the trait had worsened since her mother's death, as if he were one huge exposed nerve, picking up even the vibrations in the surrounding air. She'd tried to phone him again later, but the number was engaged, and immediately after that Robin's girlfriend had rung and he had disappeared into his room with the receiver and remained there until well after half-past ten, her father's unalterable bedtime.

She had worried all day at the surgery, finally deciding that an unscheduled visit might help to mollify him. It was only a five minute walk from Sarum Road to Alma Crescent, along streets much tidier than those in Dalston, and past front gardens that contained shrubs rather than dismembered gas stoves. Number 1 was a red-brick end-of-terrace with a crisp privet hedge and a gate with a rat-trap spring which the postman had complained about several times, but its unique glory was the double row of tiles with which a nameless craftsman had decorated the blank end wall. They were obviously hand made, and of two designs: a stiff little flower, and a bun-faced bull-necked lady with a crown. The house was named Victoria Cottage, in her honour. Iris had always loved the tiles; when the twins were little, in the difficult two years when they were all still living at home, their daily walk had always paused by the end wall, so that two mittened forefingers could point up at the queen. Robin's first word had been 'lady', though he'd applied it with equal enthusiasm to men and lamp-posts.

She gave the tiles a quick glance as she rounded the corner, and then stopped dead. The upstairs curtains were closed and the house was in darkness. Instantly, her heart was pounding and she groped in her pocket for the keys and, failing to find them, fumblingly unzipped her bag and started pawing through the contents, wondering if she could possibly have left them at home. Closed curtains meant illness, they meant her mother laid out on the bed in her best nightie with her hair brushed flat against the pillow. The keys weren't in her bag. She took a deep breath and then forced herself to search again, methodically this time, and found them almost at once, nestling between the pages of a book. The gate smacked shut behind her with its usual startling force, and as she inserted the key in the lock, some automatic spirit of courtesy led her to ring the bell just before she opened the door.

'Dad?'

She stumbled over something, a rustling plastic shape, and reached out for the light switch, sweeping her hand across the wall until she found it. The hall was full. An old bedside table stood by the coat pegs, and beside it three bin liners, tops neatly tied. There was a pair of child's wellingtons at the foot of the stairs, and her mother's sheepskin car coat hung over the banisters.

'Dad?' She started up the stairs, and sensed, rather than distinctly heard, a noise from the bedroom. The door to the boxroom was open and the contents seemed to have flowed out across the landing. She picked her way through the junk: old rolls of wallpaper, a box full of half-used balls of wool, a stained projector screen, an ancient fan-heater. Just as she reached the bedroom door, she heard her father's voice.

'Don't come in, Iris.'

'Dad, are you all right?'

'Yes, but don't come in.' He sounded almost panicky. She hesitated on the landing, her hand resting on the naked bulb of a defunct standard lamp.

'Have you been ill? Do you need anything?'

'No, no. I wasn't expecting you. I was asleep.'

'I should have phoned, sorry. But . . . why's there stuff all over the landing?'

'I was having a clear-out for the church jumble sale.'

'And you're really all right?'

'Yes I'm all right.'

There was a pause.

'Can you come back later?'

She shook her head as if trying to clear it. 'Look, Dad, I'll go and make a cup of tea. Do you want one?'

'No. I've not had my supper yet.'

She stood for a moment, swaying with indecision, and then wove her way back to the stairs. A nap at half-past six; a house strewn with junk; a missed meal. These were events without precedent. Her father was a man of iron routine, developed out of necessity over the long years of her mother's illness and now seemingly ingrained in his nature. He got up at seven o'clock; during a breakfast of All-Bran and banana he took a multivitamin and an Anafranil for his depression; at eight thirty he started the housework, beginning by cleaning the kitchen floor; at ten thirty he went out to buy a copy of the *Daily Mail* – and so on and so forth in an unvarying cycle which measured his days like the roll of a treadmill. If Iris had come round the corner to find the front door painted orange and a camel tethered in the garden she could not have felt more unsettled.

The kitchen was as spotless as ever; on his last visit, Tom had commented that you could lick the floor and not get your tongue gritty. Her father used copious amounts of bleach and the formica surfaces, a brilliant yellow when first installed in the 1970s were now the colour of buttermilk. She filled the kettle, and then opened the fridge to see what was on the supper menu; it contained only a pint of milk, a plate of cold, boiled potatoes, half a tin of peas and a single pork chop. The freezer contained a tub of vanilla ice cream, a packet of spinach and a matchbox which she knew contained her mother's rings, hidden against possible burglars. She paced around the kitchen, waiting for the kettle to boil. She simply couldn't fit the facts together. Was he concealing an illness? She hadn't seen him in the surgery for weeks, and he'd seemed as stringily fit as ever during her visits, so it seemed unlikely. Was it senility, of weirdly sudden onset? Was it a recurrence of his depression? But that had never led him to take to his bed, only created a terrible, grinding slowness, as if he were dragging a great weight behind him. The kettle rattled on the hob and started its piercing whistle, rising quickly to a painful shriek. She turned off the gas and it was as the wail dropped in pitch and died away that she heard it: the unmistakable sound of the front door closing. Immediately there was a rattle and a sharp knocking and the door reopened from the inside. Iris put down the kettle and took two steps towards the hall. 'Silly me, I got my coat caught,' said a voice, and the door closed again. Iris blinked as if slapped in the face. She knew that voice. It was Mrs McHugh, head of the church fund-raising committee, a tiny bouncing woman who wore tartan skirts and crimson lipstick.

Her father's footsteps approached along the corridor and he entered the kitchen. Two of his shirt buttons were undone and there was a red smudge on his chin.

'Do you want a cup of tea, Dad?' she heard herself asking.

'Yes please.' He caught sight of his reflection in the kitchen window, and gave his chin a wipe.

It was Mrs McHugh, who drove a mini and boasted that she swam two miles a week, who had been in her father's bedroom, with her father, in the dark.

As if on automatic pilot she rinsed out the pot; behind her she heard the fridge door opening. 'I wasn't expecting you, so there's only one chop.'

'Don't worry, I'll have something when I get back. I just called round to apologize about yesterday.'

'Yesterday?'

'I was a bit abrupt on the phone and I was worried you were upset. You were talking about the jumble sale and I . . . cut you off.'

He looked confused, as if she were talking about something that had happened years ago.

'Well there was no need to come round. You always phone me on a Monday anyway.'

'Yes but –' He had turned away and was emptying the peas into a pan. 'Oh it doesn't matter.'

'I'll get on with the supper then, if you don't mind.'

They danced round each other like strangers, her father heating the fat in a frying pan and lighting the grill, while Iris set the cloth on the table and poured out two mugs of strong tea. She sat down and watched him pushing the potatoes round the pan with a wooden spatula. He avoided eye contact and the set of his shoulders was defensive. 'You couldn't do me a favour could you, Iris?'

'Of course, Dad.' She tried to reassemble her thoughts.

'All that stuff on the upstairs landing needs to be in the hall. There's a van picking it up tomorrow morning.'

'Right, OK. All of it?'

'Unless there's anything you fancy for yourself or the boys. I've just hung on to a few bits in the box room.'

'OK Dad.' Embarrassment hung between them like a barrage balloon.

Carrying the junk downstairs didn't take long, but assembling it in such a way as to still be able to use the front door was more difficult. In the end, she moved the bin bags into the television room to create a little more space. The knot on one was loose, and she looked inside; to her amazement it contained her mother's clothes, folded neatly. She had offered to take them to a charity shop a few months ago, but her father had almost wept at the thought, and had slammed the wardrobe door and turned the key, as if Iris were about to run off with the contents. Now she crouched and put her face into the mouth of the bag, full of dresses in sweet-pea colours, and hand-knitted cardigans in flimsy, shiny wool; the faintest waft of L'Aimant was still detectable. She heard the clank and swish of her father washing the grill pan, and suddenly she couldn't face going back into the kitchen.

Upstairs, she snapped on the light in the boxroom. The remaining contents were stacked by the window, items that she hadn't seen for years: a couple of suitcases, a box full of ordnance survey maps from her father's hiking days, a little row of books from which he'd taught himself circuitry from scratch, a copy of *Mathematics for the Million* signed by the author, and a large black, flat-topped trunk with the words 'Iris Unwin, Barton Hall, University of Cardiff' painted on the lid in white gloss. She opened it. Underneath an armful of blankets were three folders of notes and a pile of textbooks: Haematology, Pharmacology, Anatomy – the latter still redolent of formaldehyde, and a huge and useless general medicine text on which she had spent the frightening sum of £3 before finding out it was obsolete. She flipped open one of the folders and looked at the neat, sloping handwriting. The subject was the Sympathetic Nervous System, and she could remember nothing about it; what she did recall, and with extraordinary clarity, was her state of mind while writing these notes. She could almost sense the wooden walls of the lecture theatre, and the fountain pen between her fingers, and the irritation of watching Lyle Kravitz, one of the American students, sitting with his arms folded and a miniature tape recorder in front of him. She could hear the lecturer, a small, wet-eyed man with a soft, rapid speaking voice that necessitated much frantic shorthand. She could also feel the concurrent knotting of her stomach, the perpetual fear that she had lived with for an entire term, and the awful, awful knowledge that at some point she would have to tell her parents. She'd half known at the time that these notes were destined to be locked in a trunk somewhere, to serve only as souvenirs.

She was distracted from her thoughts by a bobbing light in the garden. She peered through the window but could make nothing of it, apart from the fact it was very low to the ground, and close to the back fence. She turned off the light and looked again. There was a figure crouched at the bottom of the garden, holding a torch. As she watched, he stamped one of his feet several times around a small, wobbling Leylandi, one of a row that marked the boundary between her father's garden and the one beyond it.

She could hear her father coming up the stairs behind her.

'Dad, come and have a look at this. Don't turn on the light.'

He came and stood by her shoulder, and stiffened like a gun dog. 'The so-and-so!' It was his strongest term of abuse.

'What?'

'He's re-planting my trees, he's ... he's ...' He turned belligerently towards the door.

'Oh, it's Mr Hickey, is it?' She'd never actually seen the fabled fence-mover in action before.

Her father plunged back down the stairs without answering her. 'I'll get him, I'll get that ... that ... trespasser. I've got a witness now.'

Iris closed the trunk and followed him slowly. It had been a long day.

8

Chimneys like gun turrets pointing skywards, birds wheeling about them, elusive as the smoke that drifts from their dark mouths.

Duncan had reached northern Germany. The letter was a particularly thick one, and Fran hadn't opened it until the fish pie was in the oven and there was a glass of wine in her hand.

Here there are no green fields to camp in; here my tent is pitched on wasteground and in the morning no birds sing. I walk alone, I sleep alone, I wake alone.

She had first met Duncan when he came hedging with her university conservation group. He had not been there to help but to take photos for his visual arts postgraduate degree show, and in due course she went to see the exhibition of brooding monochromes into which he had transmuted their cheerful day in the country. Fran was featured in several of the photos, sweating in a sleeveless T-shirt, an axe in one hand, a branch in the other; he had taken her shots from a very low angle so that she looked like a Valkyrie silhouetted against the horizon (his words) rather than a stocky five foot two. He had been twenty-six to her twenty, dishevelled and unshaven in a fairly romantic way and he had wooed her by chalking poems on the wall of the garage opposite her flat, so that every time she'd opened the front door she could see how much he wanted her (his words again). She had succumbed fairly rapidly and when they had sex in a candlelit bath sprinkled with lavender oil it had been the most exciting thing that had ever happened to her; certainly well worth all the mopping up afterwards and the subsequent row with the landlord about the downstairs ceiling.

I wake alone, Fran; and this is your choice too, to wake alone without my arms wrapped around you, my hands cupping your breasts, my mouth whispering into the breath-light strands of the hair at the nape of your neck.

After they had left university, Duncan had stayed dishevelled and fairly romantic and had travelled a lot and carried on taking brooding photographs, whereas Fran had got a job, moved to London, and rented a bedsit. He wrote her long, flattering, poetic letters, and had turned up every few weeks with his camera and a bag of dirty washing, and carried her off to bed. He had never stayed longer than a few days, and they had never – as a consequence – had to have arguments about cleaning rotas or whose turn it was to pay the milkman. It had all been very easy. As time passed, however, she had started to resent certain aspects of their relationship; for instance, the fact that he always arrived penniless but departed with a loan of anything up to £50. Sometimes she'd see it again, sometimes not.

Walking through a landscape built from money, I wonder whether it is the same city in which I lost you, in which you ran ahead between the glinting buildings until I could see you no longer.

Often he'd be in bed when she left in the morning and still there when she returned at night, having managed to stagger no further than the corner shop for some Rizlas. If she became annoyed, if she pointed out that he might at least have shoved a couple of potatoes in the oven and done the washing-up, he would urge her to relax, to take time off, to let her life breathe, as if she were selling futures on the floor of the stock exchange instead of forking manure just off the North Circular.

Perhaps if I had held you still, pulled you close, we could have listened together to the soft murmur of the turning world.

He'd started using her already tiny flat as a storage facility for his photographs, so that her bedroom gradually filled with cardboard boxes. She'd opened one, once, out of curiosity and found it full of enormous sepia enlargements of her own left nipple.

You've been the lodestone to my lens, the strong heart and tender hands that guided my star, and now I'm wandering, my compass is broken, my map is burnt.

It wasn't, she had come to realize, so much a relationship as a bi-monthly excuse for sex, operating on a barter system. When she and Peter had decided to buy the house, she'd known it would be a turning point; Duncan and her brother had no mutual history and found each other incomprehensible. 'I don't want to sound like a fascist, Fran,' Peter had said, going upstairs with a j-cloth and a bottle of Ajax, 'but he's a complete sponger. And he's left water *all over* the bathroom floor.'

'Jesus, Fran,' Duncan had complained, lying in bed at 6 p.m. on a Tuesday with a joint in one hand and one of her buttocks in the other, 'he's such a *tightarse.*'

Sometimes she'd felt like a double agent.

Spencer had always been agog for details. 'It's like Withnail sharing a house with Prince Charles.'

'Yes, but not nearly as funny,' she'd replied.

She had been working her way round to ending it, and wondering whether she'd miss him at all, when Duncan got a job. Not a real one, of course, but a modest commission for a book of photographs of Northern European rural skylines, commissioned by the EU for their agrarian archive. 'Sign me up for ten copies!' Mark had shouted, hooting with laughter.

You could have been that compass, Fran, we could have walked these white roads together.

He'd wanted her to come with him, and she'd been relieved to find that she wasn't even tempted.

'I've got a job, Duncan.'

'You could leave it.'

'I don't want to, it's a brilliant job, it's exactly what I want to do. And I've just bought a house.'

'You could sell it.'

'I don't think we could *give* it away.'

She had told him that it was a good place, and a good time, to end their relationship (a speech rehearsed over the course of an afternoon with Spencer) and he'd taken it incredibly badly, weeping white-faced throughout the night and leaving at dawn. She'd watched him walking down the street in the milky light, unlaced boots flopping and a water bottle swinging like a pendulum beneath his rucksack. He'd phoned her from Victoria Coach Station and begged her to write and Fran, amazed to find herself enmeshed in the plot of a romantic film, had promised to do so. Since when she had dispatched factual two-siders on a regular basis to postes restantes in Finland, Norway and Denmark and, in return, had received these huge and passionate letters, heaving with poetry. They were ridiculous, she knew that; Duncan saw himself as the hero of a tragic drama which in no way fitted with the prosaic facts. But they also provided an enjoyable frisson, a flattering and mildly erotic counterpoint to a life which at present seemed to revolve around shovelling mud and paying an ever-greater proportion of her wages into the mortgage.

> *I dream of you, Fran, crouched like a wild creature amidst the green leaves and jewelled petals of the gardens you love so much. Did I lose you to nature – does only nature have your heart?*

Like a wild creature who lacks an oven timer, she lifted her head suddenly and then leapt from the chair, alerted by the faintest, slightest aroma of burning. Grabbing the casserole from the oven, she was relieved to see that the smell arose from a tiny piece of potato, separated from the rest of the herd and now fused to the side of the dish. The pie was starting to brown on top and bubble underneath, and was looking quite impressive. She'd used potatoes from the garden, and the last of the broccoli was waiting in a colander for Sylvie to arrive. Apart from the fact that she liked fish, Fran had gleaned no more details about Peter's new girlfriend.

'What type does he go for?' Spencer had asked during a phonecall.

'I don't think he's got a type,' she'd said. At school he'd gone out with a big, square girl who played hockey, and at university he'd lived for three years with a short, flexible girl who'd been a gymnast. In his mid-twenties he'd become engaged to a middle-sized, completely unsporty woman who had eventually broken his heart by deciding she was a lesbian and going to live in Wales.

'I see what you mean,' Spencer had said, when she'd explained.

Fran laid the table, and put on the water for the broccoli;

then, on impulse, she took a torch and a pair of scissors into the garden. The only flowers still blooming were the yellow plates of fennel, swaying high above the vegetables. She snipped off the last seven heads, and had just finished arranging them in a vase when the key turned in the lock.

'It's just up the stairs on the right,' she heard Peter say, and then he came into the kitchen, unwinding a long scarf from around his neck.

'Sylvie's not feeling too well,' he said, his cheeks pink from the cold.

'Oh. What's wrong?'

'Just tired, I think, and a bit stressed.'

'Oh. Do you think she'll want something to eat?'

'I'm not sure. She's been a bit upset.' He poured himself a glass of wine and stood beside the table, leafing through the morning's post.

'Why?'

'What?'

'Why's she been a bit upset?' Sometimes Fran wondered if it wouldn't be quicker to issue him with a questionnaire, and come back later when he'd filled it in.

'Oh. Problems with her landlord.' He took an olive from a bowl, looked at it carefully and then popped it in his mouth.

'What about?'

'Her cat.'

Upstairs the toilet flushed. Fran turned down the oven and put the plates in to warm. Peter ate another olive and looked at a cycling magazine. Sylvie didn't appear. Fran wiped the kitchen surfaces with the special kitchen-surface cloth and poured herself a second glass of wine. The lid of the saucepan rattled insistently as the water boiled away.

'Do you think she's all right?' asked Fran.

Peter looked up and frowned. 'Perhaps I'd better check.'

He disappeared upstairs and it was nearly five minutes before he returned, this time accompanied by Sylvie. Fran was draining the broccoli and said hello over one shoulder as she bashed the colander vigorously against the bottom of the sink.

'Sylvie's got a bit of a headache,' said Peter in a lowered voice, looming beside her.

'Oh.' Fran gave the figure sitting at the table an apologetic look. 'Sorry.'

Sylvie, one hand to her head, smiled slightly. 'That's all right. It's very nice to meet you.'

Her voice was sweet and soft. 'It's really kind of you to cook for me.'

'Oh, well, I hope you enjoy it,' said Fran, rather awkwardly. 'Pleased to meet you too.'

It was a very quiet meal; it felt almost as if someone had turned down the volume in the house, and Fran was aware of every clunk of cutlery against china. Sylvie sat at the head of the table, with Fran and Peter on either side. She ate extremely slowly and carefully, holding the knife and fork like delicate surgical instruments and conveying one tiny morsel to her mouth at a time. She had a round, pale face, rounded grey eyes, and long straight hair of an improbable silver-gilt colour. She spoke little, but listened carefully, fixing her eyes with unwavering attention on the face of whoever was talking. At one point she coughed slightly, and Peter reacted as if to a starting-pistol, flying to the sink for a glass of water and placing it tenderly beside her plate.

'Peter says you've been having trouble with your landlord.'

Sylvie swallowed what was in her mouth, put her fork down and then very gently tucked a strand of hair behind one ear. Fran looked at her, waiting for a reply, and then noticed with a shock that the grey eyes were brimming with tears.

'Oh God, sorry, I didn't mean to –'

'No, no, it doesn't matter.' Sylvie searched within the overlong sleeves of the vast green jumper she was wearing – Peter's jumper, Fran suddenly realized – and found a tissue with which she blotted her eyes. Peter watched, his face heavy with concern.

'It's been a really difficult week.'

'Oh dear,' said Fran, inadequately.

'He says I've got to get rid of my cat.'

'Oh,' said Fran.

'One of the other tenants has complained. Her son's got asthma and she thinks he might be allergic to cats and, to be honest, I hadn't properly read the terms of the lease and it actually says no pets.' Her eyes filled again. 'I know he's only a cat. I know it sounds silly . . .'

'No it doesn't,' said Peter.

'It does, I know it does.' She gave Fran a rueful, rather watery smile. 'I'm not usually stupid about animals, truly.'

'Fran likes animals,' said Peter.

'To eat,' said Fran. 'Only joking,' she added, catching his expression.

'It's just that he was a stray, so I feel he's been abandoned once already . . .'

'Oh right,' said Fran, feeling mean.

'So if he goes I'll have to go too. And things have been difficult at work, one of my colleagues is ill and we're having to cover for him, so it felt like one more problem to have to cope with. But anyway –' she shrugged gamely and blew her nose '– I'm fine really. And it's lovely to come round here this evening.' She loaded a minute flake of fish onto her fork, lifted it halfway to her mouth, looked at it, and then lowered the fork back onto the plate. 'That was really delicious, Fran, but I don't think I can eat any more.'

Fran scraped the remains of the pie into the bin and dumped the plates into the washing-up bowl. Immediately after finishing her meal, Sylvie had excused herself and Peter had followed her upstairs a few minutes afterwards. Fran had no idea whether they were going to reappear or not and in the meantime a panful of plums from the farm was stewing gummily on the stove and the custard had developed a lovely thick skin. She went out into the hall and cocked an ear up the stairs; she could just hear the low rumble of Peter's voice, but not what he was saying. She went halfway up the stairs, and a faint sobbing became audible in the gaps between the rumble. 'Anyone want pudding?' she called. There was no break in the pattern of the noise.

Iris was cleaning out the cupboard under the sink. It was the kind of esoteric out-of-sight-out-of-mind housework with which she didn't normally bother, but the u-bend had developed a slow leak and a sludge of semi-liquid washing powder now covered the interior. She had mended the leak with gaffer tape and was scraping up blue gunge with a spoon when the phone rang.

'Mu-um!'

'Hang on.' She started to rinse off her hands. 'Bring the phone through to me,' she called. There was no response. Blue bubbles sluiced into the plughole.

'MU-UM, it's for you!' Robin called again, louder this time.

She shook her hands to dry them and hurried along the narrow corridor to the living room. Robin lay on the sofa, feet hanging over one end, the phone flopping in his outstretched hand.

'It's Fran.'

'Thanks.'

'No problem,' he said, as if he'd just done her a favour.

'Are you hungry?' asked Fran abruptly, as soon as she took the phone. 'Only I've got a lot of pudding on my hands. Not literally, of course.'

Walking up to Fran's front door, Iris trod on something that made a crunching noise, and she lifted her foot to see the fragments of a roof slate strewn across the path. She held out a chunk of it to Fran as she opened the door.

'Oh fuck, not another one. And it's not even windy.' Fran cast a vicious look at the roof as though suspecting it of sabotage and then ushered her in.

Iris was always struck by the amount of space in Fran's house. Part of the reason was the obvious one – Fran and Peter had a whole two floors rather than the botched downstairs conversion that she occupied with the boys. Admittedly her flat had a large extension out the back, containing the bathroom and a third bedroom, but it had been built prior to the days of planning regulations and therefore lacked both aesthetic pretension and the usual number of sockets, cupboards and windows.

The other part of the reason was the lack of clutter: no plastic bags in the hall, no jackets over the chairs, no copies of *Viz* on the floor, no ironing on the table, no school bags apparently loaded with pig iron sitting immovably in the centre of the living room. Fran's rooms were freeways; her own were permanently covered in roadworks.

'Sorry about the mess,' said Fran, as they went into the kitchen. The room smelled wonderfully of hot cinnamon, and Fran filled two bowls with stewed plums.

'Custard?'

'Yes please.'

'Wine?'

'Yes please.'

'I'm two glasses ahead of you so I'll fill you up. Aren't you normally at your dad's on a Tuesday?' she asked incuriously as she poured.

'Yes. Normally.'

Fran looked at her sharply and handed over the glass. 'What's up? Is he all right?'

Iris took a large drink of wine and considered her answer. 'He's having an affair,' she said, and the words sounded as unlikely to herself as they did to Fran.

'What?'

'I turned up at the house yesterday when he wasn't expecting me, and I think he was in bed with someone.'

'Who?'

'Mrs McHugh.'

'Who's she?'

Iris paused. 'Captain of the women's crown green bowling team.'

Fran laughed so hard that she spilled some of her wine. 'Well, good for him,' she said, raising her glass in a toast. Iris didn't reciprocate. 'What's the matter?' asked Fran.

She could hardly explain even to herself. She had spoken to no one about what had happened at the house yesterday; had been walking around in a daze, one brain-filling emotion replacing another like a Roman Candle puffing out green, then pink, then yellow smoke. And yet underneath the successive waves of amazement and bewilderment and baffled apprehension she could sense something much more complex taking shape in her mind, not yet fully constructed, but ominous in form.

'Have you ever met my father?' she asked.

'Once. The time he came round to prune your ivy. We didn't exactly chat.' Fran remembered a thin, tall, relentlessly unsmiling man, who had ripped every last rubbery stem from the garden wall and left it as naked as a bleacher.

'Well you saw that he's not someone who finds a great deal of joy in life. He's a very serious man, he always has been, and he's never had much time for . . . for fun.'

'And what's *she* like?'

'Mrs McHugh? She's . . . frivolous.' Fran laughed incredulously. 'She is. She almost skips around –'

'How old is she?'

'Early seventies. Her first name's Tammy –' Fran snorted ' – and she wears little hair slides and sings songs at the church social.' An enduring image in Iris's mind was the sight of Mrs McHugh clad in a nightie encouraging the audience to clap along as she sang 'It's nice to get up in the morning but it's nicer to stay in bed' while brandishing an oversized alarm clock. 'She's the sort of person that people say "oh she's a one" about.'

'Well she obviously is a one,' said Fran, 'luring your dad to bed.'

Iris closed her eyes for a moment, trying to orientate herself in this new world, and Fran refilled her glass. 'Your mum wasn't anything like that then?'

'Oh no, nothing like that at all. My mother was very shy. Very, *very* shy. She hardly ever opened her mouth in public. I think she was worried about her lack of education – she thought she might let Dad down if she said anything.' Or let both of them down, in fact, her autodidact husband and his swotty daughter. She had always waved aside her own genetic input, insisting that Iris 'got all her brains from her father'. In the event, of course, it had been Iris who had let everybody down, throwing away her career and closing the book on Unwin social progress for yet another generation.

'So what's the problem – is it that you mind him taking up with someone else?'

'No, it's not that. At least I don't think it's that. It's . . .' Iris tried to pin down her thoughts. 'I think it's the first time,' she said, slowly, 'that he's ever done anything that I couldn't completely predict. It's the first time that I can ever remember him stepping outside his –' she groped for a phrase '– moral framework.'

'Is she married then? Mrs McHugh?'

Iris gaped in horror. '*Married*? No, she's a widow.'

'Sorry, when you said "moral framework" I thought you meant . . .'

'I meant they're not married to *each other*.'

'Oh I see.' Fran topped their glasses up.

She didn't though, thought Iris. She liked Fran, liked her enormously, but talking to her was sometimes like talking to someone from another continent. Everything from Iris's own life had to be explained, translated. 'It's that he's broken his own rules and he's never done that before. He's always been so inflexible; he's never believed in second chances, you have to do everything exactly right the first time. He's always –'

The phone rang and she jumped. Fran answered it and handed it over. 'Robin. Or Tom.'

'Hi, Mum.' It was Tom. 'Where do you keep the sticking plaster?'

'It's in the bathroom cupboard, top shelf. Why? What have you done?'

'Cut my hand.' He sounded pathetic.

'How?'

'I dropped a glass.'

'He was being a prat, Mum,' shouted Robin, in the distance.

'Well how bad is it?'

'It's about an inch long.'

'Is it still bleeding?'

'No, but I think there might be a piece of glass still in it.'

He sounded (as he always did when injured, or ill) about six years old.

'Well hold it under the tap for a minute, and I'll look at it when I get home.'

'Thanks, Mum.'

She put the phone down.

'Emergency?' asked Fran.

Iris shook her head. 'He's not exactly a stoic.'

'Which one?'

'Tom.'

Fran went to the fridge and took out another bottle. 'You know, don't mention it to the boys, but I still can't tell them apart. I wish they'd get their hair cut differently.' She uncorked the wine. 'Where were we?'

Iris felt embarrassed. 'I was going on about Dad. Sorry.'

'No no, don't apologize.' Fran sloshed some more wine into her glass and sat forward keenly. 'You were talking about his morals.'

'Oh.' The moment broken, she found herself suddenly reluctant to continue. Fran's eager expression made her uncomfortable; it was as though she were listening to the plot of a soap opera. Iris herself had been the focus of enough gossip in the past – 'fancy that happening to *Iris* of all people' – to want to avoid doing the same to her father.

Fran saw her hesitation. 'It's OK,' she said. 'You don't have to tell me. I'm being nosy, I know I am.'

'It's not that,' said Iris. She felt mean, and smiled to soften the severity of the moment. 'I think perhaps I need to mull it over for a while.'

'Will you say anything to your dad?'

In her mind's eye, Iris tried to construct a scene in which she and her father had a discussion about the presence of Mrs McHugh in his bedroom. 'So, Dad, are you going to see her again or was that just a one-off?' she'd ask casually, as she dried the dishes. Or 'So, Dad, sex outside marriage – have you revised your position?' as she emptied the contents of the pedal bin into the black plastic bag he was holding. Or on the phone: 'Sorry I can't come over on Thursday, it's parents' evening at the sixth form college. Incidentally, who made the first move, Dad? Did she pinch your bottom or did you ping her suspenders when she was helping you empty the boxroom?'

Fran was still waiting for her answer.

'No,' said Iris.

9

The glass bottom of the snail tank was no longer visible; there were now so many occupants that their shells formed a seamless cobblestone surface. Spencer nerved himself and dropped in a lettuce. For a few seconds it lay motionless; then with a gentle quivering it started to rotate slowly on the spot, dwindling horribly with every turn, and the air filled with the whispering champ of a hundred and thirty-seven sets of toothless gums. In less than a minute the last green shreds were just visible, drooping from the mouths of the slowest eaters, and all over the tank antennae waved in a desperate signal for more food.

Spencer retreated, fighting back nausea. The situation was out of control. Yesterday he'd emptied the lettuce section of his local supermarket in order to feed them; by next week he'd need to corner the European market.

The phone rang and he grabbed it.

'Fran?'

'Lo.' Her voice was flat and rough.

'Are you OK?'

'Hungover. Peter just woke me up.' She cleared her throat painfully. 'So what's the problem?'

'Fran, I've got to do something about these snails. You've got to help me.'

There was a long pause. 'Snails?'

'You know, the African land snails. I used to have five and now I've got a million.'

'Spence, it's 9 a.m. on a *Saturday*.'

'And it's my only day off this week, I've got to do something about it today.'

'God, Spence, I thought you'd killed them weeks ago.'

'No. I know I should have but I didn't.' He heard a sigh. 'I'm desperate, Fran. You should see them – it's like something out of *Dr Who*.'

She cleared her throat again and said, 'Hang on,' and he heard the clunk of the phone being put on the table. He perched on the edge of the sofa and looked across at the tank. The glass walls appeared marbled from this distance; it was only when you were up close that the pattern resolved itself into a mosaic of flattened grey undersides and their personal trails of slime.

'Right.' Her voice was clearer, and possessed a crisp edge, just this side of crossness. He knew she had a mug of tea in her hand.

'Good party was it?' he asked.

'No,' she said. 'That's why I got drunk. So, snails.'

'I phoned my pet-shop man during the week but he says he doesn't like snails, never stocks them. I phoned the zoo, but they weren't interested. In fact they suggested they were probably an illegal import in the first place. Then I phoned *Reptile* –'

'Spence,' she said levelly.

'What?'

'They've got to die. There is no way out.'

'Well I was thinking, what if I released them on some wasteground somewhere, wouldn't they end up –'

'*No*, Spence. God almighty, talk about affecting the eco-system! It's the Himalayan Balsam all over again, only mobile this time – in six weeks there'd be more snails than people, they'd be standing for mayor.'

'So they've got to die.'

'Yup.'

'They've got to pay for their crime of being born snails.'

'Spence, it's not as if Mark was *fond* of them. They didn't even have names.'

'That doesn't mean he didn't like them,' said Spencer, defensively. Though he couldn't actually remember Mark saying anything at all about them, favourable or otherwise.

'Oh, please, Spence,' she said fervently, 'let's not have an argument about fucking gastropods at the crack of dawn on the day I've got to carry a double bed up three flights of stairs.'

'What?'

'Look, I've got to get a top-up.' She disappeared again. While he waited, Spencer looked behind the magazine rack to check on Bill. He'd tried offering him a snail as a little snack, but Bill was sticking firmly to his diet of magazines. The tattered remnants of *Hung and Heavy* had been consigned to the bin a couple of weeks ago, but Bill had moved smoothly on to *The Lancet* with barely a change in jaw rhythm. He was there now, tackling the editorial section.

'I'm back. Feeling better by the minute.' There was a loud crunching noise. 'Toasht,' she explained, her mouth full.

'What's this about a double bed?'

'Sylvie's been kicked out of her flat, Peter's found her another one in Wood Green and I've agreed to help her move.'

'That's very kind of you.'

'Three-line whip. She can't lift things.'

'Why not?'

'Because –' Fran brought her mouth close to the phone '– *because she's a bit fragile*,' she hissed. '*She's in the house. That's why I'm whispering.*'

'Not everybody can carry six sacks of manure with one hand, you know. Your standards are unrealistically high.'

'*No, really. She has to protect her wrists.*'

'What do you mean?'

'*She's got delicate wrists and she says that if she* yeah, the snails, anyway, we ought to talk about the snails.'

'Just come in?'

'Yup.'

Spencer grinned. 'Tell me some more about her delicate wrists.'

'No.'

'Oh go on.'

'*No*. Snails. Easiest, quickest way to kill them is by squashing them.'

'What, a hundred and fifty of them?'

'You could put them in a bin liner and use a mallet.'

'That is such a disgusting image that I can't even think about it.'

'OK, then your best bet's water – boiling for a quick death, warm with lots of detergent for a slower one. Of course, you could get some slug killer from the shops, but the effect's much the same.'

Spencer was silent for a moment. He'd actually tried the boiling-water technique on a slug that he'd found outside the flats. The result had been truly horrible, the creature letting out a sort of fizzing scream before dying frothily.

'Tell you what, Spence, I'll come round during the week and do it myself.'

He was touched. 'Thanks, Fran. Why don't I give it a try and let you know the result.'

'All right. Well don't feel under pressure. Oh thanks, Sylvie.'

'What's she done?'

'Made me some fresh tea.'

'So strong enough to lift a teapot then?' He heard a door close at the other end.

'*It's not a very big one,*' whispered Fran.

'So what was this terrible party you went to?'

She groaned at the memory. 'Claud's fortieth. We went to one of those Greek places where you smash plates on your head.'

'Retsina?'

'Don't even mention the word.'

'So why was it bad?'

'Because –' he could sense her framing the sentence '– well firstly because Claud made a speech in which he thanked everyone he'd ever met in his whole life and people were practically slitting their wrists by the end of it, and secondly because Barry cornered me by the bogs and said that he worshipped me and that he'd split up with his girlfriend because he couldn't get me out of his mind.'

'I *told* you.'

'I know you did.' They'd had a long conversation about Barry a couple of weeks before, during which Spencer had unswervingly diagnosed lovesickness.

'Classic psychology – you abused him and then you were kind to him. Now he'll *never* leave your side.'

'Fantastic. Two blokes I can't get rid of.'

'A poet and an apprentice.'

'A sad old hippy and a complete dipshit.'

'How is the sad old hippy?'

'Seems to have got stuck in north Germany. He keeps sending me photos of factory chimneys.'

'It's a classic eternal triangle, Fran. They'll make a film out of it.'

'There's no one in Hollywood short enough to play me.'

'Danny de Vito?'

'Listen, mate, you've got snails to kill.'

It took him half an hour to transfer them into a bucket. The repulsive sequence of events – grip shell, wiggle shell, prod snail's front end to loosen its grip until at last it peels free, trailing a handful of glistening threads – quickly became routine, and after a while he put on a tape to relieve the monotony. It was one of Mark's, a home-made compilation he'd designed specifically to get himself into the mood for going out. It started with a string of slushy show tunes (having a bath, smoking a joint, ironing a shirt), then moved on to Motown (getting dressed, undressed, ironing a different shirt, putting it on, taking it off, putting the original shirt back on again), and ended with some red-hot soul (cockily admiring himself in front of the mirror, knocking back a shot of tequila, hitting town). Spencer had played it so many times since Mark died that it no longer made him cry and in fact he was feeling quite mellow by the time Gladys was taking the Midnight Train and the last snail had relinquished its hold on the glass. He plopped it into the bucket and turned his back on the mucoid disaster of the tank, and it was as he was crossing the living room towards the doom of the kitchen tap that the front door buzzed. He pressed the intercom button.

'Hello?'

'Helloo! Spence-a!' The small, piercing voice was like a knitting needle in the ear.

'Nina?' he said stupidly, wondering not so much what she was doing here, as how she could possibly have reached the buzzer.

'Hi, Spencer. Sorry we're late, really sorry, we had to go back for a teddy.' It was Nick's voice that jerked him back to reality, instantly filling in the blank diary page at which he had gazed uneasily this morning, sure there was something he'd forgotten.

'You hadn't forgotten, had you? You're looking a bit dazed.'

'I remember writing it down somewhere but . . .' No doubt

it was on one of the scraps of paper – invitations, appointments, reminders – that littered the top of the phone table and the floor beneath and which he daily intended to organize.

'Had you arranged to do something else?' Nick held Nina in mid-air, like a parcel that had yet to be signed for.

'No, it's fine.' He held out his arms and accepted a bag of toys and the chunky figure of his god-daughter, before Nick disappeared back to the car for more supplies.

'Hello mush.'

She wriggled round in his arms so that she could look directly at him. She had a round face, and marmite-coloured eyes behind pink-rimmed spectacles.

'I'm Nina,' she said, a little indignantly.

'Sorry. I meant Nina. And who am I?'

'You're Spence-a.' She ground an emphatic forefinger into his chest.

Nick wheeled the buggy into the living room. 'We'll only be a couple of hours. We'd take her with us but you know what IKEA's like on a Saturday – she'd have to stay in the buggy the whole –'

'It's fine. Really.'

'OK.' Nick's perpetually anxious expression relaxed a little. 'Giant teddy coming over.' He slalomed a huge blue bear into the arms of his daughter, and Spencer's field of vision was reduced to a narrow slit. He shifted the solid little package in his arms.

'What's your teddy called?'

'Teddy.' She leaned over and bit one of the bear's ears.

'What do you want to do while you're here?'

'Look at the photo book,' she said, her mouth full.

'Spencer –' said Nick, tensely '– have you . . . ?' he raised his eyebrows, by way of finishing the sentence.

'Yes, I've taken it out.'

'It's not that I disapprove or anything, it's just that she kept talking about them in nursery, and you know how people –'

'It's gone. It's in a drawer. Honestly.' The man with nipple rings had been well in the background of a perfectly innocuous beach shot, but Nina had spotted him immediately.

'Fine.' Nick nodded. 'I don't want to be the fussy parent but, you know . . .'

'Hey, Nina, what about feeding the animals?' suggested Spencer. 'You like doing that, don't you?'

'The big spider.'

'Is he the one you like best?'

'Yes.' She and the bear swung round to check on her favourite and there was a clatter as the blue legs whacked the top of the lizard's tank.

'I've got it.' Nick restored the lid to its usual position.

'Bloody bear,' said Nina.

'Now then,' said Nick, warningly, 'we don't say that, do we?' He hefted his daughter from Spencer's arms and lowered her to the floor.

'Bloody bear,' said Nina again, to test the effect.

Nick shook his head repressively. 'It's Niall's fault,' he said to Spencer, sotto voce. 'I keep telling him but he claims it's cultural so he can't help it. You know his whole family swears? Even his granny uses the –' he leaned forward and mouthed '– f word the entire time. It's a nightmare when we visit, and of course I'm the one who has to be the bad-language policeman, doling out the disapproval. It's not a role I enjoy . . .' He folded his arms prissily, looking rather like Hilda Ogden. Spencer bit back a smile.

'No swearwords here,' he said. 'I promise.'

'Thanks. Hear that, Nina?' She gave him an unfathomable look. 'Why don't you go and say hello to the spider while me and Spencer have a little chat.'

'OK.' She moved away a couple of steps. 'Bloody spider,' she said, very, very softly.

With a visible effort Nick ignored her. 'So, Spencer. How are you doing?'

'I'm all right.'

'Are you?' Nick looked at him searchingly. 'Are you looking after yourself?'

'Yes Mum.'

'You know what I mean. We never see you now. I wish we could get you out of the flat sometimes – we miss you, you know.' He curled an affectionate hand round Spencer's neck. 'I mean, what do you do in here of an evening?'

'Oh you know – sleep, study, watch TV.' Lie on the sofa. That was the correct answer; lie on the sofa with his mind revolving around a single fixed point, a dismal satellite stuck perpetually on the dark side.

'And look after Mark's zoo, I suppose.' Nick rolled his eyes.

'They're no trouble,' said Spencer, trying not to think of the hundred and thirty-seven occupants of death row, sitting in their bucket in the kitchen.

'And the list? How's the list going?'

'Oh.' He could hardly bring himself to answer. 'I'm still a bit behind on that. I did the Changing of the Guard last week.'

'What was that like?'

'Freezing.' He had got there late and seen nothing but a row of heads and an occasional bobbing bearskin. 'I don't know that it really counted. I might have to do it again.'

Nick looked troubled. 'You know, Spencer –' He paused awkwardly.

'What?'

'Well . . . it's just that the list doesn't really seem to be . . . helping you. I mean, you've given it a good shot and I honestly don't think that Mark would've minded if you didn't do it all.'

'I'd mind though,' said Spencer. 'It's important to me.'

'But *why* is it?'

'Because . . .' He reached for a reply. It was important because Mark had measured his life in lists: lists of work to do, holidays to book, presents to buy, films to see. And he had gone on making them, even when life narrowed so much that every tick was a triumph and the item 'load washing machine' took a whole morning to accomplish. His last list had read 'phone Mum, drink half litre of fluids, watch *Neighbours*' and he had accomplished all of them. 'It's about finishing things off,' said Spencer.

'Yes, but he wouldn't want you to make yourself –' Spencer felt his face set into a mulish rejection of any argument, and Nick gave up. 'Never mind,' he said.

There was a tattoo of beeps from outside and he looked at his watch.

'OK, I'd better go. Nina, are you going to be all right with Spencer?'

'Yes.'

'We'll be back before the little hand's on the two.' She looked at him blankly. 'Early days on the time front,' he said, apologetically, to Spencer. 'Niall thinks I'm pushing it.'

They waved him off at the window and watched till the red camper van disappeared round the corner.

'Gone,' said Nina, dispassionately, clambering backwards off her chair.

'Only to the shops; they'll be back soon.'

'I know.' She wiped her nose on the teddy's head and smiled unexpectedly. 'I like it here.'

'Good. So what do you want to do first? Feed the animals?' She shook her head. 'Go to the park? Play a game?' He groped for ideas. 'Make a . . . er . . . cake?'

'Look at the *photo* book,' she said impatiently.

'All right then.' He sat her on the sofa and put the album on her lap. 'Here you go.'

She flipped it open and looked at the first print, which sat on a page of its own. 'Spencer,' she said, squashing a finger against the transparent sheet that covered it, 'Daddy, Mark, Daddy, Dog.'

The photo showed the four of them coming down the slide at Kingdom of Water, Ibiza's primary aquatic theme park. Mark was in front, screaming hysterically, eyes half-closed against the spray. It had been taken long enough ago for Nick to have a fringe and Mark a small pot-belly. The dog was just visible as a dot beyond the chain-link fence.

Nina turned the page. 'The seaside.'

'That's right. It's a place called Brighton and it's got stones instead of sand on the beach. Do you like your Daddy's beard?'

'No I *don't*', said Nina firmly, covering Niall's experimental goatee with one hand and attempting to turn the page at the same time. 'I like this.' She pointed at a rucksack Spencer was wearing on the next page, the smallest object in a vast panorama of the western isles.

'Can you remember what country it's in?'

'London.' She turned over again.

The rapid progression through the pages was like watching a film on fast forward. Nick's hair lengthened, shortened, went blond, red, blond again and finally receded so far that he shaved it off altogether. Niall started off stocky, became stockier, got to a point where he realized that the correct description was 'fat' and then strenuously dieted back to stocky again. Others – lovers and friends – joined the group for a while, stayed for a holiday or two, reappeared at a party and then disappeared from the album. Mark lost his pot and gained a second earring and a red blotch on his nose, and started wanting to take the photos rather than appear in them, so that Spencer saw more and more images of himself, and fewer and fewer of Mark.

'Horse riding.'

'Yup, that was in Wales and we were all staying in a big orange tent.' It had been their last proper holiday and a rotten one to boot. He and Mark had had a stupid running argument about a bloke that Spencer had been seeing, it had poured for most of the week and the tent had been invaded by the most revolting, slimy –

He stood up. 'I've just remembered I've got to do something in the kitchen, OK? We can keep talking.'

'OK. Spencer, Daddy, Horsey, Horsey, Daddy, Horsey, Lady . . .'

'The lady was the riding instructor and she was called Ann,' said Spencer, over his shoulder. He opened the door of the kitchen and stepped on something that squashed crunchily.

'What names are the horseys?' asked Nina, from the living room.

They were everywhere. In shock, he took half a step backwards and there was another viscid crunch. From the bucket on the draining board, a web of shining trails showed their escape routes: up the wall, across the window, over the fridge, along the floor; every surface was studded with snails. There were snails on the toaster, snails lodged in the folds of the tea towel and so many snails on the chopping board that it looked like a solitaire set.

'What names are the *horseys*?'

'Oh, er, the white one was called Snowball and the brown one was called Star because he had a little white mark on his head. Like a star.' He fumbled to open a drawer and a snail came off in his hand.

'On his head?'

'Yes, right in the middle of his forehead.' He tried again, and this time located a bin liner. 'Can you see it?'

'No. Can I have a biscuit?'

'In a minute.'

He shook open the bag and reached for the Marigolds, his mouth continuing to operate with a normality that amazed him.

'The two black horses were called Castor and Pollux.' Bastard and Bollocks, Mark had called them. He had been too thin by then to find riding comfortable. 'They were a bit frisky. One of them bit me.' For the hundred and thirty-eighth time that day, he picked up a snail.

'What are you doing?'

'Just some washing-up. Very boring.' With none of his earlier care, Spencer started grabbing handfuls of escapees and shoving them into the bin liner. 'What's on the next page?'

'It's a party.'

Mark's thirtieth, held in hospital. 'How many candles does the cake have?'

'One, two, seven, five. . . .'

He threw the tea towel and its clustered occupants straight into the bag and followed it up with the cutting board.

'Fifty!' announced Nina.

'Very good. And who's that I'm holding in the picture?'

'Me!'

'And what's your Daddy Niall wearing?' He crouched down and used his special omelette spatula to scrape up the two snails he'd trodden on.

'A hat.'

'A pirate's hat, isn't it?'

'No it's not, it's a stupid hat.'

Ruthlessly, he dumped the spatula in the bag and then

straightened up and started to pull the snails off the ceiling. There were only four pages of the book left, and during the scant couple of minutes that Nina allocated them, stretched by as many questions as he could think of, Spencer became a snail-disposal machine, grimly closing his mind to the noise and texture of the task, and to the near-clinical disinfection that the kitchen would require afterwards.

'Spencer, Mark, Daddy, Daddy, Lady,' said Nina.

'The lady's a nurse called Cheryl,' said Spencer, picking what seemed to be the last snail out of the soap drawer of the washing machine, and then spotting another one in the softener compartment. He heard the book snap shut.

A moment later Nina and the bear appeared at the kitchen door. 'What you doing?'

'Just tidying up a few things.' He nonchalantly knotted the bag, and then dropped it into a second bag and knotted that. Then he shook open a third bag and encased the first two. The bin men didn't come till Tuesday and he wanted to prevent a mass breakout; Fran might read about it in the local press and then there'd be hell to pay. Just to be on the safe side he put the bundle into a fourth bag.

'Do you want some juice?' he asked casually.

'No,' said Nina. 'Look.' She pointed towards the gap between the top of the washing machine and the work surface.

'What?' He peered into it, expecting to see a couple of strays, but it was empty.

'Greeny thing. There.' This time she pointed at the toaster. It was patterned with a sort of slime version of noughts and crosses.

'Oh that's just –'

'*There*.' Now she was indicating the blank stretch of wall beneath the window.

Spencer scanned the area and then looked at her, puzzled. 'I don't –'

Her finger was lifting again, pointing over his shoulder. '*There!!*'

He spun round and this time he saw it – a flash of green, whipping past the corner of the doorframe.

He swallowed a proscribed word and hurried into the living room. The lizard had already disappeared again. The lid which had fallen and been hastily replaced by Nick seemed to cover the top of the tank completely, but when Spencer looked closely he saw a minute slit at one end, through which the narrow body must have eased itself. He took the lid off altogether and laid it on the floor, just in case the lizard possessed some kind of homing instinct.

'What you doing?' Nina was hovering by the open door of the kitchen.

'I'm looking for the lizard. The greeny thing. Can you see it anywhere?'

'No.'

'Keep looking.'

The room might have been designed for hiding lizards, the tall shelves of books with as many crevices as a dry-stone wall, the litter of papers and cushions providing enticing ground cover. Perhaps if he could approach it on a blank stretch of wall . . . he removed a couple of withered apples from the fruit bowl and picked it up in readiness. As he did so, a pale brown speck whizzed across his field of vision and then another, and he realized that a mass cricket escape was taking place from the open tank.

'There!' said Nina, pointing at the window. The lizard was hiding behind the pelmet, visible only as a vivid sliver.

'Well spotted, Hawkeye.'

'I'm Nina.'

As he approached the curtain it moved again, streaking up and across the ceiling and pausing by the light fitting, a good eighteen inches out of Spencer's reach.

'What's it called?' asked Nina.

'Lizzy,' said Spencer, off the top of his head. The escaped crickets had already started singing, now in quadrophenia.

'I want some juice,' said Nina.

'In a minute. I won't be a moment.' Slowly, carefully, he picked up one of the dining chairs and placed it under the light fitting. Fruit bowl in hand, he climbed onto it.

'What you doing?'

'I'm just . . .' Seen from so close the lizard was a piece of perfection, an emerald mosaic that breathed. It seemed completely unmoved by his giant proximity and he inched the bowl towards it.

'What you doing?'

'I'm trying to . . .' It suddenly occurred to him that trapping a lizard on the ceiling would be completely pointless unless he could seal off the mouth of the bowl. He paused to think and in that instant it was off again.

'What you *doing?*'

'I'm trying to catch Lizzy.'

It arrowed across the ceiling and changed direction at the wall, heading once again towards the kitchen.

'Nina . . .'

'What?'

The lizard flickered through the impossibly small gap between the door and the frame and into the uncluttered, manageable space of the kitchen.

'Shut the door. Really shove it.'

She used the bear, holding it in front of her like a battering ram and applying all her three-year-old weight to the head end. The door started to swing shut, and as it did so the lizard appeared again. It had doubled back on itself, re-emerging through the same tiny gap – that suddenly wasn't a gap at all but a slit too small for even the thinnest lizard to negotiate.

Half of Lizzy managed the journey; the other half stayed in the kitchen. Both fell to the ground with a tiny slither.

'Done it!' shouted Nina, triumphantly.

10

Fran had never seen professional piano movers in action before. There were none of the heaving crashes of the average removal team, the random shouts, the furrows of paint gouged from doorways, the pock-marked walls left in their wake. Instead, all was order and calm. With the aid of one little trolley, the occasional 'left a bit' and a few gently articulated 'hups', the piano was down the stairs and into the lorry with not a sign of its passage remaining. Slamming the tailgate shut, the two movers looked as unruffled as if they'd just lifted a cheese straw from one plate to another.

In contrast, Sylvie was sitting on the front steps of the house, one hand pressed to her chest, the other clutching a glass of water.

'You all right, love?' asked the older and more avuncular of the two movers, approaching her with a clipboard.

She nodded and gave him a tremulous smile. 'I love that piano so much. I know that you're experts but I could hardly bear to watch.' Her voice was breathy with anxiety.

'Don't you worry, little lady, we'll treat it like the Crown Jewels. Now I just need your signature.' He knelt solicitously beside her. Fran, returning from the hired van on her twelfth trip upstairs, had to turn sideways to squeeze by. The man glanced at her in passing. 'Any chance of a cuppa?'

'Kettle's packed,' she snapped, disappearing into the gloom of the hall.

In the empty flat, Peter was taking down the lampshades.

'Is that it?' she asked.

'Just these and the cat.'

Mr Tibbs was asleep behind the mesh door of a wicker travelling basket, his orange bulk almost filling the interior. 'God, he's fat, isn't he?' said Fran, peering in.

'The vet thinks he may have a hormonal imbalance,' said Sylvie, apologetically, from the doorway.

'Oh right, sorry.' Fran straightened up, embarrassed.

'You see, he was starving when I found him, and that might have affected his ability to break down fats. Also, he's half blind which means he can't run around much.'

'Oh.'

Sylvie came over and crouched by the cage. 'And I think he's a bit deaf. He's a sad old thing really, I know, but I do love him.' She extended a finger through the mesh and gently stroked one of his paws. 'He sort of chose me. He arrived on my doorstep in the middle of a rainstorm and never left.'

'Like the princess and the pea,' said Fran fatuously.

Sylvie's face lit up. 'Oh I *loved* that story. Did you ever try it?'

'Try what?'

'Putting a pea under your mattress to see if you were a real princess?'

'I don't think so,' said Fran.

'Fran spent most of her childhood up a tree,' said Peter, carefully sealing the top of a cardboard box with sellotape.

'Really?' Sylvie stayed kneeling, gazing up at him like a supplicant.

'Yes, a two-hundred-foot horse chestnut at the end of our road.'

'It was a sweet chestnut,' said Fran.

'So what did you do up there?' asked Sylvie.

'Just hung around, really.' She had loved the whoosh of the wind through the leaves and the heaving green canopy that had concealed her from view, but the best bit had been the climb up, and the knowledge that only the fearless and the brave were capable of joining her. 'Ate sweets.'

'Shouted rude things at people passing underneath,' added Peter.

'Did I?'

'Well you shouted rude things at me.'

'What did she shout?' asked Sylvie.

'Yes, what did I shout?'

Peter hesitated for a moment. 'You used to say I was boring.'

'You're not boring,' said Sylvie. Peter had flushed slightly.

'That's not what I call rude,' said Fran.

'Hurtful, then,' he amended. 'It was hurtful.'

She looked at him in bafflement. 'I must have been about *nine*. I'm not going to take responsibility for something I shouted fifteen years ago.'

'All right.' He hefted the box of lampshades and carried it out into the passage.

'I mean, if I had to apologize for all the things I did when I was nine . . .'

She could hear his feet starting down the stairs. 'I think we're ready to go, Mr Tibbs,' said Sylvie, whispering into the basket.

Fran raised her voice. 'Calling you boring would pale into insignificance beside breaking the wing mirror off the neighbour's car.'

'Oh that was you, was it?' His voice boomed in the empty stairwell.

'It was a dare.'

'Uh huh.'

Sylvie got to her feet. 'Fran, could I ask you to carry Mr Tibbs? He's a little bit heavy for me.'

'Sure,' said Fran. It was like lifting a bowling ball. She was halfway down the stairs before she realized there was no one following her.

'Sylvie?' There was no reply, but she could just distinguish a soft murmur floating down the stairwell, like one side of a conversation. She retraced her steps and cautiously re-entered the flat. The living room was empty.

'Sylvie?'

'Just a minute.' Her voice came from the bedroom. After a pause during which the cat sneezed, apparently in its sleep, Sylvie reappeared with a beatific expression. 'I only have one more room to do,' she said, and disappeared into the tiny kitchen, leaving the door open. Fran crept nearer, straining her ears to filter the flow of soft speech that ensued. Sylvie seemed to be thanking someone.

'. . . the day I looked out and saw a rainbow over the roofs. And for the smell of fresh basil.' There was a pause, and then she emerged, smiling. 'All done.'

'What's all done?'

'Oh . . .' she shrugged. 'It's just something I do when I move house.'

'What's that then?'

Sylvie looked at her, bashfully. 'I'm sure you'll think it's silly, Fran.'

'No, go on, I won't.' She had to know now.

'Well . . .' Sylvie hesitated, and then explained in a rush. 'I thank every room in the house for a happy memory. I read about it once and it seemed such a lovely idea. Sometimes it's for something that actually happened in the room, and sometimes it's just because you had a wonderful thought when you were standing in there. I thanked the living room because it was on the living-room extension that Peter first phoned me.' She looked at Fran as if to gauge her expression. 'Do you think that's silly?'

'No,' said Fran, sounding unconvincing even to her own ears.

'It's like a blessing. I wonder if it will feel different now, for the next person?'

'Dunno,' said Fran, wondering with a sort of reflex flippancy what Sylvie had thanked the bog for. She roused herself. 'I think we'd better get going, you know, otherwise the piano's going to get there first.'

Sylvie laughed – a breathy, tinkling sound. 'Oh Fran. You're so practical and I'm so –' she fluttered her hands in illustration. 'I'm glad, though. I'm glad there are people like you to keep my feet on the ground.'

Lugging Mr Tibbs down the stairs, Fran brooded over this last remark. What she found tiresome was the assumption that flights of fancy, however nauseating, were automatically more commendable than simply getting on with things – than shouldering the workload that enabled the Sylvies of the world to have something to get fanciful *about*; it was the resentment of the serf through the ages, ordered to prune the fairy bower at the dead of night so that no human agency would seem responsible.

It took them over an hour to drive the two miles to the new flat. A car-boot sale just off Green Lanes had jammed the flow of traffic completely, and for nearly twenty minutes they sat unmoving beside a fruit stall, listening to 'pahnd a pahnd, pahnd a pahnd, ripe and lovely, pahnd a pahnd' until the chant merged into the background noise and became indistinguishable. Fran sat with the *A to Z* open on her knee and listened to Sylvie telling Peter about the imaginary big brother of her childhood. He listened with apparent concentration, watching her face throughout, but it seemed to Fran that Sylvie could have been reciting the fatstock prices and still have received the same degree of attention. She had never seen him so intent, so absorbed in one person, but then she had never really had the chance to observe him during one of his relationships. She had still been at university when he became engaged to the Welsh lesbian, and had only caught up with him during the aftermath, when his sad, moon face had reflected only the misery of rejection. She didn't know what this raptness signified: passing lust or a more permanent and serious condition.

'What I most liked to pretend,' said Sylvie, 'was that he was my twin and he looked just like me.'

'Different-sex twins can't be identical,' said Fran.

'It was just a pretend.'

'I should have warned you, Fran's very keen on scientific accuracy.' Peter had turned off the engine and was leaning against the door, Sylvie beside him on the long seat. Fran, at the other end, put her feet up on the cat basket.

'You know, Fran, I think I might have found you a bit scary when I was little,' said Sylvie, resting against Peter's chest.

'Why?'

'Because you're so . . . confident.'

It felt an oddly double-edged comment.

'I can't ever imagine you being shy, or afraid of the sort of silly things I was afraid of.'

'What were you afraid of?' asked Peter.

'Oh –' Sylvie shook her head self-deprecatingly '– everything! Dogs, balloons popping, motorbikes, most of my teachers . . .'

'I was sometimes shy,' said Fran, defensively. 'I was shy of Peter when he came home for the holidays.' Sylvie frowned.

'I was at boarding school till I was fifteen,' explained Peter.

'Oh. And Fran wasn't?'

'No, I was a girl,' said Fran.

Peter shifted his head in the little gesture that always implied irritation. 'It was a trust fund set up by our grandfather, and because I was the oldest –'

'And the malest.'

Peter looked at her evenly and then resumed his explanation. 'Because I was the oldest I was sent away.'

'And did you hate it?' Sylvie had half turned towards him, so for a moment Fran could see only a pale sheet of hair.

He considered the question. 'I didn't *hate* it, no. But when I was eventually given the choice, I preferred to be at home.'

'How lovely, having your big brother back at home with you,' said Sylvie dreamily, gently rubbing the end of his chin with a fingertip. 'How old were you, Fran?'

'Ten.'

'And were you terribly excited?'

'For about five minutes,' said Fran. 'Until the first time he told me off.' At which point she'd realized that there were now three grown-ups living in the house, rather than two.

'But he's so lovely and tall, he'd always be able to take things off the top shelf for you.' Peter's face was soppy and slack, his eyes fixed on Sylvie's, only inches from his own. 'And he'd bring lots of friends home for you to fancy when you were a teenager.'

'What, like Norman Livesey?' said Fran, derisively, remembering Peter's best friend at school, a stork-like maths freak who wore a suit at weekends.

'And he'd lend you his lovely big jumpers,' continued Sylvie. 'And he'd help you with your homework.'

Peter roused himself. 'It's never worth trying to help Fran with anything.'

'I am *here* you know,' said Fran. 'Only a couple of feet away. You can address me directly.'

'All right,' said Peter, mildly. 'It's never been worth trying to help you with anything.'

'Why not?' asked Sylvie.

'Because she – you, Fran – don't like taking advice.'

Fran opened her mouth to speak, and was interrupted by a

loud hooting. Ahead of them a gap had opened in the traffic, and the cars behind were getting impatient; Peter calmly restarted the engine.

'It's not that I don't take advice,' said Fran. 'I just don't like people . . . interfering.'

Peter's face was unreadable. Sylvie, bemused, looked from one to the other.

'When Fran was twelve –' began Peter.

'Oh not the shed,' said Fran, but half-heartedly; she actually rather liked the story.

' – she volunteered to put up a garden shed that our step-father had bought as a kit.'

'For money,' said Fran, 'he offered to pay me.'

'It took her a month.'

'I'd never seen a plan before.'

'She refused to let me, or our stepfather, or Mum anywhere near, even when it was obvious that she was trying to force the window frames in upside down.' Fran bit back a smile. 'Eventually she had to take the whole thing to pieces and start again.'

Sylvie shook her head in apparent wonderment. 'And did you finish it?'

'Of course I did.'

'Apart from the roofing.'

'Well you can't argue with genetics,' said Fran, irritably. 'I am only five foot two.' She remembered how infuriating it had been, to stand aside while Peter and Richard, their stepfather, completed the job.

'And is it still there?' asked Sylvie.

'Just about,' said Peter.

'The roof leaks,' added Fran.

The piano lorry was already parked just outside Sylvie's new address, under a plane tree whose spiky fruits dangled from the branches like drab Christmas decorations. The older mover, looking considerably less avuncular than before, clambered out of the cab to meet them.

'We've been here nearly forty minutes,' he said, sharply, as Peter opened the door of the van. 'We've got another job after this one, you know.'

Peter got out to open the front door, and Fran lifted the basket out of the footwell. For the last ten minutes of the journey she had become aware of a low grumbling sound, like that of a food mixer on low speed. The cat had awoken and was staring at her through the mesh door, growling continuously and shifting from foot to foot. His discomfort was obvious.

'I think he wants a crap, Sylvie.'

Sylvie's hand flew to her mouth. 'Oh gosh, there's no litter. I used the last of the bag yesterday.'

Gosh? thought Fran. 'Well, are there any shops near here?'

Sylvie shook her head, eyes huge in disproportionate worry. 'I don't know. I don't know the area yet.'

'Can he go in the gutter?'

'No, he'll only go in his litter tray, or on fresh earth.' She made his pickiness sound like a virtue.

'What, even if he's desperate?'

'I think he might run away if we let him out in the road. He's quite nervous sometimes.'

Fran looked around; the street was devoid of earth, fresh or otherwise, the trees forcing their way through collars of concrete. The houses were four storeys high, the front doors reached by a broad flight of steps, and the basements by a narrow spiral staircase, approached through a metal gate at pavement level. There were no front gardens.

'Hang on.' Fran climbed out of the van and went over to the railing by Sylvie's house. Fifteen feet below was a dank strip of concrete, patched with the etiolated leaves of a bindweed that had grown along the ground and halfway up the facing wall, the main stem snaking up from an area of deep shadow behind the dustbin. The adjacent window was heavily curtained and covered by a metal grille, and the door was set back in an alcove under the steps. Fran returned to the van where Sylvie sat, hunched and guilty.

'Which flat are you in?'

'Second floor,' said Sylvie.

'Who's in the basement?'

'I think it's the woman who owns the house. Mrs Hackett. An agent showed us round, though, so we didn't meet her.' She looked mistily into the basket. '*Poor* Mr Tibbs.'

'Is there a back garden?'

'Yes. It's very overgrown. Why, what are you going to do?'

The steep walls swallowed the noise from the street, and by the time Fran was halfway down the spiral staircase, she felt as though she were wearing ear plugs. Only the clear pinking of the sparrows still cut through, the sound dropping into the well like chips of stone. The cement floor at the bottom was green with moss and the black paint of the stairway was flaking, revealing vivid splashes of rust. Fran rested the cat basket on the bottom rung and tiptoed over to the dustbin. It was lidless and empty, save for an inch or two of water and an empty plastic bag, and she shifted it noiselessly to one side. Behind lay a tiny strip of soil, the remnant of years of leaf mould that had accumulated in a gap in the concrete. The sweetish, rotting smell permeated the whole area.

Fran hesitated. The right thing to do at this point would be to knock at the door, and explain the situation to the inhabitant of the basement flat in the hope that she'd allow access to her back garden. On the other hand, only a complete lunatic would let a stranger into their flat for the purposes of letting their cat defecate.

The querulous yowl increased in volume, and Fran decided to do the wrong thing. The door was shrouded in shadow, the window crammed with curtains and cushions; it seemed certain that no one could be watching. She loosened the straps on the basket and tipped Mr Tibbs out onto the concrete, where he spread like a unbaked loaf. He looked around vaguely as if he'd forgotten what he wanted to do. Fran moved him nearer to the patch of earth and he seemed to get the idea, sniffing it delicately and then turning around with the grace of a backing caravan.

'Is he all right?' called Sylvie, leaning over the railing.

'Shhhhhhh.' Fran flapped her hand in frantic warning.

'No, it's fine.' Sylvie opened the gate and pattered down the stairs. 'The woman's not here.'

'How do you know?' said Fran, still keeping her voice low.

'The couple from the third-floor flat just stopped to talk to me. They said they haven't seen her since they moved in, and that was three weeks ago.'

'That doesn't mean she hasn't come back,' hissed Fran, exasperated.

'Oh,' said Sylvie, more softly. 'Though it doesn't really feel like she's here, does it?' They both turned to look at the choked window, the curtains arranged in heavy, permanent folds, the cushions flattened against the glass.

'It's horrible down here,' whispered Sylvie. 'Like a dungeon.'

A sudden, indefinable noise made them jump. It was the cat, kicking earth against the wall with great sweeps of its back feet.

'Oh Mr Tibbs!' said Sylvie, delighted. 'You've done your business, you clever boy.'

Dimly seeming to register their presence, he looked up at them and mewed, a half-formed sound, like a death rattle.

'There's something wrong with his vocal cords,' explained Sylvie, noticing Fran's expression. 'The vet thinks they might have been damaged by early malnutrition.'

'Let's get him back in the basket,' said Fran.

Ten minutes later, as she was leaving the first-floor flat with half a bottle of milk and a saucer, she bumped into Peter.

'What's happening,' he said, 'why aren't you helping me unload?'

'Because we can't get the bloody cat back in the basket. He's hiding and I've just cadged this to try and make him come out.' She edged round the piano, temporarily parked on the landing while the movers inspected the next flight. 'I'll be with you as soon as I can.'

'Is Sylvie all right?'

'What d'you mean?'

'I was just –' he shrugged helplessly '– just checking she wasn't upset.'

'She's fine,' said Fran, mystified. 'Why shouldn't she be?'

Peter rested the box on the banister. 'Because moving's a disruptive event, especially an enforced move. And Sylvie's very sensitive.'

'She's fine,' said Fran again, slightly irritated. 'She's getting lots of help, isn't she?'

Peter opened his mouth as if to speak, and then closed it. Instead, he lifted the box and started up the stairs.

'Look,' said Fran to his retreating back, 'I'm being nice to her, I'm getting her sodding cat back in its box, aren't I? It's Saturday, you know, I could still be lying in a bath listening to the radio . . .' Her voice trailed off as the movers reappeared round the hairpin bend in the second-floor staircase.

The older one gave Peter a glum stare. 'I'm going to have to phone the next job,' he said, 'tell them we're gonna be late.'

Sylvie was still crouched on the cement floor, making beseeching noises to the invisible Mr Tibbs. Energized after his crap, he had evaded Fran's initial grab and skittered away around the basement perimeter before inserting himself, presumably by a process of deflation, into the tiny space under the bottom step of the spiral. From there, immovable by any physical means short of a crowbar, he peered out through half-closed eyes.

'Oh, you found some,' said Sylvie, gazing at the milk as if she had just sighted the Holy Grail. She poured a little into the saucer, and placed it temptingly just out of the cat's reach. 'Here we go, Tibbsy.' A minute passed, and then another. 'I think,' said Sylvie, in a whisper, 'we should move further away, where he can't see us.'

They retreated to the shadowy alcove that hid the doorway. 'When he gets out,' said Fran, 'I want you to block that gap under the step. Stick your foot in it so he can't get back in.'

Sylvie giggled nervously and then sniffed a couple of times. 'There's a funny smell here,' she said.

'I think it's the leaf mould,' said Fran.

'But it seems stronger by the door.' She sniffed again. 'It's horrible. It's not gas, is it?'

Fran did some sniffing herself. 'No, it's definitely not gas. It's sweeter than that.' And more foetid, she thought, and quickly scanned the dark corners of the little porch for a mouse corpse, or disembowelled sparrow.

'I wonder . . .' said Sylvie. 'If she's away then maybe she forgot about something in the fridge. I remember once when I got back from holiday . . .' As she spoke she lifted the flap of the letter box and cautiously looked through. 'There was a really awful –'

The letter box snapped back so suddenly that the cat, who had just started to inch forward, shuddered back into hiding.

'Oh God, what's the matter?' asked Fran, half dreading the answer.

Sylvie turned slowly, her face white, her mouth an almost perfect O.

'There's a hand,' she said.

The next hours were a patchwork of sounds – the police siren, the booming footsteps down the spiral staircase, the crunch and tinkle as the door was broken open, the retching coughs of the officers' retreat, the miserable wail of the approaching ambulance, pointless in its haste, and finally, summarily, the thump as Sylvie's piano was set down in Fran and Peter's living room, rattling the pictures on the walls and plucking a great thrumming note from the strings.

'It's only insured for the journey as agreed in the original contract,' said the older mover, seeing Fran about to speak. All traces of avuncularity seemed to have been scrubbed from his features, despite the fistful of tenners recently transferred from her wallet into his.

Wordlessly, Fran signed the form and then winced as the little trolley ricocheted off the skirting board on the way out.

There were boxes in the hall, and up the stairs, and on the landing. In the quiet that descended when the front door closed, Fran could hear from Peter's room the soft hiccup of Sylvie crying. In the kitchen, Mr Tibbs lay beneath the table like the last rug in the shop. Fran poured herself a large glass of wine, drank half of it at a gulp and picked up the phone. She really had to talk to Spencer.

II

Iris's father was out. Again. His answerphone message, over-enunciated at dictation speed, was becoming grindingly familiar. 'I am unable to come to the phone at the moment, but you may leave a message stating the time, the date and the reason for your call, as well as your name and telephone number, and any details about when you can be reached most conveniently, and I will return your call as soon as possible. Please leave your message after the long tone which you will hear after a number of short ones.' Just before the first tone a perky voice with an identifiable Scottish accent could just be heard in the background. 'Ian, it says here you've got to press the red button and then rewind.' Mrs McHugh.

'Hi, Dad. Just to say I'm off to the parents' evening at college. I'll phone you when I get back, if it's not too late. Bye.'

'Grandad out on the razz?' asked Tom, wandering into the living room with his forearm deep in a packet of cornflakes.

'I've no idea,' said Iris, replacing the receiver. 'He's not very communicative these days.'

In the past, her father's rare evening outings had been referred to and planned around for weeks beforehand, adjustments made to his schedule, early meals shopped for and cooked, the oven timer set to ring to remind him, the bus timetable checked for potential problems; now he just switched on the answer machine (a brand-new, spur of the moment purchase, never previously mentioned as a possibility – Iris had almost dropped the phone the first time she'd heard it) and grabbed his coat. Last week he'd even cancelled the unalterable Sunday visit, explaining cagily that he 'had something on'. It was so long since Iris had had the day to herself that she hadn't known what to do with it; it had been like getting a self-assembly gift with no instructions. He had not mentioned Mrs McHugh's name, or referred – even obliquely – to that Monday night, six weeks ago, but knowledge of it infused every subject and muddied every conversation. Far from having to prise him off the phone after twenty minutes, Iris found that the calls dribbled to a conclusion in less than half that time.

'Maybe he's got a bird,' suggested Robin, supine on the sofa. Tom cackled and wandered out again, leaving a scattering of Golden Nut flakes behind him.

'Hang on,' said Iris, 'I want to finish this list.'

'Done it,' said Tom. 'I've told you everything I know.'

'You haven't. Who's your Geography teacher? I'm seeing him first.'

He slackened his jaw and pushed his tongue into his lower lip, so that he looked like one of the unluckier recipients of the Hapsburg gene. 'Mithtuh Lomakth,' he said, thickly. Robin snorted.

'Say it properly.'

'Mr Lomax. That's how he speaks. I'm just helping you to identify him.' He resumed the impression. 'Thuh Nile ith uh thlathic exthampul of uh delthuh thormathion. You're starting to laugh, Mum, I can see you.' He held out his hand. 'Goodth evthning, Mith Unwin, ith fabbuluth to thee you.'

Iris fought down a grin. 'That poor man.'

'You're laugh-ing,' he taunted.

'No I'm not. Anything else I should know about him?'

'He fancies the French exchange teacher and she's only twenty.'

'*Dirty* old man,' added Robin.

'Anything relevant, I meant.'

Tom shrugged. 'He said I could get an A if I put some work in.'

'You didn't tell me that!'

He shrugged again.

'Boffin,' said Robin.

'When did he say that?'

'Last year.'

'And you didn't tell me?'

'I forgot.'

'Oh Tom,' she said, exasperated. He grinned and wandered away with his hands in his pockets.

'Come back. Is that everything?'

'Thath all folkth,' he said, disappearing into the bedroom.

She made a note on the rough timetable and turned to Robin. 'What about you? Anything more I should know?'

He looked glumly at the floor, scratched his stubble and said something inaudible.

'Sorry, I didn't catch that.'

'I said "not that I can think of".'

'Haven't been expelled or anything?'

'Nah.'

'And just in case I bump into Stephanie's mum, are you still going out with her?'

He hunched his shoulders. 'Not really.'

'Not really?'

'Nah.' He stood and stretched hugely, drumming the ceiling with his fingertips in the annoying way that both boys had adopted. She'd made them repaint it last year, but the grubby prints were beginning to build up again. 'I'm gonna have a bath.'

'All right. I'll see you later.'

He paused in the doorway. 'How are you getting back?'

'Alison Steiner's giving me a lift.'

He nodded, apparently relieved, and padded off to the bathroom. Within a few seconds the antiquated water heater had started with a thud and a roar, to be immediately drowned by a pounding bass line. The luminous yellow splashproof radio which now stood on the cistern, and which had instantly become the boys' favourite possession, had been a birthday present from the fast-talking Leon.

'Why's there red paint all over the handle?' Iris had enquired when the boys brought it home.

'We don't ask questions like that,' Tom had said.

When the bus doors opened the wind surged in and inflated her skirt like a crinoline. The air outside was filled with whirling leaves and she zipped her anorak up to the neck and started to pull on the knitted gloves she'd bought at her father's church bazaar last spring. They had been a particularly poor purchase – pale fawn, scratchy wool, the fingers so full of bobbles and unexpected loops that it took a great deal of wiggling dexterity just to put them on – and she had only bought them out of sympathy for the home-crafts stall holder and her sad piles of lumpy garments and asymmetrical teddy bears. Mrs McHugh had been there that afternoon, of course, running the refreshments area and dispensing simultaneous rivers of tea and chat while charging an unheard-of twenty pence for slices of coffee cake. 'All in a good cause,' she'd chirped, repeatedly, as the coins clanged into the tin.

Turning the corner from the bus stop, Iris found that she'd shoved one of her fingers straight through a missed stitch in the palm, and she peeled the gloves off and dropped them into the nearest bin.

The walk from the bus stop to Broderick Gale Sixth Form

College (motto: Learn and Achieve) normally took ten minutes, but assisted by the wind, which thrust her along in a series of skittering runs, she turned the corner into Uckfield Close in record time – noting, as she blew past, that the usual F had been appended to the road sign by some felt-tipped wit. The college was a jumble of seventies prefabs clustered around a solid chunk of finest municipal Victoriana, originally the home of the Water Board. In the local history section of the library, Iris had once found a photograph of it being built. A line of dusty-aproned masons had been assembled by the photographer, and stood shoulder to shoulder, arms folded, looking like a row of bouncers. Their current equivalent was the pencil-thin figure of the vice principal (a 'tragic hippy' according to Tom) who stood just outside the double doors, swaying in the wind and extending a hand to visitors as if grabbing a lifeline. 'Good of you to turn out on such a wild night,' he said to Iris, his shoulder-length hair whipping about his head like a sunburst. Wondering what her own must look like, she went into the toilets to repair the damage.

She had combed her hair into submission and was wiping leaf mould off her shoes with a wad of damp loo roll when Alison Steiner came in, closely followed by a heavily made-up woman who went directly into one of the cubicles. Alison darted over to Iris and hissed urgently in her ear, 'Do you know who that is?'

'No. Who?'

'Tory local councillor. She's got a daughter here – Melina Scott. Do you know her?' Iris shook her head and Alison pantomimed amazement; they had known each other for fourteen years – since their sons had shared an infants' class – but she was still astonished that Iris lacked her own perpetually swivelling social radar. 'You must, she's a Goth. Dead-white face, dead-black hair, head-to-foot black clothes, earrings.' Iris shook her head again, and Alison waved a hand impatiently and continued in her habitual telegraphese. 'Never mind. Apparently the father's bankrupt – that's the reason she's here and not at Roedean. Overreached himself in property and crashed with the market. Ha bloody ha. Just desserts. Anyway, *she*'s part of the –' The toilet flushed and Alison straightened up, raised her voice to its normal, commanding level and seamlessly changed subject, '. . . car's got a battery problem. It's been a real bore. I recharged it just before I came out so it should be all right, but I might need a bit of a push. Warning issued.' She nodded briskly at Mrs Scott as she emerged from the cubicle, and then leaned towards the mirror and examined her face, as bare of make-up as a scrubbed knee. 'Would you *believe*,' she said, 'that you could still get blackheads at my age?'

The woman, radiating suspicion, applied another coat of lipstick and fluffed her hair before shutting her handbag with a noise like a pistol shot and stalking out.

'Banzai!' said Alison. 'Nearly got us. *She*'s part of the right-wing caucus that wants to close the library.'

'Oh!' Iris was stung into a response, and found herself directing a venomous if pointless look at the door through which Mrs Scott had exited. She felt deeply proprietorial about the library, as though it were only her own visits that kept it open.

'There's a public meeting about it. Tuesday evening,' said Alison, groping round in her shoulder bag and extracting a sheaf of orange flyers. 'Want to come?'

'I go to Dad's on Tue –' Iris paused mid-weekday.

'Sorry?'

'Yes, all right. Why not?' She took a flyer.

Alison gave her a sharp glance. 'So how is your father? Is he still seeing Mrs –'

'McHugh,' supplied Iris. 'Yes, I think so. His social life's certainly picked up.' To her own ears her voice sounded dry and strangely spiteful.

'Good,' said Alison briskly. 'Then you won't be quite such a slave to his routine – isn't that what you've been wanting?'

Iris was silent for a moment. The present situation hardly tallied with the controlled, incremental nudges towards freedom she'd had in mind. 'In a way,' she said.

Her friend looked at her speculatively, head cocked. 'I was thinking about you the other day – I took a seminar on attitudes to senile sexuality.'

'Oh, don't,' said Iris. 'Please.'

'Fascinating subject,' continued Alison, inexorably, her voice slipping into lecture mode. 'Most younger people, even those who'd consider themselves quite liberal, find it difficult to talk about the topic without facetiousness. We completely deny our parents that aspect of their lives. I'm as guilty as the next woman. We assume our teenagers are at it the entire time – obviously I'm not guilty of that, Lawrence, God love him, being the boy he is – but when it comes to our parents –'

'I cannot talk to my father about his sex life,' said Iris flatly.

'But that's exactly the standard response!' Alison leaned towards her, eyes burning with proselytizing zeal. 'Why not break the mould? Why not give it a try?'

'Because . . .' Unbidden, images floated into her mind of her mother smuggling sanitary towels into the house as if they were contraband, of her father clearing his throat during a hymn as a way of avoiding having to sing the phrase 'lo! he abhors not the Virgin's womb', of watching a wildlife programme dwindling into a white dot after oestrus cycles were mentioned, of her father's face when she stepped off the train from Cardiff carrying rather more than a suitcase and a copy of *Middlemarch*. 'Because I was eight and a half months pregnant before he could bring himself to mention mine, that's why.'

They emerged together into the corridor and then separated, Iris to the scrum of the arts and Alison to the echoing canyons of the science department, under whose aegis her son Lawrence was taking five A Levels. According to the twins, science students were pitiful freaks, friendless fashion-voids with bottle glasses and personality disorders. They were vastly unimpressed that Lawrence (of whom this was actually a pretty fair description) had already gained a place to study Physics at Cambridge.

'Only complete saddoes go to Cambridge,' as Tom had explained to her yesterday. She had been attempting to engage him, for the thousandth time, in a serious talk about his future, but the conversation had quickly degenerated into the usual facetious meanderings.

'I might go travelling for a bit.'

'But you haven't got any money.'

'Oh, I could grape pick or something. Or juggle.' Both he and Robin had recently, and effortlessly, acquired this skill and could keep three oranges up in the air for what seemed like hours. 'Do you know I can do it with my eyes shut now?' He'd picked up a Spurs mug and smiled dangerously.

'But even if you take a year off you could apply for college before you go. Then you'd have something to come back to.'

'Not everyone goes to college, Mum. You didn't.'

'I did.'

'Well, you didn't finish it anyway.'

'No, but if you look at most successful –'

'Richard Branson didn't.'

Iris had groped for a response. Your father went to college, she'd wanted to say and he's probably got a mansion and a yacht by now. Though she didn't know that, of course; it was just an image, part-filched from Eudora Welty, that sprang to her mind like a pictogram whenever she thought of him: Conrad standing in front of a Plantation House, the sheltering trees heavy with Spanish Moss, a horse pawing the ground at his side, a speedboat parked on the Bayou beyond.

'You've never liked this mug, have you?' Tom had said, dispelling the vision. He'd tossed it into the air and caught it with one hand.

'Seriously, Tom. This is terribly important.'

'OK.' He'd put the mug back on the table and folded his arms, frowning purposefully. 'Serious conversation. What do you need to know?'

'Have you thought about courses?' she'd said, doggedly.

He'd let the pause hang. '. . . Not really.'

'The form has to be in by the end of November.'

He'd looked startled. '*This* November?'

She'd opened her mouth to protest and he'd crowed with delight. 'Kidding!'

Robin hadn't thought about courses either, but that was because he was almost certain he was going to fail his A Levels.

'But your summer papers were fine. You got a B and two Cs, didn't you?'

'Yeah, but everyone says the real exams are different. I might go to pieces. Or totally freeze.' He had picked up the stapler on his desk and idly clicked as he talked, watching with apparent fascination as the wasted staples bounced onto the floor. 'I'll probably have to resit them. Loads of people do – it's not a big deal like it was in your day,' he'd added, reassuringly.

'But isn't it worth looking through a couple of prospectuses. Just in case? Find out if there's something you really fancy doing?' She had been aware that she was wheedling, and she'd tried to inject a note of calm reason into her voice. 'It wouldn't do any harm to put in an application, would it?'

'Well . . . I might take a year off anyway. Even if I pass.'

'And do what?'

'Travel a bit. Or just . . . you know. Chill.' He'd wiped a weary hand across his forehead. 'There's been a lot of pressure this year.'

'But what would you live on?'

'Well, Tom thinks we could do juggling. You know, in the street, for money.' He had put down the empty stapler and picked up a paperweight. 'D'you want to see me catch this with my eyes shut?'

Mr Lomax, the speech-impaired Geography teacher, turned out to be a handsome man in his forties, with a slightly prognathous jaw and a minimal lisp. Iris introduced herself.

'Ah, Tom's mum.' He assumed the look of smiling indulgence that she had become used to over the years, from the various authority figures on whom Tom had exerted his indolent charm. It always amazed her, the ease with which he strolled through life. He had none of the qualities that she had been brought up to associate with success – he wasn't brilliant or conscientious or passionate or concerned or single-minded or dynamic or even punctual, in fact he expended very little effort in any direction; if he had a skill, it was that of benign flippancy.

Mr Lomax steepled his fingers. 'Well, I expect you know what I'm going to say.'

'Lazy.'

'Yup, he really doesn't put the hours in. It's a shame, because he's quite capable of original work. When he can be bothered.'

She nodded resignedly. 'I've heard this so many times.' Tom usually completed his homework over breakfast, spooning in

Weetabix with one hand while writing an essay with the other, at a speed which indicated that he was putting down the first thing that came into his head. Any criticism of this habit, indeed any attempted discussion of exams, revision, time-tables, course content, homework requirements or even his handwriting – which was atrocious – was greeted with an indulgent smile and the phrase 'stop *worrying*, Mum', as if her concerns were a sort of trivial tic, on a par with cushion-straightening.

'But I enjoy having him in class,' continued Mr Lomax, 'he always contributes, he's very articulate. Do you know what he sees himself doing – any future plans?'

Iris grimaced. The end of her conversation with Tom had been as unsatisfactory as the beginning and she was shame-faced about revealing the outcome. 'He wants to be a million-aire by the time he's thirty, I'm afraid. Nothing more specific.'

The correct response to this admission, she felt, would be for Mr Lomax to slam his hand onto the desk and shout, 'Oh for God's sake, that's exactly the problem with this generation, they want the world on a bloody plate.' Instead, he shook his head with an almost fatherly chuckle. 'I wouldn't be at all surprised.'

Robin's form teacher, Mr Clark, was a youngish man with a pale, severe face, who looked at her without interest.

'Ah, Mrs Unwin.'

She couldn't face correcting him. In any case, she'd never really solved the Miss/Mrs dilemma; asking to be called 'Miss' always made her feel like a character out of Jane Austen, while insisting on 'Ms' required rather more assertiveness than she could generally dredge up. 'Call me Iris', the third option, sounded like a line from a Barbara Stanwyck movie. She shook hands in silence, and then waited for several minutes as Mr

Clark finished appending a note to a file, a task which he undertook with great intensity. At last he recapped his pen and with a sporty flick of the wrist, tossed the folder onto the pile beside the desk.

'Robin,' he said challengingly, placing both hands flat on the desk in front of him and leaning slightly forward, as if about to perform a handspring.

'Yes,' said Iris, uncertainly.

'Bit of an enigma.'

'Is he?' She was disconcerted. Tom was far more of an enigma to her than Robin.

'Something of a depressive.'

'*Depressive?*' It seemed an intense word for Robin's brand of mild and self-indulgent melancholy. 'I don't think I'd describe him as a –'

'Tends to be moody.'

'Well . . . he's quite quiet but I wouldn't say –'

'Mumbles.'

'Yes, he mumbles. He definitely mumbles. It stems from lack of confidence, I think.'

'Older or younger twin?'

'Older. By seven minutes.' Mr Clark frowned, and she felt as if she'd just given the wrong answer in a mental arithmetic test.

'People always assume Tom's the oldest,' she said, placatingly. 'He's always been the leader – he was the first to speak and the first to walk, and Robin was always trotting along after him, and I think that's why . . .'

Mr Clark frowned again at this excess of information, and she tailed off into silence. 'I think the main problem,' he continued, when the floor was once again his, 'is that he's lacking in confidence.'

Iris replayed the conversation in her head. 'I just said that.'

'What?'

'That's what I just said. About him mumbling.'

Mr Clark gazed at her uncomprehendingly. 'I'm not following you, Mrs Unwin.'

'I said he mumbles because he lacks confidence.'

'Yes, that's exactly what I said.'

'But . . .' She began to doubt her own senses. 'I think I said it first.'

Mr Clark looked around the room, as if for adjudication, or possibly a straitjacket, and then at his watch. 'I think we agree, then, that he's lacking in confidence?'

She felt herself dwindling in the chair. 'Yes.'

'He assumes that his opinions aren't worth listening to.'

'I know,' she muttered.

'Sorry?'

She raised her voice. 'I said I know.'

'Did you and your husband ever consider sending the twins to different schools?'

'No,' she said, startled by both the idea and the husband. 'Why?'

'It might have given Robin a little breathing space, so to speak. Away from the domination of his brother.'

'But they're in different classes.'

He gave a little moue of acknowledgement.

'And they've each got their own room at home.'

'Uh huh.'

'And it's not as if Robin's ever done really badly in school. And he's got lots of friends. And he's never been in trouble . . .' She felt like the trailer-trash single mom that she'd seen in a recent TV film, pleading to the judge after her boy had gunned down most of his classmates. Mr Clark looked at her impassively and she remembered with a surge of pleasure that Robin had described him as an 'arsy know-all git'.

'Do you know what he wants to do when he leaves?'

'No, he's – well, he's not really too sure.'

He nodded, as if the answer confirmed something, and then pulled Robin's file towards him. He uncapped his flash-looking fountain pen and wrote a rapid sentence or two in a script so rounded and neat that even upside down and from the other side of the table Iris could read the final word; it was 'mother'.

'So Tom's *sui generis* and Robin's your fault?'

'More or less.'

Alison snorted dismissively and shoved her car seat back as far as it would go, crushing a boxful of 'Save the Public Sector' leaflets in the passenger footwell. The dodgy battery had been more than a conversational gambit, and they were now in the only vehicle left in the car park; Mr Clark had been the last member of staff to drive away, gunning the engine of his scarlet MG like a drag racer. It was – according to Tom – known as the Penismobile.

'Of course, there's a ritual element to these evenings,' said Alison. 'Any actual exchange of useful information is rigorously avoided. They either tell us what we already know or avoid telling us what they think we're incapable of hearing. How many teachers, do you imagine, informed me that Lawrence is an introvert?'

'All of them?'

'That's right. As if I might somehow not have noticed. And how many told you that Tom's bone idle?'

'All of them,' said Iris, depressed.

'And how many told you that in a secret poll conducted last month, Robin was voted "sexiest boy in the year" for the second year running?'

'He wasn't, was he?'

'It's that brooding shyness, you see. Mr Clark may think it's held him back but he's quite wrong. Apparently, when he split up from Stephanie Young last month he was utterly besieged by young women. Tom does quite nicely, of course, but Robin's the one. The current phrase is "babe-magnet", I believe.'

'This is Robin we're talking about?'

'Yes.'

'A babe-magnet.' The term was half-familiar to her.

'Swept the vote. Tom came second.'

It was one of those moments, occasional but recurrent in her life, when Iris felt that she'd been issued a seat with restricted view. On her side of the pillar she could see the familiar Robin – affectionate, gentle, somewhat lacking in impetus, Tom's loyal and admiring sidekick – while the rest of the audience was being treated to the full picture, that of a Lothario. She shook her head to dispel the vision. 'They didn't say a word to me about it.'

'Most adolescents wouldn't, would they?'

'But how did *you* know?'

'Because Lawrence doesn't come under the category "most adolescents",' said Alison, bluntly. 'He comes under "utter geek" and therefore has no idea that it's infra dig to tell me things. I can't imagine who he gets it from,' she added, ironically.

Iris glanced involuntarily at a photo blu-tacked to the dashboard. Against a background of sea and sky, Alison stood smiling beside two beaky bespectacled men in identical orange cagoules; it looked less like a family portrait than an illustration of male cloning. The cagoules suddenly flared more brightly, and she turned to see the headlights of Dov Steiner's lovingly restored Alvis rounding the corner to the car park.

'Aha, talking of geeks . . .' said Alison fondly, raising a hand to greet her husband.

They stayed in the car and watched in comfortable silence

as Dov, his long face taut with concentration, crouched by the headlights of the Alvis and started to disentangle the jump leads. The night was crisping up with early frost, and he tried for quite some time to open the crocodile clips without first removing his gloves, until Alison banged on the windscreen and mouthed 'take them off' at him. She shook her head and tutted good-humouredly, and Iris wondered what it would be like to see one's child's future incarnate; Alison would never have to worry about the source of her son's peculiarities, wouldn't have to torture herself as to whether they might be the result of maternal inadequacy, or environmental deprivation, or genetic inheritance. Neither would she have to fret long into the night about how he'd eventually turn out. For better or worse, one glance at Dov was all that was needed.

Whereas she herself . . .

'I've never asked you this before,' said Alison, suddenly, as if jump leads were present inside the car as well as outside, 'and of course you don't have to answer, it's sheer idle curiosity on my part – but are the twins much like their father?'

Iris blushed. Incredibly, automatically (autonomically for that matter), after all this time, the thought of Conrad still made her blush. She ducked her head, embarrassed.

'None of my business, of course,' said Alison.

'No it's all right,' said Iris. 'I was just thinking. . . . thinking along similar lines.' He had been eighteen when she'd last seen him – exactly the twins' current age. She could remember the long chain of lampshades down the corridor of the hall of residence, each one swinging where his head had knocked it in passing; she could almost trace the dust on the spines of his textbooks, almost hear the midnight music from his room, vibrating the wall between them. The phrase in those days had been 'chick-magnet'. She smiled, a little bleakly. 'Yes, I think they probably are.'

12

There was something about the quintessential *wrongness* of green gravy that prevented Spencer from actually lifting the fork to his mouth. The pie looked all right – the pastry nicely crusty and brown, the meat in recognizable chunks – and the mash appeared to be normal mash, but the whole plateful swam in the virid sauce which the man behind the counter had scooped straight from the eel barrel with a ladle. 'What's that?' Spencer had asked, revolted.

'Licker,' the man had said, with an edge of contempt.

'Licker?'

'Yeah. It's traditional.'

Everything in the shop was traditional: the green and white tiles, the absence of a customer toilet, the almost theatrical surliness of the staff, and the orange tea, so strong that after half a mugful he felt as if someone had smacked him round the head.

He was sitting on his own at a marble table in the corner, tucked away from the draught of the door, but with an unrestricted view of the other customers. Three o'clock was an odd time to be having lunch, and besides Spencer there was only a quartet of yellow-jacketed construction workers, eating two pies apiece, and a very old man, bent low over his sponge pudding and custard. Sleet and a cold snap had left a pattern of lacy streaks across the window, through which could be glimpsed the shabby bustle of the Kingsland Road. The roofs of the cars were spattered with white and the pavement was a slab of pitted, grey ice across which the older passers-by walked with tiny steps and even the loping black youths halved their stride.

The morning Casualty shift had been a conveyor belt of textbook fall injuries – hips, wrists, collarbones and tailbones, wheeled out of the ambulances, into X-ray and thence to the winding queue for the plaster room. Mrs Spelko had attempted to speed things up by zoning the waiting area according to injuries. Spencer had heard her shouting 'wrists to the *left*, to the *left*' at a bewildered porter, and had shortly afterwards come across Vincent, his friend the psychiatrist, watching the scene with quiet wonder. 'Evidence is mounting,' he'd muttered to Spencer. 'Recurrent grandiosity and delusional behaviour – in this case she obviously thinks she's an air traffic controller. My file is building and I hope soon to have her removed under Section 4 of the Mental Health Act.'

There were now only six weeks left of Spencer's contract, and he was experiencing the unfamiliar sensation of looking forward to something – to several things, actually. To waving goodbye to Mrs Spelko, for a start; to the end of the relentless shift system to which his body clock had never really adjusted; to the impersonality of Casualty, through which patients passed with the speed and anonymity of car factory components – a door bolted on here, a wing mirror there – but most of all he was looking forward to leaving hospitals behind him; God knows he had spent too much time in those places in recent years. That smell, compounded of antiseptics and air fresheners and bedpans, that atmosphere of fear and boredom and desperate hope, the terrible rattling sweep of curtains drawn around beds, the colours never seen elsewhere – jaundiced skin under fluorescent light, iodine splotches on bleached sheets – he never wanted to hear, see, feel any of it again.

'Is there somefing wrong with that?' It took a moment for

Spencer to realize who was speaking. The man behind the counter had his back to him, and was using a large knife on something that crunched unpleasantly, but in the long mirror that lined the wall, his heavy-lidded eyes were focused on Spencer's plate.

'Yes,' said the man, 'I'm talking to you with the books. Is there somefing wrong with your meal?'

'I haven't tried it yet,' said Spencer.

'Well if you don't like it hot, you won't like it cold.'

'It's good food, that,' said the old man with the pudding, pointing with his spoon. 'Put hairs on your chest, that will.'

'Right,' said Spencer.

'He doesn't like the licker,' said the man behind the counter.

'It's full of goodness, that.'

'I told him it's traditional.'

'Licker's the best bit. Go on, son, try it.'

'It's normally ladies who won't try the licker.'

'Go *on*, son,' said the old man, as if urging a slow but willing horse.

The construction workers, having reached the fags and *Sun* portion of the meal, were watching with what looked like mild contempt, and Spencer could feel that the number of comments might soon multiply and darken. He reloaded his fork with as much pie and as little green stuff as possible, and raised it to his mouth.

'Good?' asked the old man, keenly, before he'd swallowed.

Spencer nodded, smiling, and gave a thumbs-up. The atmosphere lightened, and the construction workers went back to their paper.

'You fought it would taste fishy, din't yer?' The man behind the counter had turned, and Spencer could see he was holding a decapitated eel in one hand. He nodded, still unable to speak.

'And it don't, does it?'

He shook his head. The man looked satisfied and slapped the eel back on the counter. It flipped its tail and Spencer turned away hastily. To be honest, the bolus of flavours in his mouth – gravy browning, cheap stewing steak, unbuttered, unsalted, lukewarm mash – seemed strangely familiar, almost comforting. He swallowed and remembered: school dinners.

He opened *Microbiology for the General Practitioner* at the chapter on food poisoning, and started to read, mechanically inserting forkfuls with his left hand and making notes in the margin with his right. He had brought his textbooks to the shop as part of a new regime, instituted out of desperation. Faced with failing both his exams and his promise to Mark, he had started combining the two disciplines. Thus, within recent weeks he had revised obstetrics at the oyster bar in Harrods' food hall, sexually transmitted diseases while sheltering in a doorway during the ceaseless rain that accompanied the Lord Mayor's Show, and paediatrics while queuing to see Santa at the Hanley Cross Shopping Centre. The latter wasn't actually on Mark's list, but constituted a long-held promise to his god-daughter. Nina had been so excited at the prospect of seeing Father Christmas that she had sung 'Rudolf the Red-Nosed Reindeer' throughout the car journey and then fallen asleep in her buggy for the entire forty-five minutes it took to inch through the Pixie Glen. Spencer had found a textbook in his bag and been pleasantly surprised by the degree of concentration he'd achieved, shuffling along with the book held in front of him while a tapeloop of 'Jingle Bells' boomed from the tannoy. He'd woken Nina just before they reached the grotto and she'd been understandably cross and sleepy, refusing to give her name or even look at Santa, although she'd taken the present with a disdainful hand. The chief pixie helper had greeted Spencer by name, and he'd been startled to recognize a two-day relationship from a couple of years back, now minus a moustache, but sporting a little pointed hat and matching tunic. The helper (Simon? Stuart?) had been busy fending off the next child in line who was trying to punch him, so hadn't had time to chat, but he'd looked well; it was always a grim relief when someone you hadn't seen for a while looked well.

The really odd thing about that afternoon was that now, whenever Spencer heard 'Jingle Bells', he instantly recalled the five commonest causes of non-haemorrhagic childhood rash. It was a pity he couldn't bring a tapedeck into the exam.

'Enjoy that then?' The counter man was removing his plate, and Spencer realized that he'd eaten the lot, green gravy and all.

'Yes it was lovely,' he said mendaciously.

'Spotted dick?'

'No thanks.' He felt a pang at the missed opportunity of the question; Mark could have come up with half a dozen replies, each cheaper than the last.

'More tea?'

'No thanks, I'd better be going.' He checked his watch and saw that it was much later than he thought; Dr Petty had suggested he arrived at four thirty and it was already twenty past. He grabbed his books and coat, and hurried out into the cold.

The Christmassy decor at the Sarum Road Practice began in the car park, where someone had spray-painted fake-snow holly leaves onto the surgery wall, continued in a small way at the door (plastic Yule wreath), the doormat ('Merry Xmas' in Gothic script) and the umbrella stand (dangly Santa) and achieved full glory in the waiting room where no inch of wall was free of tinsel, no surface of beaming snowmen, and even the receptionist wore three-inch earrings in the shape of Christmas trees. She was on the phone when Spencer entered, and gave him a raking stare before pointing to a chair and resuming her conversation.

'Like I said, there's nothing in the book until Tuesday.' She was in her very early twenties, black, slightly buck-toothed and strikingly well-dressed for the job in a fuchsia crossover top and black lycra trousers, her hair teased into an elaborate weave dotted with pink and white flowers. Even her nails continued the theme, each one a deep pink, encrusted with white dots like a mini-snowstorm. As she listened to the person on the other end of the line, she examined them one by one, first from a couple of inches away and then from arm's length. 'Like I told you, there's totally nothing I can do about it,' she said, scratching an invisible stain from her thumbnail. Her tone was mildly sympathetic with an undercurrent of deep boredom. She leaned across the counter towards Spencer and put her hand over the mouthpiece.

'Are you Dr Spencer?'

He went over to the desk. 'Dr Carroll, you mean?'

'Carol?' she said disbelievingly.

'That's my surname. Carroll. Spencer's my first name.'

'Right. But you're definitely the one who's starting in February?'

'Yes, I –'

'Excuse me just one moment.' She unblocked the mouthpiece. 'All right, Mrs Latham, you're going to go for Tuesday then? Ten thirty? All right, then. Merry Christmas, Mrs Latham.' She put the phone down and made a note in the appointments book.

'OK Dr Spencer, Dr Petty's sorry but he had to go on a call. You're late.'

'Yes I know, I got lost in the one-way –' The phone rang again and she picked it up with an automatic 'Sarum Road Practice, how can I help you?'

Spencer leaned against the counter, being careful not to nudge the flashing nativity scene, and took a covert look around the waiting room. Evening surgery wasn't due to begin for forty-five minutes but the seats were already starting to fill. Compared to their counterparts in Casualty, the patients looked slightly older, slightly shabbier and slightly less likely to shout obscenities and punch a member of staff; it was odd to think that in a few weeks he would know some of their names, and in a few months be able to recite their entire medical and family histories. They sat in silence; the quiet was punctuated only by sniffs and coughs, and the occasional sharp snapping noise. It took a moment or two for him to realize that the latter was the receptionist clicking her fingers at him. She was still on the phone, but she pointed a tiny blizzard at an unmarked door next to the leaflet rack and mouthed 'wait in there', before turning away to riffle through the repeat prescriptions book.

He edged round the table where neat rows of magazines lay untouched and knocked on the door, waiting a good few seconds before turning the handle. Someone said, 'Come in,' just as he opened it and out of some strange reflex he half closed it again, banging his knee and forehead and dropping his briefcase. There was a stifled titter from the waiting patients as he picked it up again and entered the room with as much dignity as he could muster.

It was a Christmas-free zone, a large and cluttered area that obviously served several purposes – meeting point, kitchen, office – the one function flowing into the other so that the kettle was on the desk and the easy chairs piled with folders and printouts. Crouched in the corner, an open black bin liner in front of her, was a women he vaguely recognized.

'Hello Spencer,' she said, straightening up. She was almost his height – not far off six foot – with grey-streaked shoulder-length hair and a pink-and-white complexion that made her look oddly girlish. She held out a hand. 'We've met a couple of times. I'm Fran's next-door neighbour.'

'Oh, of course.' He was used to only seeing her top half over the garden wall. 'Violet, isn't it?'

She grimaced. 'Iris.'

'Sorry. I knew it was a flower.'

'It was actually one of my great aunts. The other two were called Olive and Myrtle, so I suppose it might have been worse. Anyway, welcome to the practice.'

'Right, thanks.' He was still feeling the slight disorientation of seeing someone out of context. 'So . . . you work here?'

'Yes, I'm the –' She paused. 'I don't really have a title. Practice Administrator I suppose; I do a bit of everything.' She looked rather ruefully at the bin bag.

'What have you lost?'

'Not *me*,' she said. 'Dr Petty accidentally threw away his invite to a medical dinner and he can't remember where it is, or who's giving it. And he's not sure whether he threw it away here or at home. Or he might just have lost it.' She rolled her eyes.

'One of those satisfying little tasks then?'

'Mmm.'

'I was supposed to be meeting him at four thirty for a chat and a look around the surgery.'

'I know. I organized it.'

'Oh God, well I'm sorry I'm so late.'

'It doesn't matter. I can do the showing round and Roger's chats go on far too long anyway. Tea?'

'Please.'

'I'd seen your name on our trainee list for a while, but it took me ages to make the connection.'

As she filled the kettle and washed a couple of mugs, he

wondered who it was she reminded him of, with her mid-calf navy skirt and matching blouse, her shining cheeks and bobbed hair. There was an image hovering in his head of a woman with one foot on a bus platform and the other jauntily in mid-air; a 1920s clippie, he suddenly realized – all she needed was the ticket machine and a cloche.

'Milk?'

'Please.'

She poured a little into his empty mug and set it on the table. 'Do sit down – just shove all that stuff onto the floor. I was in the middle of a tidy-up when Roger had his crisis. Have you ever met him?'

'Briefly. He was on the traineeship selection panel.' He remembered a voice that could have been borrowed from Trevor Howard, a silk tie, a tailored shirt and a great deal of mature-model-quality white hair. 'What's he like?'

'Well he's –' She hesitated, clearly weighing up a number of possible answers. 'He's rather patrician,' she said at last, and he had the feeling that she'd gone for the tactful option. 'He does tend to pronounce on things, which some patients like of course . . .'

'Right,' said Spencer, getting the picture. 'And what about the ones that don't?'

'They can see Dr Steiner.'

'And what's Dr Steiner like?'

'He's –' The same weighing-up process took place, Iris's eyes roving around the room as she searched for the correct adjective. 'He's very –' She paused again.

'Difficult to describe?'

'Odd, I was going to say.'

'Odd in what way?' asked Spencer, fascinated.

She moved her head, hesitantly. 'Well you know Mr Spock in *Star Trek* –'

He let out a great bark of laughter, startling himself. It was such an uninhibited sound, so unfamiliar to him in recent months that he'd forgotten he could make that noise. Iris was looking amazed.

'That wasn't actually supposed to be a joke,' she said. 'It's quite an accurate comparison.'

'The ears?'

'Not the ears, no. Just the general air of . . . other-worldliness. Ayesha – she's the receptionist – she calls him The Martian.'

'And what's *she* like?'

'Very efficient and confident and rather patronizing. Well, she patronizes me, anyway,' she added, humbly.

'Is she the Christmas fan?'

'Yes. It's a bit excessive, isn't it? I did try to say something but – well, to be honest she thinks I'm very old and not altogether worth listening to. And a killjoy, of course.'

'How did you keep this room clear?'

'Oh, I just reminded her that Dov Steiner's Jewish and he'd be offended if we forced Christian symbolism on him.'

'Would he?'

'No. I doubt he'd even notice.'

'Anyone else I should know about?'

'Magda, the practice nurse. But she's quite normal.'

He laughed, and again she looked surprised, as if unused to being found amusing. 'She is, you know. Well, compared to Dov, anyway. Though she's a Mormon so there are certain subjects you have to avoid.'

'Like what?'

'Oh, you know . . . wedding rings, that sort of thing.' This time, when he laughed, she looked rather pleased. 'To be honest, I've been looking forward to you coming; I do miss having ordinary conversations.'

The tea she made was only marginally weaker than that at the pie and mash shop, and Spencer sipped it cautiously. He had found that if he started night shift on a caffeine high, then by 3 a.m. even patients who were quite ill themselves started enquiring whether he was feeling all right, and by 8 a.m. he was wide awake again, ready to go through the whole dreadful insomnia cycle once more.

Iris spotted his hesitation. 'It's too strong, isn't it? I'll make you another.' He started to protest but she was already turning the kettle on again and rinsing out his mug. 'I always do that. I grew up in a household where it was one spoonful per person and two for the pot, and I've never lost the habit.'

'Where was that, then?' he asked, vaguely imagining some tea-steeped Orwellian tripe shop, though her accent was unexceptionably middle-class.

'Just round the corner from here, actually. About five minutes' walk.'

'Oh. You haven't moved far, then.'

'No,' she said, rather broodingly, her hand poised on the milk carton. 'No distance at all.'

'And your dad still lives here, doesn't he?' he asked, suddenly remembering a piece of Fran gossip.

'Mmm. That's right.' She gave him a suspicious look and Spencer felt as if he'd inadvertently prodded a tender spot. He searched for a neutral topic.

'So what's this area like?'

'Oh, it's got a bit of everything. There's nearly five thousand on the list – is this better?' She showed him a mugful of a more acceptable shade.

'Lovely.'

'Dr Petty sees a few private patients. We cover two hostels for the homeless, there are refugees coming and going, bit of TB, a few needle users, Hep B, AIDS . . .' She trailed off and their eyes met. Clearly Fran's gossip channel went both ways. 'I'm sorry about your friend,' she said.

'Thanks.' They sat in silence for a few moments, obviously both wondering the same thing. 'Perhaps . . .' said Spencer, struck by a thought, '– if you tell me what you already know about me and I tell you what I already know about you – which is very little,' he added hastily, seeing her look of alarm. 'For instance, I know you've got identical twins. Public knowledge?'

She relaxed a little and nodded. 'They're nearly six foot five, I'd have a job keeping them secret.'

'Your go,' he said.

'All right.' She thought for a moment. 'I know you recently killed over a hundred snails single-handed.' He shrugged modestly. 'Oh, and you were once an art student.'

'Only for a year. I was hopeless – I packed it in, decided to follow the family trade. I still can't draw hands. Actually –' he suddenly remembered '– I know that you went to medical school. That's right, isn't it?'

'Mmm.' It was an unenthusiastic assent. 'Only for a couple of terms, though.'

'Why did you give up?'

She looked at him. 'I was pregnant with twins.'

'Oh I *see*,' he said, feeling stupid. There was a pause. 'Your turn again,' he said.

'All right. Well . . .' She seemed to gather herself up. 'I do know that you're gay. I mean . . . I wanted to ask you. Is that public knowledge?'

He hesitated, hating the ugly, anxious gap between the closet and the world, the jump with no clear landing. Mark, who at fifteen had whipped open the door of his own closet and started giving guided tours, had once suggested that he try the other exit, push his way out through the back. 'You could check out how they treat gays in Narnia. That Mr Tumnus is definitely a poof.'

'Sort of public,' he said, at last. 'It's just that being out and being a doctor's quite a – a statement. I like to choose who I tell – I mean, I wouldn't lie if someone asked but I'm not going to hire a tannoy . . .' He felt craven, but she nodded understandingly.

'All right,' she said, 'your turn. No, actually, no. Sorry.' She shook her head and started to go pink.

'What's the matter?'

'It's just – let's not do this any more. It's all a bit too much like some awful game show. Besides, there's only one thing I ever told Fran which I'd rather she'd kept to herself, and I'm sure you know that already. It's long past being a secret.'

'About your dad?'

'And Mrs McHugh. Yes.'

'Tammy,' he said in a cod Scottish accent, to make her smile.

She didn't. 'Yes. I know Fran thought it was funny, but I've had rather a sense of humour failure about it. Sorry.'

He was embarrassed. 'No, I'm sorry.'

'Well, anyway . . .' The pinkness was fading, but she still looked unhappy. 'That's it, really, for secrets. And on my side, apart from knowing about your friend –'

'Mark wasn't a secret,' said Spencer. His voice sounded harsh, even to himself. 'He didn't hide away somewhere, we didn't talk about him in whispers. He had AIDS, he died of AIDS. Anyway he was much too loud and bossy to be a secret.' He took a swig of tea, and then another to ease the sudden ache in his throat.

There was an awful silence, punctuated only by a richly phlegm-laden cough from the waiting room. 'I didn't mean –'

Iris began, looking stricken, and Spencer could have slapped himself.

'Oh God,' he said, 'I'm so sorry. Just ignore me, I'm sounding like a tetchy old queen.'

'No, really –'

'Really. That was *such* a terrible idea, possibly one of the worst ideas I've ever had. "I'll show you mine if you show me yours" – I mean, what an awful way to get to know someone . . .'

'It doesn't matter,' she said. 'Honestly.'

'God.' He shook his head. 'Perhaps I should just leave the room and come in again. We could start from scratch, from a baseline of polite acquaintanceship.' He set down his mug too firmly, and a bit of tea slopped over the side onto his pristine cuff. 'Oh bugger.'

'I'll get a cloth.' She was on her feet straight away, rinsing out a j-cloth at the sink.

'Or maybe we could pretend we've never met before and make up an entire history – it could be quite liberating. I could say I was born in a trunk, mother in panto, father a balloon-folder specializing in giraf – oh, thanks.' He took the cloth from her and dabbed fruitlessly at the orange stain for a while.

'I made the tea too strong,' she said. 'You'll never get it out.'

'No, no – I've got some bleach at home. It'll be fine.'

'Really?'

'Iris, it was my fault not yours. And I've got loads of other shirts.'

She started to say something and then checked herself.

'Sorry?'

'I was going to say –'

'What?'

173

'Fifty. I've heard you've got fifty other shirts.'

He stared at her for a moment and then started to laugh. 'My God, now that *is* a secret. Fran told you that?'

'You mean it's true?'

'Well . . . give or take a couple.' Fran had once insisted on counting them and had arrived at the figure of fifty-two. He had not told her about the five in the linen basket.

Iris shook her head in apparent wonder. 'And are they crease-proof?'

'*Nylon?*' he said horrified. 'Iris, I'm gay. I iron therefore I am.'

There was a sharp knock and he turned to see Ayesha standing in the doorway, the fluorescent light catching her nosestud so it looked like a luminous zit. 'Am I interrupting anything?' she asked, brightly. Round the half-open door came the loud, liquid cough that Spencer had heard earlier.

'No, we were just chatting,' said Iris. She smoothed her skirt and looked suddenly official.

'Only Dr Petty just rang and said he's sorry, Dr Spencer, but he's in the garage with an exhaust problem so he won't be back before six. And also he said to tell you, Iris, that he's found the invitation in the glove apartment. Oh and that glue man's back in the surgery and three patients have walked out already. I've told Dr Steiner but he didn't take no notice. All right?' she cocked her head as if speaking to a pair of six-year-olds, and then closed the door again.

Iris sighed. 'Well that was a waste of an afternoon.'

Spencer's thumbs were pricking. 'Who was it she meant by the glue man?' he asked tentatively. He already knew the answer.

Less than half an hour before, the patients in the waiting room had been seated randomly, odd spaces between them; now they were all crammed at one end, and at the other, like an unexploded bomb, sat Callum Strang. He appeared to be asleep, his head resting against the wall and his legs spread loosely, revealing an unzipped fly and an expanse of crusted red y-front. The tattoo was less noticeable than usual, being half-camouflaged by a row of steri-strips that held a ragged cut together. Disgust and UHU saturated the air.

'How long has he been coming here?' whispered Spencer. It was a while since Callum had been in Casualty; on the last occasion he'd been plucked off the street with hypothermia, and actually admitted to a ward. He'd scarpered less than twelve hours later, taking with him thirty quid and a tube of glue from the nurses' station.

'A few weeks,' said Iris. 'He's registered at a local hostel. Dov actually runs a weekly clinic there, but he keeps turning up at surgery.'

'About his chest?'

'About his tattoo. It takes ages to turf him out again.'

'My husband says I shouldn't have to deal with people like him, he says it's not part of my job description,' said Ayesha, viciously turning the pages of the appointment book. 'We should get the *police* in to chuck him out.'

At the word 'police', Callum's eyes opened and Spencer found himself actually cringing in an attempt to avoid being spotted.

'Dr Carroll!' The words were spoken with delight.

'It's Dr Spencer,' said Ayesha, censoriously, 'and you haven't got no appointment.'

'Fuck appointments,' said Callum, levering himself to his feet. He walked stiffly over to the desk, the smell preceding him like a fanfare.

'The police can get here in three minutes,' said Ayesha, her hand hovering above the phone.

'No, don't call them. I'm sorry for swearing. I am. Honest –' he swayed forward and peered at her name badge '– Ashley.'

'It's Mrs Pershaw,' said Ayesha, leaning back as far as possible.

'Right. But I jus' wanted to say hello to this doctor, because he's the best fucking doctor ever. Sorry to swear but he fucking is.' He punched Spencer matily on the arm.

'Hello, Callum,' said Spencer, depressed. He was aware of the rapt attention of the entire waiting room.

'Will you look at my head?' He started fumbling with the dressing.

'Not just now,' said Spencer. 'How did you get the cut?'

'I did it with a tin opener.'

A Mexican wave of revolted whispers flowed along the row of seats.

'Best fucking doctor ever,' said Callum again, this time as a general announcement. 'He's the one I want to see. No offence to the robot man – what's he called, Stainer? – but I want to see this man.'

'Dr Carroll's just going,' said Iris, quickly. 'He was only on a visit, he's not working here.'

Spencer shot her a grateful look.

'Until February the first,' added Ayesha, as if Iris had just said something rather stupid. '*Then* he's working here. *Then* you can come back.' She closed the appointments book with a snap and turned to Spencer. 'That's right, isn't it, Dr Spencer?'

13

The precipitation that rattled softly against the classroom window wasn't really snow – the tiny white flakes were actually jagged pieces of ice which stung when they hit bare skin – but it looked enough like snow to have utterly distracted a class of ten-year-olds who were supposed to be engaged in botany-related artwork. Heads were craned towards the window, voices more usually dripping with infant ennui raised in thrilled speculation about sledging and death by frostbite.

'Will we be snowed in all night, Miss?' asked a small girl, hope in her voice.

'All right' said Fran, bowing to the inevitable. 'Put the tops back on the paint pots *very carefully* –' she watched hawkishly while this was done '– and now slowly and *without running* you can go over to the window and have a look.'

There was immediate chaos, twenty-two chairs shoved backwards in unison, twenty-two voices raised in instant conversation. Fran stood aside as they stampeded past. It had been too cold to take the class outside, and instead she had been supervising the creation of a Christmas frieze, messily involving gold and silver paint and a couple of bin bags full of autumn leaves, dried and kept for this very purpose. She was not particularly happy with the result so far – the paint was too runny and, far from festively illustrating their delicate skeletal structure, the frieze was a jumble of leaf-shaped blotches and unintentional fingerprints. This was partly the fault of the children's own teacher, a self-styled art expert who had urged her to let the class experiment with the correct thickness of paint ('it's important for them to grasp the point of your request') and then abdicated all responsibility for the ensuing mess ('it was just a suggestion'). He was sitting in the corner now, flipping through a copy of *British Trees* and looking bored.

Fran joined the children by the window.

Through the icy rain, the farm looked bleak and shuttered. Hagwood was battening down the hatches for winter, stepping up its provision of indoor activities and laying off part-time staff. Porky was the only visible animal, standing by his trough with his ears blowing in front of him like pennants. As she watched he took an excited step forward, snout raised, and a few seconds later Barry came round the corner of the hen house with a laden bucket, his head dipped against the wind.

'That man's going to feed the pig,' said Fran, ever alert for educational possibilities.

'What man?'

'What's he going to give him?'

'What pig?'

'He's going to give him some hard little chunks, a bit like biscuits but not sweet. They're called pig nuts and they're very crunchy and full of vitamins.'

As she spoke, Barry slipped in a patch of mud and fell over, distributing pig nuts over a wide area. There was a shout of delighted laughter from the class and he looked up to see twenty-three pairs of eyes watching his ignominy. Fran turned away and clapped her hands.

'OK, let's get back to work.'

'Oh Miss, we want to see him pick them all up.'

'No, we've had a break now so let's get back to work. We've only got twenty minutes before you go back to the coach.'

'Ohhhhh.'

As they meandered back to the tables, she kept half an eye on the window. The hail was getting stronger, sweeping up the hill in successive curtains, alternately obscuring and revealing the cars on the flyover. Barry, plastered in mud, had abandoned the spilled feed and was tramping back to the store for another load, leaving Porky making anxious little runs up and down the sty.

It was three weeks since she had told Barry – straightfor-wardly, efficiently – that she was not and never would be interested. They had been labelling jars of wild-flower seed at the time, and Barry had gone very quiet, printing and peeling labels in doleful silence and – she discovered afterwards – sticking most of them on upside down. 'Is there anyone else?' he'd asked, after a while, and for once Duncan had come in handy; with only a slight adjustment of reality she was able to cast him in the role of Odysseus, for whom she was patiently waiting, forswearing all others. Barry had glumly accepted this, and although she had half expected him to revert to his old, lazy, complacent self, he had – to his credit – kept up a modicum of the new dynamism. He was, however, still fairly useless and while it was true that any member of staff could have been unlucky enough to fall flat on their face in front of a score of children, the odds would always be on Barry.

The children had settled back into their chairs, and Fran glanced at the clock; there was just enough time for a final stab at accuracy.

'Right, now I want you to make up one last mix of paint, but only after you've listened *very carefully* to my instructions. Pick up the little powder scoop and fill it as far as the *second* mark. Which mark did I say?'

'THE SECOND MARK,' droned the class in ragged uni-son. Over in the corner, their teacher shrugged disapprovingly.

A quarter of an hour later, Class 3L departed with noisy

reluctance, leaving behind them twenty yards of gilded splodges, three gloves and a hanky, stiff with snot. Fran donned a pair of Marigolds and started to peel paint-sodden leaves from the floor. She hated this part of the winter, the dreary emptiness of the farm landscape, the enforced confinement and massed coughing of the classroom, the continual strain that Christmas decoration manufacture put on her minimal artistic talent.

'Fran? Ah Fran, I thought you might be . . . er . . .'

She looked up to see Claud hovering in the doorway. He was wearing his favourite blue jumper with the red cow on the front, rumoured to have been knitted by his mother.

'Hi. What's the problem?'

'There's a phonecall for you in the staff area . . . er, it's rather a noisy line so it took me a while to . . .'

'Thanks, Claud.' She had already peeled off her gloves and squeezed past him, feeling a little troubled; no one ever phoned her at work.

Barry was in the staffroom, trying to warm his hands under the hot tap. He nodded sadly at her as she picked up the phone.

'Hello?'

The distinctive, rasping voice came over the roar of traffic. 'Hello, little Fran.'

'*Duncan?*' Barry stiffened like a pointer sighting game.

'How are you, Fran?'

'Me? I'm fine.' She was disconcerted, he didn't normally deal in pleasantries. 'How about you?'

'I need to talk to you, Fran. Can I come and see you?'

'Come and see me? You mean, come back to England?'

'I'm here now. I'm at a petrol station on the A28, waiting for a lift.'

'*What?*' Over by the sink, Barry was pretending not to listen.

'I spent the last two days hitching to the Netherlands and then I got the first ferry I could. I have to see you, Fran, when can I see you?'

She caught Barry's eye and pointed towards the door. He nodded and started to move very slowly.

'Fran?'

'Oh – er – come straight to the house. I'll try and get off early. I could probably be there by four.' She realized, with a pang of relief, that it was Tuesday – choir practice – and Peter and Sylvie would be out.

'OK. I'll be there.'

'Are you all right, Duncan? I mean, what's going on?'

There was a pause, during which she could hear the hoots of a reversing lorry. 'I have to see you, Fran, I have to talk to you, there's something I've got to say,' he said in a rush, and put the phone down.

'Blimey.' She stared at the receiver for a moment, still absorbing the conversation.

'I'll cover for you if you want to get off.' It was Barry, who had almost, but not quite, got as far as the door.

'Oh you heard that, did you?' she said sarcastically. 'OK then. Thanks. I'll check it with Claud.'

'I hope everything's all right. With Duncan.'

'Well, obviously you'll be the first to know.'

He brightened slightly, and she sighed. 'Just *kidding*, Barry.'

She arrived back home at five past four to find the doorstep empty and a copy of the *Dalston Advertiser* on the mat. Mr Tibbs was lying on the floor of the hall as if just dropped from a height and he mewed creakily as she stepped over him. He had two or three favourite spots in the house, all of which were inconvenient to the other occupants, and one of which (fourth stair from the top) was actually dangerous. One morning

Sylvie had caught Fran gently trying to lever him off the latter with a slippered foot, and had been reproachful.

'What am I supposed to do, jump over him?' Fran had asked.

'You can pick him up,' Sylvie had said, bracing herself before doing so. 'He's a gentle old pussy cat and he loves being picked up, don't you, Tibbsy?' He had lain in her arms, inert, like a fun-fur bolster.

Sylvie had been living in the house for more than a month now. There was nothing obtrusive about her presence; she was tidy, quiet and ate almost nothing while still taking a share of the cooking and washing-up. She spent most of her evenings in the room she shared with Peter; she never watched TV, she listened to the radio at barely audible volume and she played the piano so beautifully that Fran would sometimes sit on the stairs to listen to her practise. She had even chipped in some rent, considerably easing the burden of their ever-expanding mortgage payment.

The downside was this: she held hands with Peter almost all the time, even at dinner, making Fran feel perpetually like an unwanted third; she reacted to almost any setback (running out of cat food; forgetting someone's birthday) by bursting into tears and then getting a headache, forcing the rest of the household to walk round on tiptoe and converse in whispers; she thought that Mr Tibbs was a human being; and she used the phrase 'you're so practical, Fran' at least once a day, generally in a context which implied that the word 'practical' could be substituted by the words 'unimaginative', 'insensitive' or 'crass'. Fran had never felt so self-conscious, so lumpen, so loud.

And this was in contrast to Peter's radiant, almost tangible happiness; when he looked at Sylvie, there was clearly an angelic choir on the soundtrack, and vaseline on the lens.

There had been, so far, no indication as to when she might be moving out again.

'Any luck with flat-hunting, Sylvie?' Fran had asked last week, in passing, and Sylvie had drooped her head, and reached across the breakfast table to take Peter's hand.

'Sylvie's a little bit upset,' Peter had said.

'Why?'

'She's just seen this.' He had pushed over a copy of the *Advertiser* and pointed to the front page. Under the headline 'Local woman lay Dead in Basement for Five weeks' was a summary of the coroner's report into the death of Constancia Hackett, complete with lurid sub-headings.

Fran had read it through slowly. She herself had not found it easy to shake off the image that she'd seen through the letter box that day, after Sylvie had scrambled, gasping, back up the stairs to the street – the yellow fingers curling round a door frame into the hall, the cloud of little black flies.

'No one realized,' Sylvie had said in a small voice, squeezing Peter's hand. 'She had a heart problem but no one checked how she was or wondered why they hadn't seen her. And that's awful, isn't it?' She had looked intensely at Fran, her grey eyes beginning to blur.

'Yes, it is,' Fran had replied, meaning it, and then had felt disconcerted by how wooden that 'yes it is' had sounded. She had become so used to automatically agreeing with Sylvie's airy generalizations and pointless fancies that she appeared to have forgotten how to be sincere.

'And I don't want to live in a place like that,' Sylvie had continued, 'a place where people don't care about each other.' A tear had plopped onto the table, and then another. Peter had looked anguished, and Fran had nodded, and been sympathetic, and had realized that this was not the time to ask whether, in that case, Sylvie intended to stay in Stapleton Road indefinitely, or to speculate on where, short of Shangri-La, she intended to look for her next flat. Sometimes, she'd accepted reluctantly, it was best just to shut up.

By a quarter to six, Duncan had still not arrived. Fran had put a couple of potatoes in the oven, tidied round a bit (not that he would ever notice), considered – and then rejected – squeezing a spot on her chin, and re-read his last two letters. Both had been posted from a small town near Hamburg, where he seemed to have halted his Southern progress. He had been there for at least a month, and the local landscape was becoming familiar to her through his photographs – flooded meadows, distant cooling towers, Friesian cows and half-timbered farmhouses that looked oddly two-dimensional, as if they'd been thrown up on a Hollywood backlot. It didn't look – to her eye – particularly striking or memorable, but his letters were lyrical about the fusion of the industrial and the rural. 'A sinuous dark form, twisted against the sky. Is it a tower? Or is it the trunk of a leafless tree?' as he had written on the back of one of the pictures. A tower, she would have said, from the evidence of the vast billboard next to it, advertising electric power. Duncan always laughed when she pointed out that kind of thing. 'Factwoman' he called her.

Now that she looked at the recent letters again, she realized that they contained even less information than normal. Usually, she could count on a few personal nuggets wedged between the acres of poetic maundering – her eye would snag on the word 'tent' or 'money' and she'd find a sentence or two about soggy groundsheets, or the non-availability of dope in rural Finland. She might even, occasionally, see the answer to one of the list of questions she always appended to her own letters: 'Have you seen any storks?' for instance, or 'Do you have enough waterproof clothing?' The Hamburg letters, however, contained not a shred of anything factual, no hint that he was about to abandon his journey and fly west for winter, and no clue as to his reason. They were pure streams of consciousness, paeons to the environment, lacking even the lustful reveries that had spiced up previous efforts.

She returned the letters to their envelopes and poured herself a glass of wine. What if he'd had enough of the EU project, and wanted to revert to his old work pattern? Would he want to resume the relationship where they'd left off, and if so what should she do about it? Or what if the problem were financial and he needed a loan? Should she give him a nominal amount to tide him over? Or should she tell him to get stuffed?

Or what if – God help her – he wanted to move in until this crisis, whatever it was, blew over? It would be Withnail and Prince Charles all over again, this time with the addition of Tinkerbell. She tried to imagine the four of them sitting down to a meal together, attempting to find topics in common. Maybe he'd find a soulmate in Sylvie, a fellow traveller down the pathway of the spirit. Maybe not, though. Despite the poetry, there was something very earthy about Duncan; fragility was not a quality she'd ever heard him admire.

She topped up her wine glass. If she'd missed anything about him over the last few months, it was his physical presence. He was a big bloke, tall, broad-shouldered; when she put her arms round him, they barely met. She liked big blokes, liked the reassurance of always being able to hear where they were – the heavy footsteps, the creak of chairs. She thought she'd probably eventually settle down with a big bloke. Though not Duncan, obviously.

By seven o'clock, the potatoes were on the cusp between crispy and adamantine, and Fran was on her third glass of wine. She was standing in the dark by the window of her bedroom, from where she could see the junction with the main road. Three 92As had swung round the corner since she had started her vigil, but no one had got off and she was beginning to worry. The weather had worsened and the orange halo of the street light was filled with slanting snow, the flakes too wet to settle on the pavement but showing fleetingly white along the tops of the privet hedges. She glanced in the opposite direction to the High Road and saw him immediately, slogging into the wind, hands in pockets and his head well down against the sleet.

It was lucky that she put on the landing light before running downstairs, because the cat was couched in his favourite position, his back lethally flush with the stair above. She pushed him off with an impatient foot and hurtled past to the front door.

Duncan was bearded, soaked, and frozen – so cold that she had to take his rucksack off for him, and undo the buttons on his (non-waterproof) coat.

'Fucking English drivers,' he said, barely able to move his lips, as she peeled off the coat and unwound a sodden scarf. 'Once it started getting dark no one would stop. I had to walk from Walthamstow.'

'You did *what*? Why didn't you get a bus? Or the tube?'

'No money.'

'You could have ordered a cab – I'd have paid.'

'Didn't think of it. I just wanted to get here.'

'*Honestly*, Duncan.' She rubbed his reddened hands between her own with a vigour heightened by exasperation; walking six miles through sleet was the kind of pointless dramatic gesture that almost defined him. 'I'm going to run you a bath, it's the only way you'll get warm.'

'Thanks, little Fran. Hug first?' He held out his arms, and it was like standing in front of an open fridge.

'Hug afterwards,' she said, decisively.

In the heat of the water, Duncan's body turned from white with red extremities, to red with purple extremities, and finally to a uniform shrimp pink. He lay with his eyes closed, groaning half-pleasurably at the tingle of returning blood, his hands floating just below the surface, and his bony knees jutting above it. He was thinner than when Fran had last seen him, more gristly, and a few silver hairs glistened in the scrubby beard. She added a little more hot water to the tub, and poured in some of Sylvie's blue bubble bath.

Duncan opened his eyes. 'I feel reborn,' he said.

'Do you want your cocoa now?' She offered him a mug to which she had added a large dash of brandy, and he sat up, slopping water onto the floor. The bathroom was already wetter than she had ever seen it, condensation dripping down the tiles and Duncan's clothes lying in a pool of their own making. It reminded her of the first occasion that she and Duncan had shared a bathroom. He took a sip of the cocoa.

'Fucking fantastic.'

'Are you hungry?'

'Nah.' He lay back and looked at her, with an expression that she could not read.

She felt a little uneasy. 'What?'

He shook his head and then reached out and took one of her hands. He held it loosely and turned it over, as if checking the provenance. 'What a small hand. Such small fingers.'

For one ludicrous moment, she thought he was about to whip an engagement ring from – well, from God knows where – and slip it onto her finger. Instead, reality asserted itself and he squeezed her hand and farted, creating a temporary jacuzzi effect near the taps.

'Jesus, Duncan.' She jerked her head back.

'Loud and lethal, eh? Sorry about that.'

He settled himself again and resumed his study of her face,

his own assuming a look of gentle melancholy. 'Why didn't you come with me, Fran?'

'Why? You know why. Because I had a job and a mortgage and I didn't want to live in a tent for a year.'

'But were there other reasons?'

'Well . . . yes.' She paused. All the other reasons involved wanting to see less of Duncan, but it seemed rather ungrateful to bring that up when he'd just schlepped halfway across Europe to see her. It seemed to be the right answer, in any case. He nodded significantly and took her hand again, this time sandwiching it between his hot, wet palms.

'I missed you so much, Fran. I didn't realize how lonely I'd be. The only people I was meeting were shopkeepers and gits in fast cars who tried to run me down. I was smoking a lot, and getting very low and I just wanted you there, keeping me plugged to reality. I wanted little stubborn Fran walking beside me and the dark horizon ahead. The long . . . dark . . . horizon.' He had drawn her hand closer, so that she was leaning halfway across the bath, looking into his gooseberry-green eyes. 'And then after I'd crossed the border from Denmark I started to realize that it wasn't a journey across land I was making, it was a journey through my mind. And I spent hours in there sometimes – exploring, searching . . .'

Her gaze drifted. When Duncan was in poetic mood, she always lost the thread of what he was saying and started focusing on the carnal. Beneath the bubbles his chest rose and fell, the hairs just breaking surface, and out of the corner of her eye she could just see his cock, floating palely in the deep. She wondered whether she should get in the bath too; she'd be more careful this time, more aware of the downstairs ceiling. He'd started talking about the landscape again, and she forced herself to listen.

'. . . seemed to reflect just what I was thinking. I'd see a lake and it would show me how deep my thoughts were; I'd see pylons and ideas would flash across my mind. Like electricity. I think I was going a bit mad.' He released her hand temporarily and took a slug of cocoa, before resuming the clasp and the intensity, his voice growing husky with nostalgia. 'I was looking for a sign – something to show me why I was there, and what I should be doing. And then one evening I got to this little town. It was just an ordinary place. I was going to stay there one night and then walk straight through and back to open country. I camped in an orchard on the outskirts and when I woke up the next morning I looked through the tent flap and – it was amazing.' His eyes were vivid, meeting hers and then bouncing off to examine their own private landscape. His body tensed with the memory and she watched the muscles springing into line down his belly. 'The whole orchard was in blossom. The whole orchard –'

'In November?' said Fran, incredulously, lust suddenly dissipated.

'In November,' he confirmed, almost with reverence.

'What sort of trees?'

'I don't know, but the blossom was white. And it smelled of . . . heaven. And I knew it was the sign I was looking for. I didn't feel mad any more, I just knew I was in the right place.'

'What shape were the leaves?'

'And the next thing I saw were two people coming through the orchard towards me, bringing me breakfast. It was like coming home.' He pressed her hand between his own and then released it rather theatrically, as if launching a dove.

'I wonder if –' With an effort she wrenched herself away from the subject of unseasonal blossom (although she'd have taken a substantial bet that what he'd seen hadn't been an orchard at all, but a few bushes of *Viburnum fragrans*, which flowered all winter directly onto bare stems and could only be mistaken for fruit trees by someone who couldn't tell a cornflower from a speedwell). 'So who were these people, then?'

'They were part of a community – it's called *Schone Welt*. It means –'

'Beautiful World,' said Fran, who'd done German O Level.

' – and they're artists and craftsmen and cooks and teachers. They run a restaurant and a gallery and they've converted a farmhouse and all the outbuildings to live in. Fran, it's amazing.' He was almost breathless with enthusiasm. 'The ones who brought me coffee were Hella and Auguste. Auguste is a carpenter.' He left an obvious gap for her to fill with a question.

'And Hella?'

'Hella.' He repeated the word rather slowly, as if for the pure pleasure of saying it, and then said it again. 'Hella . . .'

Fran looked at him for a moment, and then sat back on the linen basket and put her feet up on the edge of the bath. 'Oh, right,' she said, 'I get it.'

Duncan heaved himself into a sitting position, slopping water onto the floor. 'It's more complicated than that, Fran. That's why I had to see you.'

'Uhuh. Hang on a minute.' With studied calm, she mopped up the worst of the flood with a bathmat, and then blotted the rest with a couple of handfuls of loo roll. 'All right,' she said, sitting back down again. 'Carry on. You were telling me about Hella.' The word came out with the harshness of an expectoration.

Duncan took a deep breath. 'You know when something's just right, when it fits into place like the last piece in a jigsaw?' He waited, yearningly, for an answer and Fran allowed herself a teeny little nod. 'Well that's what *Schone Welt* felt like. They took me in and I was suddenly a part of it. They'd wanted someone to document what they were doing, and there I was, right where I was needed. Like a limb, an essential limb.'

As opposed to a non-essential one, thought Fran, pettishly.

'I mean, it was the first time I've ever wanted to *stay* anywhere. You know me, Fran, you know how hard it is for me to settle. But I didn't have to walk away from there to find new horizons . . . there were new horizons –' he spread his hands as if kneading stiff dough '– *within* it.' He looked at her expectantly.

'Well how come you never mentioned this, then?' she asked. 'How come your letters were still wittering on about factory chimneys and ditches and things?'

'Because part of everything, part of what I felt, had to do with Hella – and I couldn't mention Hella in a letter because . . . because she was too huge a subject to mention.'

Fran had a sudden image of a Teutonic Bessie Bunter, puffing across the orchard with a plate full of cream buns. 'Well, you're here now,' she said, more brusquely than she meant to. 'Fire away.'

'Don't be angry, little Fran,' said Duncan, placing a wet hand on her knee. She restrained an impulse to shake it off and instead took a deep breath. This was ridiculous; she was being ridiculous. Duncan, whom she didn't love, had never loved, and in fact had tried to dump only eight months ago, had clearly met the woman of his dope-fuelled dreams, and she, Fran, had turned into the archetypal jealous cow, defending her man with hooves unsheathed. She hadn't known she was capable of it; jealous of *Duncan*, for fuck's sake, with his unreadable letters and supine career plan.

She picked up his hand and plonked it back in the bath. 'I'm not angry,' she said.

'You look angry.'

'Well I'm not. You were going to tell me about Hella. What's she like?'

His face seemed to melt and then reassemble itself into a new and sloppy shape. 'She's tall, and she's –'

'No,' said Fran, suddenly changing her mind. 'I'm still not angry, but I don't want to hear any more about her. What does she do?'

'She's an architect.'

'Fine.' She nodded. 'That's it. That's enough information.' Bessie Bunter had transmuted into a Valkyrie with a doctorate. 'I'm going to check on the potatoes.'

'Wait!' He launched himself out of the water and stood dripping. 'Don't go, Fran. I had to say this face to face, I couldn't tell you over the phone. I do still love you, Fran. I'll always love you, but . . .' He looked down at her, tears in his eyes.

She folded her arms and stated the required line, 'You love Hella more.'

He nodded solemnly.

'All right,' she said flatly. She knew there was a gracious way to do this, a way that would match the drama and romance of Duncan's journey, but she was unable to find it.

'You know what I think about you, Fran, you know how much I –'

'Yeah, OK. I'm all right about it, Duncan.' Each word felt chipped from a block. He reached out his hairy arms and wrapped them around her, and kissed the top of her head, and she stood like a cross little statue until he let go.

'I'm all wet now,' she said.

While he dressed, she threw the blackened potatoes into the bin with unnecessary force, and fanned the back door to and fro, dissipating the smoke that still clung to the ceiling. The temperature had dropped and great clouds of steam billowed up by the outside drain as the bathwater swirled away. The snow was beginning to settle.

Duncan entered the kitchen rather diffidently, his drying hair sticking up in tufts like the top of a thistle.

'The potatoes have had it,' she said. 'Do you want bread and cheese? Or we've got some beans, I think.'

He shook his head. 'I'm going to go, Fran.'

'What do you mean? Where?'

'I'll kip at my sister's tonight.'

'You can stay here, I don't mind. You can sleep on the sofa if you want.'

'Nah.' He smiled. 'I think I should leave you alone. Maybe we can talk tomorrow. Go to a bar and have a real old session.'

She shrugged. 'OK, if that's what you want.'

'I'll still miss you Fran.'

'I'll miss you too,' she said, truthfully, if a little stiffly. She was used to Duncan being lyrical, or raucously horny, or melodramatic, or stoned and giggly, or asleep; she wasn't used to this sweet and dignified regret. He fiddled with the buttons on his coat, still damp after an hour and a half on the radiator. 'Fran?'

'Yup?'

'Can you lend me something for the tube?'

She saw him off into the snow with a twenty-pound note and all of her loose change in his pocket, a hot-water bottle stuffed down his jumper, and one of Peter's hats tied under his chin with one of Peter's scarves. On the doorstep he gave her a hug which lifted her off her feet, and she stood and watched him trudge up the road until he disappeared round the corner by Aashish Videos. Then she closed the door gently and wandered back into the kitchen. A few wisps of smoke still curled across the ceiling, and she leaned against the open back door with a beer in her hand, and watched the snow settle on the Brussels sprouts.

14

Iris, standing outside the library with her petition, didn't bother to target the two men who were strolling out of the covered market and along the pavement towards her, but instead turned her attention to a studenty girl who had just crossed the road and was heading towards the post office. The three successive Saturdays that she had spent collecting signatures had turned her from a nervous rookie, plastered against the library façade bleating 'Can I possibly interest you in . . . ?' at people's backs, to a focused assessor, skilled in predicting the exact response of a given passer-by, homing in on the keen and the weak with ruthless accuracy. She felt she could publish a leaflet on the subject.

The girl was in her early twenties and was wearing a jacket that looked vaguely ethnic. This was a good sign, as were her clumpy lace-up shoes. Other items of clothing that seemed inexplicably linked to an interest in the fate of the library were zipped-up anoraks, hats with brims (this included flat caps) and knitted scarves. It had been a chastening moment when Iris realized that she simply had to look out for people who dressed a bit like her. On a broader scale, there was little point in approaching males under twenty-five (unless they were actually entering the library), women under twenty-five in packs of three or more, anyone with a shaven head and anyone who hadn't put their teeth in that morning.

'Petition against library closure.'

'Huh?' The girl turned towards her.

'Would you like to sign a petition against library closure?'

She had learned to start with a statement and keep the clip-board half-concealed at her side until the person had stopped moving. Beginning with a question and an outstretched biro sent people veering away as if repelled by an invisible force field.

'It's closing, is it?' said the girl, surprised.

'There's been a steady reduction of opening hours which means that fewer and fewer people can use the library, which then gives the local authority the ammunition to cut the service entirely.' (Alison Steiner had invented this wording which – as Iris had pointed out at the Save the Library committee meeting – actually translated as 'No, it's not closing.' 'It's a pre-emptive strike,' Alison had said. 'We're saying, "It's not closing *yet* – but if we don't act now then the philistine right will shut every library in Britain and sell them off for yuppie flats."')

'OK,' said the girl, rather uncertainly.

'And it's the best library in North East London.' This was Iris's own addition, one she'd taken on trust from her father who used to claim that he'd cycled round every library in the area, comparing stock, staff and architecture. Admittedly that had been in the late 1940s, but it had become a tenet of family lore, together with her mother's 'nothing beats a nice cup of tea' and her Auntie Olive's 'three prunes a day and you'll live to be a hundred', though she herself hadn't made it past seventy-seven.

The girl took the proffered pen and clipboard and started to fill in her details, while Iris scanned the street for the next potential signatory. The last couple of weeks had awakened a competitive side of her nature that she had never known existed, and she was keen to beat last Saturday's total. A couple of hundred yards up the street, lingering beside the rack in front of the Pound Store she could see a sure-fire bet – one of

Dov's patients who was, moreover, wearing a natty (brimmed) Homburg.

'That all right?' asked the girl.

'Thanks very much,' said Iris, taking back the clipboard and then starting violently as someone tapped her on the shoulder.

'God, you're jumpy, Mum.' It was Robin and Tom, and she realized with a mental lurch that they were the two men she'd seen just a moment ago, distance turning them into unrecognizable adults. Close by they looked reassuringly unchanged, but she felt unsettled, as if something important had happened while she wasn't looking, and she had yet to catch up.

'Do you want us to sign then?' asked Robin, taking the pen from her hand.

'Oh,' she said, surprised. 'Yes please.' Neither had been keen library users for at least a decade, and when she had first mentioned the campaign Robin's response had been, 'Oh, is it still open then?' They had been hugely amused at the thought of her standing in the street 'soliciting', as Tom had put it.

Now he took the clipboard from his brother and started filling in their address with his usual speedy scrawl.

'I've been practising,' he said, finishing his signature with a huge full stop.

'Practising what?'

He started writing on the next line. 'Different signatures. I can do you about fifteen extra people.'

'What? But you –'

'No one will know and it –'

'*No*, Tom.' She tried to grab the clipboard but he turned his back protectively and stuck out his elbows.

'Honestly, I'm really good', he said over his shoulder, 'and they're all real people.'

'That's not the –'

'Mum.' She recognized the warning note in Robin's voice, and turned to see a bulgy young woman holding a large camera.

'Hi.' The woman stuck out her hand. 'I'm Lara.'

Iris shook it hesitantly. 'I'm sorry, I . . .'

'From the *Dalston Advertiser*? We spoke earlier?'

'Did we?' said Iris, doubtfully.

'You're Alison Steiner?'

'No. Oh, I see – you're a bit early. Alison takes over at two o'clock.'

'But you're doing the petition, aren't you?'

'Yes,' said Iris, reluctantly, seeing what was coming. The *Advertiser* was notoriously so short of journalists that almost any unsolicited article was printed, and Alison had recently submitted a rabble-rousing six hundred words.

'Well I just need a photo, to illustrate the piece. You know, standing in front of the library.'

'Wahay, Mum's going to be famous,' said Robin.

'Oh. You're her son?' said the photographer, her face brightening. 'Well, it would be nice to have both of you in the shot.'

'And me,' said Tom, turning round.

'God!' Lara looked as if she'd hit pay dirt. 'You're identical! Fantastic! And you're all involved in the campaign?'

'Yup,' said Tom, handing the clipboard casually back to Iris. She glanced at it and spotted the signatures of her aunts Myrtle and Olive as well as those of Fran, Peter, Sylvie and Mr Tibbs. Tom put his arm around her shoulder and smiled dazzlingly at Lara. 'Where do you want us?'

By the time Alison arrived, Iris had been dropped from the line-up altogether, and Tom and Robin were standing on the steps of the library with Lara crouched on the pavement below, angling her camera near-vertically.

'They're going to look about forty feet tall from there, aren't they?' said Iris, sotto voce.

'Any publicity's good publicity,' said Alison, 'and they can do a headline about giants of literature. Are you off home now?'

'No.' Iris remembered the task she had set herself and her stomach gave a nervous little skip. 'I'm going to the reading room, I need to write a letter.'

She sat for a while with the blank pad in front of her, biro in hand. Since the parents' evening, the idea of the letter had been a fishhook, tugging gently but persistently at her consciousness. She had thought about the Conrad of her image, the one standing in front of the pillared façade of a Southern mansion, and had realized that he was still a student, sideburns fuzzing the edges of his face, his lanky frame clad in denim; if she focused hard enough she could almost see the acne scars on his cheekbones. The mansion itself, she knew, had no basis in fact – he had once referred to 'the old family place' and she had invented the rest from the Deep South of her imagination. There was no real Conrad there; she knew nothing about him, nothing at all. He could be a senator, he could be in gaol, he could be living the sort of unexceptionable middle-class American life about which she knew very little, since it was rarely described in novels. The twins had caught up with him now; all three of them were eighteen and if they had stood in a row, Conrad would have been the shortest and youngest-looking. The thought made her uncomfortable – there seemed something vaguely incestuous about hanging on to an image of a lover who was younger than her sons. What she wanted was an update, a new picture that she could superimpose over the old one. And if that picture showed someone who was living a decent, admirable, successful life then so much the better. If the twins ever asked she would have a template to show them.

She had secured her favourite seat, a buttoned, viciously upright leather chair positioned so that light from the frosted window fell across the table in front of it. The reading room was a remnant of sombre Victoriana, held in aspic while the rest of the library had been lightened, brightened and knocked through. It held a couple of leather armchairs, three desks with inkwells attached, their porcelain interiors still a profound blue, and a row of tables, smooth-topped from a century of elbows. The room was jealously guarded by those who had stumbled across it, tucked away behind the upstairs stacks and blessed with a sign on the door which read:

Horace Saddler Reading Room
No Talking
No Children ·

Iris had studied for her A Levels in here, had used it as a sanctuary during the last few weeks of her pregnancy after she had moved back to London, and had saved it as a treat for those rare, fleeting and widely separated intervals during the twins' childhood when she was neither at work, nor looking after them, nor in transit between the two states. It was as familiar to her as her own kitchen, and far warmer in winter; the walls were lined with enormous brown radiators that looked like pieces of obsolete farm machinery, and which clanked when they moved up a gear during cold snaps. In the summer, the sash window was raised a discreet two inches, admitting the roar that filtered through the glass roof of the indoor market next door, and during periods of almost tropical heat (three times within her memory) the fan on the ceiling was switched on, and the room seemed to gain a touch of colonial grandeur. There were rarely more than half a dozen people in there, all on nodding terms with one another; today there was only one other occupant and he was deeply asleep. Iris found that the occasional snore only added to the comforting ambience.

> *Dear Sir or Madam,*
> *I am hoping you can help me with an enquiry . . .*

It seemed a sufficiently bland opening. She had obtained the address of the Bethesda Christian College Medical Faculty from international directory enquiries, but had decided to write rather than phone, as being both cheaper and less frighteningly immediate. She also found it far easier to lie on paper than in person.

> *I am organizing a reunion of Cardiff University medical graduates,*
> *class of 1977, and wish to extend an invitation to the members of*
> *your university who, in 1972, spent a pre-med term at our school as*
> *part of an exchange plan, namely Julie-Jane Vitelli, Lyle Kraviz,*
> *Donald Moray Strachan Junior and Conrad Blett.*

She had found the other names on the tiny contact sheet that had been issued as an *aide-memoire* during the first week at medical school. The students had been herded one by one in front of a box camera and the resulting black-and-white images printed in tiny rows, in alphabetical order. She had hung on to it as the only photo she had of Conrad, though he was almost unrecognizable in a Zapata moustache which he had shaved off only days after term had started; like all his compatriots he was wearing a Bethesda College sweatshirt with 'In God We Trust' printed in large letters above a coat of arms; like all his compatriots he had binned his Baptist morals almost as fast as his sweatshirt. Hysterical with freedom, far richer than any of the British students, the Americans had become the wild and dazzling centrepiece of Barton Hall's social life, the hosts of a hundred parties, the open-handed distributors of Jim Bean and joints, and Iris – lucky Iris – had been in the room *next door* to the master of revels – his right-hand maiden, the thrilled recipient of his generosity both in the sack and out.

In the event, as she'd discovered after they'd gone back to Virginia and student life had reverted to a dull round of thumping discos and warm beer, it wouldn't have made any difference if she'd been on a different floor altogether – Conrad had apparently slept with almost every woman in the entire hall of residence, regardless of proximity. There had been three rumoured pregnancies; only Iris, her bump already palpable at ten weeks, had not opted for an abortion. The confirmation that it was twins had come the same week that she'd spotted the clipping from the *Bethesda Clarion* on the medical school noticeboard, announcing Conrad's engagement to his childhood sweetheart.

> *I would be grateful if you could send me any information on their*
> *current whereabouts or, if more convenient, details of your*
> *alumnus association, who may have kept track of them.*

When the twins were small, she had dreaded and planned for the moment when they would start asking about their father. She had borrowed books on single parenting and even on adoption to find a form of words that would soften the explanation, while still conveying the truth. She had weighed the advice, jotted down ideas, adapted and pruned and tailored until she had two versions poised in readiness: a full one, and one that would cover her if the subject came up for the first time in public – in the dentist's waiting room, say, which was where Tom had first enquired what bosoms were for.

The years had gone by, the explanation had rusted gently in her subconscious, and the boys had never once asked the question, never evinced the slightest curiosity about the subject.

'We haven't got a dad,' she had once heard eight-year-old Robin inform a friend.

'Why not?' the friend had asked and Iris had braced herself for the answer.

'Dunno,' Robin had said, unconcernedly. There had been other single parents at their junior school; she could only conclude that they viewed fathers as an optional extra. Or perhaps their lack of concern was the result of their twinship and the sort of natural self-sufficiency it gave them. Together, they were a closed circuit.

In the end she'd raised the matter herself, during the summer holidays before they started at the comprehensive. She'd asked for a 'little chat' and they had sat through it in silence, wearing expressions that tempered deep embarrassment with disbelief. Then, with a degree of hesitation, not knowing what emotions might be unleashed by the sight, she had shown them the photo. And the reaction had been not resentment, or angst, or puzzlement, or grief, or anger or any of the textbook predictions. No, they had looked at the photo of Conrad and exploded into laughter. The ludicrous moustache!! The stupid surname!!!! Blett!!!! It was, apparently, the funniest name ever in the history of the universe, and became an instant term of inter-twin abuse: 'you stupid Blett', 'you've got a face like a Blett', 'you're a right Blett'.

She had wondered for a while whether the information simply hadn't sunk in, whether it was too big a topic for an eleven-year-old to absorb in one go. She'd waited for some kind of sequel – a volcano of brooding resentment, a volley of unanswerable questions – but the only follow-up had come from Robin, who had wandered into the kitchen one day when she was making a crumble.

'Mum, you know Conrad Blett?' he'd said, taking a piece of apple from the dish.

'Yes?' she'd said, bracing herself, aware that he'd avoided the use of the f word.

'Where does he live? I mean, whereabouts in the USA?'

'I don't know. He went to college in Virginia so he might have stayed in the area.'

'Is that near Florida?'

'No. Not very.'

'What about California?'

'No. It's a really long way from there.'

'Oh.' He'd wandered off again, and she'd followed him a few steps up the hall, her hands dropping flour onto the lino. 'No,' she'd heard him say to Tom in the living room, 'he's miles away from either of them.' Disneyland, she'd suddenly realized.

No further enquiries came her way. 'Blett' was gradually dropped as an insult, and aside from a bout of sniggering when they saw she was reading a book by Joseph Conrad ('Hey, Mum, you must *really* like that name.') the subject had stayed closed. There seemed no way of finding out what they were really thinking, though she imagined – hoped – that they had discussed the whole issue between themselves, in that private world to which adolescence had simply added another layer. Certainly they appeared completely unchanged by the revelation. She didn't know whether to be relieved or not; it was as if the defining episode of her life had been dismissed as a piece of minor information, on a par with (or, probably, slightly below) the latest signing for Spurs.

I very much hope you can help me – it should be a really good bash!

She winced at the phrase.

> *Thanking you in anticipation,*
> *yours sincerely,*
> *I Unwin*

It was her usual signature; she had always hated her first name.

She re-read the letter, realized that she had left a 't' out of Lyle Kravitz's surname, and turned to a blank sheet to write it all out again, rather more neatly this time.

> *Dear Sir or Madam,*
> *I am hoping that you can help me with an enquiry . . .*

The heavy brass doorknob of the reading room gave a familiar rattle and she glanced up and stayed looking, transfixed. Round the door trotted a small, white-haired figure carrying a tartan holdall.

'*Here* you are,' said Mrs McHugh, 'I was beginning to think you were hiding from me!'

Iris looked at her, stupefied.

'Are you busy?' The neat heels were already clicking across the floor towards her.

'Er, no, I've just finished.' She hastily folded the letter and scoured her brain for some tiny clue as to what might be going on. Her father was still maintaining radio silence about his relationship, and Iris's last exchange with Mrs McHugh had consisted of the words 'Happy Christmas', spoken after a carol concert several weeks ago. Mrs McHugh had been rattling a bucket for charity while dressed as the angel Gabriel.

'I've just bumped into your lovely boys outside Woolworths. Of course I've never actually met them before but I've seen photos and I think they got the shock of their lives when I called their names out across the street. I said, "Tom! Robin!" I said it quite sternly, just as a joke – of course, I didn't know which one was which. I said, "I hope your mother knows you smoke!" and for a moment they looked a wee bit sheepish, but then I introduced myself and they had to laugh.' I bet they did, thought Iris, diverted even in the midst of her confusion.

'So then I said, "I've been meaning to have a little chat with Iris but I never get to talk to her because she's always *so* busy, and we've got something we really need to discuss"' – Iris's heart sank – 'and so they told me you were in the library – but they didn't say where!' She wagged a finger in roguish admonition. 'I've been up hill and down dale and in my lady's chamber and I was just about to give up when the man at returns asked if I'd tried the reading room, and I said, "You just show me where it is, young man, and I'll call the reels at your wedding." So, here I am!' She settled herself in a chair opposite Iris, clasping her hands over a bouncily crossed knee. She was so short that her chin was only inches from the table top. 'All the years I've lived here and I've never realized this room existed. Mind you, it's just the place for a chat.'

'We're not supposed to talk in here,' said Iris, waving a straw at a hurricane.

'Och, and who's going to tell them?' There was a snore from the easy chair. '*He* looks out for the count. But we could go somewhere for a snack instead – my tummy certainly thinks it's snack time.' She patted her stomach. 'And what about your tummy?' she asked, coyly.

'It could do with a cup of tea,' said Iris. Or a very large gin, she thought.

Mrs McHugh seemed to know everybody in North London. In the three hundred yards that separated the library from

British Home Stores, she stopped four times for little chats, all of which extended to quite long chats, as Iris was introduced, explained ('Ian's daughter') and included in a conversation that was conducted at a rolling boil, one topic succeeding another in rapid succession until Mrs McHugh happened to glance at her watch. 'Whoopsy! Is that the time? Iris and I are on our way for a little chat, aren't we Iris? Can't linger as much as we'd like!' and off she'd skitter down the street again, like a tugboat that happened to be dragging a lighthouse behind it.

'Honestly, Iris, sometimes I don't know how I ever get anything done,' she said, as they walked through the automatic doors and past the vast red banners advertising the January sale. 'When Hammy and I moved down here in 1957 people said I'd find London unfriendly but you know it's quite the opposite. Have you seen that, Iris, wool coats for under thirty-five pounds? And they've got some lovely colours – I'd like to see you in a nice royal blue. That would really bring out your eyes.' They stepped onto the escalator up to the café and Mrs McHugh raised her voice to reach Iris's great height on the step above her. 'No, I think people who say London's unfriendly just haven't made the effort. It doesn't matter if someone's black, white, yellow or green, if you say "hello" they're always pleased to say "hello" back.' Iris tried to avoid the eye of the stony-faced black teenager standing just behind Mrs McHugh. 'One "hello" – that's all it needs to kick-start a friendship, and I'll say "hello" to anyone. Do you know that saying, Iris, "a stranger is a friend you haven't met"?'

It occurred to Iris, as she selected a teacake and listened to Mrs McHugh tell the stranger that she'd only just met on the cash register that English cooks never seem to use enough soda in their scones, that although Mrs McHugh talked even more than her father, their styles were completely different.

His phone monologues were an attempt to fill a horrible silence, whereas her chat seemed to be the overspill from a bottomless vat of *bonhomie*.

The scone conversation had now spread beyond the queue to include the woman who was clearing the tables, and a bottleneck was developing by the stack of trays. No one within earshot seemed to mind too much but those towards the back of the queue were getting restless. 'Cold hands for pastry, warm hands for dough,' said Mrs McHugh, deep into baking techniques. She was fishing around in her holdall as she spoke.

'Let me pay for this,' said Iris, attempting to break the blockade.

'No, no, this one's on me.' She drew out a bulging wallet and opened the purse section. 'Now,' she said, turning back to the woman at the counter, 'you won't mind if a lot of it's in coppers, will you?'

After half an hour they were on their second pot of tea, and Iris still had no idea what Mrs McHugh's little chat was supposed to be about. At the moment – and she couldn't remember how they had got onto the subject – they were talking about porridge.

'My mother,' said Mrs McHugh, 'used to put a lump of butter right in the middle, and a sprinkle of salt. It had to be unsalted butter, and sea salt, and then she'd stir the whole thing, round and round and round with a little horn spoon. I always found it rather greasy.'

Iris had been dragged across a lot of conversational ground – Scottish education, the ingredients of white pudding, getting stains off suede, how to tell the twins apart – and she had learned to use the word 'Tammy' without choking on her Earl Grey, but there had been no hint from her kidnapper that there might be a weightier subject on the agenda, or a more complex relationship between them than that of pourer and drinker. All was bubble and froth, an unstoppable fountain, deluging the listener with goodwill. The ridiculous image that for months had been floating at the back of her mind – Mrs McHugh as houri temptress, luring her father from his family, ensnaring him in the nets of her lust – popped with the finality of a burst balloon.

'Do your boys eat porridge?'

'Only with lots of sugar.'

'Yes, of course their grandpa's a bit of a sweet tooth as well, isn't he? The Cough Candy King I call him.' Mrs McHugh gave her a jolly, red-lipsticked smile. 'Speaking of whom . . .' she added, unzipping her holdall and taking out a diary. 'Twenty-seventh of March! That's what I wanted to talk about.'

'Dad's birthday,' said Iris, feeling a great wash of relief. This was a topic that she could cope with.

'Uh huh. His seventieth, which *I* always feel is a significant one though I'm sure to a young thing like you it just seems terribly, terribly old.'

Iris, who had not felt like a young thing since 1972, shook her head in polite and automatic deprecation. Her mind was already jumping ahead. A present. Mrs McHugh was going to ask her advice on a present. She started mentally running through the possibilities – a really good pair of secateurs, perhaps. Or a couple of deckchairs. She had already, on her own account, started checking out lawnmower prices.

'So I thought it might be quite exciting to organize a surprise party.'

It took a moment for Iris to catch up. 'You what?' she said, using a phrase she'd spent sixteen years trying to eliminate from the twins' vocabulary.

'A surprise party.'

'What, for *Dad*?' She realized how loudly she'd spoken when the three people on the next table all looked round.

'Nary a word from you now!' said Mrs McHugh to them, miming a zipped lip. 'We're talking secrets!' They smiled rather uncomfortably and turned away again.

'I'll tell you my plan,' said Mrs McHugh, patting Iris's hand, 'and then you can say what you think of it.' She leafed through the diary. 'It's on a Wednesday, you see, that's midweek bowls, so I could think up an excuse for not going myself – I might say I've just got a little tummy upset – and then we'd have the whole afternoon to prepare. I can invite the people from the church but I'd need your help for a few others, his cousin – Kath, isn't it? – and he's mentioned an old army friend in Wales –'

'Leslie Peake,' said Iris.

'There, you see –' she scribbled a note in the diary '– Peake. You'll have to give me his address. So we could assemble everybody in the kitchen, and when he comes back, not suspecting a thing – or perhaps just expecting a little birthday tea, nothing out of the ordinary – he'll open the door and . . . there we'll be!' Her face was suffused with enthusiasm.

For a moment, Iris saw it all: the covered buffet on the table, Mrs McHugh in a frilly blouse trying to light seventy candles without setting fire to her cuffs, Tom and Robin pink with suppressed hysteria, their eyes fixed on Leslie Peake's bizarre hairstyle, the sound of the front-door key, the excited shushing of the party guests, the footsteps in the hall, the door opening, and then . . .

What? Who would come through the door? The man who kept his tins of vegetables in alphabetical order, who stood anxiously on the pavement if Iris arrived more than five minutes late for an evening visit, who still allocated time for the television to 'warm up' before *Coronation Street*, who winced if she used the word 'bloody', who had chosen the same shade of beige with which to decorate the living room every five years for the last thirty, who regarded spontaneity as simply a case of bad planning? Or the one who'd just bought himself a video recorder, been out to the cinema every Wednesday since Christmas and answered to the nickname of Cough Candy King?

'Well,' said Mrs McHugh, eagerly, 'you know him best – what do you think?'

15

'There's a lot more space in here now,' said Fran idly, glancing around Spencer's living room instead of bending to the task for which she had set aside Wednesday evening.

'What, now I've killed half the occupants, you mean?' Spencer was lying on the sofa with the tortoise on his lap.

'Bit more than half I'd say.' She did a quick mental calculation. 'More like ninety-eight per cent.'

'Thanks,' he said. 'That's a tremendous comfort.' He tipped a little Extra Virgin olive oil into the palm of one hand and started applying it to Bill's shell. He was looking after his remaining charges with renewed care, and had found this particular tip in the 'Pet of the Week' column of *Reptile Monthly*. There had, as usual, been no mention of paper eating.

'It was *good* that you killed the snails,' said Fran. 'It was the only correct way to deal with them. You know they've just found a huge colony of them at Hornsey dump – and that's because some stupid person must have decided to cull their collection by putting them out with the rubbish. Can you believe that? They've had to mount a special extermination programme just to get rid of them.'

'Oh,' said Spencer, and then tutted disapprovingly a couple of times, not trusting his voice to say more. He turned Bill over and started on the underside.

'You know, you look like a Roman emperor with his favourite plaything,' said Fran. 'You should have someone oiling *you*.'

'My days of being oiled are over.'

'Mine too. Of course, Duncan was such a cheapskate that he always used Mazola so I smelled like a vegeburger.'

'What about Barry? I'm sure he'd fork out for some First Pressing if you gave him a bit of encouragement.'

'He's back with his girlfriend, didn't I tell you? Given up on me, thank God.' She twiddled the pencil between her fingers and looked at the blank page in front of her. After a moment's thought she wrote the number 1 and then put the pencil down.

'Do you want a beer?' she asked, getting to her feet. 'They should be cold by now.'

'Go on then.'

'I'll just shield my eyes.' She snapped on the kitchen light and blinked again at the extreme whiteness of the walls, the blinding sheet steel of the pristine work surfaces. Spencer had lashed out on a new kitchen and had chosen a style oddly reminiscent of an operating theatre.

'I just wanted it *clean*,' he'd said, a touch nettled, when she'd pointed that out. The only remaining homely touches were the photo of Mark in the park, now curling a little at the edges, and the two pages of the list. She found the bottle opener in the new lime-green revolving cutlery dispenser, and threw the tops into the chrome swingbin.

'Spence, can I ask you something?' she said, reseating herself.

He didn't answer for a moment, but held Bill up with one hand and tilted him to catch the light. 'Bit of a transformation,' he said admiringly.

'Are you going to paint his toenails now?'

'Might do,' said Spencer. 'Self-image is very important. It's a key element in eating disorders.' He placed Bill carefully on the floor and they watched as he began the trek to the magazine rack, his lumbering progress now strangely at odds with his jewelled appearance. 'Ask away then.'

'I just wondered what had happened to the Hypothetical

Blinking Man.' She hadn't asked him again after that day at Kew; she had managed to batten down her curiosity, but there had been a subtle change in him since the turn of the year, a lifting of mood so slight that it could only be spotted by an old friend, only measured in nanometres, but present none the less.

Spencer took a long swig of beer. 'Nothing's happened really. In fact, not even "really". Just nothing. I haven't contacted him.'

'So you've got his number, then?'

'No, but I know where he works.'

'Which is . . . ?'

'The North Middlesex.'

'A nurse?' Spencer had always had a penchant for nurses.

'Eye surgeon.'

'What, he's a surgeon and he's got a twitch?' said Fran horrified.

'He doesn't operate with his eyelids,' said Spencer, rather severely.

'No, I suppose not.'

'Anyway, a lot of tics disappear completely when the person's concentrating.'

'Right. It's just that I remember you saying all surgeons are psychopathic bastards.'

He thought about this for a moment. 'Maybe it's only the straight ones.'

She couldn't imagine Spencer with a psychopathic bastard. She had got to know a couple of his previous boyfriends and they'd both been rather quiet, self-effacing men, apparently content to sit in the corner at pubs and laugh at other people's jokes. 'Harpo', Mark had nicknamed one of them. 'Smiles but never speaks.' Neither of them had stayed on the scene for very long – blown over the horizon, she always thought, by the hurricane of Mark's personality.

'He did say,' said Spencer, as if struck by a new thought, 'that if I ever went to the Changing of the Guard then I should ring him.'

'You've already been, haven't you?'

'Yes, but I couldn't see anything, so maybe it doesn't count.'

'Give him a ring, then.'

He shrugged. 'I only met him the once. He probably wouldn't even remember me.'

'Balls. I bet he's saying exactly the same thing about you.'

Spencer lay back on the sofa and laced his fingers across his stomach. 'Do you want to get started?'

'Yeah all right,' said Fran, reluctantly. She looked at the piece of paper again, and added a full stop to the number 1; then, as an afterthought, she wrote 'House Meeting' at the top of the page and underlined it using a table mat as a ruler. 'Did I tell you,' she said, putting the pencil down again, 'that Sylvie's got a special saucepan for the cat?'

'No.'

'Tinned cat food makes it ill, apparently, so every morning she has to boil up tiny bits of chicken and fish in a pan that's completely uncontaminated by wheat products and then shove them through a sieve. Except that the smell makes her feel ill so she gets Peter to do it while she sits in the bedroom and sprinkles ylang-ylang on an oil burner.' It was hard to express the weirdness of the two-storey odour that ensued: upstairs smelling like the meditation tent at Glastonbury, and downstairs like a baby vomitorium.

'Do you know,' said Spencer, carefully, 'that that's the third Sylvie anecdote you've told me since you got here.'

'Is it?'

'Not that I don't enjoy them, but I wonder if you might be getting . . . a bit obsessed? After all, how much do you actually see of her? You're at work all day, you're out a lot in the evenings, and she sticks to her room most of the time, doesn't she?'

'Yes but –' Fran tipped her chair back on two legs and searched for a description that would convey the pervasive presence of Sylvie. 'What was the name of that woman poet who was ill all the time? There's a film of it. She lies on the sofa and marries some other poet. Elopes.'

'Elizabeth Barrett Browning?'

'Yup. That's the one. That's Sylvie. Honestly, Spence, you needn't laugh. In the film she sits around with the curtains closed and you're meant to feel sorry for her and think how incredibly sensitive and poetic she is, but you never see the effect on the rest of the household. You never see them being told not to flush the loo after midnight because she's a light sleeper, or having to listen to her going on about the happy place she's just this minute discovered in the corner of the living room and wants to share with you, or always having to do the washing-up really quietly because she gets a headache if she hears two saucepans banging together, or hosing her cat's crap off their winter greens *every* bloody day, or having to explain a joke three times because she's got absolutely no sense of humour, or being told by her that they're "wonder-fully prosaic" as if they're supposed to take that as some sort of compliment.' She paused for breath.

'Is that what she said to you?'

'Yes,' said Fran resentfully.

'What was the context?'

'She was talking about reincarnation. Again.'

'And . . .'

'I said I saw the world as a sort of giant compost heap . . . no, listen Spence, I thought it was a really good analogy. Stop laughing.'

'I'm sorry,' said Spencer, composing himself, 'but Sylvie's

right, that is wonderfully prosaic. "In the beginning God created the heaven and the earth and the earth was a kind of giant compost heap."'

'Yes, all right.' She found herself grinning reluctantly. 'But at least you don't use the phrase as if you're speaking to a peasant. And you don't have – who was the bloke in the film? –'

'Robert Browning.'

'– Robert Browning agreeing with every word you say. They give me this *look* and I can feel my knuckles starting to scrape the ground – give me a couple of months and I'll have forgotten how to use tools. My opposing thumbs will wither away.'

'She's really got under your skin, hasn't she?' said Spencer, bemused.

'Yes, she has, and I don't know how to cope with her, I don't have a strategy. If I say anything even vaguely defensive she folds up like a deckchair and Peter gets all hurt and disappointed. You know they write in novels "she nestles in his arms"? I swear, that is literally what she does. He probably feeds her undigested food when I'm not looking.' She took a long, soothing drink of beer. 'And the thing is,' she said, more meditatively, 'when she gets upset I never know whether it's my fault or not.'

If Spencer had been standing, he would have had to sit down.

'What?' she asked, noticing his expression.

He hesitated for a moment and then checked his watch.

'What?' she asked again.

'Just thought I'd better note the time for the records – nine fifteen, February the thirteenth, nineteen ninety-one, public expression of self-doubt from Fran Tomlinson.'

She looked at him uncomprehendingly.

'It's not something you normally do,' he said gently.

'Really? Don't I?'

'No.' He tried to swallow his laughter at her amazement. 'Sylvie's clearly having a terrible effect on you.'

'I'm sure I have *private* self-doubt,' she said, a touch uncertainly.

'Well maybe you just hide it better than the rest of us.' Though he hoped that wasn't true; he really hoped that Fran's psyche wasn't a vicious maelstrom of self-destructive angst and internal conflict, kept in check only by a meniscus of iron will. It seemed unlikely.

'Anyway, what I meant,' said Fran briskly, moment of introspection apparently over, 'is that it's impossible to know in advance what's going to upset her. Her whole life is a minefield. You mention the word "uncle" – you find her uncle's just died. You happen to say that you think tortoiseshell cats are hideous, you find out that her first ever cat was a tortoiseshell and someone reversed over it.'

'Her uncle?' suggested Spencer.

'Exactly. You mention in passing that music therapy's a complete waste of time –'

His jaw dropped.

'Just *kidding*, Spence. But it's a kind of power she has. Sometimes it feels deliberate – she wrong-foots me every time. Nothing's straightforward any more.' She finished her beer and plonked it onto the table. 'I've had enough of it.'

'I'm sure you all have,' he said, with feeling. He wondered how poor old Peter was coping with this running battle between Morgan le Fay and Jet from *Gladiators*.

'Well, yes. Hence the meeting tomorrow evening.' She picked up the pencil again. 'And it's nearly two years since we bought the bloody thing so I suppose it's time we talked through the options. What there are of them.'

'OK.' Spencer hauled himself upright and tried to look alert. 'How do you want to do this?'

'Well, you know Peter – he'll want a thorough discussion of every single permutation, even the ridiculous ones, so I want to be prepared. I want my arguments marshalled.' She thought for a moment, beating a little tattoo with her pencil on the table top. 'What about if you do the pros and I do the cons? It'll be mainly cons.'

'Fine.' He stifled a yawn. The crickets that had escaped from the lizard tank had set up a breeding colony in his room, and he was finding it difficult to sleep. The noise that he had once found soporific was horribly disturbing when it came from just behind the bedside table, accompanied by unpleasant rustlings.

'OK,' said Fran, starting to write. 'Number one – sell the house. Pros?'

'Ideal solution.'

'Cons. Completely fucking impossible.' She marked a brisk little cross by the option and then suddenly looked up. 'Did I tell you the house opposite's been on the market so long that a bat hibernated in the little gap between the two halves of the sign? A pipistrelle. First sighting in Dalston, apparently.' Her face, alight with momentary enthusiasm, resumed its expression of serious intent. 'Right, number two. Everybody moves out and we put the house up for rent. Pros? Actually, Spence, it's not even worth you saying anything, because the man in the letting agency said they had more stuff on their books than they knew what to do with and that it would have to be something "really special" to shift. When I said it was in Stapleton Road he laughed. Bastard.' She put another cross on the paper.

'I'm finding this quite easy,' said Spencer.

'Number three,' she continued, ignoring him. 'This is a

good one. *The* good one. I move out, rent somewhere else and Sylvie and Peter get in a lodger to cover the mortgage.'

'They'd need to do that, would they?'

'The payment's gone up three times in three months. It's ironic, isn't it – Sylvie's actually an essential member of the household, financially speaking. Pros?'

He thought for a moment. 'You and Sylvie would be living in different places.'

'Yup, that has to be the top one. Any others?'

'You could move out of Dalston.'

'God, yes, to somewhere on the tube. That would be nice.' She noted it down.

'And cons?' asked Spencer. 'Are there any?'

Fran paused, and considered. 'I'd miss Iris,' she said. 'And I'd really miss the garden.'

'. . . so nearer the spring I could come over once a week for an hour or two and work on it. You'd just need to do some basic maintenance the rest of the time – you know, pull up any couch grass, pick off caterpillars, nothing very demanding – and we could share the veg. Of course, if you wanted to do more than that, it'd be great.' Feeling generous and slightly noble, Fran put down her list and glanced across the table. Peter was looking inscrutable, and Sylvie sat with her eyes downcast, hands knotted under the long sleeves of Peter's favourite pullover. The silence lengthened. The meeting so far had been oddly quiet – no disagreements, no provocative statements – instead Fran had the feeling that all parties were biding their time, manoeuvring quietly for position.

'So what do you think?' she prompted.

Peter cleared his throat. 'I think we should talk through *all* the possible options before we make a decision.'

'All right,' said Fran doubtfully. She glanced at her list again;

after number four, the level of seriousness decreased rapidly, something she blamed on the combination of Spencer and alcohol. 'Before we go on,' she said, unwilling to relinquish her carefully thought-out plan, 'is there anything about the idea of you two staying here and me moving out that's specifically a problem?'

Peter looked at Sylvie, and her head drooped like a flower soused with paraquat. 'Yes there is,' he said. 'Sylvie doesn't like Dalston.'

'I don't think anyone *likes* Dalston,' said Fran. 'I don't, for a start.'

'No, I mean she wants to move away.' Sylvie nodded behind the curtain of hair.

'Oh. You mean –' hope flooded through her '– on her own?'

'No, with me. We want to move out of London.' One of Sylvie's hands emerged from a sleeve and sought one of Peter's and he took it as if accepting a gift. 'I'm applying for a job in Norwich.'

'Norwich?' said Fran, stupidly.

'We want to live somewhere where people care about each other,' said Sylvie.

'So, hang on –' said Fran, trying not to be distracted by this non-sequitur '– you want to move out, right out of London, and leave me here?'

'Yes,' said Peter.

Fran looked at her list. This was option four, and while the only 'pro' Spencer had come up with was physical separation from Sylvie, the number of 'cons' was almost into double figures, the handwriting becoming larger and more frantic as each contraindication had occurred to her.

'But that means I'd have to get *two* lodgers to cover the mortgage.'

Peter nodded sombrely.

'But that would be awful, it would be like running a boarding house – one of me and two of them. And you wouldn't even be near enough to help with any problems. What about the next time a bit of the house falls off? This place takes two of us to maintain.' The previous weekend she and Peter had spent a whole afternoon taking turns at the top of a wavering ladder, clearing bucketfuls of putrid black gunk from the guttering.

'I'd be general handyman *and* landlady. I'd have to do everything.' The future scrolled away from her – a constant round of interviewing prospective tenants, of reminding them about rent and bills and double-locking the front door, of dull discussions about who pays for bog roll and washing-up liquid ('but *I* only eat takeaways'), of clipped conversations about phone and bathroom usage and the idiosyncrasies of the pre-Cambrian thermostat, of justified complaints about lukewarm radiators and disintegrating floorboards and cupboard doors that came away in the hand. 'Oh God, Peter,' she said, with desperation, 'you can't mean it. There must be another option.'

'Well, what else do you have on your list?'

Fran hesitated; a truthful reply was impossible. It read:

5. Nobody move out, instead learn to live together in an atmosphere of love and mutual understanding.
6. Hire an arsonist and collect on the insurance.
7. Buy a fake hand and leave it on the hall floor for Sylvie to discover.
8. Smuggle Mr Tibbs to a cattery and start sending ransom notes. ('If she *really* loves him then thirty-five grand's nothing' – Spencer)
9. Lease the house to a film company specializing in suburban porn.

The last suggestion had been so appealing that they had wasted nearly half an hour thinking up titles ('Sadie Does it Herself in Six Weekly Parts', 'Those Big Boys Next Door', 'How Firm Your Courgette' (subtitled)) before Spencer had fallen asleep between adjacent sentences, and she had tiptoed away.

Peter was waiting for her answer. 'None of them is very practical,' she muttered, slightly ashamed, crumpling the piece of paper so that it would be unreadable from the other side of the table.

'So where does that leave us?'

'I don't know. With you applying for a job in the sticks, I suppose.'

'I've only just seen it advertised,' said Peter. 'Nothing's definite yet.'

But looking at his hand grasping Sylvie's, at the welded unit they formed together, Fran saw that the discussion was over and that all roads would henceforth lead either to Norwich or to some other provincial Utopia. Peter looked as implacable as when he'd forbidden her to borrow, or even touch, his new cassette player fourteen years ago and now, as then, her sole remaining option was to rage impotently.

'Of course it's definite,' she said. 'You've made up your mind, I can see you have. You decided this ages ago and didn't tell me. What was the point of even having this talk? You might as well have left me a note on the table and buggered off. "Dear Fran, please look after the white elephant, all it needs is twenty-four-hour care and a constant supply of money."'

'Sylvie and I have been discussing it for a while,' said Peter, calmly, 'but we had other decisions to make first.'

'Oh yeah, like what?' She felt poised for the next rally, tongue at the ready.

'Well . . .' He drew Sylvie's hand closer to his chest. 'Do

you want me to say, Sylvie?' She raised her head and smiled at him shyly.

'I don't mind,' she said.

'Or would you rather wait?'

'No, perhaps we should say.'

'All right then. If you don't mind.'

'No, I don't mind.'

'*What?*' asked Fran, hoarse with frustration.

'Well . . .' They exchanged complicit looks. 'Sylvie – Sylvie and I – are going to have a baby.'

Fran blinked at them.

'We thought you might have guessed,' said Peter. 'Sylvie's been getting terrible morning sickness.'

'And migraines,' said Sylvie, smiling wanly. Peter lifted her hand to his mouth and kissed the knuckles.

'But I thought –' began Fran, and then stopped. They looked at her, Sylvie a little anxious, Peter shiny with bliss. 'Congratulations,' she said, almost too late.

'Are you pleased?' asked Sylvie.

'Yes. Yes, of course I am.'

'It means you'll be an auntie.'

'Yes, I suppose I will.' She couldn't believe her own obtuseness. How many more signs would Sylvie have needed to display? A half-knitted matinee jacket? A foetal scan sellotaped to her forehead?

'We didn't want to say anything until Sylvie was at least twelve weeks pregnant.'

'It was a surprise to us, too,' said Sylvie, eyes modestly lowered.

'You're the first person we've told.'

'Oh. Well, thanks. That's brilliant. Fantastic news.' Her mouth seemed to be doing the right thing while her brain was still lying on the canvas, being fanned by the seconds.

'When's it due?'

'August,' said Peter.

'Our little Leo,' said Sylvie.

'What, you've already picked a name?'

'No, I meant the birth sign.'

Fran realized with a jolt that there would be no getting rid of Sylvie now – she might be leaving the house, but she was entering the family, and every Christmas, every wedding, every funeral would be studded with exchanges exactly like the last. She felt worn down by the burden of future feyness.

'Or it might just be over the cusp into Virgo,' added Sylvie.

'Even better,' said Fran. As discreetly as she could, she eased the shameful list from the table and shoved it into her pocket. The house discussion was now clearly moribund; two against one had suddenly turned into three against one with the baby hitting well above its weight.

'We should crack open a bottle,' she said, heavily, getting to her feet. 'I think there's some white in the fridge.'

'What about the meeting?' asked Peter, dragging his eyes from Sylvie. 'We ought to carry on with the meeting.'

'Why? What's the point?' The words came out more sharply than she intended, and the happy look faded from Peter's face. She struggled to make amends. 'I mean, let's just leave it for today. Let's pick it up another time.'

'If you're sure.'

'Yeah I'm sure.' She managed a glum smile. 'Let's celebrate.'

'Ace in the hole,' said Spencer, when she phoned him later that evening. 'They were playing with a concealed card. Totally unfair.'

'Yeah, the bastards.' Out of a sense of mild melancholy, she was sitting in the dark, watching the rain slant across the lit square of Iris's kitchen window. On the table in front of her sat Mr Tibbs, his eyes disconcertingly fixed on hers, the pupils huge and depthless.

'And are they happy about it?'

'Very.'

'And are you?'

'Give me a while. For me it's not a baby, it's a lifetime in Dalston.' Mr Tibbs seemed to be leaning towards her and she shifted the chair so that she was turned away from him.

'So when are they off?'

'It depends whether he gets the Norwich job. But they're going on holiday next month, so at least I'll get the house to myself for a couple of weeks. I bloody can't wait, honestly Spence, I'm going to run up and downstairs in the nude, and flush the toilet every –' A sudden wet roughness enclosed her ear and she jerked her head away. 'Get *off*.'

'What?' asked Spencer.

'It's the cat, he was trying to – *stop* it.'

'What's it doing?'

'Trying to lick my earlobe – he's got a thing about earlobes.'

'Why?'

'Because I smear Whiskas on them.'

'*What?*'

'I don't know, do I? Maybe he finds them attractive. Duncan always did.' Mr Tibbs was moving towards her again, neck outstretched and a vaguely lustful look on his face, the tip of his tongue just visible. Repulsed, she gave him a light shove and his back legs slid off the edge of the table, rapidly followed by the rest of him. He hit the floor with a thud and the light snapped on to reveal Sylvie standing in the doorway, hot-water bottle in hand.

'Tibbsy,' she said piteously.

'He's OK,' said Fran. 'He just fell off the table.'

'You pushed him. I saw you.' She knelt and the cat crept towards her with a death-rattle mew.

'You'd better apologize,' said Spencer, in Fran's ear.

'He was sucking my earlobe,' said Fran.

'He can't help it. The vet thinks he was weaned too early.'

'So he thinks my ear's a *nipple*?'

'Apologize,' said Spencer.

'He's only a little cat and you hurt him.'

'I didn't mean to and I'm sorry.'

'Well done,' said Spencer. 'Phone me back.' She had hung up the receiver before she realized that Sylvie was crying, blotting her tears into Mr Tibbs's orange fur.

'I'm sorry, Sylvie,' she said again. 'But he is a cat and they land on their feet. It's not like shoving a baby off a table.' It wasn't, she realized immediately, a happy analogy. 'Not that I meant to shove him off,' she added.

'You said you'd look after him,' said Sylvie in a small voice. She wiped her face with the back of one hand.

'Did I? When did I?'

'When we go on holiday.'

'Oh *then*. Well of course I'll look after him.' She tried to hide her exasperation. 'I'm not going to hurt him, Sylvie. I work with animals, I know about them, he'll be fine. I'll boil bits of chicken and everything.'

'But looking after him doesn't just mean feeding,' said Sylvie, sententiously. She was stroking the cat with long, even gestures. 'He needs to feel loved as well. Don't you, Tibbsy? I couldn't leave him if I thought he might be unhappy, I'd have to cancel the holiday.' Tense with ecstasy, Tibbsy thrust out his hindquarters and waggled his rectum in Fran's direction.

'Honestly,' said Fran, 'I'll be lovely to him.'

'Really?' Sylvie gazed up at her.

'Really.' And then, because she still looked doubtful, 'I absolutely promise.'

Sylvie nodded slowly and then got to her feet, brushing a few stray hairs from her fingers. 'I wish we got on better, Fran,' she said. 'I wish we could be friends, but I know you think I'm silly and oversensitive about things.'

Fran stood paralysed, nailed by the truth.

'My granny always used to say that I had one skin too few so I feel everything more, and I know I can often sense things that other people can't, and that makes me different.' She smiled gently, her eyes still shining from the tears. 'And I know it's hard for some people to tolerate differences.'

'Now hang on just a cotton-picking minute . . .' Fran wanted to say, but managed – by dint of massive self-control – not to. Instead she nodded dumbly.

Sylvie started to unbutton the cover of her hot-water bottle. 'Sometimes I even wish I could have that thick layer between me and the world that other people have. But then I feel I'd miss so much. It would be like watching a rainbow wearing dark glasses.' She shook her head sadly and fiddled with the screw top of the bottle. 'You couldn't do this for me, could you Fran? It's a little bit stiff.'

Fran unscrewed the plug and handed it back.

'Thanks.' She reached forward and took one of Fran's hands. 'I'd love to start again, you know, and try and really be friends. I'm sure we could. I do admire you, you know, Fran. You're so . . .'

'Practical,' thought Fran.

'Practical,' said Sylvie.

16

Identical Interest

It's not just their 'good looks' that identical twins Robin and Tom Unwin (18) share, it's also their 'good books'. The keen readers spent last Saturday petitioning outside Dalston Public Library against the reducing of library opening hours. 'We grew up surrounded by book's and the local library is very important to us' says Tom. His brother agrees. 'The library is an important local resource and it would be a crying shame if it had to close like so many other local libraries.' The twins who are both final year students at Broder8ck Gale Sixth Form College collected nearly 400 signatures including that of their mother Irish (39), to whom the boys credit for their love of literature. 'I'm very proud of the both of them,' she said.

The photo took up about a third of the front page of the *Dalston Advertiser*, was slightly out of focus, gigantically foreshortened and showed Robin and Tom clutching stacks of books and framed in the neo-classical entrance to the library. Tom was standing directly in front of a bust of Shakespeare, and the wreath of laurel appeared to be resting on his own head. The books had been plucked at random from the shelves and the only visible title was *Silas Marner*, a volume which Robin had dismissed as 'total crap' after failing to get past page twenty for GCSE.

Alison, whose submitted report – concise and racy – had been completely ignored in favour of the confabulations that accompanied the photo, had been straightforwardly delighted by the feature. Iris had mixed feelings.

'But it's on the front page,' Alison had pointed out. 'A feature about library cuts on the *front page*.'

It had certainly caused a stir at the surgery; Ayesha had spotted it first, and been unflatteringly astounded by the twins' appearance. 'But they're totally nothing like you,' as she'd put it, several times. She had made photocopies and pinned them on both the staffroom and waiting-room noticeboards, the latter with a thick accompanying arrow pointing to Iris's name (the h crossed out), and the words 'OUR PRACTICE MANAGER!!!' written in the margin.

'I don't think she ever really believed in the twins until she saw the photo,' Iris confided to Spencer one lunchtime, as they ate their sandwiches in a corner of the staffroom. 'She thought it was a little fantasy of mine.'

'Something to fill in those empty hours when you're not at work?'

'That's right. She looks at me differently now – as if I've suddenly become fully visible. It's quite disconcerting.'

'Have any of the patients said anything?'

'Oh yes, everybody says I must be very proud.'

'Of the both of them?'

'Of the both of them,' she agreed, gravely.

'And aren't you?'

She hesitated, grappling with unworthy emotions. 'I am,' she said eventually, 'but it seems so unfair. Alison and I worked so hard for those signatures. And the last book Tom read voluntarily was *Teddy Bear Coalman*.'

Her irritation was compounded a fortnight later when the boys received a letter informing them that they had each been nominated for a Dalston Young Citizens award, consisting of a certificate and £50 cash.

'I hope you'll spend it on books,' she said rather crossly, and was rewarded with loud laughter.

'You're jealous, Mum.'

'No I'm not. I just think you're operating under false pretences.'

'We're not,' said Tom, all injured innocence. 'We think the library should stay open, don't we Robin?'

'Yeah. Just as long as we don't have to go there.'

At work that afternoon, she unpinned the staffroom copy of the article to make room for a Department of Health memo on headlice treatment. She was deep into an administrative blitz, prompted by Dr Petty's absence. He was in Lisbon on a two-day drug freebie (or 'much needed international forum to discuss the place of Lamazol in the treatment of senile insomnia' as the brochure had put it) which meant that she could work in relative peace, free from the continual chatty interruptions in which he specialized.

She tucked the boys' picture into her handbag and stuck the headlice memo in its place, highlighting the key points with a marker pen. Then she drew three little boxes in the margin and stuck a post-it note on each of the doctors' in-trays, telling them to look at the noticeboard and tick the box when they'd read it. Her method was fantastically pedantic, she knew, but it kept office paper bills within reasonable limits, and moreover ensured that memos were actually read, rather than just photocopied, stacked and binned. The internal phone rang just as she had steeled herself to start the monthly drug accounts, and she picked it up with a twinge of relief.

'There's some Indian doctor calling for Dr Spencer,' said Ayesha. 'I told him to phone back after surgery but he says he wants to leave a message and I can't understand a single word what he's talking about so I told you'd deal with it. All right?' Before Iris could answer there was a click, and the wail of an ambulance filled the earpiece.

'Hello?' she said, cautiously.

'Good afternoon,' said a precise, slightly accented voice. 'I'm trying against tremendous odds to get a message to Spencer Carroll. I received a –' The siren was momentarily eclipsed by a gigantic voice shouting, 'Spleen. It's his spleen,' and the unmistakable crash of a hospital trolley hitting a door frame. 'Excuse me,' said the man, and after a few seconds she heard a door closing, pushing the noise into the background. 'I do apologize,' he said, a moment later, 'but that woman is beyond non-pharmaceutical methods of control. I had better talk quickly.'

'Right,' said Iris, for once empathizing with Ayesha. 'I'm listening.'

Spencer was also listening – albeit not very attentively – and watching Alfred Hickey's finger as it traced the route of an ancient byway that snaked right across the Sarum Road estate and over the railway line into the marshes beyond. The map on which it was marked was so big that it covered Spencer's desk and drooped over the edge at either end, and it was patched with white stickers each marked with a Roman numeral. These were cross referenced to a chart drawn up with six different colours of felt pen and covered in minute handwriting; Mr Hickey had propped it against the examination couch for ease of reference, and had thoughtfully brought a magnifying glass with him so that Spencer could read it in comfort. Eight minutes into the consultation he was still only up to V, and Spencer's attention was wavering.

'You can see,' said Mr Hickey, his nose hovering just above his finger, his eyes darting up to check that Spencer was watching, 'that the back gardens of numbers 1 through 15 were actually built right across the byway, whereas 17 to 31 incorporated the byway at the end of the garden, allowing partial access, but only partial. Of course, the key access point is the garden of *Number 1'* – he pronounced the words with loathing – 'abutting, as it does, the . . . the –' he slid the map towards him, knocking Spencer's pot of tongue spatulae onto the floor ' – the A44 which is the old trading route out to the west, previously the B243.'

His voice was a hoarse vibrato, the result of a stroke which had also left him subject to bouts of extreme agitation, bordering on mania, and intermittent paranoia. Spencer knew his history almost off by heart, having whiled away several previous visits by surreptitiously reading Mr Hickey's notes while pretending to listen to Mr Hickey's personal obsession. He was a regular visitor to the surgery, turning up at least once a week, but although he presented each time with a different symptom – a painful elbow on this occasion, but ranging in the past from insomnia to piles – the treatment required was the same in every case: twelve minutes of close attention to the latest round of his knock-down drag-out boundary dispute with the owner of Number 1.

'I've got a letter here –' Mr Hickey continued, opening a box file and rummaging through four years' worth of correspondence with the local council ' – that clearly states that the fault lies with the original estate plans, but it's actually the owner of *Number 1* who's blocked my application *over* and *over* again . . .'

Mr Hickey was one of several patients that Dr Petty had eagerly shovelled over to Spencer under the guise of offering him a full range of clinical experience; all of them could loosely be classified as 'difficult' and most of them had initially resented being fobbed off with a trainee. Mr Hickey, on the other hand, had been delighted – a fresh acolyte meant that he could start his explanations from scratch, and he had seized the opportunity with croaky intensity. And while it was sometimes hard for Spencer to feign concentration when he knew that there were another eight patients to see before the end of surgery, and only an hour to see them in, he at least had the feeling that he was providing a real service – a pressure valve that kept Mr Hickey in the community for another week.

At a calculated ten minutes into the consultation Spencer directed an unsubtle glance at his watch, and Mr Hickey took the hint and with incredible slowness began to fold the map, talking all the while. At eleven minutes he starting packing his paperwork into the wheeled shopping bag that accompanied him everywhere, and at eleven minutes forty-five seconds he levered himself to his feet and, in an unexpected move, started taking off his jacket.

'Is anything the matter?' asked Spencer, thrown.

'My elbow,' said Mr Hickey, reproachfully, 'you haven't looked at my elbow yet.'

The knock-on effect of this omission was that evening surgery overran by twenty-three minutes and by the time Spencer emerged into the empty waiting room Ayesha had already slammed down the desk shutters with audible pique and was standing by the door with her coat on.

'Could you walk me to my car, please,' she said with deliberate over-politeness, before he could say anything. 'Your friend's outside.'

'Oh God, not again.' It was the third time in as many days. Sighing, he held the door open and Ayesha stalked past him into the darkness; there was an icy wind and he buttoned his jacket as he hurried after her. The car park was at the side of the building between the bins and the railway embankment, and sitting on the low wall that divided it from the road, his face pale green in the glow of a street lamp, was Callum

Strang. He was in the middle of a coughing bout but managed a wave before gobbing on the tarmac.

'That is *disgusting*,' said Ayesha averting her head theatrically and opening the car door by touch alone.

'Shorry. Asha. I carn –' his lips laboured slowly to form the thickened words '– I carn . . .' He blinked a few times, appeared to forget what he had been about to say, and instead leaned forward and drooled a long, flecked string of saliva onto the right knee of his trousers. 'Shick,' he said, his mouth stretched ominously wide.

'My husband says I shouldn't have to put up with this,' said Ayesha, sliding into her car seat. Her voice was jagged with tension and Spencer could see her hands were shaking as she tried to insert the keys into the transmission. 'He says it's way outside my job description. He gets really mad when he hears about it, I have to hold him back.'

Spencer gestured hopelessly. 'I don't know what to suggest. You know he's banned from the surgery and I can't help it if he keeps turning up –'

'You shouldn't even talk to him. I've seen you talking.'

'But I –'

'We should just call the police.'

'The police have already said they're not in the slightest –'

'Look, I can't take it!' It was almost a shout and Spencer was shocked by her vehemence.

He held out his hands pacifically. 'OK. I'll phone social services again tomorrow and –'

Callum started retching, and Ayesha grabbed the door handle and slammed it shut in Spencer's face. Staring rigidly ahead, she reversed with a screech and then revved into the night.

'Bye. Bye,' said Callum, raising his head as though it were lead-plated. His eyes drifted until they met Spencer's. 'Hey tsocta. Tsocta Carra. I bin bad. My shest bin bad.' He started pawing at the zip of his jacket. 'Lissen to my shest.'

'Callum, you must stop turning up here.' He spoke slowly and clearly. 'There's no point. I'll only examine you at the hostel clinic and nowhere else.'

'Shucked out. Shucked me out.'

'Of St Clare's?'

'Fuckers.' His head dropped forward with a brutal suddenness that made Spencer flinch. 'Fuckers,' he said again, the word muffled against his chest.

In the staffroom, Iris was addressing a pile of envelopes, flipping back and forth through a broken-backed notebook with her free hand.

'Hi,' she said over her shoulder as Spencer entered, 'I've got a message for you.'

'Oh yeah?' He slumped into a chair and clasped his hands behind his head. 'I think I should warn you first that Callum's outside again and Ayesha's threatening to send her husband round.'

'To do what?'

'She didn't specify, but apparently he's a wild man when roused.'

Iris smothered a smile. 'I met Terence once. He's a bit roly-poly and he told me all about his upholstery evening classes. Was Callum sick, incidentally?'

'Yup, all over the pavement as per usual. Why?'

'Well . . .' She straightened her shoulders as if about to make a presentation. 'I think Ayesha's phobic about vomiting. She almost fainted once when a child threw up in surgery and it might explain why she gets so panicky about Callum – after all, he's not violent and she's never been afraid of anyone or anything else.'

Spencer paused, turning the diagnosis over in his mind, and she waited with the air of someone having their homework marked.

'I bet you're right,' he said, and she looked pleased. 'I'll have a chat with her. Good call.' He tipped an imaginary hat. 'You realize that you're wasted addressing envelopes?' Or repairing the coffee-machine, he thought, or sorting the post, or typing memos, or pointing Dov Steiner in the general direction of his next appointment, or the ninety other jobs she carried out without effort or fuss or much apparent satisfaction during the average day. 'You *do* realize that, don't you?' he added.

She looked at him for a moment. 'I'm beginning to,' she said. 'Do you want your message now? It's fairly complicated and I had to use a sort of shorthand.'

'Go on then.'

She took a closely written piece of paper from the desk and scrutinized it for a few moments, her lips moving soundlessly. 'Right, I think I've got it. Vincent Jayaram called.'

'Vincent? I haven't spoken to him for ages.'

'He said that a very flamboyant American man named Reuben had rung Casualty and asked if anyone knew a doctor named Spencer. Vincent didn't have your work number so he took the message and then tracked you down through the GP Training Scheme office. Anyway, this man told Vincent he's back in London on nun-related business, that's definitely N-U-N – I checked –' she glanced up, bemused, as Spencer laughed ' – for one night only, and did you want to meet up with him and Miles and another name that Vincent didn't catch for a good old knees-up –'

'A *what*?'

' – and he said they'd be at The Cockney pub from eight onwards, and that you'd definitely know where that was because it was on your list and that the only excuse he'd accept for your absence was a motorbike accident.' She paused and looked at him. 'That all makes sense, does it?'

'Perfectly,' said Spencer. He realized that he was grinning.

'And he – Vincent – said that even though it sounds like the worst night out he's ever heard of, as your unofficial psychiatrist he thinks it's about time you got off your backside and re-embraced life in all its forms, and that having a good time does not in any way constitute a betrayal.'

'I see.'

'And he also wanted me to tell you that Mrs –' She checked the note again.

'Spelko,' he supplied.

'Thank you. That Mrs Spelko recently removed a spleen in twenty-six minutes from first cut to closure and that her sole *raison d'être* now is to beat her own record.'

'Right.'

'And that's it,' she said, folding the note. 'I'm glad it made sense; I felt a bit like a Bletchley Park stenographer.' She handed it to him and he felt the odd liberation of being under orders.

'Thanks, Iris. Mr Turing's very grateful.'

'I don't know where this pub is, but you know it's already a quarter past seven?'

'Is it? I'll have to go straight there.' He checked what he was wearing. 'Is this all right? No stains I haven't spotted? No dangling threads?'

She shook her head. 'You look very smart.'

'Iris, this is a *date*.'

'Oh.' She blushed. 'Then you look very nice.'

'Thank you. And so do you, incidentally,' he added, remembering that he'd meant to say something. That morning, for the first time since he'd met her, Iris had been wearing an item of clothing that wasn't completely unnoticeable. 'That colour really suits you. Is it new?'

'Um. Yes.' She looked down at herself and warily fingered the royal-blue shirt. 'I bought it last weekend.'

'It really brings out your eyes.'

She gave him an odd look. 'Thanks.'

'You're welcome.' He stood up and stretched and was surprised by a sudden burst of energy; he felt as if the top of his head had been uncorked and a youthful fizz was rushing through it. 'So how come you're working so late?'

'I'm doing some invites of my own. Actually,' she looked up at him hopefully, 'I don't know whether you'd like to come.'

'What is it?'

'It's my father's seventieth birthday. We're having a surprise party.'

'Really?' He had met her father a couple of times at surgery, and he hadn't struck him as the soul of spontaneous enjoyment.

'I think he'll hate it,' she added, as if reading his mind.

'So why . . . ?'

'It wasn't my idea,' she said, a little grimly, 'but I couldn't veto it without seeming a complete killjoy. Ayesha's coming. And Dov – you'd be someone for him to talk to,' she added hopefully.

'Oh goody. There's a tempting prospect.'

'Please. It'll be just after work and it's only five minutes away, and I know Dad would really love to have two doctors there.'

'Is Tammy going to be there?'

Her mouth twitched. 'Yes.'

'I'm coming,' he said. 'Just you try and stop me.'

★

'Outside he was relieved to see that Callum had gone, leaving only a scattering of splashy mementos. He picked his way between them to the car and then sat for a while with the *A to Z* open at the narrow streets of the City, trying to remember the route which only a year ago he could have walked blindfold.

It was The Cockney Pub that had triggered the entire list. From his fifth-floor hospital bed, and with the aid of binoculars to enhance his failing vision, Mark had been able to make out the pub façade with its ineptly painted frieze of dancing pearly kings, and after a few days of ribald speculation had demanded that Spencer make a special trip to find out what went on there and what, specifically, was written on the blackboard outside.

'Eight p.m. Singalong with Mrs Harris,' he had reported back. 'Nine p.m. Roll out the Barrel, all draught beers a third off. Ten p.m. Knees Up with Andy.'

Mark had been drinking a build-up milkshake at the time and had sprayed it clear across the room on receipt of this information. From then on it had become a daily detour for Spencer, a chance to present Mark with a nugget of diversion on every visit.

'Seven thirty tonight, Cockney Bingo,' he'd announced one evening. 'And it's followed at eight thirty by Get Out Your Pearlies.'

'What the fuck's that?'

'It's a smile competition.'

'Who *goes* there? You've got to tell me who goes there.'

Spencer had found out the next evening when, sidling into the bar, he had witnessed a group of Japanese businessmen being taught the words to 'Knocked 'em in the Old Kent Road' by a man dressed as a chimney sweep.

'God knows what they must think of London,' he'd said to

Mark afterwards. 'One of them had a brochure from Madame Tussaud's so they're really plumbing the depths.'

'Madame Tussaud's is brilliant,' Mark had said.

'Is it? I've never been.'

'You've *never been*?' He had started the list that evening; he had died five weeks later.

It was as he locked the car that Spencer began to feel a creeping sense of unease: a slight lurch in the stomach, a tattoo of little pinpricks across the back of the neck. He had found a parking space in a deserted street behind St Paul's and as he walked past the darkened shops – shops that sold hunting prints and furled umbrellas and pipes of pointless curliness – the sensation gradually increased. He checked behind him but the street was empty and unthreatening, the only noise his own footsteps and the blurred roar of traffic.

He walked on, aware that with every few yards the feeling was intensifying. Cold hands, dry mouth, increased pulse rate, shallow respirations – one adrenaline-related symptom succeeded another, as his body prepared for . . . for what? This wasn't pre-date nervousness but a growing sense of dread, formless but intense, and as he turned the familiar corner and saw the hospital entrance across the square, he realized with a shock what was happening: it was a visceral time-slip. His body thought that he was visiting Mark, and had cranked up the usual awful anticipation.

His heart was pounding so hard that he could feel his sternum jump with every beat, and he took some deep, rather shaky breaths and then crossed to the centre of the square and sat for a while on a bench beside the dried-up fountain. The feeling ebbed slowly. He could hear a noisy group of men approaching along a side street, but for the moment the only other person visible was one of the meat porters from the nearby market, taking a quiet fag break beneath a street lamp. During the final days of Mark's life, when he could no longer see, or speak, but seemed to like to hear people talking, Spencer had sometimes filled the silence by giving a running commentary on the view from the window. From the fifth floor it was impossible to see people's faces, but during the day the square was busy and there were hats and bald spots and paunches to describe, and during the night there was always a white-overalled porter to be seen, for whom he could invent a name and a history and whose shoulder breadth could be awarded marks out of ten.

He gave the fattish guy under the street lamp a valedictory five.

The shouters – city boys, effortlessly loud – had reached the square and Spencer watched idly as they clustered at the entrance to a bar. The wide steel door was designed to look like that of a walk-in fridge and he realized with a jolt of grim amusement that the bar was called The Meat Locker. He also realized, a split second later, that what he was looking at was The Cockney Pub, renamed, refurbished and defunct. There was nothing remaining of the old façade, but he recognized the shops on either side, and the bricked-up window on the second floor, and when he turned his head and craned upwards he could see the window of Mark's room on Lilac Ward, the curtains still a zingy orange.

Vincent answered the phone with his usual thoroughness, giving his full name and title and beginning on the area code before Spencer could interrupt.

'Hello, Vincent.'

'Spencer, you got my message?'

'Yes thanks.'

'That was a very calm woman I spoke to at your surgery.

I was impressed by how quickly she grasped the situation.'

'Yes, she's very good.'

'Fast writer, pleasant disposition, unfussy – speaks with clarity but without excessive volume. They're all underrated qualities.'

'I'll tell her.'

'So where are you? Did you take my advice?'

'I'm in a phone box, outside what used to be The Cockney Pub. It changed hands last year. It doesn't exist any more.'

'And your friends aren't there?'

'No, maybe they went away when they couldn't find it. It's full of city types.' Spencer paused, breathing heavily. 'I just thought I'd phone you. As my unofficial psychiatrist.'

'Is it a bad evening?'

'Yup.' He had set up a little stack of ten-pence coins on the coinbox and he started moving them, one at a time, to a different spot. 'You don't mind me phoning, do you?'

'Of course not. Have you enough money for this? Do you want me to ring you back?'

'No, I've got plenty.'

'So – why's it a bad evening? Apart from missing your friends.'

'I . . . had a sort of flashback and it threw me a bit. I thought it was a year ago, I thought I was visiting Mark and I was scared shitless.'

'Why were you scared?'

'Because every time I visited I thought things couldn't get worse without him actually dying, but they went on getting worse and he was still alive.' He wiped his face with a sleeve and resumed stacking the coins. 'I'd forgotten I'd felt like that.'

'And that was last March?'

'Yes. I was working in obstetrics during the day and coming

242

here every evening.' He remembered being aware of the dismal irony of the situation; the nightly tube journey that took him from a ward full of noisy beginnings to a room where the end never seemed to come.

'Here?' said Vincent. 'What do you mean by "here"?'

'Oh. The pub's just by the hospital.' He fed a coin into the slot. 'A hundred yards and eleven months away. And I'd just, *just* started to think I was . . . I don't know, I was gaining a bit of perspective and managing to look ahead and making plans and all that five-stages-of-grief stuff and then I turn a corner and I'm back at the beginning. I'm before the beginning. And I want to know when it all stops.' His hand shook and the pile of ten-pences slid sideways, all but two of the coins dropping noisily onto the concrete floor; peering into the gloom he saw nothing but a scattering of Miss Whiplash cards.

'I have a theory,' said Vincent. 'A quasi-medical one.'

'Tell me.'

'Have you heard the proverb about grief taking a year and a day?'

'My grandmother says that.'

'Does she? Well I think she may be right. I think that perhaps that's the time it takes for the knowledge of someone's death to become wired into our neurones. Once it's there, once the permanent connections are formed it becomes part of us; we lose that constant, repeated shock – that *remembering* of it.' There was a sudden smash and a cheer from outside the bar, and Spencer hunched away from the noise and pressed the phone closer to his ear. '. . . course there's another aspect to it,' continued Vincent's clear, careful voice, 'an obvious one, a semantic one. On the day after the first anniversary, the phrase "this time last year" suddenly loses its dreadful power, because it's describing a world that lacks the person we're grieving for. This time last year, we were already on our own.'

Vincent paused. 'There,' he said, with careful lightness. 'Not really a theory, just a review of painfully collected data. It's not quite ready for publication.'

'It's pretty good,' said Spencer, his throat tight.

'Well, I think it's more helpful than being told "life goes on".'

'Or "time is a great healer".'

'Or "you'll find someone else", a favourite of my brother's.'

'Sensitive bloke?'

'Orthopaedic surgeon. Happier with hammers than words.'

Spencer fed in the last couple of coins.

'So,' said Vincent. 'What are you going to do now? Would you like to come round here?'

'No, I – thanks, but I'll probably just go home.'

'I'm sorry about your friends. I think that man Reuben tried very hard to track you down – he said he'd phoned at least five other A and E departments before he struck lucky. And he seemed very certain about this place The Cockney.'

'The Cockney Pub, it's called,' said Spencer, automatically.

'No, it's a pub, but it's called The Cockney. That's definitely what he said.'

'Oh,' Spencer felt the ground shift.

'Does that make a difference?'

'It might do. I mean, I just assumed it was the place I knew, but I suppose . . . thinking about it . . . it was quite an obscure –'

'Let me get the phone book,' said Vincent, crisply.

There were nine columns of businesses with the name Cockney in the title, and Spencer had to scrabble amidst the foetid litter on the floor for a final ten-pence piece before Vincent's finger landed on a likely candidate.

'It's on the Tottenham Court Road. It calls itself a cabaret pub,' he said, with some disdain.

244

'Fake pearly kings playing the old Joanna,' said Spencer. 'I bet that's it.'

'Number 327.'

'Right.' Spencer tried to summon up a vestige of his earlier enthusiasm. 'I suppose I should go, then.'

'Suppose? I've worked incredibly hard for this social evening of yours. You can't cancel now.'

Spencer smiled. 'I'm grateful, honestly.'

'*Go.*'

17

Spring was edging towards Hagwood Farm; the first tight buds had appeared on the hawthorn hedge, the winter aconites glowed like butterpats amongst the leaf litter, and Claud had stopped wearing the purple hat with earflaps that made him look like the Dalai Lama. Fran, leaning on her spade, watched the pale dome of his forehead bobbing ahead of a group of third-year Environmental Science students. He was leading them towards the sheep pen where Rodney and Delboy were waiting to be fed, their necks extruded desperately over the fence. They had developed a system of alternate bleating which meant they could produce a noise as continuous as a police siren and almost as hard to ignore; it increased in frequency as Claud approached, climaxed as he tilted the bag he was carrying, and then disappeared with magical suddenness as the orange chunks of mangel-wurzel bounced into the trough.

Fran resumed digging. After a cold February the ground was only just soft enough to take a spade, but steaming gently in readiness beside the vegetable patch was a four-foot high mound of horse manure, the greenish clods oozing with pongy goodness. It had been delivered that morning from the local police stables by a constable so cheerful, so flatteringly impressed by the place, so touchingly thrilled to be making a contribution, that Fran had cringed to remember that the bi-monthly donation was known on the farm as 'Pigshit'.

'Hoy, Fran.'

She turned to see Costas, the volunteer, waving a pair of secateurs at her.

'What?'

'This OK?' He held up a bundle of hazel twigs that he had been cutting into plant supports. She knew without checking that they would all be of exactly equal length, the cuts at right angles, the ends as smooth as if planed.

'That's great, thanks.'

'OK. What I should do now?'

'You could help me dig this over. I'd love to get it done before dark.'

'OK. It's work for a man anyhow.'

'What is?'

'Digging. For women it makes ugly muscle.' He mimed a grotesquely huge bicep and then walked off before she could say anything. Not that there was any point; sexism ran through Costas like a seam of coal and he was for ever extracting new lumps for her edification. He returned with the canvas bag in which he kept his own set of garden tools, the metal parts gleaming with oil, the handles silky with use, each implement wrapped in its own soft cloth. Squatting stiffly beside it, he wiped and sheathed the secateurs, and then beckoned Fran towards him.

'What's the matter?' she asked, continuing to dig.

He put his finger to his lips and looked over his shoulder with exaggerated caution to where Barry stood thigh-deep in the pond, hooking out a mass of blanket weed with a hoe. 'I have to say something,' he said. His voice dropped in pitch, the nearest he could manage to a whisper. 'Something private.'

'Really?' said Fran, unenthusiastically.

He nodded and beckoned again; with a sigh, Fran anchored her spade and went over to him.

'So what's up?' she asked. 'Is Barry being a pain?'

Costas checked over his shoulder again, and then leaned towards her. 'Barry smell,' he said in a bass rumble.

'Smell?'

'Stink.'

'Of what?'

'Pig.'

'Well that's his job – cleaning Porky out.'

Costas shook his head dismissively. 'He smell *before* he clean Porky out. He smell in the mornings when I walk on the farm.'

'Well I haven't noticed.'

'I notice when I stand next to him.'

'When do you stand next to him?'

Costas frowned as if she'd asked something distasteful. 'Men's business,' he said.

'Oh I see.' In a way that put a new light on it. If Barry could be smelled over and above a urinal then it must be quite significant. 'So, did you ask him why?'

'No no no.' Costas looked quite shocked at the idea; men's business obviously didn't include mentioning BO.

'Maybe his hot water's not working,' she suggested, her own boiler problems springing to mind.

He shrugged, and started unwrapping his spade. The secret communication seemed to be at an end and Fran glanced over at the pond, where Barry had stopped grappling with the weed and was instead bent over at right angles, one arm submerged up to the shoulder. He seemed to be groping for something, and even from this distance Fran could see that water was beginning to slop over the top of his waders. Before she could shout anything, however, he straightened up and began to pull a long muddy stick from the depths. It was the hoe. She caught Costas's eye and he shook his head and said something in Greek.

As they dug, the brisk wind pulled a succession of wispy clouds across the sky, and the sun blinked on and off like an

Aldis lamp. Fran peeled off her jumper and was immediately too cold; put it on again and the sweat started trickling down her ribs. As she took it off for the second time, a chorus of wolf whistles erupted behind her, and she spun round to see that Claud's school group had reached the vegetable patch. She put the jumper back on again.

'Didn't mean to interrupt,' said Claud. He looked strained. 'We've just got five minutes before the . . . the . . .' He gestured vaguely at the rutted strip that served as a car park. 'Just thought we'd drop by. Everyone's very keen to see your compost heap.'

'Oh right.' Fran dusted her hands and surveyed the group of fourteen-year-olds. She had rarely seen less enthusiasm on a set of human faces. 'Would you like me to give the guided tour?'

'No, that's all right. We've only got time for a quick . . . a quick . . .'

'Shag,' said someone, fairly loudly, and the class erupted.

'I think we should . . . er . . .'

'Hey, Miss,' said one of the boys, raising his arm.

'Yes,' she said, warily, alerted by the innocence of his tone.

'Did you do that?' He pointed to the heap of horseshit. This time the laugh was a cannonade, the girls screaming and covering their mouths, the deliverer of the line basking in the uproar.

Fran folded her arms. 'Yes I did,' she said seriously, when the noise had died down. 'That's what happens when you eat a lot of roughage. I didn't even have to strain.'

They were deeply shocked – she even heard a couple of gasps – and a worried-looking Claud took advantage of the sudden silence to usher them away. One or two looked back as they straggled towards the compost heap, apparently checking that she wasn't following them. Before they'd reached their destination, however, a coach pulled into the car park and the group broke and ran, streaming past Claud as if he were a bump in the road. He watched them go and then walked slowly back to Fran.

'What a horrible bunch,' she said, when he was within earshot.

'Oh, they were just . . .' He waved an arm. 'Adolescents.'

'Sorry about the cheap joke.'

'No, don't apologize. I mean I always think you're so much better at, er . . . connecting with them than, than . . . I mean one of them even asked me what "roughage" meant, though the coach came before I could really, er . . .'

'So out of evil came good,' said Fran, hefting the spade.

'Yes, you could say . . .' He sounded even more distracted than usual, and his eyeline wavered between Fran and his wellingtons. 'Er, while we're talking, I wondered if you have a moment. . . . it's just there's something a bit . . . delicate . . .'

She put the spade down again. Claud's face was clenched in the anxious spasm that meant he had something important to say. He looked at his wellingtons again.

'Er . . . I don't know if you've noticed over the last few days, but Barry has begun to . . . to . . .'

'Stink,' said Costas, helpfully, digging his way past them with a spade action so perfect that the turned earth behind him looked like a cable-knit sweater. 'Stink like a pig.'

Claud nodded, relieved that he hadn't had to say the word.

'No, I hadn't noticed,' said Fran. 'I haven't been anywhere near him – he's been doing fence posts all week.'

'Right, right.' He carried on nodding for a while. 'It's just that it's becoming rather . . . obvious.'

She guessed what was coming; at home, Sylvie might consider her an insensitive clod, but on the farm she was automatically handed any tasks deemed vaguely delicate, partly because she was the only female, and partly because Claud was too embarrassed to deal with them himself. She feigned innocence. 'So have you actually asked him what the problem is?'

'Er . . .' He looked trapped. 'No,' he said eventually, as if he'd just remembered the answer.

'Or even mentioned it?'

'Er . . . it seemed a bit . . .'

'Or even just hinted, tactfully?'

'I don't, er, think so . . .'

'So would you like me to have a word?'

His face broke into a smile of such relief that she almost felt mean for having strung him along. 'Could you? It's just that you put things so . . . so . . . and I know that Barry . . .'

He was drying his waders using the time-honoured method of hanging them upside down on sticks, in this case two six-foot raspberry canes he'd stuck into the marshy section by the pond edge. Across one of the soles he had draped his jumper, the left sleeve black with water, and was in the process of wringing out his socks when he looked up and saw Fran approaching.

'Hello, Barry.'

'Hi, there,' he said, in a tight, bright voice and backed away from her, a move so untypical that it was startling. She halted a few yards from him.

'Everything all right?'

'Fine.' His shirt was blotched with pond water and his jeans soaked from ankles to thigh. 'I got a bit wet,' he added unnecessarily.

'You could dry your stuff on the radiator in the classroom.'

'That's OK. There's a nice breeze out here.' He held out a sock to illustrate, and it stirred minimally.

She took another couple of steps towards him and he

skittered away again, holding the sock in front of him as if to ward her off.

'What's the matter?'

'Nothing.' He smiled unconvincingly and swayed on the balls of his feet, poised for further flight. Fran wondered how on earth she could edge this non-conversation round to the subject of BO. Out of the corner of her eye, she saw something moving and turned to see one of the raspberry canes starting to keel over. Barry noticed simultaneously and they both lunged towards it, hands outstretched. It was too late; jumper and wader landed in the pond for a second time and Fran found herself off-balance, one hand clutching Barry's arm for support, her face shoved against his shirt buttons.

'Jesus H Christ,' she said, jerking her head back. 'You *stink*.'

He leapt away from her, but the smell remained, almost tangible – the unmistakable odour of wet pig.

'Bloody hell, Barry. What have you been doing – sleeping in the sty?'

He froze, the muscles of his jaw clenching and unclenching as he worked through a decision. 'Yes,' he said, after a moment and then bent to retrieve the jumper.

'You've been sleeping in the sty,' she repeated, a statement this time, just to check that they'd both been hearing the same words.

He nodded. 'Since last Thursday. Not on the floor, obviously,' he added, as if to dismiss a really ridiculous idea. 'On the raised bit where we keep the bales.'

'But why?'

'Well, the straw's really warm and you can pile it –'

'*No*. I mean why are you sleeping in the pigsty?'

'Oh. Because my girlfriend threw me out. Changed the locks when I was at work.'

'And that was the *only* place you could find to stay?'

'Thursday night I slept in the classroom but I nearly got caught by the cleaner.'

'What about friends?'

'Well . . .' He looked discomfited. 'They were all Janette's friends first. And she's really angry with me.'

Fran opened her mouth.

'I can't say why,' he said quickly. 'I just can't.'

'What about bed and breakfast?'

'Not enough money. Everything's at the flat – cards, cheque-book. All my clothes.'

'What have you been eating?'

'Pot noodles.'

'Well –' she shook her head, dazed by the sheer inanity of his solution, the last possible idea that would ever have occurred to anyone else '– how long were you intending to stay here?'

He looked blank.

'A couple of weeks? Right through the summer? Put in double glazing and spend the winter there? I warn you, Porky might start charging rent.'

He grasped the point. 'No, no, it was just until Janette came round to . . . to what I did. I thought it would only be a day or two but she won't answer the door and she keeps putting the phone down on me. We just need a bit of a talk. I've sent her a letter explaining things.'

He had drifted towards her during the course of the conver-sation, and she caught a second noseful. The porcine whiff seemed to extend a good two yards beyond him.

'Couldn't you at least have washed? We've got basins here.'

'It's my clothes,' he said earnestly. 'The smell's in my clothes. I hadn't realized it would get this bad. If I could just use someone's washing machine, or borrow a pair of jeans or something, I'd be all right.'

'You can't carry on sleeping in the pigsty, Barry. Not now that I know about it.'

'But where can I go?'

Fran clasped her hands behind her head and swung round to look at her fellow workers: Costas, still digging, but shortly to return to the one-bedroomed fourteenth-floor flat that he shared with his disabled wife; Spike (re-felting the hen-house roof) whose partner had recently given birth to twins; and Claud (supposedly helping Spike but in fact looking anxiously at Fran), unlikely fount of testosterone and father of six, five of them still living at home. With a sigh of resignation, she turned back to Barry.

There was an arthritic twang as the frame of the sofa bed swung out from the crumb-strewn interior. It was a while since it had been used, and after unpleating the mattress and easing out the stiffened legs, Fran bounced cautiously on the edge a couple of times and then wriggled to the centre and lay flat. It had a distinct starboard list and she got up again and slid a folded newspaper under the right leg. The living room seemed even colder than the rest of the house, and she made up the bed with three blankets and the duvet from Peter and Sylvie's room before returning to her vigil beside the boiler. She had reached page nineteen out of twenty-six of the central-heating instruction manual without any hint as to why the pilot light sometimes stayed lit, and sometimes didn't.

Barry was next door, scrubbing himself raw, she hoped, in Iris's bath, while his clothes whirled through an ecologically unsound but in this case necessary boil wash with some specially bought biological powder.

Iris had been very understanding when they had turned up at her front door in search of hot water. 'I wasn't doing anything,' she'd said and for once that had appeared to be the case; there had been an open book on the kitchen table and a half-eaten apple beside it and Iris herself had had the slightly guilty air of a truant.

'Evening to myself,' she'd said, after Barry had been banished to the bathroom, and she was rinsing out the teapot. 'Dad's gone to the cinema again. He's decided he likes Harrison Ford.'

'And where are the boys?'

'Oh . . . out somewhere. They've been a bit mysterious lately. I'm protecting my sanity by not asking.'

'And by reading a psychiatry textbook?' Fran had said, incredulously, picking it off the table. It was the real thing: five hundred pages of polysyllables interspersed with graphs.

Iris had looked slightly embarrassed. 'Spencer lent it to me. We were talking about phobias.'

'Oh right.' Fran had suppressed the infantile twinge of jealousy she always felt when Iris talked about Spencer, the pre-school urge to shout 'but he's *my* friend'.

'Anyway, I was only dipping into a chapter,' Iris had said, dismissively. She'd poured some milk into Fran's mug. 'So how long's Barry going to stay for?'

'One night. Only. Just to make himself presentable again. If Janette won't take him back he can stay at the YMCA. I'll lend him the money if necessary.'

'It's very kind of you.'

'No it's not,' Fran had said, disconcerted. 'It's just –' she'd shied away from Sylvie's favourite word '– the obvious solution.'

She reached the last page of the manual without revelation, closed it and looked at the boiler. The little flame danced tauntingly in the window. She turned the black knob so that the arrow pointed towards the words CONSTANT HOT WATER and the flame went out again. For the ninth time she relit the pilot light and then closed the boiler door and looked at the manual, weighing it in her hands. The clue was in the colour; the paper was a mottled yellow, the pages curled at the edges, the spine a series of parallel cracks from which little threads dangled. Like the boiler, it was a museum piece. She threw it into a corner and a sunburst of pages broke loose and fluttered to the floor.

'It's a bit cold in here,' said Barry, when she showed him his bed in the living room. 'Can't we light the fire?'

'Chimney's not swept.'

'Oh. Pity.' He rested his mug of tea on the piano and bent over to fiddle with his trouser legs. He had returned from next door smelling of sweet-pea body lotion and dressed in a selection of laughably enormous clothing from the twins' wardrobe.

'They must be complete freaks,' he said, aggrieved, adjusting the turn-ups around his knees.

'Just taller than you, Barry,' said Fran, removing the mug, 'and this piano belongs to somebody who's very strict about how it should be treated. Apparently it's very old and very valuable.'

'Is it?' Barry flipped up the lid and played a speedy two-finger version of 'Chopsticks'. 'It's not bad. Keys are a bit yellow.'

'And only she's allowed to play it,' said Fran, repressively (and untruthfully), putting the lid back down again.

'Sowwy,' he said, in a baby voice. Fran frowned; the touching gratitude he'd shown when she'd first invited him back to the house had given way to a disconcerting perkiness, the excitement of a kid on a school trip.

'I'm going to cook some pasta,' she said. 'Do you want to try phoning Janette?'

His face fell. 'Yeah, all right.'

He bounced into the kitchen as she was picking the bones out of Mr Tibbs's supper, a repulsive sludge of steamed fish and vitamin powder. The cat sat at her ankles, mouth stretched in a soundless mew.

'Any luck?'

He shook his head. 'She's not in. I left a message.'

'What are you going to do if she doesn't get back to you? You'll have to collect your stuff sometime.'

'I think she'll be fine when she gets the letter,' said Barry. 'I explained everything in it, I think she'll come round.'

'When did you send it?'

'Day before yesterday.'

'Then she should have got it by now.'

'Second-class stamp,' said Barry laconically. He opened the fridge and took a good long look at the contents. 'Any beer?'

'No.' She put down her fork decisively. 'Barry.'

'Uhuh?' He turned, a piece of cheese in his hand.

'I'm serious, you know, about you only staying one night. This is not an open-ended invitation.'

'Yeah, yeah. Sure.' His vivid blue eyes widened with sincerity. 'God, Fran, I'm really grateful, I mean – you saved my life. I'm not going to take advantage.'

'Right. I just wanted to . . .' She paused. What she really wanted to do was question her own sanity. What on earth had possessed her to offer him a bed in the first place? She didn't like to think that part of the reason might have been the unexpected creakiness of the house last night, after Peter and Sylvie had left for the airport. She had realized, lying awake at 3 a.m., listening to a slithering noise that was almost certainly another tile easing its way off the roof, that she had never before stayed there alone, without either Peter's antiphonal snoring down the hall, or Duncan's long body beside her. She had never before been conscious of the absence of window locks in her own room, or the fact that only a couple of low garden walls separated the back door from the ill-lit street full of dented cars that ran behind the house. She was still slightly ashamed that she had shoved the bed-side table in front of the door before finally managing to sleep.

Something nudged her leg, and she looked down to see that Mr Tibbs, desperate for his bowl of mush, had edged so close that he was dribbling on her trousers. She gave the dish a final stir to check for bones, and then plonked it beside him.

'Can I do anything?' asked Barry, his mouth full.

'You could grate some cheese.'

'Er. . . .' He swallowed. 'I've just eaten it.'

'Never mind.'

She stirred the pasta and gave a crusty-lidded jar of pesto a cautious sniff. With only a few flabby tomatoes to cut up for a salad, it seemed a poor first meal for someone who'd just spent half a week in a pigsty.

'Tell you what,' she said, 'you could go and get a bottle of wine. Here –' she fished a fiver from her purse and handed it to him ' – there's an offie on the corner.'

'Thanks, Fran.' He gave her fingers a squeeze as he took the money.

'Do you think I've got better?' he asked, three glasses of Turkish Chardonnay later ('I got two bottles for £4.30,' he'd said excitedly on his return).

'At what?'

'At the job. Do you think I've got better at it?' He rolled his glass along one cheekbone and looked at her through it.

'Yes,' said Fran, cautiously.

'You think I'm definitely better at the job?'

258

'Yes I do.'

'Because of you,' he said, setting down the glass half on and half off a coaster. 'You made me what I am.'

'Do you want some coffee?' she said, getting to her feet and readjusting the glass before it fell over.

'No, I'm fine. I'm soooo fine.'

'I'll make you some anyway.'

He had wolfed down the pasta and then got drunk with amazing rapidity, passing straight from giggling silliness to soused philosophy in the course of about three mouthfuls.

'The thing is, Fran, the thing about you is – ' his eyes followed her as she washed up a couple of mugs ' – the thing is you're strong.'

'Do you take sugar?'

'You're small but you're strong, like a . . . a . . . diamond.'

'Sugar?'

'Or the bit that's not going round in the middle of a hurricane. What's it called?'

'The eye,' said Fran, through gritted teeth.

'So when the storm blows you're always . . . in the middle. To cling onto. Where's the corkscrew?' He looked vaguely around the table, the second bottle in his hand.

'Ah no.' She moved swiftly to confiscate it. 'You've had plenty.'

'Strong,' he said, looking up at her admiringly.

The phone rang and she went to answer it, taking the bottle with her.

'Hello?'

There was a pause and then a woman's voice, cool as water, said, 'Who's that?'

'Fran,' said Fran, and realized, in the microsecond it took to say the word, that she shouldn't have.

'In that case,' said the woman, 'you can tell Barry he's a

lying fuckwit and he'll find his stuff all over the pavement tomorrow morning.' The line went dead.

Fran looked at the receiver for a moment before replacing it. Then, holding the bottle like a club, she went back to the kitchen.

'Hey,' said Barry, giving her what he probably imagined was a winning smile.

'That was Janette.'

The smile faded. 'Huh?'

'Janette. You gave her this number, didn't you?'

'Yeah.' The implication filtered through. 'Oh . . . I should have answered –'

'When I said my name she said "in that case" she was throwing your stuff out. What did she mean, "in that case"?'

He looked alarmed. 'Throwing my stuff out? But I've got a guitar, I mean she can't –'

'*Barry!*' He jumped and knocked his glass over. 'Tell me what she meant. What have you been saying to her about me?'

'I haven't said anything.'

'Bollocks you haven't.'

'I swear,' he said, his expression so shifty that he looked like Wile E Coyote. 'Not deliberately, anyway.'

'What do you mean?'

'It was accidental.'

'What was?'

'I –' He looked at her helplessly. 'You're going to be angry.'

'I'm angry now. You've got to tell me.'

'OK, OK.' He took a deep breath. 'Can I have another glass of wine?'

'No.'

'Right. You see, I'd been thinking about you. I mean, I never stopped thinking about you even when I got back with

Janette, but I was thinking about you more because I'd been thinking . . . well, I'd just been starting to think . . . what it was, was that I'd started to think that you'd probably . . .'

Fran put the bottle on the table with a thump and sat down opposite him; he blinked at her nervously and cleared his throat.

'Right. You see, what it was, you stopped reading your letters in lunch break so I guessed you'd broken up with Duncan. If he wasn't writing to you any more.' He waited for her to say something. 'That's what I guessed,' he added, when it became clear that she wasn't going to. 'That's what I thought had probably happened.'

'Get on with it.'

'So, anyway, I . . . I kept thinking about you, and thinking I might be in with a chance again, and just – you know – working myself up, and there was one day last week when it rained and you got all wet, and you were in that black t-shirt –'

'Oh God,' said Fran.

'And that night, I was with Janette and we were – having sex – and it came to the – you know –'

'Oh God,' said Fran, again, with awful prescience.

'And I said – I said your name. Pretty loudly really. You know, shouted it. Several times.' He laced his fingers together and looked at them. 'Janette's quite a jealous sort of a person.'

Fran's first coherent thought was a vow never again to wear the black t-shirt; her second was more nebulous – a vague hope that at some time in the future she might attract someone who wasn't looking for the calm in the centre of the storm, who didn't require a lodestone, or a rock, or a compass, or a steady North Star – someone, in fact, who could read maps and stand upright all by himself, but who just liked having her along for the ride.

Barry sat silent, sneaking occasional glances at her, the

261

expression on his face somewhere between fear and pleasurable anticipation, as if – and she suddenly *knew* this to be the case – as if he thought that she would find his confession so powerful that her defences would melt and she'd hurl herself into his arms.

'Are you still angry?' he asked, after a while.

'Depressed,' said Fran. 'Deeply, deeply depressed.'

It took her a long time to get to sleep; at first she was disturbed by the sound of Barry doing the washing-up with careless vigour and then by the long, guilty silence after something smashed onto the floor. Her senses sharp with annoyance, she was sure that the next noise was the sound of a cork being drawn.

After that she drifted into a long and irritating dream, in which she was sitting in the Hagwood staffroom, reading a letter from Duncan. The letter was only three sentences long, but she could sense Barry watching her, so she sat with her eyes glued to the paper, reading the words over and over again. 'Dear Fran, I hear you are looking for lodgers. Hella and I are moving to England and would love to move in. She is expecting twins in October. Love Duncan.'

She was woken instantly, completely, by a hoarse eldritch screech, followed by a couple of staccato footfalls, an indefinable rending sound, and a final enormous thud. As she leapt for the light switch there was a galloping noise that ended just outside her door and she opened it to see Mr Tibbs, more alert than she had ever seen him, sides heaving, tail cracking back and forth like a whip.

Barry was lying ghost-pale on the hall floor, dressed only in a pair of Tom and Jerry boxer shorts, his limbs flung outwards as if trying to acquire a tan. As Fran hurtled downstairs towards him she could see his chest jerking irregularly, ominously, his mouth searching for air, his head lolling. The sound he was making only registered as she knelt beside him, her face cold with fear. He was laughing.

'Shtood on the cat,' he said. 'Ur her her her her her.'

Fran sat back on her heels, and looked at the stairs. Halfway down, just below the step that Mr Tibbs liked to think of as home, the banisters were bowed outwards as if an elephant had casually leaned on them.

'Shorry,' said Barry. 'I wash coming to shay shorry.' The heady bouquet of Istanbul white filled the air.

'Do you hurt anywhere?' asked Fran, voice like a stone.

'Dunno.' He heaved himself into a sitting position. 'No.' He put one hand on the radiator and one hand on Fran's shoulder and tried to stand up. He sat down again with a thump. 'Ankle,' he said. 'Ow.'

18

At the time, the discovery of a cache of biscuit cutters at the back of her father's pan cupboard was merely a nice little moment, a pinch of sweet serendipity; in retrospect it was the undisputed best bit of the entire day of the surprise party. It was mid-afternoon. Her father had left for his indoor bowls match, all unsuspecting and Tammy McHugh was scouring the shops of Stoke Newington for liquorice wheels; Iris, meanwhile, was meditatively mixing a batch of dough in the quiet kitchen. A fine rain pattered on the window and she could hear the regular chunking of a spade coming from Mr Hickey's garden. His head bobbed intermittently above the Leylandii but he kept his face resolutely turned away, and ignored a couple of tentative waves that she'd aimed in his direction. In surgery, he was always stiffly polite to her, but here, on his own ground, she was obviously viewed as an enemy consort.

After rolling out the dough, she rooted around for a baking tray. Her father used the same two pans for everything but behind them in the cupboard, amongst the casseroles and double boilers, were items unused – unthought of – since the fifties: milk strainers, measuring funnels, egg poachers with twirly wire handles, bain-mairies, Swiss Roll tins and a jingling cluster of nozzles for squeezing icing onto fancy cakes. She found the yellowed muslin bag of cutters nestling in the bottom of a jelly mould, and the touch of it was instantly familiar, the same mysterious bundle of jagged yet hollow shapes that she had pulled from her stocking when she was seven. She lifted it out and tipped the contents onto the table

– a Christmas tree, a teddy bear, a crown, a hexagon and a star, now all splotched with rust and possessing the sort of lethal edges that had seemed standard in post-war children's toys. Fingering the sharp angles of the star, she thought she could remember the last time she'd used them, another rainy day when the boys were toddlers and she had been desperate to find some activity to contain their bursting energy, to distract them even momentarily from their favourite game of clambering up the first two stairs and then jumping off them onto the hall floor, again and again and again. She had lured them into the kitchen and then hovered nervously as they'd squeezed and thumped the greying dough, envisaging at any moment a cry of pain and a severed finger rolling across the counter top.

She ran the star-shaped cutter under the tap and gave it a rub with a brillo pad; to her surprise, bright tin showed beneath the rust and it took only a couple of minutes to restore it to a usable state. She dried it carefully, and had just resumed her search for a baking tray when the doorbell rang.

Idling over his Weetabix that morning, Tom had predicted that half the guests would turn up much too early: 'You know old people, they always give themselves an extra nine days to get somewhere just in case a volcano erupts and destroys the bus depot.' And here on the doorstep, two and a half hours before the invited time, stood Leslie Peake, sporting a waterproof bush-hat, and carrying a bottle of wine with an ominously home-made label.

'Not too early, am I?' he asked, in his whistling North Welsh accent that broke the words into their constituent syllables and left clear air between each one, 'only I took an earlier train just in case the later one was cancelled. Wouldn't want to miss the start of the party.' He shook the rain off his mac and followed her into the kitchen.

'Cup of tea, Leslie?'

'Luffly.'

She averted her eyes as he removed the hat and adjusted his hair. Leslie's fringe ended just above his eyebrows, but it began somewhere at the nape of his neck, and several times an hour he would reposition the entire headful over the bald expanse beneath, with the action of someone settling an antimacassar.

'So are you still in Dalston then, Iris?'

'That's right.'

'Still at the surgery?'

'Yes, still there.'

'Not married yet?'

'No, not yet.' Poised with the kettle in her hand, she realized that the same demoralizing exchange would be repeated with almost every guest at the party. Iris's life, summed up in three questions.

'Don't mind me if you've got to get on.'

She pulled herself together. 'Thanks. I've still got a few things to do.' All the sandwiches, to begin with. She decided to postpone the biscuits and get on with the egg mayonnaise.

'It's potato wine,' said Leslie. 'Home-made.'

'Lovely.'

'Very potent. I thought it would bring back a memory or two for your dad.'

'Oh yes?'

'Catterick.' He tapped the side of his nose and gave a wink. 'It was supposed to be a dry barracks. Enough said.'

If only, thought Iris. She thought she could probably write an entire book on Ian and Leslie – The War Years. She checked in the oven to see how the quiches were coming on, and then delved into the fridge for the eggs.

'You know, they used to call B Block "The Still".'

'Really?'

'Oh yes. And do you know why?'

'Because it had a still in it?'

'No!' He was triumphant. 'Because there were three brothers bunking there, and you know what their surname was?'

'No what?'

'Ginn. Harry, Si and Ronnie Ginn.'

She managed a laugh. 'Oh, I see. I get it.' She poured his tea and put it in front of him, and then turned back to the stove.

'Of course, Harry was killed in Tripoli.'

'Oh dear, was he?'

'You know, Iris, I'm not as sweet as you must think I am.'

'Sorry?' She was thrown by the sudden change of subject.

'I said I'm not as sweet as you must think I am.' He mimed stirring a teaspoon.

'Oh of course. Sorry.' She placed the sugar bowl on the table.

'You've just got white, have you?'

'Oh . . . er.' She turned down the heat under the pan and started to hunt around in the dry goods cupboard, wary of disarranging her father's careful storage system.

'Doesn't matter,' he said, easily, after a couple of minutes. 'Don't want to put you to any trouble. You get on.' At least thirty seconds of silence ensued, during which Iris put the eggs into the pan and started to slice cucumber into a colander. She could feel Leslie's eyes following her.

'Haven't got a biscuit, have you?' he asked. The doorbell rang again.

'Ginn,' said Leslie. 'Harry, Si and Ronnie Ginn.' There was a chuckle round the table, and a relaxed post-anecdotal easing back of chairs, narrowing still further the tiny gangway that

Iris had been left to work in. It was a quarter to five, and there were now half a dozen premature guests sitting in the kitchen, drinking tea and listening to Leslie Peake's war stories. Only one, Auntie Kath, had offered to help Iris, but the vague air with which she was peeling the eggs, the wandering hand which hovered between the two bowls – one supposedly containing bits of shell, the other denuded eggs, the occasional cries of 'Whoops-a-daisy' and 'Now, what's *that* doing in there?', augured badly for the texture of the sandwiches.

'The Still . . .' repeated the senior church warden, appreciatively.

'So Iris –' Leslie turned to her with the benign air of a successful host ' – what time is your father expected?'

'Quarter to six,' she said, spooning mushrooms into a vol-au-vent casing.

'Oh, we're here in good time then,' said Auntie Kath, complacently. 'And when's Tammy coming?'

'She's supposed to *be* here. Helping.' Mrs McHugh had gone out in search of the finishing touch for her cake, a hand-built Victoria sponge in the shape of a vintage car. It was sitting in the living room in wheel-less splendour, awaiting the liquorice tyres with jelly hubcaps that the recipe specified. 'I'm not sure you can get those any more,' Iris had said, doubtfully, eyeing the recipe book; the photo was greenish with age and the original list of ingredients included powdered egg.

'Och, nonsense,' Mrs McHugh had said airily, clattering her wheeled shopping basket through the hall. That had been two hours ago.

'Who's Tammy?' asked Leslie.

Aunty Kath, dreaming over the eggs, seemed to click into focus. 'Ooh, hasn't he told you about Tammy?'

'He's found himself a lady friend, has he?' Leslie sat up keenly, and smoothed his fringe in anticipation.

'Well, she's –' The doorbell rang again and Iris put down the spoon and went to answer it.

'Hi, Mum.' The boys clumped in, dripping, their arms laden with bags. 'Pissing down out there.'

'We've brought the glasses, Mum,' said Robin.

'Thanks,' she said, distractedly, looking along the road. There was no sign of Mrs McHugh, but to her dismay she could see the Woodentop gait of Dov Steiner jerking into view, and behind him what looked like the entire indoor bowls team, clustered beneath a couple of gigantic golf umbrellas. They were dreadfully early – the match wasn't supposed to finish for at least another three-quarters of an hour; further-more, she realized, they must have her father with them, unless they'd run away and left him. A grumble of thunder rattled the glass in the fanlight above the door.

'What do you want us to do?'

'Oh, er . . .' She tried to marshall her thoughts. 'You could open out the dining-room table, and arrange all the plates and cutlery and glasses on it.'

'OK.'

'And get the drink out of the fridge.'

'OK.'

'And you could ask people to move out of the kitchen. Politely.'

'Are you a bit harassed, Mum?' asked Robin, curiously.

'Yes, a bit.'

'They all turned up early, didn't they?' said Tom, pleased with his prescience.

'Tom –' she said, warningly.

'Ooh, something serious.' He looked at her, his expression a facsimile of sombre attention.

'No, it's just . . . there's a man in the kitchen with a funny hairstyle. I wanted to prepare you. So you wouldn't stare.' He looked at her for a moment longer, then glanced at Robin.

'We wouldn't do that, would we, Rob?'

'Nope.'

'Well, good,' she said, unconvinced. She heard a rattling noise and turned to see Dov closing the gate.

'Hey, Mum,' hissed Tom behind her, 'there's a man with a funny head coming up the path.'

The front hall of her father's house was fairly narrow – a corridor rather than an atrium – and certainly far too small to accommodate seven members of the bowls team with Dov standing in their midst like a sentient hatstand. Her father was not amongst them and as Iris tried to disentangle the story of the afternoon there was an influx from the kitchen.

'We've been given our marching orders,' said Leslie, heading the contingent and holding a chair in front of him like a cowcatcher. 'Where do you want us?'

Iris raised her voice. 'Could everyone please move into the front room.'

'Left, right, left, right,' said Leslie, amidst laughter. There was a surge of bodies, a sudden bottleneck during which Iris was pinned against the banisters by a wall of flesh redolent of Old Spice and damp tweed and then the crush subsided into an orderly queue. From the kitchen, a number of yelping noises became audible.

Robin was actually lying on the floor, face scarlet, knees drawn up to his chest, while Tom sat with his back against a table leg. Two slices of bacon were draped over his head. 'Hey, Mum, I'm . . . I'm . . .' His mouth wobbled out of control again and he emitted a series of cheeps.

'Well, thanks for your help,' said Iris. She opened the fridge and began to take out bottles of squash and wine. 'Grandad's disappeared,' she added.

It took a while for the words to register. 'Wha?' said Robin.

'There was a power cut at the leisure centre and when the rest of the bowls team got out they couldn't find him.'

'Uh.'

'So let's keep our fingers crossed that he hasn't decided to go to the cinema for the afternoon.' She pawed through the cutlery drawer for the corkscrew and then closed it with a satisfying smash.

'So, uh . . .' Robin heaved himself up and leaned against the sink. 'Do you want us to . . . to . . .'

'Hey, Rob.'

'Wha?'

Tom lifted a hand and smoothed the bacon fringe over his eyebrows. His brother jackknifed silently to the floor and Iris picked up the bottles and left the kitchen. The phone and the doorbell rang simultaneously just as she'd squeezed between the bodies and deposited the drinks on the table and she waved the corkscrew at Leslie.

'Rely on me,' he said, taking it with a gallant bow.

Ayesha was at the door, her swirl of stiffened hair pearly with raindrops, a silver helium balloon with '70' written on it floating above her. 'You're the only person on time so far,' said Iris, over her shoulder as she hurried back to the kitchen. Tom was just reaching for the phone and she snatched it from the cradle before he could get there.

'Hello?'

'Iris?'

'Tammy? Where are you?'

'I'm back at my house. Listen, dear, there's been a wee bit of a problem – I've got your dad with me.'

'Is he all right?'

'Oh yes, he's fine – it's not a *physical* problem. It's more psychological.'

'What do you mean?'

271

'Well it was just bad luck really. You see I'd popped into Woolworths for the liquorice sweeties and you know it's just opposite the leisure centre? I thought there'd be no chance of bumping into him but would you believe there was a power cut and – '

'I heard. The rest of the team's just got here.'

'Well. Your dad spotted me coming out of the shop and he was a bit puzzled because you know I'd only just rung him to say I had a bad tummy and I was going to miss bowls and have a bit of a lie-down instead and the next thing he knows, there I am dashing along the high street with my face on and all dressed up for a party. So anyway, he wanted to know what was going on.'

'Oh. You told him, did you?'

'I had to, dear,' said Mrs McHugh gravely. 'He thought there must be someone else.'

'So what did he say?'

'He's not keen. Not keen *at all*. He says it's all too much fuss and bother and he's sitting in the front room with his arms folded.'

Iris felt a sour surge of triumph. 'I knew he'd hate the idea,' she said, and her voice was fat with satisfaction; she saw Robin shoot her a startled look. From the front room there was a burst of laughter and the doorbell rang again. The feeling of triumph dissipated and she felt suddenly wretched.

'You know there are nearly twenty people here already,' she said, 'practically everyone's turned up early and I haven't even finished the food yet.'

There was a rattle from the door knocker and a further ring on the bell, and Robin unfolded himself from the floor. 'I'll get it.'

'Well I can't seem to budge him,' said Tammy, 'you know what he can be like. And between you and me I think he might be a bit –' she lowered her voice '– *embarrassed* about introducing me to his old friends. You know, the thought simply hadn't occurred to me but of course he's a bit old-fashioned about all that sort of thing. Anyway I thought that maybe if you –'

'Hang on.' Leslie had popped his head round the door of the kitchen and, seeing her on the phone, started to mime something – something circular, about five inches high, hollow, a container of some kind . . .

'Raiders of the Lost Ark,' said Tom in a muffled voice.

'Glasses?' hazarded Iris.

'That's the one.'

'In the bags by the stairs. They're on hire.' He disappeared again. The front door slammed and she could hear the shuffle of footsteps in the hall.

'Mum,' shouted Robin, 'someone wants to talk to you.'

'Tell them I won't be a minute.' The doorbell rang yet again and continued ringing, as if someone were leaning on the bell push. Tammy said something inaudible and Iris stuffed a finger in her free ear.

'Sorry?'

'I said maybe you should have a word with him.'

She hesitated, the noise drilling through her head; she could hardly remember the last time she'd had a proper conversation with her father, one that wasn't bulging with unvoiced topics. 'All right then,' she said, reluctantly.

'I'll go and get him.'

As Iris waited, the doorbell stopped at last and then re-started immediately, stopped again, started and was finally replaced by the sound of knuckles on wood.

'Will somebody *get* that?' she called. 'Robin?'

'I'm not supposed to,' he shouted back.

'What? What are you talking about?'

'Sorry, Iris.' Spencer, looking damp and harassed, came into the kitchen. 'I asked him not to.'

'What?' The doorbell started ringing again. 'Why?'

'Because it's Callum Strang. He followed me from the surgery.'

'But –' She heard the snap of the letter box and the unintelligible roar of Callum's voice.

'What does he want?'

'To thank me.'

'To *thank* you?'

'Yes, I gave him a free baseball hat that was kicking round the surgery and he's very happy about it. I'm sure he'll go soon. He'll get bored and wander off.'

'Do you want me to ring the police?' shouted Ayesha.

'Give it five minutes,' shouted Spencer back.

The doorbell began a series of little trills of varying length, and Iris closed her eyes for a moment and imagined herself all alone in a field, sitting quietly with a book. She opened them again and looked at the phone in her hand.

'Tom.'

'What?' He was still sitting on the floor, bacon on head.

She covered the receiver with her hand. 'You're articulate. Persuade your grandad to come to his own party.'

'All right.'

'Tell him that we're all longing for him to arrive, and that Leslie's brought home-made potato wine just like they had at Catterick and tell him –' she took a deep breath '– tell him you've already met Mrs McHugh and you think she's lovely – and I think she's lovely, and I think it's about time he introduced her to everyone.'

'I've already met who?'

'Dad's girlfriend. She told you and Robin off for smoking in the street.'

He gaped at her.

'She's about four foot eleven. Tartan skirt, white hair, Scottish accent?'

'What, *her*? That's Grandad's *girlfriend*?'

'Yes.'

'Jesus, she could talk for *Europe*.'

'Yes.'

'He probably had to snog her to get her to shut up.'

'Tom –'

He grinned. 'It's all right, I won't say that.'

She was sitting on the edge of the raised flower bed in the back garden when Spencer brought her out a glass of wine.

'You've rumbled me,' she said.

'Ten minutes is far too long to spend wrapping up a lawnmower.'

'Especially when it's already wrapped and in the shed. It was just an excuse.' She took a sip and choked. 'Good God.'

'It's made from potatoes, apparently. Can I join you?'

She shifted up the damp wall a few inches. The light was beginning to fade, and she had been sitting watching the yellow square of the kitchen window as if it were a mute television screen. Ayesha had found an apron and was putting the vol-au-vents in the oven, Auntie Kath was washing up and Robin was doing a wholly inadequate job of the drying. In the corner, his back to the window, Tom was talking non-stop while fiddling with something shiny on the work surface.

'What's Tom doing, do you know?'

'Flirting with Ayesha, mainly.'

'No sign of my father, I suppose.'

'Not yet. I wouldn't worry, they're having a riot in the front room – no one's even touched the squash.' He shifted round so he could look at her. 'Are you all right, Iris?'

She nearly said 'Fine' and then stopped herself. 'Not really.' The admission, slight as it was, was liberating. 'I've been jealous,' she said, and was still surprised at the thought. It had emerged, fully formed, as she sat on the wall in the twilight.

'Jealous of whom?'

'Dad.'

'Really?' He looked at her carefully. 'This isn't anything to do with his new lawnmower?'

'No.' She managed a smile. 'No. I mean . . . anyone else would be pleased, wouldn't they, if their father had managed to start enjoying himself after years of –' she searched for the right word '– grimness. But all I could think was how unfair it was.'

Spencer said nothing, and in the silence Iris could hear a soft sawing noise from a nearby garden.

'You see, I had all these little changes planned for this year. I had a whole campaign in miniature and I was . . . easing myself into it. And then Dad just *did* it; he dived in, he altered his whole life in one go and I've been –' Dumped, she thought; it was a teenage word but it seemed horribly appropriate. He'd broken her routine as well as his own, and she'd found nothing with which to replace it.

'And because I was . . . jealous' – she still couldn't quite believe the word – 'I didn't let him talk about it, I wouldn't give him the satisfaction of telling me. I avoided the whole topic, and because he's not very good at real conversation he never found a way to bring it up.' He had tried a couple of times, she winced to remember – had edged round the subject on tiptoe, and then given up when she'd failed to respond. 'I should have been happy,' she said. 'For me as well as for him.'

'You can't be happy to order,' said Spencer. 'It doesn't work that way.'

'I know. So anyway, here I am, still in exactly the same place. And there he is . . .'

'He had a bit of help, you know,' said Spencer.

'What do you mean?'

'You were trying to do it from scratch. There's a huge difference between starting something from scratch when you're trying to do a million other things at the same time, and being swept along by someone else. Your father didn't instigate this change. He didn't make the first move, did he?'

'I don't know,' said Iris.

'Can't you ask him?'

She paused. 'No,' she said, honestly, and he laughed. 'We've only ever been able to talk about certain subjects – work, or study. Or the garden. Or the twins . . . There's lots of things we've never talked about at all.'

'What you need,' said Spencer, 'is someone who talks the entire time, to act as a go-between. Someone Scottish, maybe.' He raised an eyebrow.

'Maybe,' she said, smiling a little.

Spencer leaned forward suddenly. 'What's going on in there?'

On the yellow screen the picture had jumped. Tom was reeling round the kitchen, frantically waving his hand.

'Oh,' said Iris, with a flash of insight, 'he was using the biscuit cutter.'

'Should I go and see if he's all right?'

'Gosh, he'd love that – an in-house doctor rushing to his aid. No, I'd leave it.' Tom had doubled over, and was cradling his hand to his chest, face contorted with pain. The next stage, she knew, would be a wobbly legged stagger to the nearest chair and a whispered request for a glass of water.

'Are you *sure*?' She could feel Spencer tensed for action beside her.

'Honestly. If it were anything remotely serious he'd be on the floor. Anyway, look – Ayesha's coping.' Ayesha had found the first-aid box on the windowsill and was searching through it.

'It's a bit like being at the cinema, this,' said Spencer, relaxing back. 'Drama, suspense, pretty girl, two quite staggeringly good-looking boys –'

'Do you think so?'

'Oh *please*. As I was saying . . . two heroes – both an absolute credit to you, may I say – one mortally injured, the other – his *doppelgänger* – brutally unconcerned, a heroine trying to administer succour but being held back by the unbelievable length of her fingernails, the heroes' mother off boozing somewhere, the –' Leslie walked into the kitchen holding an empty plate ' – the arrival of the comic relief.'

Iris's snort of laughter was interrupted by a liquid cough, just feet away.

'Hello,' said Callum, leaning over the wall that separated the garden from the street. The logo on his hat – 'Hello *Lamazol*, Goodbye Insomnia' – was a luminous hot-pink squiggle in the twilight.

'Oh *no*,' muttered Spencer.

'Jus' passing.' He rested his can of cider on the wall as if it were a bar, and looked at them interestedly. 'I've got a hat,' he said to Iris.

'I can see.' It was actually a huge improvement, turning him from a freak into an averagely dishevelled wino. 'It's very nice.'

'It's fucking fantastic,' corrected Callum. 'Are you two married, then?'

'Not yet,' said Spencer.

'Engaged?'

Iris stood and smoothed her skirt. 'We were just about to go in, Callum.'

'Hey, Dr Carroll. Is that blokey your dad?'

'Which blokey?' said Iris, startled.

'Hiding behind the bush.' Callum gestured towards the bottom of the garden, and an arc of cider shot across the grass. 'With the spade.'

'What's he talking about?' asked Spencer, sotto voce.

'It's probably just Mr Hickey,' whispered Iris. 'Let's go.'

'That's Mr Hickey's house?'

'Yes.'

'Bloody hell. So your father's the legendary hedge mover?'

'It's not my father who's responsible,' hissed Iris, instantly partisan. 'It's Mr Hickey who keeps moving the hedge.'

'Hey!' shouted Callum, wavering along the wall towards the end of the garden. 'Are you Dr Carroll's dad?'

There was a rustling in the Leylandii and Mr Hickey stood up, spade in hand, his face a pale coin that rotated slowly towards Spencer.

'Oh God,' said Iris, with foreboding. Spencer raised a hand. 'Hello there.'

Mr Hickey stared at him, wordlessly.

'I think we should go in,' said Iris.

'No, I'd better have a word with him, he'll think I've swapped sides. It'd ruin our relationship.' He set off down the garden with Iris reluctantly following. Mr Hickey had been busy; the quiet sawing, the rhythmic thump of the spade that she had heard earlier was translated into the absence of a small cherry tree that had definitely been there that morning, and the new, nearer positioning of the much-travelled Leylandii. Along their bases, humped with fresh earth, a thin wire gleamed. As they approached him Mr Hickey stepped over it, into his own garden.

'Hello,' said Spencer, with the puppyish air of a *Blue Peter* presenter.

Mr Hickey looked at him, his lips trembling slightly as if on the verge of invective.

'Dr Carroll's just here for a party,' said Iris, quickly, 'he doesn't know my father at all, and he didn't even know you lived here.'

'No,' said Spencer. 'I had no idea. Truly. Your own garden looks lovely – may I have a look?'

Mr Hickey moved his head very slightly, in a plane that was marginally more vertical than horizontal.

Spencer stepped over the wire and there was sudden clunk and he fell down.

There was a spade lying on the ground in front of him, and it was ballooning and receding in perfect synchrony with the pain in his head.

There was a lot of shouting and someone stood on his foot and then said, 'Sorry, Dr Carroll.'

There was a bubble of nausea rising up his oesophagus and he half sat up and suddenly Ayesha was running across the garden towards him holding a white box with a red cross on it. Then he vomited and Ayesha suddenly seemed to be running away from him again.

Someone said, 'Lie down, Spencer,' and put something cold on his head.

Someone said, 'If he's fucking killed him I'll fucking kill him the fucker.'

Someone said, 'Hello, sir, you've had a bit of a knock.'

Someone said, 'Look, Callum, if I give you another hat will you go away?'

He opened his eyes and there was a pot of pink antiseptic on a tray just by his head; the smell seemed to seep right into his nostrils, up through the nasal turbines and straight across the olfactory plate so that it soaked directly into his brain. He sneezed and the pain bounced off the inside of his skull like a squash ball. He lifted his hand to his head and encountered another hand.

'You'll knock off the dressing,' said Iris.

'Oh hello.' She was standing beside him, holding a paper cup the size of a thimble.

'Hello, again.'

'Have I said hello before?'

She smiled rather tensely. 'A couple of times.'

'Can I have some water?'

She gave him the thimble and he downed it in one. There was a moment's hiatus and then he threw it back up again.

'Oh dear,' said Iris, and wiped his chin.

He opened his eyes and the darkened room was filled with Mrs Spelko. 'Keep them open,' she ordered, looming over him with an opthalmoscope. There was a dazzle of white light as her breath roared on his face and her bosom pressed him into the couch, the name badge indenting his chest like a library stamp.

'Fine,' she said, straightening up. His ribs creaked back into place and a pink puddle drifted across the ceiling, dancing when he blinked as if attached to his eyelids. 'Now watch my finger. Watch it. *Watch it.* Up, down . . .' She traced the sign of the cross over him. 'Can you remember what happened to you?'

He thought for a while. 'Did I fall over?'

Mrs Spelko seemed already to have left the room; Marsha, the night sister, was there instead.

'Someone hit you with a spade.'

'Oh.' Now that she said it, it rang a distant bell. 'Am I all right?'

'We're just waiting for your films,' she said.

'Films.' He could only think of pools of oily water, the colours revolving slowly. His right foot started hurting.

For a while he was sure it was the sound of the sea, the soft slushing of waves on Brighton beach, and he thought he might be drowsing on a sun lounger next to Mark, but then he heard the words 'Mrs Spelko' and realized he was listening to a whispered conversation.

'Of course, just to add to the general picture she has the bedside manner of a water buffalo. I can only imagine she was trained in communication skills by the SAS, with General Patton as a special advisor. Would you like one of these biscuits?'

'No thank you.'

'You're probably wise, they've been in this tin for at least six months. You know, lately I've been wondering whether my obsession with Mrs Spelko might be a touch sexist.'

'What do you mean?'

'Well, would I be as critical of a man who behaved with the same ostentation? Do I subconsciously prefer women to work quietly – to add to the growing good with unhistoric acts, so to speak.'

'Oh. That's *Middlemarch*. That's Dorothea Brooke!'

'That's right! My God, well spotted. Of course Dorothea would have made a superb doctor. Very calm, very able, but without the corrosive ambition that blighted –'

Spencer opened his eyes and the whispering stopped; there was an X-ray of a skull on the lightbox opposite him, the cranium a flawless dome, the teeth a constellation of fillings.

'Hello, Spencer,' said Iris.

'Hello, Spencer,' said Vincent. 'How are you feeling?'

'Um . . .' He reached a cautious hand to his head, and found

282

it to be roughly the same size as usual; it felt enormous. 'A bit fuzzy,' he said, at last.

Vincent nodded at the X-ray. 'Did you know you had a deviated nasal septum?'

'Playing rugby. When I was fourteen.'

'It's a brutal game. There's no skull fracture, incidentally.'

'Good.'

'They're keeping you in, though,' said Iris. 'We're just waiting for a bed on the ward.'

'Oh. What time is it, then?'

'Nearly midnight.'

'Is it?'

'I'd better go,' said Vincent. 'I have to write a report on your assailant.' He stood and formally held out a hand to Iris. 'It was a pleasure to meet you. You know,' he said, turning, 'Iris is the person I told you about – the one who took the message? I recognized her voice immediately.'

'Oh,' said Spencer, following none of this explanation. His foot had started hurting again.

'*And* I've discovered that she knows first aid as well. So many skills. Anyway . . .' He leaned over and gently squeezed Spencer's shoulder. 'Look after yourself,' he said, 'and try to avoid socializing with patients. It's never a good idea.'

Iris had gone rather pink.

'What did he mean?' asked Spencer. 'About patients?'

'Oh.' She seemed to collect herself. 'You might not remember, but Mr Hickey hit you with a spade and then Callum Strang climbed over the wall and started a fight with him and accidentally trod on your foot. That's not broken either but it's a bit bruised.'

'Did –' he struggled to remember something about the evening '– did your father ever turn up?'

'Yes.' She looked at him, her expression unreadable. 'He arrived at the same time as the two police cars and the ambulance.'

'Hey,' said Spencer, closing his eyes again. 'Great party.'

19

'He's fine, honestly. He's been eating like a horse.'

'Has he been sick at all? He had a bit of sicky-tummy just before we left.'

'He's been sick once. In the garden.' It would have been in the kitchen if she hadn't yelled at him, just as he began the preliminary heaves.

'Oh *poor* Mr Tibbs.'

'Really, Sylvie, he's fine. I've been combing him and . . . stroking him and . . .'

'Loving him?'

Fran looked across at where the cat lay against the door of the refrigerator, his new favourite place since Barry had trodden on him. Yesterday, when she'd needed to get some milk out, Tibbs had lashed at her ankles and drawn blood. 'I've done my very best,' she said, honestly. 'Are you having a nice time?'

'A beautiful time,' said Sylvie, gravely.

'Well . . . good. I'll see you on Friday then.'

'Oh – Peter wants to talk to you. He's got a little bit of news.'

There was a pause; Mr Tibbs stretched lavishly and started to sharpen his claws on the polished wood floor.

'Hello, Fran. Everything all right?'

'Yes fine.' She had decided to postpone passing on the long list of things that currently weren't in any way all right, until their return.

'I thought I'd better tell you,' said Peter, 'I gave Norwich a ring today. I've got the job.'

'Oh. Well done.'

'So, er . . . I'll have to give in my notice. Six weeks.'

'Six weeks.'

'Yes.' There was a flurry of whispers. 'Oh – Sylvie wants another word.'

'Fran, there was just one more thing. I know it's a lot to ask but I wondered if you could clean the piano keys.'

'Sure. You mean dust them?'

'No, they're ivory so you need to wipe them very gently with lemon juice. It keeps them white, you see.'

'Lemon juice.'

'Just enough to moisten the cloth. I always do it once a week.'

'Right.'

'Thanks, Fran.'

Barry was still in bed, his bandaged foot protruding from beneath the duvet. He looked up hopefully as she came into the front room.

'No, I haven't made you any tea,' she said. 'We're out of milk. Listen, Barry, I'm going over to my friend's flat to tidy it up before he comes back from hospital.'

'Oh. OK.'

'And what are you going to do today? Any plans?' She picked her way between the heaps of clothing to the window and opened the curtains. The light was flat and grey and the sash rattled in the wind.

'It's really cold in here,' said Barry.

'Do you need another quilt on top of that?'

'No, I mean it's cold when I get out of bed. I can practically see my breath – look.' He attempted to demonstrate the fact.

'Jumpers,' said Fran. 'Exercise. The heating engineer's coming on Tuesday.' She caught her foot on a discarded t-shirt and stumbled into Barry's elbow crutches. They slithered down the wall, knocking over a pile of books and nudging his guitar to the floor with a hollow boom. 'You could clear up in here, for a start.' The mess was a daily reminder of the humiliation she had suffered on his behalf, scrabbling around on the pavement for his belongings, stuffing them into a waiting minicab while Janette screamed abuse at her from the window of the flat above.

'I'll try,' said Barry. 'But my back's aching a bit from this bed. And you know, it's quite tiring standing up on one leg.'

'Listen, there was a bit in the paper last week about an amputee who went up Everest so I think you can probably manage to fold a couple of shirts. You've only got a sprained ankle.' For a split-second she wondered if she could ask him to clean the piano but the potential for disaster seemed too great – she could almost see Sylvie's expression as pips squirted from between the keys.

'What time are you coming back?'

'I don't know yet.'

He looked at her pathetically over the top of the duvet, and she sighed. 'Look, I won't be long. And I'll get some milk and something for lunch on the way back, OK?'

'Thanks, Fran,' he said. 'I really, really owe you.'

'Too right,' she muttered, closing the door and glancing up at the botch job she had done on the banisters.

The day after Barry's fall she had inspected the damage and found the stair carpet littered with friable shards that turned to dust in her hands. The broken edges of the uprights were as soft as cork and when she had taken a torch into the cluttered cupboard under the stairs and played it on the ceiling, a myriad little holes stared back at her. Woodworm. It was like finding out that that zit under your arm was actually a symptom of the plague. 'It's lucky in a way,' Barry had remarked later, watching her grimly lash together the uprights

287

with Sellotape and a length of washing line. 'Otherwise you mightn't have found out until it was too late.' She hadn't deigned to reply.

The bottom deck of the bus was packed with extravagantly hatted black ladies on their way to church and the top deck was empty apart from a strong smell of marijuana, which someone had tried to disperse by opening all the windows. Fran slammed them shut, one by one, and then sat hunched and misanthropic in the front seat, left leg jammed against the heater, head stuffy with tiredness.

She had been kept awake the night before by the wind, which had teased up a corner of the corrugated-iron shed roof, and rattled it at irregular intervals throughout the small hours. In the past she might have put on her boots, taken a hammer and bashed it back into place, darkness notwithstanding, but last night a feeling of impotence had kept her under the eiderdown – a sense that it would take more than a couple of 3-inch wide-topped rust-proof carpentry nails to hold back the JCB of fate; with her current luck, if she repaired the roof then the shed would collapse.

Towards dawn the wind had dropped a bit and the roof had settled down to the odd clank but by that time she was wide awake, and had gone downstairs and made a cup of tea. Wrapped in a quilt and seated at the kitchen table, she had read through the house insurance policy from 'A **guide** *to* **peace** *of* **mind**' to '. . . ask a member of staff for a "Customer Complaints Form"' and confirmed her suspicion that wood-worm was not covered under the terms of the policy. Indeed, the booklet gave the impression that the claims department would laugh derisively – possibly even jeer – if she phoned up with the news. She had put the policy back in the house folder (though in retrospect it would have been of far more use

288

folded in four and wedged into the gap in the shed roof) and made a list of pest control firms from the phone book before trailing her quilt back to bed and dozing unsatisfactorily for a couple of hours.

She hadn't slept properly in days. For a start, she had spent five and a half hours in Casualty after Barry's dive down the stairs, most of it spent sitting next to a man with a cold. 'I think it might be flu,' he'd explained to her, sneezing vastly, as though that were a reasonable explanation for his attendance. The only good moment of the night had been when some huge madwoman in a white coat had barrelled out of a side room and shouted at him that upper respiratory tract infections were a GP problem. Fran had almost applauded. The very next evening, just as she was going to bed, Iris had phoned to tell her about Spencer, and she had spent all night worrying. The next day she had visited him, and had come away from the hospital marginally happier but with definite symptoms of the man-in-Casualty's cold, and after forty-eight hours of stertorous breathing and a set of sinuses apparently stuffed with concrete, she could have definitively reassured him that it wasn't flu.

As the bus ground towards Islington, weaving between the Sunday pedestrians sleep-walking to the paper shop, the differential in temperature between her left leg and the rest of her body served to wake her up a little and she began looking forward to a cathartic session of scouring and polishing, an altruistic chance to vent a little frustration; it was disappointing, therefore, to walk into the flat and find it already tidy. Admittedly Spencer had been in hospital for only three days, but she had visualized a build-up of dust – a palpable air of neglect that she'd be able to dispel with a combination of vigour and furniture polish. As it was, there seemed little to do beyond cosmetic tweaks; even the sofa cushions had been plumped. It was far neater than Spencer normally kept it and she wondered if he'd taken on a cleaner.

She went over to inspect the animal tanks and found them looking like illustrations in a textbook, the interiors decorated as if for a photo shoot, the food trays heaving with life. The spider was mid-way through eating a caterpillar, the still-twitching corpse held between its pincers like a corn on the cob. In the tank next door, the chameleon kept both eyes closed as if revolted by its neighbour.

Mark's instructions were still on the wall, but the ink had faded from black to a purplish-brown, and the corners were dog-eared. Spencer had crossed out the columns devoted to the lizard and the snails and had added the word 'magazines' to the bottom of Bill's feeding list. Fran picked a hardened ball of blu-tack from one corner and rolled it between her fingers and thumb as she wandered between the other rooms. Aside from anything else, they were so beautifully warm; she'd almost forgotten what it was like to have central heating. The kitchen was pristine, the bathroom marred only by a couple of streaks of toothpaste on the tiles, and in the bedroom the duvet was plump and inviting. She sat on it for a moment, just so she could reach across and straighten the pillows.

She opened her eyes when she heard a key turn in the lock, and was shocked by the darkness of the room. Her body felt slack and satiated and she lifted her arm as if the watch were made of lead. It was half-past five. There was a jingle of keys and the front door slammed, and then an Irish voice said, 'Oh God, oh for fuck's sake would you ever fucking believe it.'

'Niall?' she called.

'Who's that?'

She sat up and peeled a flattened piece of blu-tack from the corner of her mouth.

'Jesus,' said Niall, when she had lurched into the hall, 'are you all right?' He was holding a Tesco's bag in one hand and a dripping carton of milk in the other.

'I fell asleep.'

'You've got a big crease down the side of your face,' he said. 'Hang on while I get this bastard decanted and I'll make you a cup of tea.'

She inspected herself in the bathroom mirror; a fold of duvet had impressed a red dent between eye and chin and her eyelids looked like uncooked pasties. She splashed some water on her face and shuffled into the kitchen.

'So what are you doing here anyway?' asked Niall, filling the kettle.

'I came to clean up the flat but someone had already done it.'

He froze, his hand on the tap. 'Did Nick not phone you?'

'No. Why?'

'Oh Jesus, he's such an amnesiac – I told him to ring you. We brought Nina round yesterday to feed the spider – God, she loves that spider – and Nick took one look at the flat and got the Mr Sheen out. Couldn't resist it. You know the old joke, don't you – how do you know if you've had gay burglars? The place has been hoovered and there's a quiche in the oven.'

'Oh,' said Fran, not quite awake enough to laugh. 'It doesn't matter, anyway.' She yawned hugely and then remembered something. 'Wasn't Spencer supposed to be getting out tonight – weren't you supposed to be collecting him?'

'It's tomorrow morning now,' said Niall, lining up groceries on the counter. 'He was sick after lunch and they said he'd have to stay in another night. He claims it was the raspberry mousse and nothing to do with concussion but the sister on the ward is having *none* of it and when we left he was having a massive sulk.' He took a rolled-up magazine from the bottom of the bag and waved it at Fran. 'I said I'd stock up for him, and I'm going to put together a little –' his voice became arch and motherly ' – welcome-home tray.'

'Oh nice.'

'Fruit, chocolate, bottle of Bailey's, video –'

'Porn mag,' said Fran, as he unfurled the front cover of *Horn*.

'A fella's gotta relax,' said Niall unblushingly. He looked critically at the large man in small pants on the cover. 'Mind you, he's never really gone for blonds. Except Reinhardt, do you remember Reinhardt?'

'He was before my time, I think.'

'He was nice enough but Mark – aka he who must be obeyed – decided he was boring so that was it for the poor bastard, big elbow and first plane back to Dusseldorf. Jesus.' He put a large spoonful of tea in the pot, looked at it critically and then added another two. 'This'll wake you up.'

'Thanks.' She yawned again and leaned against the washing machine to watch Niall put the groceries away. She had never spent time alone with him before, or even met him unaccompanied by Nick, and away from the restraining presence of partner and daughter she sensed that the leash was slipped and they might stray onto a topic that was normally avoided. 'He was quite bossy sometimes, wasn't he?' she asked, dangling a little bait.

'Mark?' Niall's expression was incredulous. 'Bossy doesn't cover it. He was a fucking tyrant.' He shook his head at the photo of Mark on the kitchen cupboard. 'And jealous – Jeeesus, was he jealous. You didn't know him when he and Spencer were an item, did you?'

'No.'

'Oh God, well if Spencer so much as turned his head in the direction of someone who wasn't actually first cousin to the

Elephant Man, he'd go out of his fucking mind – there'd be tears, tantrums, he'd chuck plates about, kick holes in the sofa, you wouldn't fucking *believe* it.' He paused for breath and looked at her expression. 'You didn't know that?'

'No.' She felt slightly shell-shocked, as if the bait had been picked up by a fifty-stone marlin, ripping the rod from her hands and heading out to sea. Spencer had tended to keep his social life segmented – Fran in one section, work friends in another, gay friends in the third and largest – and the segments had mingled only at times of celebration and disaster. As a result she had only ever experienced small doses of Mark, although even those had been intense and memorable. Well or ill, he had been at the centre of all activity, conducting events with mouthy relish; all instructions had been issued by him, all movements checked with him and although she had never seen him crossed, there was an element of Niall's description that did not surprise her.

'I mean, don't get me wrong,' he added hastily, seeing her expression, 'I loved the man, we all did, he was a massive laugh and there's a big hole left in the world now he's gone, but he was a . . . you know, a manipulator. He couldn't leave other people's lives alone, it was always fiddle fiddle fiddle. Especially with Spencer. You know me and Nick have lost a really good, close friend – the best, you know – but Spencer's lost a fucking navigator as well. I'm not surprised he's been wandering round all year like someone burned his *A to Z*. And this *bloody* list –' he rapped his knuckles against the paper as if to admonish it ' – it's just so typical of Mark. Wouldn't even let being *dead* get in the way of running other people's lives.' He clonked a couple of tins of beans into a cupboard and banged the door shut. 'I've worked my bollocks to the bone this year trying to get Spencer out the house, but he won't go anywhere unless it's on the list. It haunts him, y'know, and he doesn't enjoy it, it's like some bloody penance. I'd think he was a Catholic if I didn't know better.'

'Yeah,' said Fran. 'He was fretting about it when I saw him yesterday – he's worried that he's missed a whole weekend, he thinks he'll never catch up now.'

'How many's he got left?' asked Niall. 'He can't be too far off.'

'I dunno.' They both peered at the heavily annotated columns.

'What's that scribble in front of Cockney pub?'

Fran looked closer. 'I think he's crossed out "the" and put an "a".'

'What's that about?'

She shrugged. 'God knows. He's ticked it, anyway.'

'There's nothing next to the Tower of London,' said Niall.

'Or rowing on the Serpentine. Or Highgate Cemetery.'

'Or the zoo.'

There was a pause as they scanned the items again.

'I think that's it,' said Niall.

'So it's only four items altogether. He could get those done in a day, couldn't he?'

'Easy.' He looked at her. 'With a bit of help, maybe.'

'You think we should give him a hand?'

'Yeah. A little shove along the way.' He said it with flippancy and then hesitated, thinking it through. 'I do, you know. I think he needs to get them out the way, and once they're done, we could start luring him into the world again, find a nice, boring boy for him to shag. He likes quiet lads, you know – it's a bit fucking ironic, really.' He poured the tea, a vicious dark-brown stream. 'Here – get this down you.'

'Ta.' She sipped it and her stomach growled audibly and she felt a twang of guilt at the thought of Barry, waiting cold, hungry and clueless for her return; he would have expected her back hours ago. 'I ought to get going really,' she said. 'I've got another invalid at home to cook tea for.'

'I'll give you a lift and we can er – what do those City bastards say? Crunch numbers?'

'Huh?'

'Make plans for Spencer. I've just got to check the menagerie first – you haven't seen that tortoise have you?'

'No.'

'Nor me, and Nina *scoured* the place for him yesterday. Still,' he added cheerfully, heading for the tanks, 'they can go without food for years, can't they? How do you think the others are looking?'

'Fine,' said Fran, running a professional eye over the inmates. 'Though the chameleon doesn't do much, does he?'

'I haven't seen it move *once*. Hardly worth having.' They watched it in silence for a few moments. 'Doesn't even open his eyes,' added Niall. A few more seconds of total stasis passed.

'You don't think –' said Fran.

'Don't say it,' interrupted Niall, sharply. 'Don't even think it. Clear your mind of all electrical activity. Walk away and don't look back.' He took the car keys out of his pocket. '*Run.*'

He dropped her at the all-night Turkish supermarket, and by the time Fran was fighting her way along the High Street, the two shopping bags acting as counterweights in the buffeting wind so that she swivelled with every gust, it was nearly half-past seven. She had bought a copy of *Time Out* in the supermarket, flicking through it first to glance at the accommodation adverts. There were pages and pages of them and she had been shocked by the size of the competition; there were so many others in exactly the same fix, desperate to pay the mortgage, wanting n.s. lodgers who would share bills and hswk, and who wouldn't mind if there was no dbl glzg, shwr or easily accessible tube stn. Or cntl htng, she reminded herself as she passed the blur of the video shop's spinning sign. Or bnstrs. Or the presence of a new, large and ominous crck in the dng rm clng. In fact, apart from the vegetable garden, she couldn't think of a single asset that might be abbreviated into service and used to tempt a prospective tenant; it might even seem foolish to an outside eye that she had already given notice (2 weeks, crutches or no crutches) to the ready-made lodger who was already living there – after all, most landladies would be grateful to have someone who was, at least, reasonably polite, technically employed and moderately house-trained. She crushed the thought. It was too dreadful to contemplate being grateful to Barry for anything.

There were leaves all along the pavement in Stapleton Road, not the shrivelled singletons of autumn, but sappy bunches of five and six, torn from the trees by the wind and forming a sprung carpet of crossed stems. Fran picked her way carefully between them and then paused to blink away a speck of dirt that had blown into one eye. Another landed on her lashes and she picked it off. It smudged between finger and thumb, and as she wiped it off a third speck landed on her upper lip. She looked up to see where they were coming from and flinched from the shock.

Above the poorly pointed brickwork of number 33, above the dodgy guttering and the gappy slates and the wavering line of the roof ridge, the Apocalypse had arrived. A bank of smoke had turned the pinkish London sky a true night-time black, and from the mouth of the chimney a tongue of flame quivered, the wind pulling a spray of orange sparks from its tip and briefly brightening them before they blew to extinction. The lips of the chimney pot were blackened and a triangular chunk had broken away, leaving a gap through which a whiter flame was visible. A faint but constant roar, audible even against the wind, was punctuated by odd little cracks and tinkles that seemed to have no physical origin. Fran dragged her eyes to the front of the house and for a moment it seemed incongruously normal – the living-room curtains drawn, the hall light shining through the frosted glass of the front door – but there was an odd, blank look to the upstairs windows and with a jolt of realization she saw that it was smoke, pressed against the glass and obscuring the normal contours of Peter's room.

She started running, the bags banging against her knees until she dropped them by the hedge and threw the front gate open, fumbling in her pocket for the keys. She jabbed at the bell over and over again, trying to open the door at the same time, but there was no response and in the end she needed both hands to guide the unsteady key into the lock. She was shouting Barry's name as the door opened, and she stumbled into the hall where the air seemed smudged and grubby as if viewed through a dirty lens. The smell was acrid, almost industrial, and it caught the back of her throat like vinegar fumes. Her eyes started to water.

'*Barry!* Where are you?'

She ran to the door of the living room, flung it open and saw flames. There was a second of horror, and then she saw the fire as it was: a baby fire, tame, tucked away in the grate, caged by a makeshift guard of two oven shelves taped to the surround; only just big enough, in fact, to ignite a hundred years of soot encrusted to the inside of the chimney. She looked around, wildly; the sofa bed had been folded and the room tidied by dint of shoving everything bar the furniture in one corner. Barry was not in it.

She ran into the hall again, and then, prompted by some dim memory of a fire lecture, spun round and slammed the living-room door. She took a deep breath, coughed, took another breath and then shouted his name as loud as she was able. In the quiet that followed she could hear the soft and ominous roar.

He was not in the kitchen, and the door to the garden was bolted from the inside. She shouted again, then took a tea towel, wet it under the tap and holding it in one hand, like a weapon, ran to the foot of the stairs and looked upwards. The landing light was on, and smoke hung like a theatrical curtain, a yard above the top step. It was not as dense as that which filled Peter's room – she could see through it to the doors of the bathroom, and the junk room and her own bedroom at the back of the house – but she knew her own stupidity in approaching it. She should be outside, she should be phoning the fire brigade, she should be alerting the neighbours. Instead, she wrapped the tea towel around her mouth, and finding that the ends were too short to tie at the back, tucked them into the neck of her jumper; it might be that the whole business of wet tea towels was at best obsolete and at worst an urban myth, but for the moment it was a talisman against the fire, and with the soaking cloth in place she climbed the stairs, dropped to her knees and crept under the curtain.

It was only a few feet to the bathroom door, and she reached up and yanked it open.

'Barry?'

It was in darkness but enough light bounced off the white enamel to show her that it was empty, and she backed out again and crawled along to the junk room. It was a jumble of looming shadows, a craggy landscape of trunks and suitcases, odd pieces of lino and stacks of newspaper, and a swift glance assured her that no one on crutches could even have got past the door. The tea towel was dripping down the back of her neck and a smell of wet carrot peelings held the acridity at bay but her breaths were rapid and scared and with every second the urge to run back downstairs again was stronger. The door of her room was slightly ajar and as she crawled towards it, she knew where she would find Barry; he had been hinting for days about the discomfort of the sofa mattress, and she was suddenly sure that he had taken advantage of her absence and was asleep in her bed. Or perhaps more than asleep. Heart thudding, she pushed the door further open and saw, in a band of light shining in through the window, the quilt stretching flat and unoccupied. There was a scrabbling noise from the far side of the room, and from beneath the dressing table two small green circles emerged. Mr Tibbs.

Fran knelt for a moment, trying to compose herself, and bit a fold of tea towel to moisten her mouth. Surely Barry wouldn't have gone into Peter's room? Surely he wouldn't be in there now, lying on the bed by the chimney breast amidst the smoke that must have curled through the ventilation brick and filled the space with such deadly uniformity? What would happen if she even opened the door – would there be some dreadful escalation of the fire if she gave it an extra dose of oxygen? She hesitated. The cat crept towards her and pressed himself against her knee, and from just below the window she heard the familiar screech of bolts that signalled the opening of Iris's back door. She raised herself slightly and peered over the frame. Diagonally below her was Iris's kitchen.

Diagonally below her, one of the twins was flapping the door, evidently trying to get rid of cigarette smoke.

Diagonally below her, sitting at the table, having a fag, drinking a beer, laughing – actually *laughing* – while the other twin tried out his crutches, was Barry.

Barry was next door.

Impelled by amazement, her forehead clonked against the glass, and the twin by the door glanced upwards, did a visible double take and then starting shouting.

The cat tried to climb onto her lap and she grabbed it and headed for the door. As she scuttled, bent double, towards the stairs, Mr Tibbs panicked, somersaulted in her hands and tried to scale the front of her jumper, whipping away the tea towel in the process and raking her cheek with his claws. She jerked her head back and tried to drop him but his back legs were entangled in the wool and he kicked frantically and painfully until she wrapped her arms around him in a bear hug and ran down the stairs into the hall. The bell rang as she was freeing a hand to open the door and there was Tom – or Robin – on the doorstep, and Robin – or Tom – shouting over the hedge that he'd called the fire brigade, and then she was hustled, coughing, into the windy street.

Someone took a photo of her as she stood on the pavement opposite the house, wedged between Tom and Robin and about fifty thousand other people who had suddenly appeared out of nowhere, and it wasn't until the flash left her blinking white silhouettes of the fire engine that she realized she was still holding Mr Tibbs and that her arms were beginning to ache under the weight. She looked at him and he looked back at her with his usual half-witted intensity and then the old lady who lived at number 21 and to whom she had never previously spoken came up and congratulated her on her bravery and offered the cat a refuge in her back kitchen. One of the twins had to detach him claw by claw before Fran could hand him over.

She felt strangely calm, shielded from the moment by sheer disbelief. The transformation of the suburban curve of Stapleton Road into a cockpit of frenetic activity – seething with uniforms, splashed with blue light, hemmed by the tapes of police barriers, criss-crossed by flaccid lengths of hose which arched into life at the twirl of a stopcock, the whole crowned with flame and smoke and arcing water – had the choreographed drama of a film set in which she was simply a spectator, craning her neck to see what was going on, as keen as the next person not to miss anything.

'The chimney's going to go,' said someone, and with a kind of swooning elegance the whole stack crashed through the slates and a girl behind her screamed excitedly. There was a puff of black dust from the newly opened hole, and a flicker of light, and then suddenly the maw was filled with flames.

'Jesus,' said a twin and a thrilled murmur ran through the crowd.

At ground level there was a flurry of activity, and then the arcs of water shifted and converged and great clouds of white vapour began to boil from the hole.

'Oh, it'll go out now,' said someone, disappointed.

'Where's Iris?' asked Fran, suddenly.

'Round at Grandad's,' replied a twin.

'Where's Barry?'

'Over there.'

Through the shifting crowd she caught a glimpse of a drooping figure sitting on a garden wall, forehead resting against his crutches, eyes on the ground.

'What was he doing round at yours?'

'Borrowing some milk. Only he locked himself out.'

There was a noise like smashing crockery and she turned back to the house and saw a cascade of slates dropping into the garden, followed by a length of guttering which bounced off the porch and came to rest halfway across the garden wall.

'I put that up,' she said, almost indignantly.

The exposed roof beams looked like a broken toast rack and through the smoke she could just discern a big old suitcase that had belonged to her father and a roll of left-over loft insulation that had sucked in the water like a sponge and expanded to twice its width.

Then there was another crash and both items disappeared.

'Upstairs ceiling's gone,' said someone, casually. In Peter's room, water started running down the inside of the window.

'I painted that room,' said Fran. 'And I put up the coving. And I got all the gunge out of the ceiling rose. It took me ages.'

'What?' asked one of the twins, his eyes still fixed on the devastation.

'That's my house,' she said, and burst into tears.

The woman who had taken in Mr Tibbs gave Fran a nauseatingly sweet mug of tea which she drank, and one of the twins gave her a hug and a miniature bottle of vodka which she also drank, and the combination made her feel both better and worse: chemically buttressed against the immediate situation, but vulnerable, for the first time, to the awful practicalities that lay ahead. To one phone call in particular. A second miniature vodka appeared from somewhere and she took a nip and eased her way back through the thinning crowd towards the barrier. The hoses had been turned off and a new noise had replaced that of the pumps – a steady dripping, emanating from every sill and ledge and remaining gutter of number 33. The façade was largely intact and the house shone in the massed headlights, the newly washed bricks as red as when they'd first emerged from the kiln. The firemen had lost their intensity of purpose, and those not engaged in checking or packing equipment were standing around in a kind of post-coital stupor, gazing at the damage with what looked like admiration. Fran leaned across the striped tape towards one of the watchers.

'Excuse me.'

'What is it, love?' He was a heavy-set man in his forties, with bloodshot eyes and a mournful expression.

'That's um . . .' She gestured. 'That's my house.'

'Is it?' His face fell further. 'You the owner?'

'Yes.'

He shook his head. 'That's a real mess, that is.'

'I know.'

'If you'd kept your stack re-pointed we might have saved your roof, but . . .' He sighed. 'I'm sorry, love, I really am. We did our best.'

'I know,' she said. 'I'm not blaming –'

'I mean that must be the worst chimney fire I've seen in ten years. Alan!' He called over to a colleague. 'I'm just saying that's the worst chimney fire I've seen in ten years.'

'Oh yeah,' said Alan, wandering over. 'Easy.'

'Ten years. And that was in . . .'

'Walthamstow,' said Alan. 'Lovatt's Lane. That was a stack collapse.'

'But it fell the other way there. Missed the roof.'

'Hit the shed.'

'Oh yeah, that's right. Killed a rabbit.'

'Can I ask you something?' said Fran.

'What's that then, love?'

'There's an old piano in the front room downstairs. Do you think it'll be all right? I mean, do you think it'll still be playable?'

Alan frowned.

'Oh don't get him started on pianos,' said the other one.

'How near is it to the fireplace,' asked Alan, a wary note in his voice.

She shrugged. 'Couple of yards?'

'Couple of –?' He looked as if he could hardly believe his ears. 'And I bet you keep the lid up as well, don't you?'

'What?'

He exhaled slowly, and when he spoke again it was with an air of weary irritation. 'Pianos need *care*. That's what I'm always telling people – they're delicate, they're complex mechanisms. If you keep a piano that close to an open fire, it'll *already* be ruined. Every time it's lit you get an expansion of the metal infrastructure and then –'

'It's never *been* lit before,' said Fran, exasperated. 'That's the whole point. I had a complete tosser staying in the house and he –'

'It was me. She means me,' said Barry huskily, limping towards them like a cut-price Spartacus. 'It was all my fault. I was a bit cold,' he added, undercutting the nobility.

'I told him the chimney wasn't swept,' muttered Fran.

'Yeah, but . . . I didn't really know what that meant,' he said, humbly.

The firemen exchanged glances. 'In that case,' said Alan, 'it *might* be salvageable . . . depends how much water's come through. Keys'll be filthy, mind, from the smoke. You could try cleaning them with lemon juice.'

'Thanks,' said Fran, heavily. She looked at Barry.

There was something about his pallor and the hopeless set of his shoulders that reminded her of the day that Porky had escaped and she had yelled at him. She had been furious with him then, and had been equally furious when he had given her phone number to Janette and when he'd broken the banisters, and when – only a couple of days ago – he had failed to clean out the bath and left the fridge door open all night and forgotten to give her three phone messages. Over the months, as they had teetered from one trivial incident to another, she had used up an enormous amount of emotion on Barry. Now, though, with the knowledge that she had actually – and pointlessly – risked her life for him, had almost died saving a cat, was standing in the street because he had *burned her house down*, she realized that there was nothing left in her armoury. She'd wasted her ammo on small fry; today's events were in a different league and for once she was floun-dering for a response.

'Sorry,' said Barry.

She sighed. 'You great idiot.'

'I didn't mean to.'

She could think of no appropriate reply to this. He edged a little closer. 'What are you going to do now?'

She considered the question for a while, and the answer seemed to rise up with a sound of trumpets, with banks of choirs and a thunderous organ. 'I'm going to live somewhere else,' she said.

20

The poster drew Iris like a siren song. She had left the house with the sole intention of going round the corner to the Greek bakery and buying a bag of warm white rolls, but ten minutes and a quarter of a mile detour later she was once again walking past the covered market towards the library in search of her third fix in as many days. 'Surprise!!' the twins had shouted the first time, after they had led her the last few yards blindfold, but she had found each subsequent viewing almost as extraordinary as the first.

It was huge – six foot by three – a vast black-and-white photo, artistically grainy so that the images seemed to drift into focus as you approached. Tom was slightly in the foreground, only his head and shoulders visible, and his right hand which was holding an open copy of *Utopia*. His expression was intent, lips slightly parted, eyes apparently drowning in the text. Just behind him, in the same pose and wearing the same expression of counterfeit concentration was Robin; in his hand was a copy of *The Shining*. Tom was wearing a white t-shirt, Robin a black one, and the poster caption read: 'We're all different. Local libraries – here for everyone. Let's keep it that way.'

'It's not just us,' Tom had explained. 'They've used five sets of twins but they said we gave them the idea for the campaign.'

'The photographer said we were brilliant,' Robin had added.

'They didn't pay us but they let us keep the t-shirts.'

'And they said we could keep the books.'

'Did you?' she'd asked faintly, unable to tear her eyes from the image.

'I kept *The Shining*,' Robin had said, 'but I couldn't get into it.'

She'd gone back the next day with her father and he had stared at the poster in silence for some moments.

'Has Tom read *Utopia*?' he'd asked, eventually.

'No,' she'd said, with absolute certainty.

'They should have asked you and me to do it, Iris.' She had been quite touched by the suggestion.

This time, in the early quiet of a Saturday morning, with the pavement almost deserted and only the odd car swishing along the High Street, Iris could do what she had wanted to do from the first moment she had seen it: stand and gape. In the frozen moment, detached from the twins' usual accompaniment of thuds and smells and amiable thoughtlessness and raucous laughter, away from the sheer ordinariness of their presence, she could look at her sons with amazement. They were beautiful; the camera saw it and so, now, did she. The combination of her own nondescript genes and Conrad's borderline-handsome ones had come up with a couple of racehorses, glossy and perfect, flawless even in gigantic close-up. She almost had to remind herself of her relationship to these monochrome gods; she knew now that it would be hard to counter their latest career plan, vacuous though it was. They had been planning it for weeks without telling her.

'We're just going to give it a year,' Tom had explained over the washing-up yesterday. 'The photographer said he'll do us a portfolio cheap and then we could take it round to agents and magazines and things.'

'And models are getting younger,' Robin had added, earnestly, as if he had researched a paper on the subject. 'Like the top male model in Europe's only twenty and he's a millionaire. I mean, the juggling idea was probably a bit stupid –' he shook his head over the folly of youth ' – but this could really work

307

because, you know, we've got a gimmick. That's what the photographer said.'

'And instead of going to college this year we could go *next* year,' Tom had said, cunningly.

'So where would you live while you're doing this?'

They had looked astonished at the question. 'At home, of course. With you.'

'You don't *want* us to leave, do you Mum?' Robin had asked.

'. . . then there's the bloke who lives above Iris, he might be half of a couple, I'm not sure.'

'We'll say that's five, then,' said Spencer, counting on his fingers.

'And the family the other side – there's three of them, and I think a grandmother lives there too.'

'And the three of you in the house, of course. So that makes twelve people homeless, thirteen if you count Barry . . .'

'It's only temporary for the rest of them,' protested Fran, 'until they shore it up, or flanch the side walls or whatever it is they do.'

'Still, it's a messy old result, isn't it? A lot of inconvenience all round.'

'What d'you mean?'

'Well . . .' He shrugged. 'You should really have hired a professional arsonist – these amateurs aren't worth the tr –'

'Shhhhh.' She looked around, torn between outrage and laughter, but the only people within sight were a tour party over by the catacombs, following their leader through a water-stained door into a vault. 'Please, Spence, you mustn't. Really. You shouldn't even *think* about that list – I've tried not to.' Though she had actually lain awake in a cold sweat one night, on her camp bed in Spencer's boxroom, imagining the insurance investigator coming across their shameful, drunken suggestions miraculously preserved in the bottom of a bin somewhere.

'Sorry,' said Spencer, contrite. In the fortnight since the fire he hadn't always found it easy to judge Fran's mood; for a couple of days she had been as subdued as he had ever seen her and they had sat together on the sofa, convalescing dozily in front of the TV. Gradually Spencer's head had cleared, and Fran had regained her usual energy and started working through the practicalities, but when not engaged in haranguing the insurance company she veered between wordless brooding and a near-hysterical joie de vivre, when all subjects were fair game and no jokes off-limits. This was not quite one of those times.

'Sorry,' he said again. 'It'll be our secret.' He squeezed her arm reassuringly and took a bite of egg McMuffin. They were sharing the flat-topped tomb of Florence Alderton, spinster of this parish, which occupied the crest of a hill within Highgate Cemetery.

Around them lay a carefully managed wilderness of ivy and angels and uncut grass still heavy with dew. Fran had drawn up a strict timetable for the day, but they had both overslept with the result that breakfast had been taken on the hoof and the ninety minutes allocated to the cemetery slashed to a perfunctory twenty, of which they had already spent ten admiring the view.

'I got a card yesterday,' said Fran, after a while.

'Oh yes?'

'The silver envelope with the mauve ink?'

'I saw that. Who was it from?'

'Mr Tibbs.'

Spencer glanced at her to gauge how he should take this. She looked perfectly composed.

'What did he say?'

309

'Oh, you know – he's settling in nicely, his owners have found a lovely house with a garden for him in Norwich, he can never thank me enough for saving his life, he's sorry that he ever doubted my regard for him. The usual sort of thing cats say.'

'What's his handwriting like?'

'I think he dictated it. There was a note from Sylvie too, and their style's quite similar.' She caught his eye and then looked away again.

'We shouldn't make fun,' she said. 'She and Pete have been so bloody nice about everything.'

'No, we shouldn't. *I* think it's quite touching, actually.'

There was a second or two before they exploded. Over by the catacombs a row of faces turned to stare at them as they honked and spluttered, and Spencer ducked his head and wiped his eyes with a coat sleeve. 'Come on,' he said, grabbing her hand, 'we've got a list to get through.'

Iris held the bag of rolls to her chest like a hot-water bottle and turned down the short cut between Dora Avenue and Beryl Close. It had worried her, how quickly she had slipped back into living at her father's house, how she had never once turned the wrong way out of the surgery or attempted to catch a bus to Dalston at the end of the day instead of walking the five minutes to Alma Crescent. Of course, it might be a sign of springy adaptability but she suspected the reverse: an easy backwards fall into the past.

Her list of resolutions for the year was, of course, laughably defunct and its failure seemed to be symbolized by the clothes she was currently wearing; during the hasty packing session that they had been allowed by the safety officer, she had been so busy supervising Tom and Robin that she had ended up stuffing any old items into her own suitcase, with the result that she was now wearing a selection of garments that were dowdy even by her own standards. 'You won't mind me saying this, Iris,' Tammy had said – wrongly as it turned out – when she had popped in as usual yesterday evening, 'but that's really not a colour that brings out the best in you.' Over the past few weeks she had come to the conclusion that she'd simply been tackling the wrong set of problems, window dressing instead of wielding a wrecking ball. Or a flamethrower, she thought, remembering Fran. That was how to do it – root and branch, foundation to attic, rip it up and start all over again. Well, that was how someone like Fran would do it, anyway; she herself had commenced a little tentative, diffident, wrecking-ball research, a long-term demolition project, so to speak, the sort that was only carried out after extensive consultation with the inhabitants, causing minimal disturbance to the environs.

She turned the corner into Alma Crescent and involuntarily slowed her steps. A familiar figure was standing shakily by the gate, Leslie Peake's waterproof bush-hat pulled well over his forehead. 'Hello, Callum,' she said, approaching him cautiously. It seemed to take him several seconds to register her voice, and then he swung his whole body round towards her and rocked a little, adjusting to the new position.

'Docca Carroll.'

His eyes were unfocused and there was a sticky patina in the hollow of his cheeks, and the smell of ammonia and glue flooded the air around him. She thought he had lost weight even since the last time she had seen him; his features seemed sharpened and shrunk.

'Dr Carroll doesn't live here, Callum.'

'Wanna see him.'

'He's not here.'

'Where?'

'He'll be starting back at the surgery on Monday. The day after tomorrow.'

'Mun?'

'Yes.'

'Mun.' He reached inside the slack waistband of his trousers and before she could even wonder what he was doing, pulled out the Lamazol baseball hat and held it out to her.

'You've still got it then?'

'Yuh.' He replaced it as carefully as his coordination would allow, and then turned slowly and began to shuffle back up the street, pausing at intervals to cough and spit and painfully catch his breath again. She stood and watched him go; this was the third time he had turned up at the house, and after the second – one of his more lucid visits – she had phoned Spencer to tell him. 'I think he thinks he saved your life.'

'How's he looking?'

'Terrible. Worse than ever.'

'Yeah. I imagine it won't be long now.'

'Until what?'

'Until he dies.'

'Oh.' She was startled by the bluntness of the statement.

'Sorry,' said Spencer, 'that must sound a bit callous, but he's been dying since the first day I saw him. It's only ever been a matter of time, there's never been anything I could do for Callum.'

Except you were kind to him and you gave him a hat, thought Iris. Which is more imaginative and more truly helpful than anything Dr Petty or Dov Steiner could have come up with.

She watched Callum's wavering progress as far as the corner, and then, suddenly remembering the cooling bag of rolls, turned towards the house.

*

Judging by the cake crumbs, Nina and her fathers had been at the Serpentine Café for some time.

'Sorry we're late,' said Spencer, pulling up a chair. 'There was a very long queue for the Crown Jewels, and we felt we ought to see them.'

'A queue? In *April*? Jesus Chr –' Niall looked at Nina. 'Sorry.' He held out his hand and she gave it an admonitory tap. 'New regime,' he said to Spencer. 'We were hauled into nursery for a ticking-off.'

'So what was the Tower like then?' asked Nick, crisply.

'Crowded,' said Fran.

'Good shop, though. Some good spending opportunities.' Spencer undid the top of his backpack and put it on Nina's lap. 'Here you go. See if you can find anything in there that might belong to you.'

'A present?'

'Yes.'

'What do you say to your godfather?' asked Nick, as she rifled through the bag.

'Spankyou very much.'

'Don't look at me,' said Niall. 'She picked it up at nursery.'

'It's a lady!' Nina pulled out a model of a Beefeater on a little stand. 'With a beard.'

'It's not a lady,' said Spencer. 'It's a man. In a dress.'

Nick rolled his eyes.

'What are you going to call him?' asked Fran.

Nina thought for a moment. 'Fluffy.'

She looked startled by the burst of laughter.

'Come on little 'un, come and help me get some more coffee.' Nick lifted her off the chair and she trotted after him, still holding the Beefeater.

'So Fran, how's the new landlord? A bit of a bastard, I've

heard,' said Niall, relaxing the language barrier as soon as his daughter was out of earshot.

'No, he's very tolerant,' she said. 'I haven't exactly been fantastic company.'

'You've been fine,' said Spencer. 'And you've already done me a favour. D'you know Fran found Bill?'

'No! Where?'

'Right at the back of the cupboard under the sink where I keep the pet supplies.' He tried and failed to keep a reproving note out of his voice.

'Ohh,' said Niall, getting it. 'That was me, wasn't it? Inadvertent lock-in by the eejit rookie zoo-keeper. Is he OK?'

'He seems to be.' His reply was a little stiff; Niall was taking the near-death of one of his charges rather lightly.

'Spence, he's tried to get back in twice,' said Fran. 'He ate half a packet of reptile anti-fungal powder while he was there and it's his new favourite diet; he won't touch magazines any more.' Shortly after the rescue, she had carried out an experiment in which she had placed Bill equidistant to the box of powder and a couple of pages of *Horn* and he had virtually sprinted towards the former.

'So, I've cured him of his wank-mag habit,' said Niall, triumphantly. 'Fantastic. And how's the rest of the brood?'

'We buried the chameleon last week,' said Spencer. He had been changing its water when it had simply fallen off the branch, apparently in an advanced stage of rigor mortis. 'So in exactly a year I've managed to whittle a rich and varied collection down to Bill and a spider.' He saw the other two exchange glances.

'Now listen.' Niall put a hand on his arm. 'You've done Mark proud, you've kept them alive a fuck of a lot longer than he ever managed. You know what he was like – he treated them like a set of light bulbs – if one died he'd just replace it with another one the same size. He'd have *pissed* himself at the idea of burying a lizard.'

'Chameleon,' corrected Fran.

'Chameleon, lizard, Puff the bleeding Dragon – if it died it was in the bin. No sentiment involved, in the bin and then straight down the pet shop with his Access. It's true, isn't it?' Spencer was silent and Niall gave his arm a little shake. 'Isn't it?'

Spencer was thinking two things; the first was that six months ago, maybe even six weeks ago, he would have become quite defensive at the implied criticism of Mark, whereas now it seemed a reasonable and even amusing comment and in no way a mean-spirited betrayal of his memory. When had that transition occurred? The other thought was more pertinent.

'When Mark went into hospital the first time,' he said, 'I offered to look after the animals and he talked me through it. Do you remember he had a couple of geckoes then? The ones that walk up the side of the tank?'

'I remember,' said Niall.

'Well he referred to them as seven and nine. It turned out that that was the number of replacements he'd got through since the original pair. I hadn't even realized – they all looked the same.'

'You see.'

'To be fair to Mark they really were delicate,' said Spencer. 'I mean, he was only in hospital three weeks, but I was already up to eight and ten by the time he got out. He never knew.'

'Good man,' said Niall. 'Mind you, I think we all thank Christ that you're a doctor and not a vet.'

Tom grabbed the rolls and was tearing the first one open and slathering it with jam before she could get her coat off.

'Grandad's only got All-Bran and porridge and *prunes*,' he said with disdain. 'There's just nothing to eat here.'

'Can you get a plate?' she asked, as he bit off a great mouthful, scattering crumbs across the floor, and he opened a random cupboard and stared blankly at a stack of casserole dishes.

He closed it again, and opened the next one to reveal a row of glasses. 'I can't find any.'

She got the plates herself, and the knives and the butter and the napkins, and made herself a pot of tea before sitting down at the table.

'Where is your grandad?'

'In the garden,' he said, pasting butter onto a second roll. 'Reinforcing the new fence. Putting up gun turrets.'

She pulled a pile of letters towards her and spotted her own name and address on the top one, partially obscured by a red stamp that said 'REDIRECTED'. 'When did this come?' she asked; they had been waiting for their post for two weeks.

'Just now, when you were out. A whole bunch turned up at once, the postman had to knock on the door. Hey, you know we're getting that Young Citizens Award.' He waved a typed letter at her. 'We can spend that hundred quid getting our pictures done, can't we?'

'Or you could give it back,' she suggested mildly, leafing through the pile in search of something that wasn't a bill, 'so it could go to somebody more deserving.' There was one hand-addressed letter, a card by the feel of it, in a tasteful pale grey envelope, and an A4 manila package from the States with 'In God We Trust' printed in purple across the flap. Her stomach lurched. She had tucked the memory of her request to Bethesda College so far into the back of her mind that it was like seeing an unwelcome visitor on the doorstep, one whom you had casually but insincerely invited to visit. She put it to one side.

'I bet we could save more libraries by modelling than by doing petitions. I'll give you a bet if you want.'

'Mmm?' she said, half listening, and then, 'What's this?' At the bottom of the pile, one of the letters had been opened and the contents – a yellow booklet – half-stuffed back again.

'Oh, Grandad thought it was for him. It was in with the other post and it said I Unwin on the front.'

She eased the booklet out and turned it over. The title was in large, bold lettering: **London Area Authority Grants and Bursaries for Medical Students studying in the United Kingdom**. She jammed it back so hastily that the envelope split and the booklet uncurled on the table again, rocking slightly as if to draw attention to itself. Tom looked at her, roll halted midway to his mouth.

'What's the matter?' he asked.

'Nothing,' she said, with unconvincing lightness, turning the booklet over so that the title was hidden.

'I've already seen it, Mum. Who's going to be a medical student, then?'

'No one.'

'You're not thinking of me and Rob, are you?' he said, derisively.

'What?' asked Robin, loping into the kitchen.

'Mum's being mysterious. She's got a thing on medical students.'

'What thing?'

'A thing on grants for medical students. A pamphlet.'

'Why?'

'It's just for work,' she said, coming up with a useful lie rather too late for it to be believed.

'Well why did they send it here, then?'

'Who's going to be a medical student?' asked Robin, still half asleep, sliding into a chair. 'You need sciences for that, don't you?'

'Ayesha. Is Ayesha going to medical school?'

'You need three As or something, don't you?'

'She can examine me any time she wants,' said Tom, salaciously, licking jam out of his third roll.

'Or what's the name of that fat nurse who does the warts?'

'Oh God, yeah. She'd be like Mengele, wouldn't she?'

'Who?' asked Robin, who'd given up History at fifteen.

Iris, refilling the kettle and inventing a little washing-up so that she could stay out of the conversation, was torn between relief and a certain resentment. While she had wanted to keep her embryonic research project a secret for the time being, it was galling to hear her sons speculate on every possible recipient of a student grant apart from the obvious one.

'Or – what about this, Tom – maybe they're sending Robodoc back to college.'

'*I must examinate you*,' said Tom, in a Dalek voice.

'*Examinate!! Examinate!!*' They revolved around the kitchen for a while, blasting imaginary patients.

'Or what about the nit nurse –'

'Or that glue bloke –'

'So go on, Mum, who's it for then?' asked Tom, coaxingly, after they had run through the entire surgery.

'Well . . .' She dried her hands slowly and looked at her sons; their faces were turned towards her but she wondered who they were seeing. 'You know, there is one person you haven't mentioned.'

'Who, Dr Petty?'

'No,' she said patiently, and then, when it was clear that they were never, ever going to arrive at the correct answer unprompted, she told them.

'*You?*'

She had never seen them look so identical, jaws sagging, eyes like marbles.

'Yes,' she said, defensively. 'After all, I used to be one, didn't I? I got two As and a B.'

'But –' it was, inevitably, Tom who found his voice first ' – you're too old, aren't you?'

'Not necessarily.' It was Spencer who had shown her, casually one day at lunchtime, a couple of months ago now, a newspaper article about a woman of fifty who had just qualified as a doctor. 'She hadn't even done sciences at school,' he'd said, and Iris had secretly taken the paper home with her and cut out the picture of the comfortably pear-shaped heroine, standing by the hospital steps in her white coat, poised to add to the growing good with unhistoric acts.

'I'm only thinking about it,' she said. 'I've no idea if I'd get a place. Or a grant. I wasn't going to tell you yet, but . . .' But I have *some* pride, she thought.

She could see the idea sifting through their heads, being sampled and tested, like a dud coin for toothmarks.

'Wouldn't it be weird, though?' said Robin. 'Like, everybody else would be eighteen.'

'I spend quite a lot of my time with eighteen-year-olds, you know,' she said, gently.

'Durrrrrr,' said Tom, to his brother.

They looked at her again, weighing, testing.

'You never said anything about it before.'

'I never seriously thought about it before.'

'So why are you doing it now?'

She hesitated. 'Because I've realized it's possible,' she said, and then – because it was a better and truer answer – 'because I'm tired of small changes.'

'You'd be a better doctor than Petty,' said Robin. 'He

doesn't listen to *anything*. And you'd be better than Robodoc.'

'Thank you,' she said.

'My arse would be better than Robodoc,' said Tom. 'Hey, Mum' – struck by a happy thought – 'you can have *our* grants. We don't mind not going to college, do we Rob?'

'No,' said Robin, keenly. 'You can go instead of us.'

'Yeah, you can move out and we can keep the flat,' added Tom.

'Now let's not –'

The back door opened and her father came in and stamped his feet on the mat, at first with his usual thoroughness, and then with a gradual diminution of effort as he sensed the atmosphere.

'Is something the matter?' he asked.

'No,' she said, brightly. 'Would you like some breakfast?'

'Not for me, thank you. I've had my oats.' There was a stifled laugh from one of the boys.

'I'm sorry about opening your letter, Iris.'

'That's all right.'

'Something for work, was it?' He had started taking off his shoes, but her prolonged silence made him look up. The twins glanced between their mother and grandfather as if at a tennis match; Iris dithered over her serve.

'Well, no,' she said at last, unable to prevaricate. 'Actually, it was for me.'

She had expected surprise. What she hadn't expected was that her father's face, defined by those long, sad, disappointed grooves which not even Tammy had managed to French-polish away, would flower into amazement and pride and joy. 'Oh Iris,' he said. 'Oh Iris.'

'Lady Muck!' said Niall as they passed mid-Serpentine. Spencer, sitting in the stern with one hand trailing indolently in the frigid water, gave a gracious wave with the other.

'Meet you back at the jetty in ten minutes,' shouted Nick, his arm tightly round his daughter, as Fran's strenuous rowing stretched the distance between the boats. There was a sudden wail from Nina, and Spencer craned round to see the Beefeater once again bobbing in their wake.

'Third time,' said Fran.

'Are you trying to break some kind of record?' asked Spencer, as the far shore shot towards them.

'I know how keen you are. . . . on doing things properly,' she said between oar strokes, 'so I thought we should at least. . . . go once round the block. . . . Fuck!' She caught a crab and the oar bounced out of her hand. 'Ow. Shit.'

'Are you all right?'

'Yeah.' She shook her hand and swore a bit more, and picked up the oars again with a less determined air.

'I'll still count it,' said Spencer, 'even if we don't go all the way round. I counted the fish market, and I didn't get there till two minutes before it closed.' A flat-faced man had given him an unsold coley before slamming a grille in his face. 'It still got a tick.'

'Spence, I meant to ask you something about the list – why did it say "a" cockney pub, instead of "the" cockney pub?'

He felt his mouth curve into a smile.

'What?' she said, intrigued. 'What did I miss?'

'I never told you about that, did I?' He had wanted to keep that evening to himself for a while, to mull over its implications in private, and then he had got in the way of a spade and the moment for sharing had been postponed.

'*What?*'

'I met the Hypothetical Blinking Man again.'

She dropped both oars. 'Fuck getting to the other side. Tell me about it. When? Where? What was it like?'

'Well . . .' He leaned back against the gunwale and looked at her eager face. 'I think there might be rather more than ten minutes' worth.' He checked his watch. 'Five now.'

'Summarize.' she ordered. 'Stick to the facts. Keep it concise. Where did you meet him the first time?'

'On a London Pride tour-bus.'

'How did you get talking?'

He wondered how to put it. 'We shared a nun,' he said.

Questions boiled on Fran's lips.

'Four minutes,' said Spencer, meanly.

'All right, we'll do that later.' She made a visible effort. 'Who got back in touch first?'

'A friend of his did. An American who'd been there at the. . . . the nun incident. He told me to meet them in the Cockney Pub.'

'And?'

'I went to the wrong one.'

'And then?'

'I went to the right one.'

'How long now?'

'Three and a half minutes.'

'OK, you can take this bit more slowly. All yours.' She folded her arms and waited to be entertained.

Spencer ran through the events in his head. The first few minutes had been a cavalcade of embarrassment, the thought of which still made him blush. 'You've got to picture the scene,' he said. 'It's not like a pub at all – it's more like a theatre, and there's a box office outside. It costs ten pounds for a ticket.' The woman in the feathered hat who had taken the money had said to him with open derision, 'It's all coach parties in there, you know, it's not a *club*.' His ticket had been torn by a man in a bowler hat and braces and then Spencer had walked through a swing-door and found himself in hell.

'They pick on late-comers,' he said. 'Or they picked on me, anyway. There's a little stage with tables all around, and waitresses dressed as pearly queens, and when I went in there were two men singing "Any Old Iron" . . .' The noise had been gigantic, cacophonous in the confined space, and it had taken him a few seconds to realize that everyone had turned round to look at him. 'And then –' He baulked at the next bit.

'Tell me tell me,' said Fran.

'They made me get up on stage.' He remembered feebly bleating, 'I've come to meet some friends,' and then stumbling up a couple of steps and finding himself facing a wall of heat and light and dimly discernible faces.

'To do what? *Sing*?'

'No. I had to push a pram full of scrap metal round the stage. And wear a hat. And every time they sang "you look sweet, talk about a treat" I had to throw toffees into the audience.' It had been like some acid nightmare of his youth and had gone on for at least five verses. The sight of Reuben dancing into the footlights shouting, 'He's with us, give the poor man back to us!' had been a vision more beautiful than he could express and he had been led like a lamb through the applauding audience to the mercifully secluded table at the back of the room. 'Us' had been Reuben and Greg and Miles, the latter still amiably blinking, his moustache now nearer Groucho than Orwell – an improvement, oddly enough.

'So what happened then?' asked Fran. 'Did you meet him – your man?'

'Yes, I met him. We had a nice evening.'

'And? Is there an and?'

'Well. That's the funny thing.' It *had* been a nice evening – inevitably dominated by Reuben, still vibrating with the thrill of having given evidence in a real live courtroom earlier that day ('They wear wigs, they really and truly wear wigs!') – a friendly, flirty, silly evening, a perfect way to dip a toe into something which might become deeper. 'I liked him very much, I really did.'

'But? Not fanciable?'

'It's not that. It's just – he's quiet and sweet and unobtrusive, and –' he shrugged, a little embarrassed at the admission '– I realized I don't want someone like that. Maybe I did when Mark was around, maybe I could only look for a contrast. But now he's gone I want . . .' not another Mark. Mark was irreplaceable – he had his own stained-glass window in Spencer's head through which the world would always be coloured – and God knows he didn't want a repeat of the tearing jealousy that had shot through their relationship, but he wanted . . . '– someone I can't ignore. Someone who changes everything. Someone bigger than me.'

Fran lifted an oar and clopped it onto the water again.

'Where are you going to find someone like that, Spence?'

'I don't know. Do you think I'm making life difficult for myself?'

'Life *is* difficult,' she said. 'Nothing's ever as simple as you think it's going to be.'

Watching her start to row again, Spencer thought that that was probably as much philosophy as he would ever hear from Fran and, like her, it was short and to the point.

'So what about you?' he asked, as the jetty and the small, bouncing figure of Nina came into view. 'What are you looking for? What do you want?'

The oars rose and fell twice more while she considered the question, her eyes intent upon some inner list. 'I want a big garden,' she said at last, with decision. 'A really huge garden. South facing. And someone to dig it with.'

'Anyone in particular?'

She shook her head. 'I'm going to find the garden first. One thing at a time, Spence.'

From the window of her bedroom, a half-opened bill in her hand, Iris watched her father show Tammy his new fence, put up to forestall any boundary discussions – or indeed, any casual intercourse whatsoever – with the new neighbours. Mr Hickey, once he was deemed sane enough to be discharged from the local psychiatric hospital, was being moved to somewhere less controversial, but her father wanted to take no chances. He tested a section with his hand, and then inspected it dourly while Tammy chattered and bobbed next to him, a robin beside a stump; they looked oddly comfortable together. Tammy had confided in Iris recently that she had always gone for 'serious men'. 'I like them to have a dark side, dear,' she'd said cosily, over the washing-up, 'a little bit of mystery. I never knew what my Hammy was thinking and it kept me on my toes. So to speak.' She had actually winked at that point and Iris had resisted the temptation to run from the kitchen with her hands over her ears shouting 'please, please don't tell me any more' and instead had smiled back.

The inspection finished, her father turned towards the house and, glancing upwards, caught Iris's eye. His expression softened, and Tammy offered a little wave, and they disappeared from her field of vision.

She had come upstairs partly to escape that expression, the huge leaping excess of joy with which he had greeted her inchoate plan, and which even the boys had noticed. 'No pressure there, Mum,' as Tom had remarked sardonically when her father hurried off to phone Tammy with the news.

'I might not get in,' Iris had said, almost to herself, and Robin had laughed.

'You sound just like me, Mum. Of course you'll get in.'

'But what if I don't?' Like an old, familiar satchel, she had felt the weight of her father's expectations.

'Well . . .' He'd shrugged, untroubled by that particular burden. 'You could go and do something else, couldn't you?'

'Like juggling,' Tom had suggested.

She finished unfolding the bill, glanced at the total and set it to one side with the rest of the post. Only the package from Bethesda College and the slim grey envelope remained to be opened; she hesitated between one unknown and another and then, bracing herself, picked up the former, unpeeled the flap, and slowly withdrew the contents as though they might bite if roughly handled. It took her a moment to assimilate what she was holding, and then she was swept by a wave of relief, followed by one of disappointment. What she had half hoped for, half dreaded was a specific answer to her general question – an address, a telephone number, a cheery letter from Lyle Kravitz promising to ring up his old buddy Conrad with the news that she'd been asking about him. Here, instead, was a cheaply produced magazine and stapled to it a compliments slip which suggested, in perky handwriting, that the Bethesda alumnus association (most recent copy of the journal enclosed) might help her with her enquiry. She detached the slip and flattened out the creased cover of *The Valedictorian*. 'Jesus is Lord' it said, in smaller letters under the title, as if crediting the proprietor. The cover photograph was captioned 'White Water Bonding' and showed a group of middle-aged people – old Bethusians, presumably – propelling a raft along a churning gorge. The contents page listed accounts of weddings and christenings, dances and fund-raising evenings, and the message from the editor was a paeon to the latest triumph of the college football team.

With mild curiosity she began to flick through the magazine. The Old Bethusian social calendar was crowded with healthy pursuits, many of which she would have assumed had died with Mark Twain: cook outs, hay rides, dinner dances with charity raffles, frog-jumping contests, Christmas Concerts and covered-pie parties. Paging slowly through, she looked carefully at the faces in the crowded snapshots, their features blasted to pale uniformity by the flashgun. None seemed even vaguely familiar, but then of course Conrad might have changed out of all recognition, he might be fat, bald, pony-tailed, bearded, it was even possible he might be dead; she turned the penultimate page and saw, with an impact that seemed to scoop the air from her lungs, that he was none of those things. A little more jowly, perhaps, his hair thinner, the odd crow's-foot pinching the corner of his eyes, but fundamentally unchanged. 'Afterword' – said the headline – 'last page thoughts with the Reverend Blett'. Fundamentally unchanged apart, that is, from the dog collar. It was a byline photograph, a head and shoulders that took up nearly a quarter of the page, and Conrad was smiling slightly, his eyes fixed on a high and distant horizon. 'I spent last week at a conference' ran the text '– no, don't yawn, don't turn away, because it was a vital conference, centering on one of the most important issues that our church can deal with – a Bible-centered approach to family planning.'

Spencer stood by the glass wall of the Bat Zone and watched chunks of darkness detach themselves from the ceiling and fly in great loops around the interior. He was trying to remember something that Mark had once said about bats, some caustic comment about the size of their ears and their resemblance to an ex-lover of Spencer's, but the exact phrase, and what had prompted it, kept slipping from his mind; whether it was due to time or concussion he wasn't sure, but he realized that he could no longer rely on Mark's internal commentary, running like a bass line under every thought. It was as if he were further away now, shouting through cupped hands, and only some of his words were audible. Big ears, he thought, no chin, high-pitched squeaks. Perhaps it had been Reinhardt.

He heard the rumble of a buggy and turned to see Nick and a sleeping Nina approaching.

'We've found it,' whispered Nick. 'It's in the other wing. And it's much bigger than I thought.'

It wasn't until the afternoon that Iris remembered the grey envelope. She had not read any more of Conrad's article – had not tried to find out where a split condom slotted into the Reverend Blett's world view – but instead had smuggled *The Valedictorian* out of the house in a shopping bag and buried it deep within a skip half a mile from Alma Road, safely removed from where the products of a non-Bible-centered approach to family planning could ever see it. Her lovely, accidental boys.

If they ever decided that they wanted to know more, then she could point them in the right direction, but for now she thought they could probably amble on without him; the idea of using Conrad as an example – a lure to lead them towards academia – seemed ridiculous now, a panicky manoeuvre from another era. In any case, they had always done exactly as they wanted, had walked their own path in matching size thirteens and used their combined charm and weight to shoulder down any door they fancied opening.

The house was empty when she returned from the skip, Tammy and her father out at an antique fair, the kitchen still littered with the remains of her lovely boys' breakfast. They had left her a note commenting on the lack of cheese in the fridge, and pointing out that she still owed Robin £2.50 for a milk bill from the week before. She did the washing-up, removed three pairs of shoes from the hall, turned off an idly running bath tap and retreated to the bedroom again.

The envelope was still on the desk and with little anticipation she ran a finger under the gummed flap. There was a postcard inside, a painting of a large-featured, plain woman, who nevertheless gazed at the viewer with the slightly pleased air of one who knew herself to be attractive. Iris checked the caption; George Eliot. The message was sparse, and neatly written in black ink.

Dear Iris,
I wonder if you would care to visit the original of this, in the
National Portrait Gallery. If so, I would be delighted to accompany
you.
Yours sincerely,
Vincent Jayaram

There was a telephone number under his name.

She read the postcard a second time, smiling at its courtly formality, and then a third because she still couldn't quite believe it, and then she placed it, picture upwards, on the desk and wondered if she would ever grow out of the habit of blushing.

The sloth hung in semi-darkness, looking to an inattentive eye like an old doormat caught on a branch.

'Do you realize,' said Niall, after looking at it for a while, 'that it's actually got mould growing on it?'

'It's algae,' said Fran.

'They're different, are they?'

'Yes, one's a chlorophyll-producing plant and the other's a saprophytic – one's green and one's brown,' she amended.

'Oh right. But it's safe to say that neither of them grows on anything that's likely to go jogging?'

'Yup.'

'So, Spencer, what was Mark really trying to say here?'

'Hmm?' Spencer had been looking at the list of sponsors framed beside the cage. Aside from his own name there was a pleasingly apposite firm of bed manufacturers. 'Well . . . I think he was trying to tell me to get up earlier and stop sagging round the house, both of which I've had a stab at. On the other hand, his first choice was an elephant, so you can make of that what you will.'

There was a heavily muffled pop from the corner and a spattering sound as Nick, hidden from the surveillance camera, juggled a half-bottle of champagne and a set of plastic glasses.

'He did say I was to treat it like a brother.'

'Can't help you there,' said Niall, 'I'm an only son. Nick –' he took a glass from his partner ' – Spencer's supposed to treat this creature like a brother. Any tips?'

'Er –' Nick topped up Spencer's glass before handing it over ' – it depends whether he's older or younger than you. Older, offer to play in goal in the back garden. Younger –' he checked to see that his daughter was still asleep ' – tell him on Christmas Eve that Santa just died in a horrific sleigh accident.'

Niall's jaw dropped. 'You *didn't*.'

'Right, thanks,' said Spencer. 'Fran? Suggestions?'

'Burn his cage down,' she said firmly. 'He'll thank you for it in the end.'

'Well, I'll er . . . think about it.' He raised his glass. 'Here's to Mark's list, anyway.'

'Done, dusted, and eaten by Bill with just a soupçon of anti-fungal powder,' added Niall.

'Mark's list.' They drank, a little solemnly.

'You don't think,' said Spencer, after a moment, 'that Nina would like a spider for her birthday?'